THE HALTER

THE HALTER

A NOVEL

DARBY McDEVITT

DIVERSION
BOOKS

Diversion Books
A division of Diversion Publishing Corp.
www.diversionbooks.com

For more information, email info@diversionbooks.com

First Diversion Books Edition: February 2026
Trade Paperback ISBN: 979-8-89515-088-7
e-ISBN: 979-8-89515-089-4

Design by Neuwirth & Associates, Inc.
Cover design by Jonathan Sainsbury // 6x9 design

Printed in the United States of America
1 3 5 7 9 10 8 6 4 2

Diversion books are available at special discounts for bulk purchases in the US by corporations, institutions, and other organizations. For more information, please contact admin@diversionbooks.com.

For Kloé.

For Calvin.

For Elsa.

You can't simulate the consequences of simulation.

HAROLD LASSWELL

1

I WAS STANDING OUTSIDE ROOM 601, waiting for another gunshot. The hotel's exchange vents rattled on high, blowing summer trash reek into the stuffy hall. The only human sound was a muted moaning on the far side of the door. I reached for the knob and turned it gently.

The room I entered had an arctic theme—ivory whitewashed walls, a frosty shag carpet, bleached linen curtains. In one corner was a gray leather recliner, occupied by a bent wick of a man in a suit with a black crust of gelled-back hair. He slouched forward, holding a gun in his clawing hands. A weapon so large he might have torn it off a tank.

The swinging door hit the far wall and rattled. The man's head snapped up. Splashes of blood and clots of gore covered his slender face. He raised the gun.

"Was it you?" he choked.

I shook my head slowly. "It's never me."

He gave the gun a sloppy flick, his finger kissing the trigger. I raised my hands and stepped sideways into the room, watching him carefully. Behind that radiant red mask was a young face with sharp angles and hollowed out cheeks. This was William Brighton—Billy—the man I'd been tracking for three weeks.

I took another step into the room. The pistol jittered.

"Stop," he said through a cage of teeth.

"Billy," I said gently. "I'm here to help."

He twitched, his own name slapping him like a wet hand. His lip trembled and his eyes got moist. A second later, his shoulders dropped, and he sunk back into the chair.

"What the fuck am I doing?" he mumbled.

Taking advantage of the pause, I closed the door and twisted the deadbolt and fixed the chain. I peeped through the spyhole and waited. A minute passed. Nobody appeared.

When I turned back, Billy's eyes were closed, and he was holding the gun across his lap. A rosy chunk of viscera fell from his cheek onto the lapel of his jacket. He didn't flinch.

I looked around. Across the room, a curtain fluttered in a light breeze. The window behind it was open to the sultry evening air and the gauzy fabric roiled like a creamy ocean surf. Wafting through was a sweet stink of garbage and piss. The curtain bucked and shivered. That's when I saw Billy's trouble—a stain of blood wicking up the curtain's fabric from the floor. The source lay out of sight, obscured by the bed.

"Billy," I said firmly.

He opened his eyes. I pointed at the bloody curtain.

"You mind if I look?"

His vacant eyes vibrated. He swallowed and shook his head once and looked down at his bloody hands.

"It's not my fault," he whispered.

"Of course not."

I rounded the foot of the bed. The first thing I saw was a pair of dark leather loafers, toes askance and pointed at the ceiling. A supine slab in a tailored tan suit lay on the ground, arms at his sides.

From the shoes to the fine suit and the silk necktie, this was a man of means. His pinstriped fabrics and icy diamond cufflinks told a story of conspicuous wealth. But from the neck up, everything was a mystery. In place of his head was a moist, pulpy mash of seething matter with the form and colors of a half-eaten burrito, heavy on the hot sauce. His thinking days were done.

Beyond the body, a spray of bone and skin and clumps of black hair streaked across the carpet, as if the man's head had erupted in the middle of a nap. I moved back to the bed and sat at the corner. Billy watched me without interest.

"Okay," I said. "Walk me through this."

Billy lifted his eyes to the ceiling, as if the words he wanted were etched in the stuccoed plaster. As he ruminated, he lifted the gun from his lap and set it on the ivory desk to his right. He sighed.

"I got a call last week. Some geezer on the city council, repping Staten Island. Married with four kids. Seemed straight as an arrow. Boring even."

"I see where this is going."

"Someone has videos of him doing filthy things on a farm in Quebec."

"Blackmail."

"Yeah."

"So why are we at a hotel in Manhattan?"

"I was sent here to negotiate an exchange. The video for money."

"That's a little outside your job description, isn't it?

"How do you mean?"

"You're a cop."

Billy shrugged. "The money was good."

"So who fucked up here?"

His lip curled. "I came through the door. This meathead jumped me."

"Why?"

He frowned and glanced at the pistol on the desk. "I don't know. I guess the gun spooked him."

"You came in hot?"

"Wouldn't you?"

"Not the best way to start a negotiation."

He blinked a few times. "I was just being careful."

I nodded and looked around the room again. From my vantage on the bed, I could see a sliver of the bathroom door. It was ajar with a mirror attached to the inside panel. From this angle I could see the bathroom sink and an overnight kit bag with some of its contents spread on the counter—a toothbrush, a bottle of cologne, a pillbox. This told a new story. The victim was a guest, not a goon sent to negotiate.

"How'd you know to come here?" I said. "To this room, at this hotel?"

"A phone call," he said. "They sent me to the front desk. Told me to give my name to the concierge."

He twisted sideways and fished a folded paper from his coat's pocket.

"A kid at the front desk gave me this."

He offered me the paper. Apart from some newly smeared blood, it was clean and crisp. I unfolded it. It was stationery with a watermarked monogram of the hotel. Below the header at the paper's center someone had written a single number—109—with a thick-nibbed pen.

"Nothing else?" I said. "No name?"

Billy shook his head.

"Just that. Told me it was a room number."

I looked at the paper: 109. My gut fluttered. I was so surprised, I almost laughed.

"Billy, think carefully. What room are we in?"

"601," he said, pointing at the paper in my hand. "Like it says."

I looked at the number. 109. I turned the paper upside down. 601, but only if you missed the watermark. I folded the paper and handed it back and he dutifully tucked it away, not even curious.

"So what now?" I said.

"What now?" he scoffed. "It's game over. I can't come back from this."

"Tell me what that means."

"It means I'm done," he said, pressing a hand to his forehead. "Gotta start over. From the beginning. Fuck me."

"You're upset maybe. At yourself. Or something else."

He grimaced. "I'm fucking pissed," he said. "I want excitement. I want a good time."

"Does that look like a good time?"

He sighed and stuck a finger in the corner of his eye and fished out something to stare at. "I don't know," he said. "I just want to feel clever, you know?"

"You don't usually feel clever?"

He stared at me in silence for a moment, thoughts swirling behind his eyes. If a coherent idea was forming, he shook it away.

"Are you supposed to be here?" he said.

I laughed once and slapped my thighs and stood. "Billy, everything is gonna be all right."

"Yeah?"

"You're going home a hero."

"How do you figure?"

I crossed back to the door to play the scene out.

"It's obvious," I said. "You came here following a lead, this man attacked you without provocation. Lucky for you, you got the better of him. End of story. And unless this guy has a badge too, you're in the clear. Back on the clock tomorrow morning."

His eyes twinkled with the first signs of hope.

"That true?"

"Cops always win. I'm surprised I have to explain it to you."

His eyes fluttered and a dim look of hope cracked his face. I'd pulled him back from the brink with a good story. Now was the time to take advantage of it.

"The first thing we're gonna do," I said, "We're gonna take a break. Get you back home."

"Home," he mumbled, like he was already in bed, all tucked in.

"You okay with that? You ready to go home?"

He sniffed and dragged the back of his hand under his nose. Then he nodded.

"Sure, I could go home."

I crossed to the white desk with the phone. Billy's gun was within reach. I could smell burnt powder from the fatal shot.

"Your wife's been asking about you," I said brightly. "She'll be happy to see you."

His face went slack, and his eyes darkened. I saw it happen, but I didn't really see it. I should have.

"My wife?" he said.

God, I should have fucking seen it. I lifted the phone and dialed an outside number. "Let's give her a call."

The phone rang once, then squelched dead. I looked down. Billy's finger lay heavy on the switch, and his eyes were dark and empty. He leered at me, possessed by something ugly.

"I don't have a wife," he said flatly.

My gut twisted. *Sure. I could go home.* He didn't mean his home *outside*, where his wife and three-year old twins were waiting for him, worried sick. He meant his home *inside*, to whatever dingy squat he was renting in this handcrafted, twentieth-century fantasy New York. He was fully invested, and there was no going back.

I lifted his finger from the cradle and laid it aside.

"I'm messing with you, Billy. Let's get room service."

Billy didn't answer. He rocked himself out of the chair and strode across the room. I laid the receiver back on the phone as I watched him.

"Billy?"

He walked to the corpse with a swaying nonchalance and stopped a few inches from its loafers, surveying his butchery with bored detachment. Then he pivoted to me. His slathered face bloomed with a pearly grin and wild eyes.

"Now I know what you are," he said. "I know why you're here."

"Can we talk?"

"I told you," he said, shaking his head. "I'm starting over."

He turned from the body to the billowing curtains and stared beyond the dark frame into the noxious seething of a humid, lamplit Manhattan.

"They say it doesn't hurt," he said.

My chest tightened. I lunged forward, my arm outstretched. I yelled Billy's name. But he was too fast and too far away. The curtain rings rattled as he leapt through. In half a second he was gone, out the window and plunging through the night air.

I stumbled, almost tripping over the stiff's legs. When I righted myself, I tore back the curtains and stuck my head out the window. Just in time to see the impact.

Billy's body hit the sidewalk with a pulpy thud. A woman walking her beagle ten feet away shrieked and fell backward. The dog went nuts, snarling and jumping and biting the air. A few seconds later Billy's broken corpse began to glow with a cool gray light. Trails of vapor curled up and away from the body like steam from a street vent. The glow reached its peak and with a soft flash the body vanished, leaving no trace.

The beagle's barking cut short. It stopped moving and took a seat, mechanically placid. The woman climbed to her feet, mumbling a private curse. She swiped at her backside with an open hand and tightened the dog's leash around her wrist and gave it a flick. Together they trotted off, ambling down 23rd as if nothing unsettling had transpired. As if a man hadn't just slammed into the ground at terminal velocity an arm's length away. As if Billy Brighton had never existed.

. . . Surrogate reality. Surreals. A beautiful portmanteau. Slang homegrown in the underbelly of an online forum for aficionados. A meme that generated its own center of gravity. Corporations hated the term. Hypo made a marketing push for Hypo Reality. Then Hypospace. They wanted the market for themselves. Like Hoover or Escalator or Band-Aid. Nobody cared. We just laughed. Pushback from the underground. Surreal *was our word and we used nothing else. We guarded it fiercely.*

The first surreals were pretty basic. Sensory explorations. No narrative, just experience. Hosted at dedicated venues in the early days. First one in Seattle was a place just off Pioneer Square, First and Jackson. Isn't there anymore.

An early SR called Solar Winds *was the first blockbuster. Wowed us like a communal lucid dream. We soared through interstellar night, jumping between eight planets and their moons. Orbiting the sun in real time. Full-scale replica of the solar system, but we could adjust our size for easy traversal. We started at one to one for contrast, then continued growing. At the one to five hundred scale, we towered above mountains and cities. Miles high in a few seconds. Kept growing. Up and up. Balancing on a suspended earth like it was a basketball in the void. We could fly around at will, zipping between planets. A sense of scale like nothing before. Poked our noses in Jupiter's perpetual storm. Took showers in the icy mists of Enceladus. Sat in silence on Ceres like the Little Prince himself. Beautiful.*

Ten years after their debut, SR theaters started closing down. How quickly that format came and went. Commercial consoles took their place. Once we had them in our bedrooms, the mischief began. Sometimes we'd go phishing for morons with more money than brains. I even wrote an illegal sniffer to torment the assholes who harassed me and my friends inside. When the modding scene took off, we stopped bothering civilians. Cracking Hypo surreals wide open and rearranging them to satisfy our own ideas were more interesting. We made funny stuff at first. Running a wild west surreal but we're all riding dragons instead of horses. Or a spy thriller and we're all packing Nerf guns. Or a cooking sim but the vegetables are the size of elephants. Good times.

It wasn't long before we started thinking bigger. We took an interest in dynamic systems. Physics, weather, biology. How they interacted and overlapped. If the rain fell a little harder, would the hills erode faster? If the ambient temperature was two degrees higher would the rivers jump their banks? If a butterfly flapped its wings, that kind of shit. We felt powerful working with these variables. The deadly vastness of our understanding, pushing buttons and pulling levers. Changing the force of gravity. Altering the weak nuclear force. Tweaking the universal constant. Watching the world fall the fuck apart.

Then we'd put it back together.

The power of Gods in the hands of teenagers. What could go wrong? . . .

2

A PULSING TUNNEL OF WHITE LIGHT stretched before me, an amoebic black void at its end. I fixed on the spot. Slowly it grew bigger, surrounding then swallowing me. I shuddered, seized by a wild lurching sensation, as if I was falling.

My eyes opened to a blur of wooden beams and tarnished piping. I lay on my back, stretched out on a lumpy futon, staring at the exposed timber ceiling of my office. My head throbbed, and I could feel my legs and arms stacked beside me like dry kindling. It took a minute to regain their full sensation, beginning with a dull ache, then pins and needles, and finally a warm itch.

I sat up and took a deep breath and clawed around the nape of my neck for the Y-splitter. I pulled to break the magnetic catch keeping it snug against my spine. Rubbing my eyes, I looked around blinking, waiting for my vision to clarify. I fixed on a poster hanging on the back wall of my office, a supersaturated image of a Martian landscape in ultrafine topographic detail with an inspirational quote set against the sky. I stared at the words, focusing my quavering eyes on the sans-serif font.

Imagine Life.
Imagine Home.
Imagine Red.

As a mere ad slogan, it was poetry. An invitation to a new future, a calming reminder of the generational dream of colonizing Mars, now in its twelfth successful year. The very concept soothed and centered me.

When my head was clear, I shambled to the SR console sitting on my cluttered desk behind piles of manila folders, strewn pens, and stacks of books. A pop-up message on the screen said the report from my last session was available:

Program: The Five Borough Blues

Session Time: 3 hours, 17 minutes, 23 seconds

Below this was a readout of numbers detailing my heart rate, blood pressure, and a table of cognitive measurements I never cared to understand. Maybe I should have. I felt like shit. Three hours in a mainstream surreal, with a heart rate never rising above a gentle jog, was an average day for a guy in my profession. And yet, for the past few months, whenever I exited surrogate reality, I felt like a man hammered flat on a hot anvil.

I closed my eyes and rubbed my aching neck. With each push my fingers rode over the convex nodes tacked to my spine just under the skin—a pair, each no larger than a gelcap aspirin. The ache subsided so long as I moved my fingers, and returned the moment I stopped. It was a fight I couldn't win, not without chemical aid.

I yawned and grabbed my phone from its charging station at the edge of the desk. I tapped it on. Four new messages while I was inside. I ignored these and opened my list of contacts and swiped around until I found the number I wanted. I hit call.

A woman answered, a fragile voice.

"Officer, hello. Did you find him?"

"I'm a halter, Mrs. Brighton. Not police."

"I'm sorry, I thought . . . "

"I did find your husband."

"Oh thank God."

"Finding him was the easy part. The hard part is convincing him to come home."

"Convincing him? You can't just pull him out?"

"It doesn't work like that."

"Or turn it off? For Christ's sake, it's a computer program, not a maximum-security prison."

"It's more than that. It's a networked digital service."

"What's the difference?"

"I can't make a phone call and ask a multibillion-dollar entertainment joint like Hypo to shut down their servers because a grieving surreal widow wants to see her husband once every couple weeks. That's basically their customer base."

"Could we cancel his subscription?"

"We could, but I doubt that would cure what's ailing him. Step one is to convince him to log out and come home. To face himself and his family. Right now, he's moonlighting as a cop on a server called the Five Borough Blues. And he has no interest in coming—"

"The five what?"

"Boroughs. In New York."

"Oh, good lord."

"Bear with me. If we can't get him out the easy way, we escalate to step two. We find out where he's logged in—a second apartment, a storage unit, or a seedy motel in Surrey. They almost always stay within a ten- or fifteen-mile radius of home."

"This is insane."

"It can feel that way. Your husband's an addict, Mrs. Brighton."

She went silent, until a string of wet sobs broke through.

"Look," I said gently. "A man can live for weeks like this. And sometimes he'll wise up and come home on his own."

"I see."

"But without help, they almost always relapse. Surreality is a powerful lure."

"What can we do?"

"I gave you a pamphlet when you visited the office, with the names of addiction specialists. Billy will need counseling when we pull him out. Get everything ready. It's all right there, just follow the instructions."

"I will."

"We're gonna find him, okay? We're gonna bring him home."

"Thank you, Mr. Stark."

"I'll be in touch."

I tossed my phone aside and sat back, running Billy's last minutes through my head. *Sure, I could go home*, he'd said, and I fucked it up. A rookie mistake. It was bad form to talk about the outside world with guys committed to the fantasy they craved. Hypo's algorithms were designed exactly for that purpose—to partition the real from the imagined as cleanly as possible. Mainstream surreals suppressed all the rote details of reality. You didn't worry about your real family or debts. You didn't feel hunger or the urge to piss. That's why sessions were capped at four hours per day. But with an alternate account you could dive right back in. So Billy had been living happily in his cop fantasy for months and nothing rational was going to interfere. I wasn't optimistic.

I sifted through the case files scattered around my desk. Billy's lay on top. I opened the folder and flipped through my notes. A month ago, Billy's wife had come to my office worried sick about her husband, a real estate agent serving West Seattle. The story she rattled off was so typical I could have narrated it myself. A year before, Billy had taken a sudden interest in surreals. A friend of his had a Hypo subscription. Billy asked if he could try it out. A single session later—aboard a nineteenth-century brig with a crew of dingy whalers—was all it took to dig the hooks in. The following week Billy joined Hypo, bought the hardware, and got wired. The basic starter package. Within a month he was running two, sometimes three, sessions daily.

At our first meeting, I asked Billy's wife to describe his evolving habit. They mirrored the three stages of surreal addiction with perfect accuracy. The first was *Infatuation*—in the early days he spent all his spare time logged in, but he could generally be relied on for basic responsibilities: work, chores, sleeping at the right hour. Stage two was *Distraction*. That came a few months later. Billy was getting to work late and leaving early, or finding excuses to skip it altogether. At home he was missing meals and neglecting his wife and the new twins. Mrs. Brighton had tried to intervene at this point, but Billy's defensiveness and generally brittle nature made her afraid to push too hard, a decision she regretted once stage three hit. *Obsession*, the vanishing act. That was last month.

As Mrs. Brighton told it, she had come home to find their bedroom in disarray, clothes strewn about, a selection of his wardrobe missing along with his largest suitcase. Her husband had disappeared, leaving no indication of his destination nor the length of his absence. Three days passed with no word. That's when she called me.

As a licensed surrogate reality deprogrammer—a halter—I have legal privileges that let me skirt some of the privacy protections typically afforded the public. All I need is the written approval of a spouse, immediate family, or legal guardian and I can access redacted session reports of any SR visitor on regulated channels. Unregulated SRs do exist, but the back end of this technology is so expensive and the install base of legit companies like Hypo is so large and profitable, only two of my shades in the last four years were dipping their toes in dark streams. The legit ones are addictive enough to ensnare most mammalian brains. And now they had Billy.

I closed the file and tossed it on my desk and sifted through a pile of loose letters on the opposite corner. Three rent due notices, a credit card bill as long as my arm, and my annual Hypo subscription fee, raised yet again this year to bring me only the finest in modern surreal entertainment. A mountain of bills, and a few invoices to serve for halting services rendered. With luck, I was hoping to be in the black for a week or two. But this Brighton case had just set me back. It was beginning to look like a wash.

As I contemplated the difficult month ahead, my phone rang. It wasn't a number I knew. I cleared my throat and answered.

"Kennedy Stark, go ahead."

A slurring voice. "You the halter I read about?"

"I don't know what you read, but I am a halter. How can I help?"

"Fuck man, I got a brother that's in trouble."

"That's a start."

"Can you help him maybe? Kick this fucking habit?"

I grabbed a pen from the desk and flipped a rental notice to its blank side.

"Tell me about him. What's his name?"

"Bryce. He's losing himself in those things. Thinks he's some kind of secret agent or something. Barely shows his face except to shower and whatever."

"Is he logging in from home?"

The guy scoffed. "Yeah. Just lays in his room all day. It's giving my mom hell. She leaves food outside his door. Fucking pathetic."

Stage two, I wrote.

"It's probably best we talk in person," I said. "You have time next week to meet somewhere?"

"Man I don't know. Uh, I work and shit."

"Okay. Why don't you give me your number, and I'll call you next week."

He gave me what I asked for. When the call ended I tacked the letter to the cork board beside my desk and gave my phone another glance. Four messages awaited my answer. I pocketed the phone and rose up. It was Friday and I had worked well past my drinking hour. Fighting a yawn, I switched off the SR console and grabbed my jacket and hat and went out.

I left my office by the alley entrance. A drifter with skin the color of squashed raspberries and a loofah of gray hair was sleeping under a filthy blue tarp in the door's recess, using a camo backpack as a pillow. I stepped over him and made my way up the street. A brisk walk was usually the best antidote for the headache that followed a few hours in SR. But tonight the sour funk of the algae blooms—what locals called the Puget Sound gag tide—was spreading over the neighborhood like a flap of rancid lox. After a few blocks my headache just got worse, and my options were limited. I had an oxymask back in my car, a cheap vinyl thing I bought at a Seven-E. But the canister had been empty for months.

Searching for nightlife, I strolled down Ballard's main drag—a neighborhood built by Swedes almost two centuries back, and ruined by everyone else. The gag tide was less noticeable here, but only because the smell of rotting garbage was so prominent. Unhurried crowds looking for bars and live music loped along the narrow sidewalks. I pulled out a pack of cigarettes and lit up. As the flame pulsed, I had the pricking sensation that someone was watching me. I turned around just in time to see a stout man in a trench coat staring directly at me from the end of the block. He turned sharply and disappeared behind a building. Throngs of Friday revelers flowed by in two directions, heedless of my paranoia. I waited for a moment. When the trench coat didn't reappear, I walked on.

Between drags, I reminisced of fresher days. Memories of Seattle before the algae blooms—the clean and delicious air, the bruised and pulpy skies, the beauty and the sweetness. I hadn't smelled or seen one of those days in years. I doubted they'd ever be back. There was no denying the creeping sensation that time was running out for this world. A feeling of slow decay dominated every new day. We were now at the mercy of forces set in motion many generations before. Escape of any kind was an appealing alternative and a deadly drug. Hence the growing need for guys like me.

I stopped outside the Cavern Cafe, a 24-7 greasy spoon at the western terminus of Ballard Avenue. I took a long pull off my cig and flicked it unfinished to the street and looked behind me. No trench coats anywhere. A tiny bell above the door sassed me as I crossed into a dank world of midnight breakfasts and foggy dreams.

The Cavern Cafe was a long and narrow joint that smelled of fry grease and evaporated vomit. A battered linoleum lunch counter ran along the right side and there were half a dozen tight booths on the left. At the back of the diner was a doorway into the Cavern's seedy second hemisphere—the Headlamp Tavern. Feeling a rising thirst, I moved down a center aisle as cramped as a rail car. A copy of yesterday's newspaper was folded on the counter. I snapped it up and tucked it under my arm and moved on.

The Headlamp was a murky mirror image of its sister diner, a diabolical dream world of red lights and black walls, parallel in form to the restaurant except for the booths, in place of which were a row of minute round tables built for lovers. Along the far wall was a pocked bar glinting with an epoxy finish. There were people sitting at the other end of the bar, but nobody I knew. At the tavern's far end was a single booth built into an intimate alcove. A tin lamp shaped like a rocket's thruster swayed from the ceiling, throwing blood red light over the couple sitting underneath.

They were a stylish pair with an artsy look—an elegant matriarch in her early fifties and a handsome young dandy pushing thirty hanging on her elbow. The woman was tall and slender and sinewy, with marbled eyes and a narrow nose. Her bobbed hair was so black it swallowed every color that struck it. The dandy was her lavish accessory—a compact, pink-skinned gentleman with a coiled bush of tawny hair you could scrub dishes with. He had a mustache as thin as a wire twist tie and icy eyes that would melt down his cheeks in the sun.

Shadows shifted in my periphery. The bartender was upon me, a massive goon with a head as round and sleek as a cannonball. I didn't recognize him either.

"What do you want?" he asked in a way that made it a single word.

"Where's Andy? Friday nights are his."

"No idea," he growled. "What are you drinking?"

"He was here yesterday."

"Order or get the fuck out."

"Old Fashioned. Two cherries."

He threw a perfunctory look across his shoulder.

"I don't know where they keep the cherries."

"Andy does, ask him."

"Who's that?"

"All right, tough guy. Pretend you have cherries and leave 'em out."

The bartender grunted and turned to the well. While waiting on King Kong to mix my drink, I spread the newspaper over the bar and scanned the headlines. Most of them told a story of a world in crisis, the same old screaming panic from yesteryear. Stock markets flailing up and down like an ultraviolet wave. A tight and testy election with accusations of fraud from all sides. The world's climate creeping to a new average of 1.8 degrees warmer. And a company out of Japan testing a helicopter car with the overblown hope of getting it to market next year. Everything depressed me. I was about to bin the paper when the headline of section B caught my eye: *Meet the Newest Martians.*

This was more my style. It had been sixteen years since the first humans landed on Mars—a joint effort between the United States, China, and a handful of private corporations. A few years after this momentous event, a company out of Austin called Imagine Red began the delicate process of establishing permanent habitations up there.

Six successful trips in the past twelve years, with only a single death following a freak accident at the original camp. Four days from now, the seventh expedition would touch down, bringing the total number of humans living on the red planet to forty-one. Enough to call it a village.

I read through the article wearing a painful grin. I'd been dreaming of these days since I was a kid, but my childhood passed in an era where space travel was a rich man's hobby. A lot had changed since then. Now we were crossing the solar system and settling down on celestial terra firma with ease. That I didn't see it coming was my biggest regret—I might have picked a different career otherwise. Thankfully the engineers at Imagine Red were taking it seriously. There was an urgency to their mission, an existential thrust. With so many people spending time logged in and checked out on earth, the prospect of colonizing another planet seemed like the only rational answer to an extinction-level trend.

A screech of laughter interrupted my reading, cutting across the room from the rear booth. I looked back. The older woman and the dandy were roaring with glee, heads thrown back, the woman with sophistication and the man squirming in his seat like half a lemon on a juicer.

The bartender returned with my Old Fashioned. He set it down three feet from my hand and held out a subdermal chip reader, an old one the size of a pack of cards.

"Fifteen dollars."

I held up my thumb to show him a scar in the low light.

"I'm not chipped," I said. "Put it on my tab."

I reached for the drink. The bartender swept it away with his massive hand. He loomed over me, his vile breath fogging my corneas.

"Chips or cash only," he said.

"Andy lets me keep a tab."

"Say that name one more time and you'll eat my knee."

I pointed at the cash register. "Kennedy Stark. See for yourself."

The man's face twitched at hearing my name. He grumbled something and pushed the tumbler forward with a plump finger. Next to his hand, the glass looked like a thimble.

"Your drink's paid for."

I looked down, wondering if it was made of something funnier than liquor.

"What's the catch?" I said.

The bartender sniffed and glanced at the back booth. "Talk to those two," he grunted. "Make 'em happy."

I turned to look. The elegant pair was staring straight at me, drinks raised and eyes sparkling. I answered with a nod and turned back to the bartender.

"What's the play?" I said.

"Just shut up, drink, and listen to the lady."

"That's all?"

"That's more than enough."

. . . I designed my first surreals at sixteen. From the ground up. Artful little things. My best one simulated the evolution of the eye, from early amoebic life to our human present, offering a first-hand experience of each leap forward. I got good responses from the people who tried it. Applied to university on the strength of that demo. Once admitted, I didn't want to go. I'd proved my point. The self-taught wunderkind with a chip on her shoulder had no need for validation. But my father insisted.

Visit the school, Delia, he said. Just have a look. Tell me what you think.

He was right. When I saw the facilities, I changed my mind. A high-tech playground. Irresistible. So I went for three years. Did interesting work, if not groundbreaking. Stuff I was proud of. But it was no place to develop as an artist. Lots of pressure to collaborate with corporate donors. Job offers from big tech fluttered in every few weeks. Slimy headhunters dangling ridiculous salaries under my nose. I'd never stoop like that.

Stoop like what?

Pritchard Locksley asked me that. The first time we met at my thesis exposition. Me and fifteen other graduates. He was one of the judges. Look, I said, proud of myself, so assured. I make Art with a capital A. A for the Axe that chops at the frozen sea inside us. That's Kafka. That's all I want to do. But the prospect of making art is always in tension with the corporate stranglehold on whatever medium you're working in. The mainstream wants you docile and thirsty, and every new medium makes that easier to achieve. Every new advance invents a way to hijack another sensory organ. Books, then painting, then photography, film. Sight, then sound. They even tried smell-o-vision once. Now we have surreals. There's a real danger here. The end goal has always been simulation. Anesthetization. But we cannot give in, as much as people yearn for it. As much as people crave it, we have to convince them that their lives are worth living. Worth augmenting, not escaping. The potential for art is huge in this domain. But so is the potential for abuse. Don't give in to passivity. Don't give up on the life you're living. Find yourself. Love yourself and all your dirty edges.

Locksley was grinning like an idiot when I'd finished my rant.

What's your name? he said.

Sekhmet, I told him. Who cares?

And what's the name of your project?

This Little World, I said. For now.

We should collaborate some time, he said.

Why, I said. Who the hell are you?

He looked at me with a leer I would soon see too much of.

I'm the guy who's gonna sharpen your axe, he said . . .

3

THE DAME AND THE DANDY WAITED FOR ME WITH SMILES. Holding my drink, I grabbed a chair from a nearby table and dragged it to their booth and sat. The dandy tittered and shivered, like I'd just pulled off a triple axel in jeans. The woman smirked, batting lashes the size of hand fans.

I raised my glass.

"To new friends."

The pair answered my call, and we drank. I finished mine in half a second. The dandy nibbled the rim of a greyhound with fresh, slurping sounds. The woman finished her Kir Royale in a single breath and set the stemmed flute on the table with a click. She raised an arm and looked past me, snapping twice.

"Another for me please, Rick."

The dandy tapped the middle of the table to get my attention.

"Rick is one of ours," he said with a smirk.

"One of your what?"

The dandy giggled. The woman put a calming hand on his thigh and made a sound like rushing water. The dandy froze and his crooked smile flattened. Turning in my seat, I raised my hand and snapped.

"Rick," I shouted. "One last thing."

Rick looked up from the drinks he was pouring. He scowled when he saw it was me.

"Top-shelf bottle of bourbon for the table," I said. "Something that tastes good with imaginary cherries."

His nostrils flared but he obeyed, pulling a pretty bottle from the back row.

I looked back at my hosts. "If that's okay . . ."

The dandy laced his fingers and leaned forward across the table.

"Is it the preference of every halter to drink bourbon?" he asked, baring a perfect set of white teeth. "Some sort of brand signifier or something?"

I shook my dead tumbler to rattle the ice.

"Other way around," I said. "Drinking bourbon is a gateway to halting."

"I love drinking," he cooed. "Maybe I'd like halting."

I shrugged. "You have to like people too. Do you like people?"

He frowned. "In what sense?"

"Are you willing to spend forty hours a week in surrogate reality, talking logged-in loners off virtual ledges? Would you let a man dressed as a sunflower cry digital tears on your shoulder so he can tell you how depressed he is?"

The dandy grimaced, "Ew."

The dame folded her bare arms over the table and cocked her head. "*Halter* is a curious term," she said. "Where does it come from?"

"I've wondered that myself," I shrugged. "Maybe the halting problem—a computer science puzzle about whether a program will halt eventually or run forever. That's sort of how I approach the shades I help. Can I stop their obsession? Or will they run forever?"

Auntie nodded thoughtfully, a warm light glowing in her eyes. "I like that," she said. "I thought it might have something to do with horses. The headgear. Your firm hand on a short leash, leading people to safety."

"That's nice, too. Hadn't thought of it, but that's the idea."

"So what's the draw?"

"I have a knack for it, I guess. Folks seem to trust me."

"You have a big heart."

"Bigger than my take-home pay."

She clowned a sad face. "If it's that bad, why bother?"

"Of all the jobs I could be doing," I said, rotating my tumbler on the table, "This is the only one that might get me into heaven. It's helping people, that's all. I just like helping more than hurting."

"That's sweet."

"At any given moment, there are seventy-six million people on this planet logged into surrogate reality. A small, but statistically significant, percentage are what your doctor would call clinically addicted. I do what I can to help them."

She nodded with wonder, looked me over as if I were for sale, then made a slight gesture at the hand wrapped around my empty tumbler. I looked down. My thumb was poking over the rim and the thin scar down its pad was clearly visible.

"When did that happen?" she said.

I raised my thumb to show it clearly.

"I never liked being chipped," I said. "Made me itchy around electric sockets. So I pulled it out, just to be sure."

"Funny," she said, raising her own thumb and eying it closely. "I do love mine. No need to carry cash, an ID, or a medical card. It just works."

She smooched her thumb with a wet smack and opened her hand with a flourish, throwing the kiss in my direction. I pretended to catch it and put it in my pocket.

"Any more questions before I get to mine?" I said.

"What got you into halting?" she said.

"I was a private investigator a few years ago. One day a lady comes into my office claiming her son is obsessed with Queen Cleopatra. I tell her it's natural for a young man to find Elizabeth Taylor attractive, but that he should develop better taste in cinema. So she tells me all about the Last Pharaoh, a surreal simulation of Ptolemaic Egypt. Her kid's been playing as one of Cleopatra's guards and now he's in love."

"Sounds kind of sweet."

"It takes me five weeks to find the kid in real life. When I do he's logged in from a storage unit one town over. Weighs ninety pounds. We pulled him out, but he died on life support a week later. Dealing with the fallout of that one is how I learned halting was a licensed profession. You take a test, you pay a yearly fee. I liked the angle, so I signed up. A year later, I let my investigator's license lapse. I was getting five times the work pulling people out of SR."

"How many more clients have you lost in all that time?"

I snorted and shook my head.

"Shades, you mean. Clients are the ones who hire me," I said. "Shades are the people I look for."

"How many shades have you lost?"

"It's my turn," I said. "How about some names first?"

The woman puckered her lips to fight a smile and held out a cupped paw.

"I'm Auntie," she said. "It's nice to finally meet you."

I took the hand and squeezed it softly, then turned to the dandy. He was still slurping his greyhound like a mutt. I offered my hand, but he blushed suddenly and pulled his hand below the table. Before it disappeared, I noticed his right thumb was missing at the knuckle. I withdrew my hand.

"Does that make you Nephew?" I said. "Or Cousin?"

"We're not related," he said, throwing Auntie a furtive glance. "I'm Friend."

"Just a friend?"

"Just Friend."

The table darkened suddenly, and a bottle landed hard enough to rattle the fillings in my teeth. Three stacked tumblers followed. My bourbon had arrived. Rick slid Auntie's second Kir Royale across the table. Then he stepped back, his arms pulled helplessly to his sides. I'd never seen a big man look so fragile.

"Anything else, ma'am?"

Auntie shook her head. "No. Thank you, Rick. Add it to my tab."

"Very good, ma'am."

Rick, you son-of-a-bitch.

Auntie made a brusque shooing motion. Rick folded in half and blew away. I popped the bourbon's cap and poured myself a slurp and laid out the other two tumblers. I offered my guests a tipple. Auntie declined for both with a curt gesture. I set the bottle down and scooped up my drink.

"All right, Auntie. What do you do?"

"I suppose I'm something of a detective myself," she said languidly. "I find people, rare talents, and I put them to work, depending on the needs of my client."

"That being who?"

"Politicians mostly. I help them choose their running mates, their cabinets, their experts. I find men and women of skill and introduce them to people with money and political capital."

"And tonight you're looking for me?"

"That's right."

"I'm not sure how I can help, but it feels nice to be wanted."

Auntie smirked and gave her partner a nod. Friend reached into his jacket and pulled out a tattered business card and waved it under my nose. I took it. The corners were fuzzy, and the colors were faded but it was immediately familiar.

Kennedy Stark—Surrogate Reality Deprogrammer
You may be lonely, but you're not alone.

"This is old," I said, turning it over. "My first one."

"That's right."

I laid it on the table. "Where'd you find it?"

Auntie grinned and her tongue rolled across her bottom lip. "We'll get to that."

"Why all the secrecy? I have reasonable office hours."

"This job is delicate."

"They always are."

Friend giggled. Auntie produced a cigarette and lit it. She took one puff and held it to one side. Ghostly ribbons of smoke coiled around her head.

"Tell me about the slogan, *You're lonely, but not alone*," she said. "Where does that come from?"

I hesitated. There was something in her expression that suggested a trick question. I decided to be honest.

"A woman I knew," I said. "Called herself Dee. She introduced me to surrogate reality. Showed me the highs. Showed me how low it can drag a man."

Auntie raised an eyebrow. "Were you the man dragged low?"

"Yes, ma'am."

"And where is this woman now?"

"No idea. She disappeared."

"Have you looked for her?"

"I did. For a little while."

"Any luck?"

"What do you think?"

Auntie paused to pluck a thread of loose tobacco from her lower lip. She handed her cigarette to Friend and reached below the table. She pulled up a single five-by-seven photograph and laid it face down on the table.

"How about now?"

I flipped the photo and my heart pumped ice water. It was a picture of a young woman curled up on a recliner in a heavy wool sweater, looking up from a hardcover book into the camera. She had a narrow face, a proud Roman nose, and a tangle of wavy brown hair pulled back into a ponytail. Her skin was smooth with an olive tint, matching her hazel eyes. She looked about twenty-five, but had the poise and weariness of a woman much older and more jaded—a nun or a professor. This was her. The woman who disappeared. Dee. The one that got away.

Still in shock, I looked at Auntie. She saw everything on my face. My worry, my confusion.

"Something wrong?" she said.

I swallowed and looked at the photo again. The woman's stoic eyes dragged me in, holding me. Always serious, never joyful. Exactly as I remembered her—aloof, intelligent, beautiful, a bit disappointed by everyone.

Auntie cleared her throat and reached across the table to tap the bottom corner of the photo.

"Notice anything else?"

I looked closer. It was my business card, sitting on the corner of a table just behind the girl. My chest constricted. Had she been looking for *me*?

"This was taken at her father's house in the spring," Auntie said. "The last known photo of Delia Walsh. Ring any bells?"

Dee, Delia. She never told me her last name, but it made sense. The pieces fit, but I couldn't see the whole puzzle.

"The only Walsh I know is Washington's senior senator," I said.

Auntie nodded. "Senator James Walsh's only child."

Feeling myself growing warm, I handed the picture across the table. Auntie shook her head and shooed it back.

"That's yours," she said. "You'll need it."

"Need?" I said, trading my gaze between the pair. "Is she missing?"

"You beat me to it."

I looked at the photo again, then tucked it away in my jacket.

Auntie smiled and tapped the table with a slender finger.

"Time to show him, Friend," she said.

Friend reached into his own jacket and pulled out an envelope and laid it flat. I looked but didn't touch.

"That's a retainer," Auntie said. "Ten thousand to find Delia and bring her home. If you succeed, it's ninety more."

"If you're talking to me, I assume she's in a surreal somewhere."

"That's right."

I looked down at the envelope. I didn't know what ten thousand in bills looked like, but the bulk was large enough to start me salivating.

"Do you know where she's logged in?" I said.

"We do, in fact."

"You don't need me, then. Grab her when she comes up for air."

"We'd like you to do that."

"Why?"

"Because she seems to trust you."

"Okay. So where is she exactly?"

"Pocket that cash and we'll get there."

"Are you allergic to straight answers, Auntie?"

She batted her lashes. "Not when they're readily available."

I nodded and palmed the envelope. Auntie shot a hand forward and coiled her fingers around my wrist. Her glinting stiletto nails clicked against the table.

"Tomorrow morning, 9:00 a.m.," she said. "We'll send a car."

"All right."

"We have a deal?"

I nodded. Auntie sighed and withdrew her arm. Drawing back she stretched and squeezed out a tiny, squealing yawn, hiding it with the back of her hand. She turned to Friend.

"It's getting late, darling."

Friend nodded and the pair moved in unison, each sliding out of the booth on their own side, dragging their coats behind them. I stood as a courtesy. Friend rose to his full height, just a finger over five feet, and wrapped himself in a trench coat. When Auntie stood, she towered above the both of us, an easy six and a half feet. She yanked a fur shawl from the bench and tossed it over her shoulders with the speed of an attacking cougar.

"Thanks for the drink," I said.

Auntie reached out and tweaked my chin with a little snap. Winking, she said, "She got away once. Don't let it happen again."

With that she left, swaying across the room to join her Casanova. Bartender Rick was leaning against the ice machine, nose buried in his phone, a wet towel over his shoulder. Auntie clapped once.

"We're done here."

Rick stuffed his phone away and shot forward dutifully, tossing the dish towel on the bar and stepping behind Auntie like a well-trained bloodhound. When he reached the door, he grabbed a leather jacket from a wall hook and dove into the Cavern's sallow brightness.

When I was sure they'd gone, I picked up the envelope and pried it open. Inside was a tight stack of crisp hundreds. The count looked right.

I stuffed the envelope in my jacket and checked my watch. It was just past nine. I looked down at the bottle and wondered how much of that whiskey could get between me and nine a.m. without causing trouble. Making a quick calculation, I topped off my glass. As soon as it was gone I poured another. And another.

. . . *When I was six months out of school Locksley contacted me again. Breathless intensity in that conversation. A man on the hunt.*

Delia, he said. It's Pritchard. Surreality is coming up. You want to introduce This Little World to a broader audience?

Surreality. Annual SR convention held in Seattle. A favorite of Devs and Fans and a trawling ground for VC leeches.

I considered it, I told him. Until I missed the submission deadline.

I'm on the selection committee, he said. Deadlines are an illusion.

So he snapped his fingers, and I was in.

The premise of This Little World was pretty simple. It was a surreal generated by the action of the users' thoughts. My code could read minds, so to speak, and render the contents of a person's imagination in a way that felt like lucid dreaming. It was a novel idea but not unprecedented. Three years earlier I had tripped in a surreal called Simphony that rendered polyphonic orchestral scores based on the user's verbal and mental instructions. I took that idea and broadened the spectrum.

Over the convention's three days, This Little World made waves. The buzz was kind, but the headlines were overblown. Go spelunking in your brainpan! Psychosis surfing is the next big thing! Get high on your own supply (of neuroses)! The attention annoyed me, but Locksley saw the bigger potential of what I'd built long before I did. I wouldn't catch on until much later.

Two weeks after Surreality closed, Locksley invited me out for drinks at one of his humid First Avenue haunts. The Pink Door, a burlesque dinner theater downtown. I arrived after a show had just finished and Locksley was already buzzing with excitement for the offer he wanted to make. As soon as I took a seat he huddled in, arm over my shoulder as if we were planning the assassination of someone very popular.

I'm working on something new, Dee, he said. Something that will change the world. And I want you to be a part of it.

What's the pitch? I said.

Just say yes, he said.

I shook my head and lifted his arm from my shoulder and laid it like a hock of ham on the table in front of us.

First and foremost, I said, I work for myself. I follow my interests. If I work with you, it's because I have something to say. And I can walk away at any time. I retain all intellectual and material property rights. So think carefully about what you're offering.

He leaned back and clapped slowly with a drunk grin spreading across his cheeks.

Hallelujah, he said. I am talking to the right woman . . .

4

BACK WHEN I WAS A PRIVATE INVESTIGATOR, I spent most of my days chasing fraud claims and infidelities in equal measure. I was good, but the job was easier and less romantic than any television fantasy had prepared me for. Investigative work was mostly about three things—scouring the internet for loose data, reviewing surveillance footage, and waiting. And the pay was shit. I was living for the job, hour to hour—in the moment as most gurus advise—letting my life slip quietly by. Without a goal to nudge me forward, each day was a fresh opportunity for circumstantial happiness. I didn't desire anything. I had nothing to strive for, nothing to work toward, nothing worth losing. Joy wasn't something to be pursued; it either happened, or it didn't.

The day I met Delia—Dee as she introduced herself—I felt something different. Something worth striving for.

I was tailing a literature professor named Koontz from the University of Washington at the behest of his wife. She suspected him of the usual extramarital experiments. I had a hunch he was just a studious bore, and for the better part of three weeks my assumption played out. Koontz was a creature of habit. He spent mornings in lectures, lunches at a café on the Ave with rapt students, afternoons in his tiny office, and he was always on a bus headed home by eight p.m. It was those extended office hours that worried his wife. But after weeks of tailing him I had seen nothing untoward and was ready to write up a clean bill of fidelity.

It was a Friday when he finally broke his pattern. The sky was gauzy and spritzing rain. Around five p.m. he appeared outside his office unexpectedly and marched south across campus. I tailed him down a thoroughfare fluffed with fallen cherry blossoms until he veered into a hulking brick building with tightly packed square windows. A sign above the door read *The Allen Center for Computer Science and Engineering*. I followed him in.

The interior was open and airy. Koontz moved fast across a bright atrium to a central staircase and scurried up. When he reached the third floor he ducked through a passage that took him deeper into unseen annexes. I sprinted to catch up and peeked through the door just in time to see him enter an open classroom. I moved down the hall and glanced inside.

Koontz was just past the door, his back to me, talking quietly to a woman seated behind a long table piled with books and fliers. I passed and stopped in front of a corkboard pinned with conference announcements and tutor offerings. I feigned a freshman's interest and waited.

Five minutes unfolded. Then ten. Koontz never reemerged. I backtracked past the classroom door, and I peeked inside. The woman Koontz had been talking to was alone at her table, reading from a gargantuan book. Koontz was nowhere in sight.

I walked in. The woman didn't look up. Her book was more interesting than anything that might come through that door. I couldn't tell if she was a student or faculty. She looked young but dressed older. She had brown hair as coarse as a horse's mane pulled back in a simple ponytail. Her eyes were as large as quarters, and she had freckled olive skin and a large Roman nose. She wore a baggy, beige wool sweater and tight black jeans. I found her gorgeous in a way that felt ancient and pagan.

I cleared my throat. She closed the book over her finger and looked up. I read the title: *The Complete Works of William Shakespeare*.

"Here to volunteer?" she said.

"I must be."

"Do we have you on file?"

"I doubt it. I'm new to the area."

"To the university?"

"To Seattle."

"Welcome to suicide city."

"That's a morbid greeting."

"It's a morbid place." She stretched sideways and snapped up a piece of paper from a short stack and started filling it out. I stole a look around the room, searching for signs of Koontz. In the room's far corner was an emergency exit. I bit my lip. Koontz was long gone.

The woman spun the form and pushed it across the table. A liability waiver. She laid her pen across the page.

"You can fill the rest of this out."

"What sort of danger am I facing?"

She waved her hands as if casting a spell. "The standard SR ailments. Nausea. Temporary memory loss. Fatigue. Headaches."

"No worse than a night of clubbing."

"Without the volcanic vomiting," she said. "Is that okay?"

"Nothing I can't handle."

She sat back and pulled her book closer. "Let me know when you're done."

I nodded stupidly and scooped up the paper and walked it to a student's desk. I filled the form with improvised details and returned.

"I was supposed to meet a friend here," I said, capping the pen and laying it down. "Leonard Koontz. He told me this sort of thing was right up my alley."

The woman looked up again. "You know Dr. Koontz?"

"I do. And his wife. Good people."

"They are. You just missed him."

I feigned a frown. "I'll catch him later I guess."

The woman nodded and reached below the table. She fumbled around in a backpack or shoulder bag. When she found what she needed, she straightened up and held it out.

"He'll be here tonight."

Pinched between her fingers was a thin keycard made of hard plastic, about the size of a credit card. There was a barcode and a street address etched on one side, followed by THIS LITTLE WORLD. BETA 1.4 in bold block capitals.

"This Little World," I read aloud.

"Doors open at five."

"What is it?"

"An experimental surreal. One of many we'll be testing this weekend."

"I've read about surreals. Never tripped though."

She smirked sourly, somehow perfecting a new look. "You've read about mainstream surreals," she said. "The latest middlebrow opiate. We're doing something new. Something serious."

I palmed the card and slid it into my pocket. "Sounds interesting," I said. "And if Koontz is going, I'll be there."

She nodded. "He should be." She bent forward and looked down at the filled-out form. "Samuel?"

"Sam is fine."

"Hello Sam, I'm Dee. We'll see you there."

Her eyes bore into me with a questing intensity. Feeling anxious suddenly, I turned as if to leave and walked to the door. When I stole a look backward she was back to reading her gargantuan book. I wanted to say something to keep me in her thoughts, but I had no idea what that might be. So I left.

AROUND NINE THAT EVENING I left my apartment and hailed a cab. The driver sped us down Third Avenue, through the financial guts of Seattle and the nineteenth-century kernel of the old city, past a pair of arenas, coming at last to the dark industrial sprawl of rain-racked warehouses and graveled avenues.

The cab pulled into a massive but mostly empty parking lot at the foot of the abandoned Starbucks central offices, a looming brick and glass edifice some eight stories high with a squared-off clock tower at its center. Most of the building was dark, but a weak light glowed in the lobby. I paid my driver in cash and the cab sped away, leaving me alone with the brown noise rush of overflying jets and the hollow ring of offloading cargo in the harbor to the northwest.

I entered the building alone. The lobby was spacious and quiet with soaring columns and twisting beams of gnarly, burnished wood. A plain white sandwich board with an arrow pointed toward the central elevators. Text below the arrow read:

LSRC Beta Tests. 7th Floor. Invitation only.

At the elevators, a grizzled man in a tattered security vest checked my passkey at the elevator. Accepting it as authentic, he swiped his own keycard over a wall-mounted reader. The elevator door opened, and I stepped inside.

I debarked at the seventh floor. Directly opposite the elevators were two husky security guards standing before an enormous double door. They stiffened as I stepped out. I held up my access card. One of the men gestured wordlessly at a sensor embedded in the wall. I thanked him and swiped.

Beyond was a waiting room packed with two dozen people of various ages and attitudes. There was a second greeting desk here with the fading phrase *Coffee Tasting Labs* faintly visible against its front panel, remnants of missing letters pried off and discarded. Behind the desk was a young woman with a springy halo of curled hair and a crooked smile.

"Welcome to the Locksley Surrogate Reality Consortium," she said. "You can register here."

She slid a touch screen tablet across the counter. I hesitated before entering Samuel, the name I had given Dee. A lie that felt worse now that I had to repeat it. I punched it in anyway. A second document appeared—a liability waiver.

"Any risk of me dying in here?" I said.

The woman smiled. "Not likely," she said. "It's a formality."

"What happens if I don't fill this out?"

She pointed at the doors I had come through. "You go back the way you came and enjoy the rest of your evening."

"Just checking."

I signed the waiver and hit enter. The tablet beeped and she took it from me and looked it over.

"Thank you, Samuel," she said. "Someone will be with you shortly."

I took a seat as far from other people as possible and waited. A few minutes later a pale young man in a lab coat appeared and called someone's name. An older man about Professor Koontz's age stood up and scurried through another door. The young man followed.

Thirty minutes passed like this—the young man entered, called another name, and ushered them out. Finally he called me. I hopped to my feet and hurried through the door, eager to get on with this. The young man guided me down a long, high-ceilinged hallway with windowed doors spaced every twenty feet. Each door had a placard that read *Coffee Lab* followed by a number. I walked softly, listening for clues as to what was happening behind each. But the place was oddly silent.

The young man stopped us at 723. He opened the door and stepped aside to usher me through. The so-called lab was nothing more than a tiny cafeteria—an intimate space with polished stone floors and wood paneled walls. There was an island counter in the middle of the room and another longer counter with an embedded sink on the far side. Between the island and the sink counter was a massage chair with vinyl cushions. On the floor beside the chair was a bulky computer console with a monitor and keyboard perched on a tall metal end table. Running from the computer was a cluster of half a dozen wires, bound together with Velcro strips and coiled in a pile upon the ground.

My host gestured at the massage chair.

"Take a seat and we can begin."

I sat with caution, and he crossed to the computer. He tapped out something, then turned and lifted his eyes to the corner of the room. There was a small camera there. He gave it a thumbs up and turned back to the keyboard.

"All right," he said, still typing. "Are we ready?"

I nodded and leaned forward, pushing my face into the padded circle. As soon as I was prone, I felt his hand on my neck. He folded my collar into my shirt and something wet swabbed my skin, chilling it.

"You'll feel a slight sting," he said gently. "It won't last."

His grip stiffened. A second later two chilly needles pierced my neck, about two inches apart. I flinched but the man held firm and the pain subsided.

"All good?" he said.

"Good enough," I grunted.

"Here we go."

I opened my mouth to ask what I should expect. But it was too late. I felt a quick shock before a sucking emptiness swallowed me. A hollowness. I had only enough time to wonder, *Am I dying?* Then nothing but darkness.

I opened my eyes. I was back in the tasting lab, standing alone beside the massage chair. My host was gone. Everything else looked the same. The computer console, the piles of wires, the wood paneling. The camera was there too, watching me with its glazed eye.

I crossed to the door and slipped out. The hallway was just as empty as when I'd first walked in. But something felt different. A persistent low rumble shook the building from somewhere deep within the earth, like an earthquake forever in its earliest stage. As I gathered my thoughts, a long low moan drifted down the hall from somewhere ahead. I knew that sound well. It wasn't from pain. I moved toward it.

The moaning got louder as I approached a set of operating room doors at the hall's far end. Dark silhouettes flashed and flitted across its pair of narrow windows. A placard just below them read *Exhibition Theater*. I pressed my nose to the glass and peered in.

A bright spotlight shone on a bare island counter at the center of a spacious viewing chamber, illuminating a familiar pair fucking in full view of an audience. The man was Professor Koontz, supine on the counter, his unbuttoned dress-shirt hanging like gray jowls over the side. The woman straddling him was Dee, naked from the waist down, riding him with slow grinding thrusts. Koontz's arms were upright and locked straight, his hands clawing beneath her fluttering blouse. Dee leaned forward and sucked hungrily on the professor's lips. He gnashed back. Their passion was seismic. I watched for too long before realizing this was the evidence I needed to conclude my case.

I pulled out my phone and swiped on the camera and took aim. I waited for Koontz to come up for air to get a clean shot of his face. Dee rose up in the throes of passion. The professor turned, gasping. I snapped a picture, then flipped to the photo album to review it.

The last image in the set was a dark and grainy photo of a man asleep in a twin-sized bed. He lay on his back, naked and sprawled like a broken starfish, with crumpled sheets and a duvet bunched up on the floor. I pinched the picture to zoom in, hoping to make out more detail. As I narrowed in on the man's face, he moved, groaning and stretching. A pool of saliva darkened his pillow. He rolled to one side. A slash of moonlight brightened his stubbled face. It was me.

Someone knocked on a distant door. Four hard hits. I rose up from the bed, smacking my lips and looking around. Four more knocks. I yawned and planted my feet on the cold hardwood and rose with effort. My bedroom bucked like a brig in a storm and my tongue burned with the faint taste of battery acid. I dragged myself across the room, not walking so much as willing myself forward. I floated down a dark hall toward a pinpoint of light in a tunnel of murky shadow. I pressed my face to the peephole.

Dee stood on the far side, fidgeting with her arms wrapped around herself and throwing nervous looks at something down the hall. Something spooked her and she threw herself against the door, beating it with her fists.

"Kennedy, please!" she screamed. "Let me in!"

I tore off the chain and threw the door wide. Hard yellow light flooded my apartment. A figure stepped forth from a cloud of swirling fog—William "Billy" Brighton. He raised a gun to my face and leered with unholy glee.

"Leave me the fuck alone," he hissed.

I opened my mouth. The gun went off. Fractals of red and white lightning bloomed around me, obscuring everything. I fell backward, missing the ground and plunging into a void without resistance or the rush of wind. Just a nauseating descent into nothingness.

I halted suddenly. From sixty to zero in an instant. Still blind, I groped around. A soft warm sand flowed between my fingers, and a rank odor filled my nose. At a distance I could hear the crash and retreat of an ocean surf. I pushed myself to my knees and squinted through the glare. The light faded. My vision returned.

A dirty beach stretched before me in all directions, sprouting like a fetid garden with plastic trash and heaps of fermenting kelp and the rotting carcasses of shapeless sea life. The sky above pulsed with clouds the color of infected tissue. I stood and took a deep breath. That was a mistake. The stench of death and the reek of the blooms burned my lungs. My head spun. I gagged. Gasping for cleaner air I pulled my shirt collar across my mouth. To my surprise, I found an oxymask hanging from my neck. I slipped it on and pulled the strap taut and twisted the valve's knob to open the flow of sweet air.

A few short breaths steadied me. My head stopped spinning. I looked out across the beach at the frothing pink ocean and the rancid horizon beyond. The algae blooms had overtaken all. The view in all directions looked like a digital video generated by a careless algorithm using unrelated prompts—*Beach*, *Strawberry Daiquiri*, *Dead Squids*, *Bird Shit*, *Sadness*. Absurd on its face, but a plausible picture of a dying Earth's future.

I stepped among the wrack and death spawn with a feeling of growing disgust and anger. A faint wailing reached my ears, a mere whimper on the wind. I searched for its source but saw nothing. This cry was soon joined by a second, then a third. A growing chorus of agony swelled around me. Drowning disembodied voices, followed by screams. People in abject pain. I moved faster down the beach, searching for someone, anyone I could help. Someone I might pull to safety. But there was no one.

I ran on. The air grew hot and syrupy, sticking to my skin as the moldering mounds of organic decay grew higher. My shoe came down on what looked like a pile of dead jellyfish and sank with a splat, burying my leg to the knee and sticking me fast. I fell forward and rolled onto my back through a goopy stew of brine.

High above, throbbing clouds of pink and orange slid through the sky. They parted for a moment, revealing a pastel orange disc. It was Mars, closer than I'd ever seen it. I raised an arm and opened my hand, but it was just out of reach.

The sky flashed suddenly. A painful light that obliterated all detail. The screams grew louder. A unified choir of terror.

I pushed myself up and pulled my leg free of the muck, losing my shoe to the sucking mass. I reached out to recover it but stopped. The air was warming fast. I turned to look inland. A flickering ribbon of yellow and white rippled across the jagged horizon. It expanded as I watched, growing wider and taller. I pulled myself to my feet, holding my shoe like a blunt weapon. But what use would it be against the horror that approached? A roaring wall of fire, tearing across the land like a stampede of a million hellish horses. Closer and closer it came. The screams rose in pitch, tearing at my ears. The air crackled and a hot wind hit me across the face, knocking me back.

The wall of fire rose high above me like a crashing wave. I raised my arms. Then it fell. It burned. A scalding pain. My flesh afire.

I screamed, adding my voice to the dying choir—

"Easy now . . ."

I opened my eyes. I lay flat on the floor of the coffee lab, head throbbing from the base of my spine to the wells behind my eyes. My tongue felt burnt and swollen. A hand touched my shoulder. It was Dee. She pressed a palm to my forehead. Someone else entered the room. Dee thanked them and shifted her position and pressed a rubber straw to my lips.

"Electrolytes," she said. "Drink."

The liquid was sweet and faintly fruity. When my strength had returned, Dee helped me to my feet and guided me from the room and down the hall through a set of double doors that opened to a terrace overlooking the front parking lot. An imperial purple glowed in the eastern sky. Morning birdsong scored an airy song. Dee eased me down on a broad wooden bench and stood back to survey me.

"How do you feel?"

"Like I've been hit by lightning."

She said nothing for a moment, resolved to watch me, studying the effects of her exhibition. "Describe for me what you just went through," she said.

"It felt like someone cranked my subconscious through a meat grinder."

"Did you understand the visions? Did they mean something to you?"

"Yeah," I said. "They scared the shit out of me."

She ruminated then helped me to my feet. "Are you strong enough to walk?" she said.

I wobbled before stiffening. "I think so."

"Come. Some exercise will do you good."

We left the building by a service entrance at the back and meandered down a dusty service road toward the city to the north. It was a calm, cool morning. I struggled at first to find my footing, but Delia was patient, and always there to lend a hand.

After a few blocks, my head was clear, and I was walking without aid. Sensing my improvement, Delia prodded me with questions about my experience in her surreal. She wanted a complete accounting, so we spoke of little else over the course of our stroll. I was a willing captive to her interrogations, and the more I talked the more I found myself recalling minute details of my experience—specific sounds and smells and surges of emotion. Delia listened with a questing intensity. She was studious and thorough, with an artist's sense of purpose and eye for detail. She had the mind of a scientist, and I was her sprawling dataset. The more I told her, the more she could calibrate her surreal for future subjects.

After an hour of walking, we reached Pioneer Square and Seattle's original waterfront. Coming to a broad public pier jutting into the Puget Sound, we strolled its length and took up residence on a salt-blasted bench overlooking the lapping frothy waters. The gag tide was dormant, and the sea winds smelled of brine and creosote. Our conversation moved from technical topics to the personal. Light and friendly conversation commenced. She asked about me, where I was from and where I was going. Inquisitive questions that punctured the softest parts of me. This turn to kindness surprised me. So much so that my hands began to tremble. When I swallowed, cold air went down like raw cotton.

"It's rare to meet someone like you," I said. "So smart and serious, so kind and beautiful. With your head in the right place . . ."

She cocked her head with a wary look. "You don't know me."

"I know enough," I said. "I feel it. You're someone who gives a shit. Who wants to help. In a world going to hell, that means a lot."

"You think the world's going to hell?"

"You saw my feed," I shrugged. "It's all I think about."

She nodded solemnly. "These are rough days," she said. "But I suspect every generation feels that way."

I shook my head violently. "It's not just a feeling. The scars are everywhere. Right outside your window. The blooms, the wars, the famine, the hurricanes. Everybody's logging in to escape the inevitable explosion. They're fleeing their own lives because everybody's fucking terrified. Terrified and lonely."

"Maybe. But we're together in our isolation. A solitary ensemble. Lonely but not alone. The day we understand that is the day things get better."

I dragged my shoes back and forth over the splintering wood of the pier. "People don't know themselves anymore. Everyone's playing a role. Acting for an audience they don't even have."

She smiled and laid a hand on my shoulder. "Including you, Kennedy Stark? The alcoholic gumshoe with a heart of gold?"

My stomach churned. "You know my name?"

Dee winked. "Like you said, I saw your feed."

I drew a shuddering breath. "Can't hide anywhere."

"Not from yourself."

I swallowed hard. I had nothing else to say. Dee watched me a moment longer, then stood and took out her phone. Rosy morning light brightened her face with a newborn's tint. She dialed a number and waited. I closed my eyes and rubbed the back of my neck and listened as she ordered a cab to our location. Then we walked back to the street in silence.

When the cab arrived, Dee opened the door and guided me in. Hanging on to the frame, I swung inside and turned to say goodbye. She gave me a wave and a nudge.

"Scoot," she said.

I slid left and she slipped in and shut the door. The driver asked for a destination. I gave my address. He nodded and we headed north. Dee was silent for most of the drive. When the cab reached my apartment, I waited for her to say something. I wanted her permission to leave.

"Does your head still hurt?" she said finally.

I laid my hand on my neck. I hadn't noticed the pain for several hours, but when I focused my attention, it was still there—a mild, itching burn. I nodded. Dee reached into her jacket and pulled out a small amber bottle. She popped the top and tapped out two pills—pale green diamond lozenges.

"This should help."

They went down hard, like whole grapes. Dee held out her hand.

"Thank you for today," she said. "You've been a big help."

"Will I see you again?"

"Goodbye, Kennedy."

I took her hand to shake it. She pulled me in and brushed a soft kiss against my cheek. Without a word I slipped from the taxi and shut the door. The car shot off. I watched the silhouette of Dee's head through the window, waiting for a last glance backward. It never came.

Looking up at my building, I felt a sudden sadness. I had nothing to return to—no joy, no ambition, no happiness. Nothing but dirty rags hanging from the lowest rungs on the hierarchy of needs. I turned away and walked to a nearby bar and drank in a brooding silence. Well into my second double bourbon, I realized the terrible mistake I'd made. Delia's painkillers did not play nice with alcohol. Soon I was spinning and reeling. I stumbled out of the bar onto the street. My legs were gelatin pillars, puppeteered by an epileptic god. I made it half a block before I pitched headfirst into the sidewalk.

I woke hours later on a gurney in the recovery ward of a hospital. My head was pounding. A fiery pain ran down my spine and into my limbs. Outside the day was darkening. Through the window, between a pair of skyscrapers, I could see the last embers of sun slipping behind the Olympic mountains far across the Sound.

I struggled to sit up and looked around for an emergency call button. A nurse appeared before I found it. She gave me the full story as she'd heard it. I'd been brought in by a pair of men who claimed to have found me face down in the street somewhere in Belltown. She asked what drugs I'd been taking. I described them as best I could, but the nurse was stumped. She took my temperature and left. A short time later a doctor visited. He asked the same questions, palpated my abdomen and checked my pupils, and told me I was free to go.

It took a week to feel normal. When I did, I set out to look for Dee. I couldn't get her out of my head. Her beauty, her intelligence, her generosity. The overwhelming feeling of completeness I had felt in her presence. I missed her.

I began with a visit to the abandoned Starbucks building. I went at midday. A single receptionist greeted me in an otherwise empty lobby. She told me the SR event had already ended. They'd packed up and moved on. The space was now available for rent at a reasonable price.

Next I scoured the University of Washington for alumni named Dee, or women whose name began with a D. But the sample size was too large and in many cases I could never find a picture or portrait to accompany the name. I even visited the classroom in the Allen building where I had first met her. A programming class was underway. Dead end.

Further internet searches turned up nothing. I was stumped. Dee's total lack of digital footprints was remarkable for someone so plugged in to technology. The possibility that she was a complete and utter fantasy crossed my mind, but that couldn't explain our first meeting at the university.

Eventually I came around to the unwelcome idea that her name wasn't Dee at all. I had fed her a string of lies to get close. She might have done the same to entice an oblivious test subject. This hypothesis was oddly comforting. It turned a bland act of ghosting into an elaborate and premeditated conspiracy.

A comforting way to preserve my ego, I suppose. But it didn't dull the shame.

. . . It was the first time I'd ever seen Locksley scared. Standing in the lobby of my building, pacing and shaking, the threat of litigation at the forefront of his mind. His major weakness on full display. When I emerged from the elevator, he tore the sunglasses from his face.

What the hell happened at the Beta Lab last night? he said. Is this gonna bite me in the ass?

It's nothing, I said. We handled it.

I hear we fried some guy's brain, he said. We got a vegetable on our hands?

Jesus, no, I said. It was a volunteer from the University. After an hour inside, he succumbed to a cascade of catastrophic ideation. It freaked him out, like a bad psilocybin trip. But he's fine, I promise. Probably sitting in front of his TV right now with a warm bowl of soup and a bottle of ibuprofen.

Locksley stopped pacing, but his voice was still pitchy and quick.

Catastrophic ideation, he said. I don't want that on the warning label of any surreal associated with me, okay?

We always knew this was a possibility, I said. It happened and it worked itself out. It's the nature of the beast. But it's not dangerous.

Right, he said. Right. He pointed at the elevators. Can I come up?

I shook my head. I didn't trust his energy.

Sorry, I said. My roommate has guests.

He nodded, still staring at the elevators like he might bolt past me anyway. Then he shook himself like a dog tossing off water. He was calm again. Almost placid.

Anyway, he said. Let's iron this out in the next build.

Or shelve it entirely, I said. Work on something new.

He laughed. Sure, he said. And all that money I spent to help you improve This Little World, what was that? A donation?

You spent that money on me, I said. As we agreed.

Look, Dee, he said. I'm more than happy to let you experiment in whatever direction you want. But This Little World is key to our next phase, and I need you to take it seriously.

Then tell me what the next phase is, I said. Maybe I'll give a shit.

You can't stand the suspense?

I'm losing patience, I said. Most of us are. You have dozens of the brightest designers in North America working under you, but all we've been doing for two years is endless beta tests, endless bug fixes, endless iterations for no apparent reason. You should know better than anyone that deadlines are motivating. Deadlines let you finish things and walk the fuck away. Because I'm getting sick of This Little World. And I'm ready to move on.

Locksley listened, nodding and grinding his jaw. I think he finally understood. He could do that sometimes. Less and less nowadays. But back then, he could really listen when he wanted to. Because he did seem to want the best from us. From me.

You're right, he said. You deserve an explanation.

We all do, I said.

That's right. All of you . . .

5

THE MORNING AFTER MY MEETING WITH AUNTIE, I woke with the first rays of day. The sky was clear, and birds were singing sweetly, and I wasn't half as hungover as I wanted to be. As I lay abed, Auntie's challenge swam in the cold creek of my thoughts.

She got away once . . .

I scraped away the morning's sourness and freshened up. Sitting down to toast and coffee, I pulled out my phone and tapped it on. Four messages from yesterday craved my attention, so I called in. The first two were from Melina Brighton, recorded when I was stalking her husband in the Five Borough Blues. We'd talked already, so these went in the bin. The third message was from a potential client with another suspected virtual infidelity. I hit save. The fourth was a hang up. I binned it and kept eating.

I was rinsing dishes when my phone rang. I answered to a man's voice as smooth and slow as peanut butter.

"Kennedy Stark?"

"That's right."

"A car is on its way. Twenty minutes."

"I'll be ready."

"Pack a bag."

"Oh yeah? How long am I staying?"

"That's up to you. Twenty minutes."

The line went dead.

I pulled a dusty valise from my closet and brushed it down and threw in a few shirts and pants and pairs of underwear. I folded up two nice jackets and added a tie for good measure. Last to go in was my black vinyl bathroom kit, always packed and ready for speedy departures.

I parked the valise by the front door and returned to my studio bedroom. I tucked the picture of Delia in my jacket pocket, then pulled a thousand bucks in hundreds from Auntie's advance and stuffed it into my wallet. I slid the envelope with the remaining nine thousand dollars under the mattress of my Murphy bed. Now I was ready to go. I moved to the door and grabbed my bag and set out.

I was on my stoop barely five minutes when a slate gray sedan pulled up, an electric Ford Boson a few years old. The driver's seat was empty. The car rolled to a crackling stop and fell silent, idling like a stone, all circuits on standby. There was nobody inside, front or back. Self-driving.

I opened the driver's door. The interior was clean and streamlined and so ultra-modern it would be out of date by next Wednesday. I threw my bag on the passenger seat and climbed in. The moment my rear hit the upholstery an artificial voice greeted me with perfect gentility: "*This vehicle is reserved for Mr. Kennedy Stark. Please state your name clearly.*"

I spoke my name as clearly as possible.

"*Voice print identified. Welcome aboard Mr. Stark. Please fasten your seat belt.*"

I sat back and buckled up. When the belt clicked, a dashboard screen the width of my forearm blinked on, displaying a map of northwestern Washington State traced with today's route. My destination was a point in the north Cascade mountains almost three hours away called the Diablo reservoir. A red button labeled *Go* blinked at the bottom of the map.

I didn't press it. Getting cozy, I took the steering wheel in both hands and gave it some torque. It budged barely a centimeter before snapping back to center. I laid my hands on my thighs and looked around for something resembling an electronic eye. I fixed on the rearview mirror.

"Who's paying for this ride?" I asked the car.

The car said nothing. The button labeled *Go* continued to blink.

"Are you a dumb smart car or one of the clever ones?" I said.

Still the car said nothing. I pressed the button.

The steering wheel folded in half and retracted, and a panel dropped to conceal it. The Boson eased into a smooth roll and moved down the street. Turning left and left again it joined a trickle of traffic heading west.

We passed the Lake Union Autonomous Zone, now in its seventeenth anarchic year, and hit the interstate on a ramp heading north. Now on the straight and narrow, I settled in for a long, lonely drive up I-5. Clawing at the car's screen, I tapped around to find some music and settled on something beaming out of California. I made it ten minutes before they cut in to talk about the next round of drought evictions in southern California. It was hard to sympathize with people like that—people who refused to leave even after they'd been warned, when they knew what was coming for months and years. But I felt bad for them all the same. People fighting to live where water is scarce—where it's shipped in for a couple hundred bucks a gallon—is exactly what they were doing on Mars right now. Human ingenuity meets idiot pride, I guess. Brave and stupid all at once.

Turning the volume down to a whisper, I knocked the seat back and crossed my arms and closed my eyes.

I opened them again to find a light rain falling over the rolling evergreen foothills of the North Cascade mountain range. Lush, humpy towers of rock rose from the earth like the mossy backs of sleeping trolls. Deeper in the mountains we passed the lichen green of Gorge Lake as the road began to rise, curving up a cliffside that brought us to the sloping face of the Diablo dam.

Slowing down, the Boson veered off the highway and crossed the dam to the river's north side. Leaving the paved road, it crept down a hidden service trail overgrown with wild grasses and spiky shoots of knapweed. After a few dozen yards it opened onto a broad rectangular lot packed with gravel. There were two SUVs parked here—one black, the other liquid silver—at the lot's southern edge, a steep grade that dropped to the river valley far below. The lot's remaining sides were bounded and bulked with wild foliage. My Boson pulled in on the near side of the pair of vehicles and came to a stop. The doors unlocked with a gentle clack.

"*We have arrived at your destination.*"

I patted the dash and slapped on my hat and stepped out. A sweet piney breeze kissed my face as I stretched and looked around. Due west, a narrow footpath cut through a tangle of blackberries. It was the only obvious way forward. As I approached, I noticed a toppled wooden sign rotting among the leaves. In faded letters it read *Gondola for pass holders only*. I continued on.

The path brought me to a trampled clearing at the westerly edge of the bluff where a squared-off log cabin overlooked the dam and the dribbling river. The cabin had a ticket booth built into its front-facing wall and a sign above its window read *Welcome to the Diablo Gondola*. To its right was the topmost pulley tower of a gondola lift. A rusting passenger car hung from its twisted cable, creaking mournfully. Beneath this noise was the hushed sound of people in conversation. I moved closer.

On the cabin's south side, two men in matching beige trenches stood at the lip of the cliff staring down. Apart from their identical outfits, they were opposites in every regard. The big one was boulder-shaped—a broad middle with narrow shoulders and a tapering rear planted on two trunky legs. A cloud of bluish smoke clung to his head like a gathering storm. His partner was short and slender with a coat draped over his shoulders like it was hanging from a wall hook.

I approached slowly, digging my heels in the gravel to make some noise. The skinny one twitched but didn't turn.

"Glad you could make it, Stark," he said.

"Saturdays are slow," I said.

The big man didn't move but the other turned around, smiling generously. He had a friendly face with smooth dark skin and energetic eyes. His close-cropped hair was thinning up top, with a salt and pepper tinge around the temples. Hanging from his neck was a bespoke suede oxymask in periwinkle blue.

"Come here," he nodded. "Take a look."

I stepped between the pair and looked down. A hundred yards away, at the bottom of a treacherous slope of jagged stone and rough grass was a hulking ash gray edifice that resembled a photo negative of the Parthenon in Athens. But this version looked unfinished—more British brutalist than Greco-Roman classical. It was blocky and faceted, as if a 3D model of the original Parthenon had not been fully rendered, leaving behind a low-polygon approximation of a more detailed building. In spite of this simplification, it retained all the basic elements of the original—a few dozen pillars laid out in an open rectangle, a walled inner sanctum lacking windows with a single dark entrance at the front, a triangular roof with a carved frieze above the front steps.

"Pretty gaudy," I said. "Some tech billionaire's fantasy mansion?"

The skinny one shook his head and pointed, "Look at the frieze."

I looked again. Etched in the shadows and hues of dark stone was a title: THE FORUM-GATE IX.

"The Forum," I said.

"Heard of it?" said the skinny one.

"Never."

"Only the most well-funded high-tech project in this country's sordid history."

"Well don't I feel dumb?"

"You'll catch on," he said, offering his hand. "I'm Toots." We shook and Toots gestured at his partner. "That's Wallace."

The boulder named Wallace raised his chin and grunted.

"You two friends of Auntie?" I said.

Toots reached into his jacket and pulled out a badge. *Federal Bureau of Investigation*. The tin glinted, despite the overcast light.

"Friends of Uncle Sam," he said.

"Cute," I said. "So why am I here, Toots?"

Toots bit his lip to suppress a smile. "Because you couldn't resist," he said.

"Let me ask another way," I said. "I'm a halter. I trawl digital streams. So why am I in the middle of the Cascade mountains staring at an unfinished vanity project?"

Toots raised a slender finger and pointed at the Gate. "Delia Walsh is inside that vanity project. Four months and counting."

"Inside? What that mean exactly?"

"She's logged in."

My eyes narrowed. "That's an SR theater?"

Toots nodded. I looked down at the structure and laughed. "Bullshit. Four months in SR would put her in a coma."

"That's one theory."

"You want me to prove it?"

"If you're up to it."

I wagged my head. "I don't buy it. The longest SR session on record is thirteen days with hibernation tech. And that guy came out with permanent memory loss and partial motor impairment. Four months is impossible. Maybe the body could handle it, not the brain."

"That's true for consumer grade tech," Toots said. "The middleware shit that Hypo peddles. This is something else. Something new."

I stepped closer to the edge. The looming building seemed to breathe and heave in the diffuse daylight. Toots stepped in behind me. I could feel him close, like a heat lamp on low.

"Admit you're curious," he whispered.

"Sure," I said, turning. "I'm curious why anyone thinks four months in SR is a fruitful use of brain cells. But the world's full of all kinds."

"Such as?"

"The singularity quacks. The ones who call us bags of meat and waterskins. Addlebrained evangelicals dreaming of ditching their bodies to go full digital."

"Exactly. The Forum was funded and built by those quacks. A whole collective of tech bro shadow investors eager to jump-start the silicon phase of human evolution."

My gut twisted. There it was, plainly stated, the technocrats' fantasy—the mass migration of human minds into simulated worlds. That a disinterested federal agent could articulate this ugly idea so easily was cause for worry. Like it or not, the concept was going mainstream. It didn't matter who scorned the idea and who embraced it—the more people knew about it, the harder it would be to squash.

In the brief time I knew Delia Walsh, she didn't strike me as the type to yearn for physical annihilation and a digital afterlife. But we only spent one day together, and one day is only enough time to fall in love. It takes the rest of a man's life to really know someone.

Toots watched me with an amused pucker, waiting for a reaction.

"Delia worked with SR," I said. "Does she work in there?"

Toots pushed his hands into his trouser pockets and kicked a patch of gravel down the escarpment. "As far as we can tell," he said. "She was one of the Forum's original Engineers, one of a few dozen at least. Got the place up and running, designing and coding surreals unlike anything on the market. Something of a wunderkind, I guess. My point being, she knows the Forum inside and out—every line of code, every psychedelic dream, every secret path."

"You mean she knows how to hide."

"You got it. That's why we need somebody with experience in this domain. To get in there and find her without attracting too much attention."

"Is she in legal trouble?"

"In what sense?"

"Four years in this line of work, I've never seen the FBI concerned with run-of-the-mill surreal addiction. If the Feds want her, I figure there's something else."

The big man Wallace turned suddenly, face wrinkled with anger.

"Ain't your fucking business," he growled.

I stood in silence, waiting for a slap. Wallace turned back and resumed his quiet vigil. I looked at Toots. He shrugged.

"Considering who Auntie works for," I said, "I'm guessing Daddy Walsh has something to do with it."

Toots's lips tightened across his teeth. "Does that change things for you?"

"No skin off my back," I nodded. "So where do I start?"

Toots made a fist and pumped it. "That's the spirit," he said. "Follow me."

He set off, back toward the overgrown path, and I followed, leaving his partner standing sentinel at the cliff's edge—silent, aloof, possibly asleep.

—

BACK IN THE GRAVEL LOT, Toots crossed to the black SUV—the closest of the pair—and opened the passenger door and leaned inside. He pulled out a leather attaché case and walked it to the front of the vehicle and laid it on the hood. When he flipped the catches his eyes flashed.

"For your eyes only," he said. "Take a look."

I joined him. He pried open the case and pulled out a thin folder and handed it over. A paper label ran across the top, printed with a name and descriptor: *Jonathan Pike, Auditor*.

"Private money alone didn't make the Forum possible," Toots said. "They pumped in a mess of our tax dollars too. That means Uncle Sam has a seat on the board, and always will until that debt is paid off. Until then, the Forum is obligated to undergo a federal audit once a year."

He tapped the folder in my hand.

"That's the name of this year's auditor," he said. "Have a look. You may recognize him."

I opened Jonathan Pike's file. Clipped to the corner of a short stack of documents was a pristine driver's license—Idaho State with my face prominent, a photo of me I didn't recognize. Artificially generated, I assumed. I scanned the vital stats. Date of birth, height, weight. Everything was mine except the name.

"He's a looker," I said.

Toots nodded. "Mr. America himself. A small business attorney from Boise. Schooled at Gonzaga in Spokane. Has a wife, two kids, gold standard private medical insurance. An honest family man, from what I hear."

I thumbed through the papers behind the license. Toots narrated my discoveries.

"It's basic stuff," he said. "An up-to-date CV, a letter of introduction from the Treasury Department, a detailed background check. Look it over, get to know yourself."

"It's a bit more homework than I'm used to."

"There won't be a quiz, Stark."

I scanned the pages, reading snippets of text half seriously, a pastiche approach. I wasn't convinced this level of detail was important. What mattered was present appearances. The perception of being the right person in the right place.

"Tell me about auditing," I said. "Any special tips or tactics?"

Toots shrugged and shook his head. "We could pay an alpaca to do this job," he said. "The less you say, the more nervous they get. It scares them shitless to think you're hiding something. Just ask an oddball question every so often, something from left field to worry them."

"'How many gigawatts of power does this place draw every hour?'"

Toots snapped. "Christ, you're a natural."

"What if they start asking me questions?"

"Just play dumb. That's all they expect of us."

"That's too bad."

"It sure is. You ever hear a US senator fumble his way through a hearing on technology concerns? You ever hear a congressman talk about medical science on the floor of the House? It's like listening to a microwave boil water. They're insipid. The Dunning-Krueger effect masquerading as an empire. But we don't audit these guys because we want to know something. We do it to remind them who's holding the purse strings."

"Okay. So what's my jurisdiction?"

Toots leaned back against the hood and crossed his arms. "That's the beauty of this arrangement. With some exceptions, you can go where you like, see what you like, do what you like. They can't stop you."

"Sounds straightforward enough. I'll spend a few hours in each surreal until I sniff out a lead. If she's well known, someone'll turn her in."

Toots laughed once, a single muted bark. "You good at math, Stark?"

"I do my own taxes."

"What happens when you take any number away from infinity?"

"What are you saying?

"I'm saying the Forum is big. This place has no boundaries. No end. Or none that I know of. It just goes on and on and on, filling up with one madman's dream after another."

"Okay, so what's that do for my prospects?"

"Hell if I know," Toots said, rubbing the top of his head. "I suspect you'll narrow it down your own way. Like any halter would. Just don't make a big fuss. Don't make it obvious what you're really doing in there. "

"That's true for every job."

"Awesome."

"So when do I start?"

"You pack a bag like I told you?"

"In the car."

"Good. We booked a room for you back in Burlington. Cascadia Inn. It's nothing fancy. Barely habitable actually. But it's all part of the fun. Go there, get some rest. In the morning one of us will bring you a passkey. You'll take that to the Forum shuttle stop and hitch a ride. By this time tomorrow, you'll be inside. Making progress or losing your goddamned mind."

"Looking forward to it."

"Any other questions?"

I thought about it. "Not a question," I said. "A request."

"Okay."

"If I find Delia, you can keep the ninety thousand dollars. I don't want money; I want a favor."

Toots raised an eyebrow and crossed his arms. "Shit," he said. "You're about to say something weird, aren't you?"

"If I find her," I said. "I want a spot on the next colony shuttle."

Toots froze like a paused video. Only his eyes narrowed slightly. "To Mars?"

I nodded. "NASA nominates civilians all the time. It's part of their partnership with Imagine Red," I said. "A high-school teacher went up last year. A painter the year before. Then a journalist and a chef. Surely they can find a use for someone with SR experience and a good grasp of human psychology."

Toots bit his lip. "You surprise me, pal," he said. "In spite of all my snooping you managed to throw me for a loop."

"Yes or no?"

Toots snapped the briefcase and dragged it off the hood. "You think you're being generous?" he said. "A trip to Mars'll cost a lot more than a hundred thousand dollars."

"It won't come out of your budget," I said. "NASA contracts Imagine Red."

"It's still taxpayer money."

I snapped my fingers. "Well what do you know? That's me."

Toots grinned as he rounded the car to the driver's side door. He opened it and tossed the case onto the rear seat, then came back around the door, holding it open.

"I'll do my best," he said. "But it's not our call in the end."

"I get it," I nodded. "I just want a shot, that's all."

Toots laughed suddenly. "Jesus, you got some kind of cold feet," he said, pinching the air. "This close to finding the girl of your dreams and your first instinct is to flee to a planet a million miles away."

"One hundred and forty million."

Toots clucked. "She hurt you bad, I guess."

He looked past me and lifted his chin and pounded the hood of the SUV.

"Pick up the pace, Wallace," he shouted. "We got a busy night."

I turned to see Wallace emerge from the overgrowth, swatting at the ferns and vines. He snarled as he shuffled across the clearing. When he reached the SUV he pulled open the passenger side door and squeezed inside like a melon in a mason jar.

I looked at Toots. He was staring at his phone with an annoyed expression.

"Both of you in one ride?" I said.

He looked up. "What's that?"

"Who's driving the other car?"

He glanced at the silver SUV behind him. "That's Delia's. Been there four months at least."

"A minor detail," I said with a grumble. "You might have said something earlier."

He pocketed his phone. "I was getting there."

"Have you looked inside?"

Toots rounded the door again and climbed into the driver's seat. I followed until I was standing between the two cars. Toots hung a hand on the door, eager to leave.

"We sniffed around," he said. "You're welcome to look."

"With your permission."

"Granted. Any last questions?"

"Just one. Is this a wild goose chase?"

Toots bit his lip and bobbed his head to a beat deep within himself.

"It's a long shot, to be honest," he said. "The Forum isn't surrogate reality as you know it. It's a madman's experiment. A perpetual novelty, with no limits and no restraints. The people who go in there, they always come out . . . diminished. Less than what they were."

"Have you been inside?"

He scoffed. "No way, brother. Ain't enough money in the world . . ."

He winked and pulled the door shut. I stepped back. The engine turned and the SUV roared to life. Throwing me a salute, Toots backed the car into a jerking three-point turn and peeled out, raising gouts of beige dust in its wake.

Standing alone in the midst of a forest clearing, beside the abandoned vehicle of the woman I'd been hired to find, I flipped through the documents Toots had given me. *John Pike, auditor.* A new identity, adopted in the blink of an eye. I'd never gone properly undercover, but the prospect was intriguing.

I squared off the papers and closed the folder and walked it to the Boson and tossed it on the front seat. Then I turned my attention to Delia Walsh's SUV. For the first time in years, it was time to play detective in real life.

. . . When Locksley brought us to the Forum, he stopped us on the stairs to deliver an impromptu speech.

When I was a young man, he said, beaming with pride, I realized that internet forums were the most important popular medium of the twenty-first century. Books were dead. Television was middling. Video games were pretenders to cinema's vacated throne. Music was insipid, most of it generated by soulless algorithms. And video essayists confused narcissism for style. But the internet forum was a different beast. A popular medium most likely to reach a broad audience. They were democratic in a way that no political body had ever been. They were self-governed—not always equitably but mostly in earnest. And the best of them had a built-in sorting mechanism that migrated its strongest content to the fore. Internet forums were the embodiment of the ancient Athenian ideal. Every voice considered and evaluated.

They were toxic waste dumps, someone said. You're crazy.

Locksley nodded with considered certainty. It's true that over time they siloed themselves off from the real world. They became echo chambers, curated to death. Soon they lacked the churn and friction of real life, they avoided the conflicts and compromises that enrich and educate us as we move through our lives.

He paused thoughtfully and stepped back, making a sweeping gesture as he ushered us forward.

Rest assured, he said grandly, I will not let that happen here in my Forum. Within these walls hides the promise of true freedom. True expression. A place where all things are possible. Please watch your step.

With that brief christening, we entered the Forum. And for better and worse, our lives were never the same.

I explored alone that first day, my mood swinging constantly between awe and anxiety. As far as surrogate reality goes, the Forum was a massive advance of existing tech. What surprised me most of all was its fidelity.

The experience of being inside was indistinguishable from real life. In traditional SRs, you could feel a certain persistent detachment, as if staring at the world through a pair of greasy glasses. In the Forum I felt human. I felt like myself.

I visited every available theater that day, two dozen or so. Far fewer than we have now, but I saw enough to know the world was about to change. In the span of a few hours I lived life as a cat; I wandered the streets of London with a narrator describing my every action; I debated ethics with a pantheon of pre-Socratic philosophers; I ran seven pandemic simulations of a flu variant that I designed myself; and, I took a nap in Napoleon's bed. I can't think of a single more dizzying day in my life. The fundamental power of the Forum was impossible to ignore. It offered an intellectual and emotional experience unlike anything I had ever known.

It was evening when I exited, just a dim orange glow at the rim of the surrounding mountains. I'd been inside almost seven hours, an impossible feat in a mainstream surreal. Yet here I was, feeling rested and rejuvenated. As the other Engineers emerged one at a time, a small group coalesced on the steps outside. We compared our experiences. No one was unimpressed. Locksley appeared soon after to light applause. He absorbed it honestly. Almost humbly.

He hoped we were impressed, he said, because we were his designers. All the work we had done over the past two years, he wanted for the Forum. He was counting on us to make it better.

Six months, sixty theaters, he told us. That's my goal for the Forum's opening.

We clapped, some cheered. We were ecstatic. We could see the future. It was us.

And for the first time in almost a year, I was eager to get back to work . . .

6

I CIRCLED THE PARKED VEHICLE, scanning the big details. Delia had kept it in good condition. It had a nice silver finish, waxed and buffed and free of dents and scratches, now dulled by a heavy dusting of jaundiced pollen, a strong sign the car hadn't moved since early spring. Next I noticed the fuel door—a gas engine. That surprised me, but not for any reasons I could prove. Delia seemed like someone partial to electric engines, so if pressed I'd have guessed it was a gift from her father.

I continued circling. New tires. Expired tabs. Tinted side and rear windows. I cupped my hand to the glass and leaned in close. In the overcast light, I couldn't see much. I moved to the front and bent over the windshield. The dash was dusty but clear enough. There were a few books and loose papers on the passenger seat but nothing that looked valuable. Out of curiosity, I tried the driver's side door. It opened.

I slid halfway into the driver's seat, keeping one leg planted outside. The cabin smelled of citron and dark leather and the fit was tight. I lifted the books on the passenger seat and read their titles. Most were coding handbooks, well outside my understanding. I opened the glove box, and a tangle of receipts sprang out and dropped to the floor mat. I picked up the pile and sorted through nearly a dozen. A few were receipts from stations around Seattle, but most originated from a single station in Burlington—Skagit Gas & Goods. Tugging at the strips like strands of Christmas ribbon, I noticed a message had been scrawled on one with a thick-nibbed marker. I flattened it out.

DON'T FORGET: 5.5.11

The number format appeared to be a date. May the fifth, *Cinco de Mayo*, twenty eleven maybe, possibly some earlier century. Without more context it was just a guess. But the size and boldness of the script gave it an urgency I didn't want to ignore. I folded the receipt in quarters and pocketed it and stuffed the rest of the strips back in the glove box. Last, I checked the sun visors. Nothing there.

I exited the SUV and shut the door and took a last general look around. There was nothing else out of the ordinary. But the longer I lingered, the more its aura darkened. It felt like the origin point of a cliché tragedy. Seven times out of ten, an abandoned car meant a body was not far away. Considering all I'd learned today, that was probably true, in one sense or another.

I walked back to the Boson and crawled inside and knocked on the screen. It brightened with an insipid welcome message.

"My turn to drive," I said. "Can I drive you myself? What do I say, manual? Manual control?"

The dash panel slid open, and the steering wheel telescoped out. I took hold and the engine whirred to life.

"Thank you," I said.

I'm not sure why.

—

DRIVING WEST, I retraced my route over the mountain pass. Bars of golden sunlight cracked the low gray clouds and burned away the rain. By the time I'd reached Burlington it was midafternoon, and a clear sun covered all, giving the day a feeling of renewal.

Skagit Gas & Goods was a compact shoebox station made of brick with a single pump on a cracked and weedy lot. No electric charging stations, just an old-fashioned petrol well with a dingy convenience store. I rolled past the pumps to find parking. Stacks of dented propane lined the front of the building, housed in a battered and rusting cage. Beside this cage was a bench propping up the sagging bones of a man in his seventies. He appeared to be asleep but as the Boson rolled past, his lids lifted slowly like velvet stage curtains. He watched me with delirious interest as I pulled into a spot in front of the door. When I stepped out I waved. The man's eyes fluttered and closed again.

Turning from the building, I walked to the pump and stopped to survey the street beyond. Months ago, Delia had stood right here, taking in the same view and the same moment of meditative silence. It wasn't obvious what attracted her to this particular station. This part of Burlington was unremarkable in every possible way—a prefabricated district with the bland stamp of national franchises that could have been any street in any suburb in America. Directly across the street was a strip mall hosting a mattress seller, a sporting goods outlet, a state bank, and a pet store. A detached Starbucks took up space in the middle of the parking lot, abutting the main road. To my right were two car dealers, to the left an auto mechanic. Nothing here told me a story, just a handful of sad anecdotes.

I walked back to the store and went in. It was hot inside. Two walls of battered refrigerators hummed like angry hornets. A flock of black flies circled in the frosty light above the entrance. Waiting behind the cashier's counter was a scrawny young man in his twenties with greasy blond hair and a set of teeth as wide and spaced out as a garden rake. I crossed to the counter and grabbed a pack of gum and threw it down.

"Prepaying?" he said.

"I drive electric," I said. "Just the gum."

He glanced out the window as if to corroborate my story. Then he squeaked out a sheepish giggle. "I like the smell of gas," he said randomly.

I plucked a hundred-dollar bill from my wallet and laid it down. The cashier wrinkled his nose and opened the register. As he counted out my change, I pulled out the picture of Delia and set it on the counter. When the cashier saw it, his hands stopped moving. He turned to the window, then looked down at the picture again and grunted incoherently.

"You know her?" I said.

"Ah yeah," he nodded. "She used to come in a couple times a week."

"She's my cousin."

"Ah. Cool."

"You know her well?"

He wagged his head hard. "Not really. She wasn't very chatty. Just here to buy gas. Sometimes water."

"What time usually? Early? Late?"

The cashier crossed his arms and shifted uneasily. "Is she okay?" he said.

I took up the picture and stared at it with a look of concern before sliding it back into my jacket.

"We're all a bit worried," I said. "Her mom and dad just want to hear from her. To know she's okay."

"Ah jeez," he frowned. "She always seemed so nice. Way more than her friends."

"Which friends?"

"They'd be with her sometimes. Drunk usually. I don't think she ever was."

"Were they drinking nearby?"

The cashier raised a bony arm and pointed out the window. "Yes sir. Antony's Pizzeria. Behind the Starbucks, you can't see it from here."

I looked anyway, but he was right. "Are they open now?" I said.

"'Til midnight usually," he nodded.

He finished counting my change, an inexplicable pile of bills and coins. I peeled off a five and slid it back.

"Thanks kid. I might come back."

"Okay. If I see her, you know—" he said, trailing off.

I moved to the front door and pushed through. Halfway out, the cashier shouted after me: "T-tell her Cody says hello, if you find her first."

I nodded. "Okay. I will."

"Cody from the gas station," he clarified. "That's me."

THERE WERE NO CARS PARKED IN FRONT OF ANTONY'S, so I slid the Boson into the nearest spot and hopped out. The exterior had the lonely vibe of a money laundering front—blackened windows painted over with flaking exclamatory fonts advertising cheap pizza and cheaper beer. A redundant backlit sign above the door glowed a sickly green: *Antony's Pizzeria – Pizza – Beer – Spirits*. I entered with optimism.

Once inside, the natural light of day scuttled to the corners and died. The joint was a shadowy cave that smelled of stale beer and tomato sauce, overlaid by the odor of pine-scented floor cleaner. Near the door were digital gambling cabinets and a neon-bright claw machine. The main dining area was a single large room with a dozen black tables for four. Along the right wall were a trio of dart boards and four video game cabinets with titles that hadn't been swapped out since the 1990s. A pair of teenage boys were huddled around *Street Fighter II: Hyper Fighting*, their knees buckled and bodies jerking and palms slapping the deck.

I walked to the back of the long room. There was a bar here, separated from the dining area by a horizontal brass pole on three legs, like a hitch for a cowboy's steed. A sign on the pole read *Under 21—No Admittance Beyond This Point*. A woman was tending bar. Early thirties, thin-armed and ruddy featured, with dirty blond hair parted down the middle like two whisk brooms hanging from her head. She was leaning against the counter on one elbow, her back arched, staring up at a TV attached to the wall, watching football.

At the far end of the bar, heaped on a stool, was a lumpy man with a cloud of wavy gray hair and pockmarked skin. Somewhere around fifty, he wore a beat-up black and cream letterman's jacket with the word *Tigers* and the number "27" sewn on the back in a puffy orange font. He was staring at the label of his beer, picking at it with pale fingers and yellowy nails, glancing only occasionally at the flashing screen.

I mounted a withering stool at the bar's opposite end. The man looked up and looked me over. He snorted and took a drink. The bartender turned, surprised to see someone else. She grabbed a coaster and tossed it my way.

"Get you something?" she said.

"Just a beer," I said. "Something local."

She scratched her head and looked over at the glass-fronted fridge. "Kokanee?"

"That's Canadian."

"Canada's local."

"Lay it on me then."

She pulled out a frosty bottle and cracked it open and slid it my way. I took a long noisy drink. It was cold on my tongue and colder going down.

"Twelve dollars," she said. "Chip, plastic, or cash?"

I pulled out a twenty. She took the bill and gave me eight. I left a dollar on the table and put the rest away. Through the whole transaction I could feel the old man's eyes roaming over me with a humid sort of irritation. Beer in hand, I turned to meet his gaze. His eyes were pink and glazed like a squid's mantle. I waved to see if he was conscious. He blinked.

"What?" he mumbled.

"You all right?" I said.

"Just wondering who the hell you are."

"Just a man looking for a drink."

"Sure you are," he snorted. "Like all the others."

"What others?"

He exhaled and swiped his hand down his face, as if washing away a tortured expression. "After they built the Cube on South Burlington, guys like you started showing up in crowds. Nice suits, fancy cars, big wallets. Swarming this town like biblical locusts. Up to something funny, I just know it."

"The Cube?"

He squinted, looking for malice in my question. "Don't get pissy, that's just what I call it," he said. "Seems like every time I walk past, there's guys hanging around it. Rich guys who gather in the early mornings. Sometimes at night."

"What are they doing?"

"What are they—Jesus, you're asking me? You know what they're fucking doing. Don't make me say it."

"Not sure I do."

He grimaced. "Queer shit, you know what I mean? Don't make me say it. I won't fucking say it."

The bartender slapped her hand on the counter, rattling the bar. "Randy," she yelled. "Enough of that shit."

"Okay, okay. God damn, I know your weakness."

The bartender sighed and gave me a scolding look.

"I'm not here looking for any cubes," I said, "I just came to see a friend."

The bartender softened. "Randy's ex-military," she said. "Has a salty way of speaking his mind."

Randy growled. "Fuck's sake, Iris. You don't have to tell every goddamned johnny that comes through that door."

Iris smirked and took up a rag to start cleaning. I turned to face Randy.

"What branch?" I said.

Randy squinted, weighing the value of a response as he sipped his beer. "Marines," he said finally. "Five years active duty. Would have stayed on longer, but I lost most of my sight in this eye." He tapped the cheek below his right socket with a finger that looked like a stripped chicken bone. I leaned in to see, but there was nothing outwardly odd about it.

"How'd it happen?" I said.

"A blow to the head, I think."

"You don't remember?"

He shrugged. "I remember waking up to a lot of blood and some asshole telling me I was a lucky son of a bitch."

I raised my bottle. "Amen to luck."

Randy coughed and wiped his face with a greasy hand. "I guess you're all right," he said, raising his bottle. "Amen."

I downed my drink and shook the bottle. "Randy, I'm having another. You want one?"

"I want ten."

I gave Iris a wink. "Let's get you started," I said.

Iris smiled and pulled two frosty Kokanees from the fridge and racked them up. I pushed my empty forward and grabbed the colder bottle.

"Cheers," I said.

Iris nodded and grabbed a tattered rag from below the bar and ran it over the counter, watching me carefully. After a pause she straightened up. "You from Bellingham?" she said.

"Seattle. Drove up to meet a friend."

"In Burlington?"

I shook my head and poked the bar top with a stiff finger. "Right here. At Antony's."

Iris exploded with a short laugh and swept a strand of loose hair from her eyes. "Who's luring you up from Seattle to drink at this shithole?"

I shrugged. "She said it was her favorite dive. Delia Walsh, you know her?"

Iris's eyes flashed and she stepped back, leaving her soiled rag in a heap on the counter. "I do."

I straightened up, unfolding my lie as lazily as I could. "Haven't seen her for a few years," I said. "But we talked a couple months back. I told her I was moving to Seattle in the fall. She said to come visit if I could. Said she was working just outside Burlington, so I thought I'd surprise her . . ."

Stopping short, I took a long drink to cap my story. Iris kept nodding and smiling as if waiting on me to expand it, but I had nothing left to say.

"So here I am," I said, throwing up my hands.

Iris crossed her arms. Her smile faded to a look of pity.

"Well shit," she said. "I hate to say it, but you might be outta luck. She used to come in once or twice a week for years. But that stopped over the summer. Haven't seen her since May. Or June maybe."

I frowned. "Yeah that tracks," I said. "She stopped answering my calls."

Iris clamped her jaw and wrinkled her mouth, as if swallowing a howl she didn't want heard. "Shit. I hope she's okay."

I nodded solemnly and reached into my pocket. I pulled out the receipt with the dated message and held it up.

"This mean anything to you?" I said. "It was hers."

Iris stared at the paper for a while. "DON'T FORGET. Five, five, eleven," she said reading aloud. "Is that a date?"

"Might be."

"Hmm. Nothing comes to mind."

"*Cinco de Mayo*? Or someone's birthday?"

Iris squinted and shrugged. "Not sure. Can't be Delia's birthday. She'd be way too old."

"Right."

"I don't know, sorry. I wish I could help."

"Don't sweat it."

I pocketed the receipt and took another quick swig, letting our befuddlement drain out together. Iris palmed the rag and returned to wiping.

"Did she have any friends I could call?" I said.

"Yeah, maybe a few . . ." she said, trailing off.

She looked around the bar randomly until a switch flipped in her head. She crossed to the register and punched the drawer open and lifted the money tray and took out a postcard. She read one side, flipped it over, and read the other. Then she walked it back and laid it on the bar, picture side down.

It was old and yellowing and creased in a few places, with corners worn down to velvet nubs from overhandling. Scribbled across the back was a list of four names. Each name was in a different hand—*Delia*, *Saint*, *Francisco*, *MG*—and each was followed by a row of fluctuating dollar amounts, all but the last number in each series crossed out.

"Bar tabs," Iris said. "For Delia and her friends."

She pointed at Delia's name. The final amount of fifty-three dollars was crossed out. The remaining names all had outstanding debts, the largest of them owed by someone called Saint—a flat three hundred.

"Delia was always paid up within a few weeks," she said. "The others not so much."

I flipped the postcard over. A generic photo of Mount Rainier on a sunny, cloudless day. Nothing revelatory. I flipped it back and read the names again. *Delia. Saint. Francisco. MG.* I recited them in my head several times, committing them to memory.

"They still come here?"

Iris cocked her head to read the names. She nodded.

"Francisco sometimes. Saint's a nickname. Not sure what his real name is, but I haven't seen him either. And MG . . . I barely remember the guy."

"Were they friends or colleagues?"

"How do you mean colleagues?"

"Did they work together?"

"Oh, yeah. Definitely," she said, bouncing her head. "They were always talking about work. Computers and stuff. It was hard to follow."

"But you tried?"

"Sort of," she blushed. "They're pretty smart."

I pushed the postcard back across the bar.

"Did Delia ever hint that she was leaving?" I said.

Iris returned the postcard to the register and came back. "No," she said absently. "I mean, we weren't the best of friends. But we did talk. I wish she'd said something."

Iris fell silent, thinking on something secret and remote. Then she took up her rag and tossed it in the sink and opened the dishwasher to start stacking pints. "She's bound to turn up . . ." she said with a smile.

I watched her work for a while, then took a passing glance at Randy. He was asleep against the bar, his face buried in the crook of his outstretched arm. I drank slowly, planning my next move. I had three names to chase down—*Francisco*, *Saint*, *MG*—but not out here. Best wait until I was inside the Forum.

When my second beer was too warm to stomach, I stood and threw a twenty and a ten on the bar and slapped my hat on.

"Thanks for the company," I said.

Iris gave a curt wave. "Hope you find her," she said. "Tell her to stop by if you do."

I tipped my hat and headed out. Back in the Boson I sat back, and crossed my arms.

"Cascadia Inn," I said. "Pronto."

The steering wheel packed away and the car obeyed without complaint, backing out of the spot and rolling to the road. It was too damn easy. I hated it.

. . . Most of us moved into a condo complex in Mount Vernon, a tiny town about ninety minutes east of the Forum's gate. This closed a door on that part of my life. Leaving Seattle behind for a promising future. I had a clear goal ahead of me. I had colleagues. I had a production deadline and milestones to hit. I even had a stipend. Holy shit, I had a real job.

I worked almost seven days a week for the six-month run up to the Forum's opening. Not because I had to. I wanted This Little World up and running on the Forum's hardware as soon as possible. I imagined its improved power would elide or iron out some of the original's imperfections. A fool's hope. The delusion of confusing art with craft. In retrospect, the Forum's hardware made This Little World substantially more dangerous. I wish I'd seen that sooner.

The strangest thing about designing surreals for the Forum was the workflow. With mainstream SRs, ninety-nine percent of the work was done outside the simulation. You fire up a desktop computer and bang out some code. You sculpt objects and design worlds with 3D modeling software. You populate natural landscapes with procedural generation tools. You write code in real life to make things happen in virtual life. You compile all this work and press play. When you're confident about the product, you jump inside and take a long painful look at the mess you made. You sniff around, make some notes, and jump back out. Rinse and repeat.

In the Forum, we did our work inside the simulation itself. We were a part of it from the start, with a suite of tools at our disposal. Tools that obeyed our commands like magic. Verbal instructions took physical form. Slight gestures moved mountains. A swat of the hand could annihilate an entire continent. As a designer and a coder, I loved this method of working. With tools like ours, it wasn't strictly necessary to understand programming logic. But I did, and that gave me a conceptual advantage and a speed that few could match.

But even with all these incredible tools and resources on hand—tools and resources that could literally build Rome in a day—Locksley wasn't entirely satisfied. He wanted a faster turnaround. Quicker concept to execution. He looked forward to a day where ordinary people could dream up an idea in the morning and see it running by lunchtime. High-tech champion of the average man.

I'm cooking up a new feature, he told me about three months into our work. Machine learning mixed with an AI interpreter. Someday soon any Tom Dick or Harry will be able to sit down and explain in natural language exactly the kind of theater they want to design. And my tool will do the work.

I admired the foundation of his ideas. It was hard not to. He wanted the Forum to live up to its namesake. A public space for every idea under the sun. And we believed him. He believed himself. He hated the phrase "marketplace of ideas" because the underlying metaphor was nakedly transactional. He pushed for a "forum of ideas," where anyone could pose a question, test a theory, or disprove an assumed fact without censure or constraint.

It sounded so pretty when he said it like that. Even prettier when we repeated it. We should have known better.

For the first few months, I was so focused on my work, so obsessed with getting This Little World up and running, that every minute away felt like squandered time. Sixty, seventy hours a week was exhausting but somehow I managed. I didn't have much else to distract me. On the rare nights I clocked out early, me and a few other designers would pile into our cars and make the five-minute drive to a grungy little pizza parlor in the heart of Burlington. Antony's Pizzeria. Quiet, unassuming, cheap. A perfect place to disappear. The late-night staff and the clientele had little interest in who we were or what we were doing.

Our after-hours gang grew to nine at its peak, about a month before the Forum went live. A few of them I might even call friends. Francisco was a programmer in his thirties working on a surreal he claimed would usher in a new era of personal responsibility and ethics. He talked a big game, but after a few drinks he'd usually get introspective and properly self-conscious.

*Then there was Jude. A quiet phenom from Oregon State University. A towering, lanky kid who walked with a stoop like his height embarrassed him. He was soft-spoken and coolly clever. Clever enough to keep everyone's expectations low by telling us nothing about his current project. Nothing but the name anyway—*Your Double.

They were a spicy bunch from the very start. Argumentative and arrogant and deadly smart. They challenged me in the best way possible, even when I resented them. They were family, in a way, and Antony's was our second home. Our sacred hollow. We felt safe on those stools, amid the smell of pizza and stale beer. And there was a strict enforcement about who was invited.

No Locksleys allowed. That was the golden rule . . .

7

THE BOSON BROUGHT ME DIRECTLY to the Cascadia Inn, a dilapidated motor hotel with exquisite views of I-5, an A&W burger joint, and the rear loading dock of a hardware retailer. The car rolled slowly past the motel's front office and the five empty spaces out front.

"Stop here," I said.

The Boson rolled on, moving with apparent purpose over the vacant tarmac. Half a dozen more empty spaces presented themselves. The car ignored them all.

"Park here," I shouted, hitting the dashboard. "I have to check in."

The Boson did not park. It rounded a corner and crept along the motel's longest edge. We were moving so slowly I could have opened the door and stepped out with my eyes closed and run circles around the stubborn thing. We passed another few vacant spaces.

"For fuck's sake, stop!"

As we drew near the end of the lot, the car slowed, veered wide, and slotted expertly into the adjacent space.

You have arrived at your destination.

"Not mine," I mumbled.

Leaving my bag in the car I jumped out and backtracked to the office. The Cascadia Inn was a run-down relic from the glory days of motor vehicle travel. Early 1980s construction with white, pebble-salted walls. Exterior walkways with black railings chipped and rusted in so many places they looked like oversized cinnamon sticks. Each room could be accessed by a door that opened to the outside, and each one was pocked with dents, chips, and painted over with inscrutable graffiti tags. There was a staircase at the corner of the building beside an alcove marked with a sign that said *ICE*. The bulky ice machine within lay on its face with a dim bulb flickering above it.

An anxious teenager at the front desk handed me a pair of keys for room 114, exactly where the Boson had parked itself. When I entered my room, a sour rush of mildewy air poured out. I left the door ajar and flipped on the light. The room was a smoke-stained box with faux wood vinyl walls and a ragged low-pile carpet in olive green. All it needed was a pair of taxidermied elk and a foosball table to complete the disco era basement look. The lone double bed had a stained orange duvet and a matching pair of pillows. A nightstand made of driftwood held up a tarnished brass lamp. Opposite the bed was a small wooden desk, a tiny floor fridge, and a flat black television mounted to the ceiling.

I tossed my bag on the bed. A short hall at the back of the room led to mirrored closets and a stained bathroom. Everything smelled like wet, unwashed underwear. I returned to the bed and flipped on the television and surfed to a daytime soap opera with the word *Desire* in the title. I emptied my suitcase to the blather of men and women telling obvious lies. After unpacking my clothes, I counted out eight hundred of the thousand dollars I'd brought and stuffed it into a pair of socks and pushed it to the back of one of the drawers. A bit of caution for a job that seemed as dangerous as a day at the dog park.

By early afternoon I had settled in, but my brain still buzzed with a restless urge to work. The Forum would be off-limits until tomorrow when the Feds returned with my credentials. The best I could do was prepare.

I turned down the TV's volume and fell onto the bed. Propping myself up with a pair of pillows, I emptied the contents of the John Pike folder onto the duvet. John Pike's driver's license fell out first. I stowed this in my wallet and started sifting through the rest of the material. Amid legal documents and falsified biographical material, I found a letter of introduction from the US Treasury Department, addressed to the Forum's current CEO, a man with the improbably pompous name Pritchard Locksley. The text read like boilerplate corporate-speak, reminding the CEO of his fiduciary duty to open the Forum to a yearly audit by an accredited government official. It further outlined the rights and privileges of this executor, one being a mandatory meeting with the current or acting CEO at the auditor's request. I noted this detail as possibly useful. John Pike's name appeared for the first time three-fourths of the way down the letter, but revealed no new information about my elusive alter ego. The less said the better, I suppose. It left space for my roaming imagination.

I flattened the letter atop the scattered documents and reached for my phone on the nightstand. I tapped the screen and pulled up a web browser, searching for the name Pritchard Locksley. One hundred plus pages of relevant articles swamped the search engine. I swapped the results to an image search to get a look at the man. The pictures that came back were mostly candid photos, depicting a man with a face and a demeanor that dared bad luck to find him. The bulk of these photos spanned thirty years of his ostentatious career—a patchwork that documented a continuous wave of success. In every decade he was slender and ruddy faced with a wide toothy grin and a bouncing bouffant of natural curls—brown in the early days, a peppery silver more recently.

I tapped back to the search field to refine my prompt: *Pritchard Locksley Forum*. This returned a surprisingly small number of results—

just two pages. A majority of the results were five-year-old articles from a range of computer science blogs and online journals, announcing the founding of a new surrogate reality initiative, designed and operated by Locksley and his team. The text in every instance, however, was nearly identical—a printed press release without commentary or critique. Further down the search list was an interview with Locksley almost a decade old in which he mentioned the concept of a digital forum in an extended riff on the structure of participatory democracy in ancient Athens, adding that such a model would be impossible to implement in the modern world without the proper technological innovations. The rest of the interview contained nothing of use, but I got a good sense of Locksley himself. A brilliant but irascible man incapable of hearing the word *no*.

The final result on page one was a media link—the first video of the bunch—with a run time of a few minutes. I clicked through and expanded it to fill the tiny screen. The video opened on a lecture setting—Locksley standing on a tight proscenium stage with an ultrawide digital display behind him and no discernible audience in front. A title appeared—*A Forum for the Future of Mankind*—with Locksley's name emblazoned below.

The camera cut in close. Locksley welcomed his viewers with a smile, the beaming grin of a man eager to sell me something I don't need but will forever want.

Life is not a game of chess, he began. *It does not unfold according to simple rules and so few pieces. Life is dense and complex, sprawling and untidy. Our understanding of how we live, and why, is deeply imperfect.*

He spoke with a languid energy, like a California surfer starting a new career as a car salesman, standing stock-still as he gestured and exhorted, his large eyes pulsing behind a pair of frameless spectacles.

If we could see every branching path that lay before us, we might be kinder and more careful about the decisions we made, the rules we followed, the laws that we enforced. But we cannot. Just as young Alice, we see through the glass of our future darkly.

But what if there was a way to better predict the future of our actions? To test our well-intentioned laws and regulations before they were implemented? In ways that could not harm us?

The camera cut away to a collection of vague graphic vignettes made to illustrate Locksley's premises—data points moving along a grid, bouncing like billiard balls off one another, some exploding into clouds of dust, others gaining speed.

What if we could devise new laws and observe their results from a safe vantage? Not to hypothesize the future, but to live it. To have such a power might save us from the catastrophe of good intentions gone awry. Ladies and gentlemen, we now have such a tool.

I call it the Forum.

A diagram of the Forum's gate appeared, one draftsman's line at a time, sketching out a blueprint of what I had just seen in the mountains a few hours earlier.

The culmination of almost twelve years of bleeding-edge technology and exhaustive research, the Forum is not merely the next revolution in surrogate reality technology—it is a moral and ethical revolution of unprecedented utility. An immersive social environment built for the purpose of social engineering and rehabilitation. It is a tool capable of simulating human society in all its complexity, down to the very atoms of our existence. It is a place where reality begins anew, where life is duplicated, and where anything is possible.

A politician toying with the idea of decriminalizing narcotics may run a simulation that does just that. He may even participate in the experiment himself, to get a street-level understanding of the leviathan he has unleashed, without fear of injury or harm to anyone. An architect may test a radical new design—for a bridge, a skyscraper, or the layout of an entire city—to test its feasibility, its integrity, and the elusive experience of living within it for years at a time. A psychologist may probe the darkest corners of the human mind, and tinker with it as a mechanic might probe a broken engine. Subject populations of participating humans to unlimited stressors in fully simulated environments, and witness the results in real time.

Locksley was getting a little long-winded, and I was eager to see if he might drag anyone up on stage with him. Delia, if I was lucky. I pressed my finger to the scrubber and dragged it to the video's end.

Locksley was still talking, still alone.

—a vast and wondrous place. And soon it will be yours to explore. If you would like to be a part of this journey, reach out. We have only just begun. And we'd be happy to bring you along for the ride.

The video cut to black, giving no further context to what I had just seen. Searching for the website that hosted the video brought me to a defunct web page with broken links and misaligned formatting. From what I could tell, it was some sort of investor lure, a basic recruiting pitch to inspire the right people to donate to Locksley's secret project. Regardless of the site's deteriorating state, I tapped every link I could find, searching for leftover data, something I could use for leverage once I was inside. One page vomited back a wall of garbled code, within which was the name of Locksley's company at the time of this recording—the Locksley Surrogate Reality Consortium, abbreviated to LSRC.

Another page with the title *Coming Soon . . .* displayed a list of colorful phrases accompanied by broken image links—titles like *The Death of Desire*, *Canny Valley*, *Hello Worlds*, *Pain Possession*, and *The Relativity of Everyday Things*. The list was long—about sixty entries in all—and meant nothing to me until I reached the bottom of the page. Third from the end was something I recognized immediately. *This Little World.*

This put the list in perspective—a list of SR simulations, I assumed. I clicked on *This Little World*, but it wasn't a link. I clicked the broken picture icon, and it brought me to a blank page with the same shattered icon in the top left corner. I stared at this vacuous data point, a remnant digital fossil, searching for a secret meaning.

On a hunch I stepped back to the previous page and opened the settings tab of my browser. I scrolled to the bottom of a long list of options until I found *View Source*—a command that would give me a view of the web code behind the current page. I tapped it and a burst of plain text crawled up the screen. Most of the code was made up of symbols and truncated commands, curt instructions dictating the formatting and content of the current page. But there were more useful bits of data strewn throughout—commented code in plain English, hidden descriptions of functions, and file names. Again I scrolled to the bottom of the page. Three lines beneath the encoded text for *This Little World* was the file name of the missing image: *Engineers_Walsh_Lopez_04.PNG*.

The obvious inference was that this had been a picture of Delia Walsh and someone with the last name Lopez. The plural *Engineers* suggested that Lopez had the same position as Delia. And the title of the page—*Coming Soon*—gave the impression that this page had been created at some point before the Forum's official opening.

It wasn't much of a lead, but it was a vector—a direction with some velocity. Between the bar tab at Antony's and this image file, I had cobbled together a small list of Delia's associates—*Saint, Francisco, MG, Lopez*. If I couldn't find Delia right away, maybe I could find her colleagues in one of these sixty surreals. It was a daunting number—commercial venues used to host six on average—but it was mercifully fewer than the hundreds of thousands Toots had warned me about. With luck and efficient sleuthing, I might sweep through a dozen surreals each day until I found someone willing to talk.

I killed the source page and continued my search of the site, but nothing else came up. Finally, I did another broad search for *Locksley Surrogate Reality Consortium*. Nothing appeared but the website I had just left behind. There were no other mentions of Locksley's company anywhere, a strange result for an organization building what Toots had implied was the future of surrogate reality. Searches for LSRC were similarly useless, returning only a handful of mentions of a motorized scooter group in Baton Rouge called the Louisiana Street Racers Club. Another dead end.

I switched off my phone and threw it across the bed. I wasn't tired but I'd lost my patience. I'd reached the limits of what internet sleuthing could achieve. Old-fashioned footwork was always more effective, inside or outside a surreal. And easier on the eyes. But it was getting too late for that.

I lay inert, splayed out atop the bed on what felt like a polyester duvet, listening to the calm swish of cars running through rainfall outside. A cool white light poured into the room from the A&W's sign next door. I stood and went to the window. It was late afternoon, but the sky was a dimming slate, and the restaurant was almost empty. With little else to do but watch television and commit the biography of Mr. John Pike to memory, I contemplated a quick visit for a hamburger and fries.

Ten minutes later I was still standing at the window, scanning the darkened sky and watching my breath against the window, hoping with all my heart that this was the last halting job I ever did on earth.

. . . It was midnight, about two months from launch, when Locksley called me with a vague proposition. I was drinking at Antony's. I think Francisco was there. MG as well. Maybe Trueboy and Ryle. I took the call outside so Locksley wouldn't hear the clatter of bottles and calls for takeout.

Can you get up to the Forum in thirty minutes? he said bluntly. There's someone I want you to meet.

It's a little late for a meet-cute, I said. Can it wait until tomorrow?

Come on, he said. Five days a week you're still here at sunrise. What's another couple hours?

I'm winding down early today, I said. No harm in that.

Where are you now? he said.

Some greasy spoon halfway to Everett, I lied.

Fine, he said. First thing tomorrow, come find me.

Roger that, I said.

What? he said.

I'll be there, I said. Will your friend?

He's always here, he said and hung up.

The call cut off. I flipped my phone to silent and went back inside.

Francisco was holding court over the others, waving his hands like a conductor to underline his points. I took my stool and hit my drink and listened:

Artificial Intelligence, he said, And I mean real fucking A.I., not these net-trawling bottom-feeding machine-learning vomit bazookas we've installed in every toaster and dildo—real A.I. doesn't scare me in the least. Not as an artist. Capital fucking A.

I looked at Iris, the bartender, and bent my wrist to my mouth. Keep his drinks coming, I whispered.

Iris winked. She crossed to the fridge.

Francisco blathered on: Donald Barthelme once said—I'm paraphrasing here—if computers ever learn to make art well enough to imitate a human, if they can fucking fool us, then artists will just respond by making things machines cannot. That's the fucking dance. That's the glory. That's our entire purpose. To be human and to fucking prove it. And this dance will go on until the last person on earth is breathing. So don't you believe the fear mongering. Let's fucking be the best of our species.

He pounded the table and seemed genuinely shocked to find a second bottle of beer sitting beside his first. He drank hungrily.

Artists won't be out of business, I said. But craftsmen already are, and that's the bulk of the market. That's the bulk of what's flooding the world now—competently crafted bullshit.

The bottle popped from Francisco's mouth.

The market, he said. Pshhh.

The bottle went back in.

I'm just saying, I said. A world without good art was never the worry. Most people's fears are more mundane.

Okay, he mumbled. So what are they afraid of?

A world without any reality at all . . .

8

I WOKE TO A DRY KNOCKING. A glacial predawn light seeped through the blackout curtains into the dark room. I slipped from my bed in nothing but a T-shirt and boxers and padded to the door and eyed the peephole.

Agent Wallace of the FBI stood on the far side, glaring through the glass. I slid the chain and opened the door a crack. Wallace said nothing. He held out a box the size of a deck of cards. Matte black with a small glossy logo that resembled the Forum's columned gate. I opened the door farther to take it. An inch from my fingers he let go. The box hit the sidewalk and fell flat.

"Oops," he grunted.

I pointed down. "You dropped something."

"That's your passport, John Pike," he said. "DNA encoded. Good for two weeks of access to the Forum." He turned to go. "Shuttle leaves in one hour. Good luck."

"From where?"

He stopped. One corner of his lip curled skyward. "Are you asking me to do your job for you, dick?"

"You might point me in the right direction."

He nodded slowly and raised his arm like the crosstree of a great frigate and pointed vaguely north. "That way."

"Did I murder you in another life, Wallace?"

He faced me and planted his feet like two trees. "It makes me fucking retch," he snarled. "One hundred fucking grand to play internet tag with an ex-girlfriend, and I'm struggling to pay my car loans. Whose daddy did you jerk off to get that kind of deal?"

We locked eyes until the absurdity of this conflict washed over me in waves of suppressed laughter. I stepped outside and scooped up the box. Wallace watched me with an acidic glare. I backed through the door and closed it halfway to stave off the cold.

"You know I didn't ask for this job," I said. "But it's a good gig, so I'm taking it. Any other man in my position would do the same."

"Find the fucking girl," he growled.

He spat at my shoes and marched down the length of the motel. I watched until he disappeared around the corner, then closed the door and slid the chain into place. I walked to the bed and flipped on the nightstand lamp and opened the box with care. Directly beneath the lid was a gorgeous glassy surface, reflective but with a luxuriant depth. I tilted the box into my hand. A thin device the thickness of a soda cracker fell out. It was light but durable and comfortable to hold. After a few seconds in my hand, the screen lit up with the same stylized icon as the one on the box, an almost cartoonish rendering of the Parthenon's front face. After a few seconds the logo faded, and a greeting took its place.

Welcome Jonathan Pike.

Below this was a white button labeled *Get Started*. I pressed it.

The words faded to black. A voice kicked in.

Welcome to your first day in the Forum. An experience unlike anything you have ever known awaits you. Please listen to the following instructions to make sure your first visit to our facilities is safe, secure, and rewarding.

A stylized map of the earth appeared. It expanded smoothly, zooming in to my current position. It paused briefly to show the state of Washington, until a red star appeared on the spine of the Cascade mountains, a short leap from the Canadian border.

The Forum facility closest to your present location is Gate Nine, located in the Skagit Valley of the north Cascade mountain range, accessible via Highway 20. Please note that—except under specific circumstances—we do not provide on-site parking. Access to the Forum is limited to drop-offs and shuttle service only.

The red star flashed before disappearing and the map began to move again, zooming and panning to the west until the individual streets of Burlington were visible.

Our complementary shuttle service covers most of Washington State and parts of British Columbia. The nearest stop to your present location is located in Burlington at the intersection of North Burlington Boulevard and Hansen Place.

A shuttle icon appeared at the intersection of two streets, what looked like a ten-minute walk from the motel.

This service runs seven days a week, with pick up times at 7:32 a.m., 10:46 a.m., and 1:17 p.m. daily. For further information, please refer to the Resources section of your Forum passport. We hope you have a wonderful first day.

The map faded to black, and the lone icon returned and stayed there until the device powered down on its own. I set the passport on the nightstand with care. Lying there on a chipped wooden surface it looked all wrong, like a priceless slab of burnished platinum on a butcher's block. I opened the nightstand drawer and stowed it away, giving me just enough peace of mind to get ready.

According to the nightstand clock it was 6:35 a.m., roughly an hour before the first shuttle. I flipped on the TV to a newscast and went to the bathroom. After a scalding shower I toweled off and lathered up in front of the sink for a shave. I had just scraped the first lanes down my cheek when a droning voice from the television caught my ear.

In just four days, Imagine Red's latest colony shuttle, Cupid 7, touches down on the surface of Mars, and channel four will be there to cover it.

I hopped to the bedroom, foam sliding down my neck. Images of igniting rockets and the faces of stoic astronauts panned across the television screen.

Join the Pacific Northwest's number one television network as we bring you coverage of the next landing, interviews with Mars's newest inhabitants and veteran residents, and an exclusive look at Imagine Red's road map for the next ten years. It's a night of wonder you won't want to miss.

The promo ended with a final stark image—a pocked and rusty landscape with a cluster of capsule-shaped habitations in the foreground and the colossal cone of Olympus Mons rising in the far distance.

Wednesday 15, 9 p.m. PST.

The segment ended. I switched off the television and returned to the bathroom. As I finished shaving, images of rolling red hills and sherbet orange skies shimmered in my thoughts. The dream of a new world, a blank slate. If I could finish this job and Toots came through, Christ, I was set. No more worrying about what might have been here on Earth. On Mars every day would be a fresh step forward on a planet with no history, for a people with no relevant past. Human society, year zero.

After shaving I dressed hurriedly, picking out my freshest shirt to go with my worn-out suit. Once dressed, I returned to the nightstand and opened the drawer. I took out the passport and pocketed it. At the back of the drawer was a Bible placed by the Gideons. I opened my wallet and pulled out Kennedy Stark's credit cards and everything else that bore traces of him. I tipped the Bible sideways and slipped the stack of cards underneath and checked my wallet again. All that remained was John Pike's driver's license and his medical insurance card and a loyalty punch card from a café back home. I closed the drawer. The clock read 7:05 a.m. A good time to get started.

Outside the air was chilly, with a freezer burn fragrance. To the east, behind the Cascade's ragged peaks, the sky had brightened to a cerulean. With time to spare I left the motel on foot, walking east down a busy arterial. I turned north at the first intersection and moved at a swift clip for ten minutes, passing a gas station, a Subway sandwich joint, a payday lender, and a sprawling high school. Beyond the school, past a narrow strip of verdant woods, I discovered a stout unmarked building with no signage or common features set back from the street at the far end of a narrow parking lot.

Built from the same dark material as the Forum's Gate, it was a dense cubical structure of shadowless gray, elevated on a six-foot platform with broad stairs rising to meet it. There were no windows on the street-facing wall, just a single dark rectangle cut through its center, like a frame awaiting a door.

I crossed the parking lot to the cube's base. A blue Maserati with plates that said YES PLZ was parked out front, the only car in the entire lot. There was nobody inside. When I reached the stairs, I took out a cigarette and lit up. In the silence between breaths, I listened to the ticking and popping of the car's cooling engine.

At 7:25 a.m., I ashed my smoke and climbed the steps. On closer inspection of the cube a simple optical illusion revealed itself. The front face of the structure was not a flat square but a shallow concave of four joined triangles that pushed into the body, with a rectangular tunnel punched through its middle, making a tunnel fifty or sixty feet long. I went through.

On the far side I exited into sunlight. There were four benches ahead—steel planks grouped in two pairs that faced one another across a tiny flagstone square. Beyond this was a paved cul-de-sac that opened to a narrow back road. Sitting on one of the benches was a pale young man in a powder blue tracksuit. He had long wavy brown hair, gleaming with product and pulled back in a nubbin of a ponytail. On his wrist he wore a gargantuan silver watch and on the front of his hoodie was the phrase *Dr. Yes Please* stenciled in black. The moment he saw me he attempted a smile but ended up looking worried.

I sat and composed myself, crossing my arms and rolling my shoulders. "Morning," I said.

The man twitched and began fiddling with his watchband. I waited for him to look up. When he did, I raised my wrist and tapped it. He blinked to process my question, then checked his watch. His face brightened and he looked out across the cul-de-sac at the road beyond. He smiled and pointed.

A stubby black bus sped down the road to our position. The young man stood and gave me a thumbs up, then hurried to the curb's edge. I stood and took my place a few meters behind him. A queue of two.

The bus entered the cul-de-sac and squealed to a stop and opened its doors. A driver stepped out, a stocky man in his thirties decked in a navy-blue jacket with shining brass buttons and crisply pressed trousers. On his head was a matching pillbox hat tilted to one side, like a wedding cake suspended in mid-fall, with a mess of brown curls poking out beneath. When he beckoned, the young man took a dutiful step forward and held up a passport identical to mine. The driver scanned it with a small handheld device and nodded. The young man scurried into the shuttle.

The driver motioned to me, and we repeated the ritual. I held out my passport and he scanned it. Then he asked for a piece of ID. I produced John Pike's license. The driver squinted through his examination and gave it back. He waved me forward.

The shuttle's interior had the charm and atmosphere of a velvet-lined coffin, with thick curtains blacking out the windows entirely. Only the front windshield offered a view of the outside. There were soft benches on both sides of the cabin, each wide enough for two people. In the gloom I could see the murky outlines of half a dozen other passengers. The cabin hummed with low chatter.

The driver stepped aboard and took his seat. The door closed with a sharp hiss. I crept to the rear. As my eyes adjusted to the dark, I saw my young friend seated in the rearmost row. I dropped onto the bench directly in front of him. As soon as I was down, the bus shuddered and jerked forward.

A few minutes into the drive, a breathy voice tickled my ear, accompanied by the cloying scent of pink bubble gum.

"Seven thirty-two on the dot," he said quietly. "Nobody runs a route as tight as these guys."

"A good sign."

The young man wheezed, and the bubble-gum smell redoubled. "No doubt, no doubt. First sign of a solid operation is efficiency. When the trains start running late, armed revolution is not far behind."

"I've heard that."

"It's hard to understand, but the world is interconnected in ways we don't always see. You have to look deep. Locate novel causalities, as Locksley likes to say. That's the key to survival."

"Sounds like you know your stuff."

He snuffled with pride. "That's from Locksley's book, *The Absence of a Rule Is a Rule*."

"Right . . ."

"The truth is out there. But you gotta study, learn, hone your mind. And bring that truth to the Forum. That's what we're here for."

The shuttle took a wide, sweeping turn, throwing the young man back into his seat. He stood again as the shuttle returned to a stable velocity.

"So what's your deal?" he said "Engineer? Citizen?"

"Not something I can talk about," I said.

"Cool. I respect that. I'm doing high-tech shit. Bleeding edge. Raw as fuck."

"I'm all ears."

"We're recruiting if you're interested. Let me know and I'll hook you up. Get you on the list."

"I'd have to know more."

"Totally," he said, growing excited. "See, me and my partner . . . my *business* partner, not . . . well, we had this idea that if everyone in society had their basic pleasures met, there'd be less strife, less conflict, and a lot more harmony. You get it?"

"I think so."

"So we had this idea to make our own theater and test this concept. A theater called the Pleasure Dome. After the concept of pleasure rationing. You know the idea?"

"Tell me."

"The idea that men are more productive when their, you know, needs are satisfied." He lowered his voice. "Sexual needs."

"I get it."

"We got a grant and everything. It'll keep us going 'til next spring."

I turned for the first time and looked for this man's face. In the dark I could see the vague outline of his cropped hair, fleshy cheeks, and the glint of tea saucer eyes.

"So what's the general idea?" I said. "A bunch of guys sitting around eating burgers, drinking beer, and fucking things?"

The young man snickered and clawed his hand over the top of the bench. He pulled himself up until his elbows were hanging over the front and he pointed at the slogan across his chest. *Mr. Yes Please.*

"That's our motto," he said. "*Yes please.*"

"It's very polite."

"In our theater, you can indulge in whatever pleasures you want. Whatever you crave. Then we measure your satisfaction levels."

"How do you measure satisfaction?"

"It's self-reported."

"How accurate is that?"

"Self-reporting is a time-honored source of data," he said defensively. "What a man believes can be more important than what is true."

"Well said."

The young man made a shuffling noise and eventually produced his passport. He thumbed it a few times and held it forward. The crisp, translucent screen displayed the words *The Pleasure Dome* on one line and the word *Share?* on the next. He pressed it and pushed the passport in my face.

"Tap me," he said.

I held up my own passport and tapped one corner against his screen. A pleasant chime sounded, and a message appeared. *New Theater Acquired. The Pleasure Dome.*

"Boom. You're all signed up," he said. "Visit anytime."

I tucked my passport away. "I'm pretty busy this week," I said. "But I'll see what I can do."

"Cool, cool," he said, falling back into his seat and closing his eyes. "I'll be there. Day or night."

Mercifully alone, I slid to the darkened window and kicked my seat back a couple degrees. I didn't sleep, but the rumbling lull of the shuttle offered a restful alternative, akin to a sensory deprivation tank.

An hour later the shuttle bumped off the highway and across a steel bridge to a buckling road. I knuckled my eyes and sat up, looking forward through the shuttle's front window. Out ahead was the blocky base of the Forum's Gate and its towering black pillars. The shuttle came to a smooth stop and the door opened. The stout driver stood and faced the rear.

"We have arrived gentlemen," he sang, before stepping outside.

Gentlemen. An interesting tell.

The cabin filled with the soft patter and shuffle of debarking passengers. Only I stayed seated.

"The Pleasure Dome. Don't forget."

The young man slapped my shoulder and winked as he passed. I let him go before following. Outside, the sun was bright, and the sky was clear. Chilled air hit my lungs. When my feet touched the ground, the young driver held out a hand to stop me.

"Just a moment, Mr. Pike," he said cordially.

I moved to one side. Two more men exited behind me and snaked single file with the others down a flagstone path to the Gate. When the last of them were out of earshot, the driver turned and gave a deferential nod.

"Welcome, sir," he said. "You'll find everything you need in the Atrium."

"Thank you."

"If you like, we can call a private car for you this evening. Do you have a preferred time?"

"What time do the shuttles leave?"

"We have three afternoon departures: Three-thirty, Six-thirty, and Ten p.m. And two in the mornings, Six and Eleven. But we offer our auditors a personal driver, when requested. You are free to leave any time you like."

"Let's make it seven."

"Very good. And thank you again."

He bowed and touched his hat with a flicking gesture. Then he bounded back into the shuttle. The engine coughed and the vehicle rolled away, tires crunching over gravel and dry pine needles.

Alone, I turned to the Forum's Gate. It loomed like a living shadow, a spectral expression of the evergreen forest and the mountainous terrain beyond. The last of the shuttle's passengers were halfway up the Gate's perimeter steps, wending between the heavy columns. I hurried to catch up.

Behind the columns, I stopped before a smaller interior chamber. A narrow door opened to a long corridor that dropped away at a shallow angle. A gauzy light filled the shaft as the indistinct shapes of men wavered in its thickness, en route to their secret surreals—*theaters* as Mr. Yes Please had called them—with secret plans in their secret heads. I followed, one gentle step at a time, descending toward a shimmering rectangle of light at the far end. By the time I reached this bright terminus, all ahead of me had passed through. I was alone. I looked back up the long shaft. There was nobody behind, just a distant white tile of the faintest sunshine.

I now stood before a smooth sheet of warm light that appeared almost solid. I strained to see what lay beyond, but the light was opaque in its brightness. The passport vibrated in my pocket. I took it out and held it up. A pastel rainbow swept across its screen, leaving behind the Forum's logo and short greeting:

Welcome John Pike.
Step into the light.

I held the passport firmly in one hand and reached for the light with the other. My fingers passed through without friction, vanishing beyond the point of contact. It was warm to the touch. Comforting. I took a deep breath and stepped through.

The world flashed white, and a low hum filled my ears. My body buckled. I seemed to fall backward, only to be scooped up by something. A gentle catch. I was floating now. Drifting.

Then nothing.

. . . Locksley gave me the name of a theater and nothing else. Told me not to worry, said I'd find his friend easily enough. He was right. When I emerged from the portal of light I stepped into a serene pastel beachfront scene lit by rosy magic hour light with a caressing breeze. Standing dead ahead was a slight man in a pair of black faded work jeans and a blue denim jacket, with a psychedelic cravat twisted around his neck. He had long stringy hair and a big handlebar mustache, both of which the ocean wind just couldn't resist.

I moved to meet him. Warm sand slid around my heels and between my toes. Somehow I was barefoot, which surprised and delighted me.

I'm Mikkonen, the man said, extending his hand. We shook as I looked him over.

Locksley thinks you can help me, I said.

I hope so, he said.

All right, I said. So what do I call you? Assistant? Intern? Co-designer?

Assistant is fine, he said. I require no adulation.

I'm not in the habit of adulating anyone, I said. Do you know my work? My theater, This Little World?

I do, he nodded. I was quite impressed. May I ask where the title comes from? It strikes me as very whimsical.

This Little World is whimsical? I said.

Disneyesque, yes.

It's a line from Shakespeare, I said. Richard the Second, the final act. A needy king has been deposed and is now awaiting his end in a dungeon beneath his former castle. He's bored and anxious. To bide his time he conjures images of people and places and things, building in his mind an imaginary world to distract him from the very real fact of his encroaching death.

Interesting.

I recited the passage: My brain I'll prove the female to my soul / My soul the father; and these two beget / A generation of still-breeding thoughts / And these same thoughts people this little world / In humors like the people of this world / For no thought is contented.

Mikkonen nodded thoughtfully. I see the parallel, he said. Solipsistic mental conjurings, borne of anxiety or hardship.

It's a good play, I said. A portrait of self-absorbed narcissism. But the metaphor doesn't quite mirror my theater's function at this point. I might pick something else.

I think you found a fine name.

You sure? Disneyesque sounds like an insult.

Disney is a very successful organization, he said, unblinking. Why would that be insulting?

Forget it, I said. It's my turn. What kind of name is Mikkonen?

Finnish, he said.

For the first time I noticed his accent, flat middle-American.

You're not Finnish, I said.

No, I do not believe so.

You don't know?

I would have to look into it. People of Finnish descent may have been involved.

Are you always this eccentric? I said. Or just when you're nervous?

I do not get nervous, he said.

I guess that's my answer . . .

9

I EMERGED INTO A GRAND OPEN-AIR PLAZA, a hundred yards wide, and too long to see the end of. A warm light suffused the air, cast from a sky of Mediterranean blue. White sandy flagstones paved the ground and marble walls some twelve feet high surrounded the entire space. Behind these walls rose the heads of shaggy palm trees, while the Cascade mountains I'd left behind were nowhere to be seen. It was an impossible geography made possible because none of it was real. Somehow without hooking up to a console or any equivalent device, I had crossed into surrogate reality. The transition had been as discreet as it was painless.

I examined my hands. They looked like my hands, felt like my hands. I sensed none of the hallmark defects of consumer grade SR feeds—a frequent sluggish feeling from the latency of the brain-CPU interface, the slightly watery vision, the intrusive physical sensations bleeding in from the real world. None of this was present in the Forum and the difference was extraordinary. In older days we might have used terms like *hi-res* or *high-definition* or *increased fidelity*. But there was more to it. I felt as real and sturdy here as I did before entering. Better, even. I began walking. Not in any particular direction, simply luxuriating in how relaxed and comfortable I was.

Around the plaza's perimeter, soaring Doric columns stood like the posts of an unfinished fence. Between each was a broad sofa with fluffy beige cushions and scattered piles of pillows. Dozens of idle patrons of the Forum—men exclusively—lay upon these sofas like Roman Senators, lounging or napping or contemplating their passports in a blissed-out calm. Nobody seemed to notice me, or if they did, nobody cared.

At the center of this plaza, a second quadrangle of pillars outlined an interior perimeter, partitioning the space into two distinct sections—the outer promenade and the inner square. Between the pillars of this inner configuration were numerous free-standing door frames that looked like oversized cricket wickets with familiar walls of light illuminating their middle void. Each frame's lintel glowed with a word or phrase, while large screens suspended above each displayed feeds of kinetic images too random and surreal to comprehend—scenes of cars racing down rain-slick tracks, of discharging guns, of women showering, of vast quantities of food, of explosions. Shots of wild nature, expensive toys, happy children, giddy pets.

As I watched these scenes with puzzled interest, someone behind me cleared their throat. I turned to see a withered old man in a checkered black and brown flannel shirt shambling toward me from the same freestanding frame I had exited. He was short and hunched forward with a spray of ivory hair rising from the back of his skull to his forehead, as if his face had been caught in a bleached baseball mitt. He had a pair of tortoise shell bifocals resting on a bulbous nose, always in the process of slipping off but never falling. He smiled and lifted his hand.

"Hello, hello, hello," he said, obviously delighted.

"Good morning."

"John Pike, I presume?"

"That's right."

"I'm the Forum's Sysop," he said, extending a quivering hand. "System operator. I keep the code clean and the lights on. And you, I've been told, are this year's auditor."

"I must be."

We shook. He pushed his glasses up his nose and squinted at the passport in my hand.

"You made it inside, that's a start," he said. "Would you like a full tutorial?"

I held it up. "I could use a few pointers."

He blinked rapidly and stepped closer to gain a view of the screen. His breath smelled of mothballs and cheap coffee, and his forehead gleamed with a coat of oil that suggested he'd just been roused from a long nap. Strange details to render in a surreal, where sterile, idealized avatars were the norm.

"Touch the screen," he said, pointing. "And draw a circle around the Forum's logo."

I did. The glass burst to life with sound and color, then faded to black. An introductory message scrolled up from the bottom of the screen.

Welcome . . .
To the future of society . . .
To the next phase in evolution . . .
To the source of all dreams . . .
To the Forum.

After fading to black, the name *Johnathan Pike* reappeared at the screen's top edge. Below this, *Auditor*. At the screen's center was a lateral field with the icon of a magnifying glass. At the bottom was the word *Menu*.

"This is your home screen," the Sysop said. "To navigate the Forum, touch the search field there and type the name of any theater you wish to visit. You can search by subject or keyword. Whatever you like. Now press the *Menu* icon."

I did so. A short list of options appeared.

Favorites
Recent
Citizens
Support
Exit

The Sysop took a heavy breath. "First is *Favorites*. Any theater you search for, any theater you visit, can be tagged as a favorite and they'll appear here. *Recent* refers to theaters you have entered in the past ninety days. *Citizens* will show you a list of Forum users you have met or interacted with. You can also curate a list of friends through this tab."

"Citizens?"

"What we call members of the Forum. In keeping with the Hellenic theme."

"Beautiful."

"We think so. Now *Support* will lead you to a list of help options should you require aid. And *Exit* gets you out of the Forum entirely, turning any nearby portal into a door to the outside."

He pushed his glasses up the bridge of his nose and stepped back.

"Are you familiar with surrogate reality?" he said with vague concern. "Surreals, Meditators, Immersives, that sort of thing?"

"I've made a few trips. But I'm not a regular."

"Have no fear," he said, snapping his fingers. "You'll catch on. The Forum is quite different from anything you've seen before."

"I'm here to learn."

"That's the spirit. Any immediate questions?"

"How does this place work, exactly?" I said. "I didn't plug in anywhere."

The Sysop slapped his forearm as if it were a hock of ham. "Ah yes, that does throw people off. Colloquially we like to say you are *in storage*."

"Storage."

"It's a metaphor, of course. The truth is rather technical." He stepped back and made a display of himself, floating one hand up and down his frame. "Total physiological and mental replication," he said with a flourish.

"Meaning?"

"Commercial SRs hijack your sensory systems, feeding data of virtual places directly into your brain stem. In a very real sense, they're all in your head. The Forum is different. Every atom in your body—and the atoms of every hosted microbial organism, for that matter—is replicated virtually."

"It's not a signal feed?"

"No sir. Here you have been—for lack of a better term—cloned and uploaded."

"Down to the atom?"

"I don't mean literally cloned, of course. It's perhaps easier to say that your organic brain is controlling a digital avatar."

I looked at my hands again. They still felt like mine, and I still felt like me. I tried to will the sensation away, but it wouldn't leave. Shaking my head, I turned where I stood and gestured vaguely at the space around us. A perfect feeling of vitality. I gave the Sysop a bewildered smile and he smiled back.

"So where are we now?" I said, looking around.

The Sysop waved his hands through a wide arc.

"This is the Atrium. A social space. You'll find freshman Citizens here, wandering around, getting their first taste of what the Forum has to offer."

"I guess I'm in the right place . . ."

The Sysop smirked and poked at his glasses and swooped in close, back at my side. "Indeed," he said. "It's time for a quick tour. Would you press the search icon there?"

I tapped the magnifying glass. A keyboard popped up, as if it were any old smartphone.

"Search for something," he said. "A keyword of any kind. Anything that pops into your head."

I unfixed my eyes and stared into the distance. A word emerged with no precedent. *Narcotics.* I started typing—*N, A, R.* Below the search field, names that sounded like films or novels with artsy titles began to appear:

Narcotic Dreams
Narrated Life, The
Narwhal Mating Habits
Nasty Habits

I stopped typing and tilted the screed so we could both see.

"What am I looking at?" I said.

"A partial list of the theaters hosted here. Each is a unique and immersive experience, designed by one of our hundreds of thousands of Citizens. Pick one. Whatever you like."

My interest in Narcotics waning, I tapped the next item on the list—the Narrated Life. The list disappeared, replaced by a short paragraph.

The Narrated Life. Designed by Amber Ripley. Can objective verbal exposition aid our understanding of ourselves? Can it foster empathy and cooperation between our own interior conflicts? The Narrated Life puts this important question to test in a riveting full-world simulation.

Public Theater.

The Sysop edged in close to get a look at my screen.

"Excellent choice. You see there? *Public* means anyone can visit. You'll often see *Private* as well. Admission to a private theater requires a moderator's approval."

"How's that happen?"

"The press of a button sends a request. Then you wait. Or you can tap your way in if you meet the administrator in person."

"I see. Can I load this one now?"

The Sysop smiled and wrung his hands together. "Load, ha. No, we simply walk there. Look . . ."

He clapped a hand on my shoulder and spun me around and pointed at the lintel of the nearby portal. Displayed in faint glowing letters was the name of the selected theater, *The Narrated Life*.

"Move closer," he said, giving me a slight push.

I took a few steps. The title above the door grew brighter. I took a few more and it burned pure white. When I returned to my original position, the phrase faded to half brightness.

"Every portal in the Forum leads everywhere else," said the Sysop. "Determined by what you have selected on your passport."

"And if I don't have anything selected?"

"You return here," he said, raising his arms. "And by default, the Atrium leads back outside . . ."

I stared at the portal and its blazing center, overwhelmed by the labyrinthine promise of this place. A sudden burst of laughter seized my attention. Fifty feet away, two Citizens stood before an active portal at the Atrium's center. The title on the lintel read *Thirty-One Days*. The men watched the sizzle reel with awe. Harrowing scenes of nature's power and indifference played out across the screen. A dank forest beneath wounded skies. Raging rivers and gouts of rain. Lighting rippling and thunder crashing. Images of men in distress.

Drenched and wounded and weeping. Ripped clothing and makeshift shelters. A frantic black beetle pinched between a pair of dirty fingers and the grimacing lips of a man with nothing left to lose. A shout, a holler, a scream. Arms raised to the sky. A tagline comes crashing through. Bold booming text: *Do you have what it takes to survive . . . Thirty-One Days?*

I turned to the Sysop. "A survival challenge?" I said.

"I believe so," he said "The portals along the center of the Atrium are fixed to specific theaters. Our greatest hits, so to speak." He pressed his hands together and looked down the length of the seemingly infinite space. "Today we have over two million theaters in operation. A majority are devoted to scientific research and study. Probing questions, creative concerns, esoteric topics . . ."

"Such as?"

"Hm. *Baby Babel* was a recent favorite. Testing the hypothesis that a population of a hundred babies will develop their own language if left to their own devices for five years, without outside intervention."

"That raises a few ethical questions, I'd imagine."

"It would anywhere else," he said brightly. "But nothing is real or permanent within the Forum. It's all perfectly simulated, that's the advantage." He reached forward and prodded my shoulder. "You're not really here," he winked. "And neither am I."

He waited for a reaction, but I was beyond surprise. Clearing his throat, the Sysop adjusted his glasses and gestured to the passport in my hand. "If you have no other questions," he said, "I have one last feature to share. Would you please hold up your passport?"

I did so. He lifted his own to demonstrate.

"As auditor," he continued. "There is one feature unique to your device. Try holding it with a vertical orientation like this. Screen out, as if showing off a photo."

I mimed the gesture, rotating my passport sideways so I could see the result. As soon as the device was vertical, a picture of an ornately detailed badge appeared in golden monochrome, a parody of what a cop might carry.

"There it is," the Sysop winked.

I tilted the passport backward. At about eighty degrees, the image disappeared, and the search bar returned. I toyed with this move, rocking the passport back and forth. The badge came and went with a quickly fading blink.

"That simple motion activates your auditor's badge," the Sysop said. "Should anyone question your presence in any theater, show them this. They'll get the message."

"I'll try not to let it get to my head."

The Sysop laughed. "Oh, I'm sure you'll do fine," he said. "Now, return to your search results. Our tour must commence."

I glanced at the screen and poked around until I found my way back. The theater called the Narrated Life was still highlighted. The Sysop held his own passport aloft.

"Give us a tap," he said.

Just as I had done with the young man on the bus, I touched the corner of my passport to the Sysop's. They collided with a pleasant glassy click, and a digital chime rang. The Sysop glanced at his screen, then turned it around for me to read. *New Theater Acquired.*

"You have just shared your discovery," he said. "Now we may proceed."

He referred me to the portal once again. *The Narrated Life* still glowed on the lintel above. The Sysop tucked his passport in his shirt pocket and with a spring in his heels skipped through the curtain of light.

I waited a moment, then followed.

. . . Mikkonen's input in that final month was invaluable. He knew the Forum inside and out. Could snap his fingers and create entirely new pathways, new interfaces, new ways of manipulating data. We had a funny way of working together. Hours of silent cooperation. A word here, a gesture there, and everything fell into place. There were times I wondered if he was reading my mind. If such a thing were possible inside the Forum—which I didn't doubt—then it was happening here.

Three weeks before launch, This Little World was finally up and running. I was confident the port was an improved version in every way. But we needed to test it. So Locksley organized a session. He invited a few dozen colleagues and friends to participate. Investors and politicians and developers, all of them attached in some way to the Forum's genesis. They'd all been inside before, which helped speed things along. The awe of first contact can take a few hours to settle in. I wanted results as fast as possible.

On the scheduled day Locksley gave a little preparatory talk in the Atrium before everyone dove in. He stressed how different my theater was from anything they had experienced before. He told them it would respond to their thoughts in real time, shifting and warping with the currents of their mind. This could be disorienting, he said, borrowing my standard metaphor: like a trip on psychedelics, but infinitely more personal.

For this reason we had designed and implemented a kill switch of sorts. Users who felt overwhelmed or lost in the simulation could simply close their eyes and cover their ears and speak aloud the phrase "Take me home." If executed properly, the simulation would shut down and a portal leading to the Atrium would open.

With that, our subjects went through.

Three hours later a hyperventilating crowd of men mobbed me in the Atrium, eager to share their experience. It was no different than listening to someone describe a dream—mysterious and unexpected and not the least bit interesting to the one listening. But it was clear my theater had affected them. Some had spent time with family and friends who had passed away. Others reported embarking on long journeys through vivid memories of childhood. A few described being in the thrall of abstract emotions rendered in four dimensions. Little of it meant anything to me, but it was clear the theater was operating exactly as I had designed it.

The problem was, I was beginning to worry that the reason I had built This Little World was total bullshit . . .

10

STEPPING FROM THE PORTAL, I found myself at the base of a blackened bronze fountain under a carbon-colored sky in a bustling square full of darting people and circling cars. Rising around me were buildings I wanted to call Victorian or Edwardian. It was hard to say because so many of their facades were obscured by gargantuan flashing screens and giant posters advertising clothes and films and theatrical diversions.

I looked at the fountain, a slow recognition taking shape. At the peak of its thin spire was a winged man of classical form, lurching forward with a bow in his hand and a long towel flapping immodestly along one thigh. Under him was a large circular bowl with a dozen brainless pigeons squatting and shitting recklessly around its rim.

Without warning, a disembodied voice thundered in my head. A voice not my own.

Kennedy Stark found himself in London, standing slack-jawed amid the crowds of Piccadilly Circus, his mind shaping a vague recollection of having been here once before. Long ago, sometime in his early twenties.

It was a stout, handsome voice. London business class. Hearty and sonorous and built for storytelling. And it knew my real name.

He tensed at hearing a voice in his head, worried and confused by the precision of its understanding.

Fuck. It was reading my mind.

A profanity stained his thoughts. He spun around, first right, then left, searching for the source of these interior auguries. But the prescient narrator was nowhere to be found.

"Jesus Christ."

He blasphemed against beliefs he did not hold, his anxiety rising.

"Mr. Pike?"

Someone called to him. Stark looked about, hackles raised and goose-flesh forming, suspicious of everyone and everything.

"Over here!"

It was the Sysop calling to him, standing beside a crimson ticketing booth outside the entrance of a musical theater. The ruddy little man waved, smiling without guile. Stark closed his eyes and shook his head and beat his palm against a temple, as if attempting to dislodge something.

The Sysop approached, a knowing look knotted upon his face.

"It takes a while to get used to," *the Sysop said.*

"What the hell is going on?" *Stark grumbled, baring his teeth.* "There's a voice in my head."

"That's your narrator," *the Sysop said.* "The main feature of this theater."

The Sysop clasped his hands together, barely suppressing his delight.

"The concept is remarkable," *he went on.* "Everyone who enters here is endowed with a personal narrator, designed to give an objective accounting of the user's life in real time."

Stark found the idea absurd, intrusive. But the proof was there within him. The voice was loud and clear, spanning his consciousness like a sturdy bridge of stone.

Stark winced.

"I can barely hear myself think," *he said.*

The Sysop tapped his chest.

"You can adjust the volume," *he said.* "Check the theater settings on your passport."

Stark dragged his passport out and tilted the screen. It popped on. The theater's title appeared with the same vital information as before. The Sysop leaned in nose first, like a blind mole in search of food.

"Scroll down," *he said.*

Stark flicked up. A short column of buttons appeared.

Narrator Volume
Narrator Voice
Frequency
Interior / Exterior

Stark tapped the volume button. A slider appeared. Relief rolled over him like a drifting fog. It was set to seventy-five percent. Stark pressed the slider with his index finger and swiped left. The volume of the voice—

—faded rapidly and disappeared. I could hear my own thoughts again. And the surrounding traffic and the din of crowds and my heart beating in my temples. The Sysop drew his arms behind him and smiled.

"Most theaters are customizable to one degree or another."

"It was narrating everything I did. Everything I thought."

"That's the idea."

"Did you hear it too? My narrator?"

"No, everyone is privy to their own private narrator."

"So what's the concept?"

"This theater is testing the hypothesis that an objective outside assessment of a person's behavior can have a, let's say, therapeutic effect."

"I wanted to claw my brains out."

The Sysop frowned. "You're not the first to say that," he said. "But it's a bold idea, just the sort of daring experiment the Forum makes possible. That was always Locksley's dream."

I looked up and gave a quick scan of the area. "Why London?"

The Sysop pushed his glasses up his nose and looked at his passport. "I believe the director is English," he said, tapping at the screen. "Yes, Amber Ripley. Her name is there in the theater description. And if I recall she has a particular interest in full-world simulations."

"Full world?"

"A one-to-one scale with the real world."

My jaw slackened. A one-to-one replication of the entire world and its dynamic systems was an impossible feat with commercial surreals—not only would it require unheard of amounts of computing power to run, but the sheer amount of labor it would take to design and craft such a place was thousands of times larger than anything on the commercial market.

"Hold on," I said. "I could board a plane at Heathrow and fly to Seattle in here?"

"That's right."

"Would I meet a simulated version of myself?"

"I don't believe this theater simulates real people, but I can find out."

"How many real people in here," I said.

"I believe this one caps at five hundred."

I tucked my passport away and looked around, watching the crowds pass us by. People staring at their phones, talking into them, hauling shopping bags, staring at the ground, at the sky, at nothing, lost in thought, or focused on the destination. It felt just like the real London I had visited years ago—same vibe, same smells, same people. Odds were most of these people were artificially intelligent ciphers, but I couldn't tell the difference at a distance.

I turned slowly where I stood, marveling at the depth of detail in everything. A double-decker bus zipped by, rattling as it went. A bobbing flock of pigeons strutted in formation a dozen feet away, pecking at pebbles in search of anything technically edible. I watched people and surveyed the shops. A Boots pharmacy, a Whittard's tea shop, a Pret A Manger serving ready-made lunches. The cloud cover was thick with occasional golden breaks and the brown air smelled of exhaust with peaty undertones. It seemed an excessive amount of detail for a theater with such a narrow purpose.

"As you can see," said the Sysop with pride, "The Forum is capable of incredible feats, and we are using our generous federal funding to expand the limits of human knowledge in every direction."

"It's impressive."

"Down to the minutest detail," he chuckled, tapping the bridge of his glasses. "Would you like breakfast before moving on? I know a good spot near Leicester Square . . ."

"Breakfast in a surreal? What would be the point?"

"We take great pains to simulate nearly everything a Citizen might desire in the Forum, hunger included. Eating is not strictly necessary here, but most feel there is a certain satisfaction in the ritual nature of mealtimes."

Hearing the words *ritual nature* triggered a tickle in my throat, a familiar craving I had never felt in a commercial SR. Even my addiction had followed me here, an astounding feat of simulation. I reached into my jacket for my smokes, but the pack wasn't there.

The Sysop tilted his head. "Something wrong?"

"My cigarettes didn't make it in."

"Yes, sorry. There's no smoking allowed in the Forum's common areas."

"It's a simulation. Why would it matter?"

He laughed nervously. "It bothers people," he shrugged. "But to clarify, smoking is forbidden only in public spaces. There are many individual theaters that do allow it. The Smoking Lounge is one. A theater that celebrates tobacco in all its varieties. I can send you a list if you like. They'll appear in your *Favorites* menu."

"I'm fine for now," I said. "But I may need a toilet later."

The Sysop blushed and drew his head back. "That's certainly not necessary here . . ."

"The ritual, like you said."

The Sysop lifted his passport and thumbed it idly, stammering as he spoke. "Well, I'm sure there are one or two theaters devoted to the, ah . . . to the evacuation of . . . well, the call of nature. Would you like me to inquire?"

"That was a joke," I said.

"Ah, thank God," he sighed.

A steady beeping stiffened him suddenly. He punched his arm forward to reveal a hulking silver wristwatch beneath his sleeve, an odd redundancy considering the clock on his passport.

"Well, well, I'm afraid I have a meeting I cannot put off," he said. "Do you feel you have a firm grasp of things? Enough to begin your day?"

"I think so," I said. "I do have one request."

"By all means."

"My minders in D.C. asked me to look into the evolution of the Forum over the past few years. They'd like to understand its growth rate and its active user base, and they're curious about the evolution of the surreals in—"

"Theaters," the Sysop cut in. "We prefer the term."

"Theaters, right. We're interested in how they've changed over the years. What subjects and themes did your original theaters explore, versus what's on offer today."

The Sysop's eyes flashed, and he pulled his hands to his chest as if in prayer.

"A very interesting line of inquiry," he said. "Indeed, quite a lot has changed over the years. The theaters we see these days, they push boundaries we wouldn't have dreamed of crossing in the early days."

"That's exactly the sort of thing we're curious about," I said. "Would it be possible to get me a list of these original theaters? I'd like to begin my audit by tapping the source, so to speak."

The Sysop squinted and kneaded his hands together. "Yes, that's certainly possible," he said. "It shouldn't take long."

"I'd be grateful."

"I do know that only a handful of our original theaters remain active. There were nearly sixty in the beginning. I'd be surprised if more than twenty were still functional."

"Whatever you can dig up."

The Sysop raised his chin to the sky, as if absorbing some divine revelation. "You know, your request suggests the idea of a Forum retrospective," he said airily. "Revisiting our original content. The classics. Getting a sense of where it all began and where it's going. A marvelous way to celebrate our fifth anniversary next year."

I said nothing as he ruminated on the idea, chasing it among his racing thoughts. He clapped his hands together and gave me a beaming smile.

"I'll run this up the chain," he said. "As for your list, midafternoon by the latest."

"Perfect. Thank you."

"Until next time, Mr. Pike—adieu."

With a final salute he sauntered to the glowing exit tucked away in a narrow alcove between a dinner theater and an Italian Café. He stepped through without looking back and vanished in a flash of light.

Now set free, I looked around and contemplated my next steps. Elbow to elbow, masses of men and women surged, cutting around me like a rough current. Dank breath and fast chatter mixed in the air. I felt penned in like a farmyard animal. But, in truth, I was probably alone, the only real person for tens or hundreds of miles.

I pulled up my passport. The screen brightened, opening to the setting controls. I scrolled down and pressed the button labeled *Interior / Exterior*. The slider was set to fifty-fifty. I dragged it to the right, one hundred percent *Exterior*. Then I scrolled back to the volume slider and raised it to sixty—

Stark lifted his finger. It hovered above the screen as he listened. A few seconds passed. He nodded and pocketed the passport and raised a palm-facing hand before his face. He splayed his fingers and wiggled them all at once in a waving motion, then one at a time. He made a fist, held it, clenched hard, released. His eyes narrowed.

"This is wild," *he said.*

Pocketing his hands, Stark resumed his walk, now westward bound. He moved at a steady clip, past sundry shops and services, surrounded by pedestrians in perpetual motion. He rounded the street-level entrance of an underground station. He passed a money exchange, a sweetshop, a Gap, a Bubba Gump, a musical theater showing The Book of Mormon. *He crossed a narrow street and threaded up the bottlenecked entrance to Leicester Square and made his way to the fountain at its heart.*

Perched on a dais at the center of the fountain was a statue of Shakespeare in casual repose, leaning elbow-wise against a pile of books, his chin in hand, absorbed in pensive thought. A scroll sculpted in stone unfurled below him, hung frozen against the wind, inscribed with a brief maxim, a quote from Twelfth Night, *act four, scene two.*

"There is no darkness but ignorance."

If Stark recognized the line, he made no outward sign. He cleared his throat and lifted his passport again. He opened it to the theater's settings and navigated back to the Interior / Exterior slider. He swiped left.

How long, he wondered, could a person stay in the Forum like this without needing water or food? He recalled the Sysop had used the term in storage. *The very suggestion made him squirm. Did the Forum provide some sort of passive nourishment to its shelved Citizens? By what means was it delivered? Orally? Intravenously? Were there needles in his arms or tubes down his esophagus? And where were the bodies kept? Stretched upon a bed with wires in their ears? Or floating in a vat of preserving agents?*

Don't think about it, he thought. You're here to find Delia. Focus.

A surge of trepidation filled him from heart to limb. He realized a narrator with perpetual access to his thoughts could reveal them to the theater's administrators, blowing his carefully constructed cover. They might learn his name and his motive as easily as reading it off a page. The more he dwelled on this, the more fearful he became. With each worried thought, more evidence of his deceit accumulated. He knew he had to leave. Immediately.

Willing himself to run, he darted through people and traffic back to the theater's exit. His mind swooped and spun as he hurried on. Soon the exit appeared before him, the mere sight of it offering relief to the chaos hounding him. His pumping legs ached as he leapt through. He yearned for the relative quiet of his own mind. In a few seconds, he would have it—

WHEN I REENTERED THE ATRIUM, the shock of losing my narrator took some minutes to wear off. The eerie silence of a mind returned to my complete control was difficult to accept. I was relieved, yet I had never felt so empty.

I checked my passport for the time. A tiny clock in one corner said it was approaching 10:00 a.m. I crossed to the Atrium's outer wall and took a seat on an empty sofa. I watched dozens of meandering Citizens come and go through myriad portals arranged to pique their curiosity. Their flow was steady, and their vectors were insistent. A man would appear suddenly, bursting from one portal and shaking himself free of whatever lingering sensations had followed him through. Then he would stretch, glance around to get his bearings, and walk briskly to an adjacent portal, diving through the light barrier into a new adventure.

Sufficiently rested, I strolled the outer promenade, browsing the preview screens of portals, invitingly arranged. The Scent of Success advertised looping reels of enormous quantities of cash, both stacked in neat towers and strewn loose in large piles, intercut with extreme close-ups of noses and flaring nostrils. The advertisement for a theater called *Aflame* was even less forthcoming—shots of assorted random objects consumed in flames. I considered entering to satisfy my curiosity, but the next theater had a title too evocative to pass up: *The Psychogenic Implications of Quantum Gravity*. The teaser was inscrutable—images of vibrating atoms evolving through a series of lightning strikes into epileptic neurons. A total mystery . . . so I entered.

Passing through, I found myself in a massive circular room about a mile in diameter with a domed transparent roof. Another blue sky glowed high above, seen through an enormous geodesic dome built from clear glass. I stood at the room's perimeter on a semicircle ledge no more than a dozen feet wide, situated high above the floor. A few hundred feet below was a wall-to-wall mass of pillows. Millions upon millions of pillows in uncountable colors and sizes, piled at a depth impossible to judge. There was no sign of the floor and nothing else in the room as far as the eye could see.

I crept to the edge and looked down. There was a ladder off to one side, hanging from the ledge and dropping down until it disappeared into the crush of pillows. As I stared into this pliant abyss, a pair of jogging footsteps pattered behind me and slapped to a sudden halt.

"Shit!"

I turned just in time to see a man in his forties grind to a quick stop behind me just an arm's length away. Gulping for air, he backed off, heaving and panting in a blue polyester pajama suit peppered with gold stars. He raised his arms and doubled over, slapping his thighs.

"Sorry," he said, breathless. "Didn't see you there."

"My fault," I said. "I'm just looking around."

He chuckled and shook his legs, first one then the other. "Was trying to get a good lead," he said pointing at the pillows below.

I shifted to one side, keeping my eyes on the portal, fearful of what else might come rocketing through. Pajama man did the same.

"What's the experiment here?" I said.

"Experiment?"

"The purpose of this theater. What's it for?"

Pajama man scratched his bulging belly and tugged at the hem of his shirt as he looked out across the cavernous room with a look that bordered on love.

"Some quantum shit, I think."

"Quantum shit."

He scuttled to the edge of the platform and looked down. "The main idea is to gather speed and launch yourself as far as you can." He hunched at the cornice and squinted as he swept his eyes across the enormous space. Suddenly he pointed.

"I see you, Juice!" he shouted. "Bombs away, bitch!"

A distant voice called back. "Fucking do it!"

Cheers filled the room. The man backed away from the ledge and bent low like a sprinter ready to bolt. He gave me a last sturdy look.

"*Carpe diem*, brother," he said.

A parting wink and he was off, exploding forward into a run. In three long strides he hit the platform's edge and bounded off, leaping through the open air. He pumped his legs and whirled his arms like a helicopter losing a battle against gravity.

"Woo!" he bellowed, a doppler foghorn all the way down.

When he struck bottom, the impact threw a dozen pillows skyward like drops of dew off a struck leaf. Pillows farther from the point of impact heaved and rippled. The man disappeared.

Again the theater erupted with screeches and victory cries. I scanned the field of pillows for their source. The floor was a mesmerizing pixel field of jagged color, impossible to parse. Yet somewhere down there were people, crawling and lounging among the downy softness, waiting their turn to take the plunge.

I turned to go. Before I could reach the portal, the hooting of the monkeys below became more uniform, their voices pulsing in rhythmic unison, a single syllabic shout. I halted to better hear it.

Jump!

Jump!

Jump!

Jump!

I walked out.

FOR THE NEXT FEW HOURS I bounced from one theater to another, awaiting the fulfillment of the Sysop's promise. Without a list of early theaters still in operation, finding Delia or one of her colleagues would take some time. The defunct website I'd found listed sixty theaters or so. If I could pare it down to at least half that, I'd stand a better chance.

I hated the contingency of relying on someone else to move a case forward. I liked active, intentional work—cases I could solve myself. I liked to be in control at every step, not at the mercy of a massive bureaucracy that resented my very presence. If there was an advantage to this pause, it was functional. I now had some time to get a feel for the Forum as an ecosystem, to experience its full scope, the breadth of its inquiries, the depth of its capabilities.

Driven by whim, I wandered for the next few hours. Each theater bore titles as evocative as their contents—*Algorithm Zoo*, *Day of the Meteor*, *What Would Jesus Drink?*, *Songs for Your Health*, *What's My Gerrymander?*, *Super Schleppers*.

I visited a theater hosting a steaming bubble bath the size of Lake Superior. I found another that served eighteen thousand flavors of ice cream from tubs the size of Olympic swimming pools. I ducked into an eternal Beatles concert starring perfect replicas of the Fab Four on a stage the size of a flatbed truck in a cavernous underground venue with a max capacity of two hundred. With each theater visited, my opinion of the Forum grew ever more divided. It was a technological triumph, but the bulk of its content existed only to satisfy a basic hunger for entertainment or escapism.

I found some solace in a theater called Brains in Jars, a simulation that offered no more or less than its title implied. The entire theater was a tiny, unadorned cement room dimly lit by halogen tubes glowing a bilious green. Small tables about eighteen inches square were arranged to fill the space in a perfect grid, standing ten across and twenty deep. Upon each table was a large glass jar containing a pinkish-blue human brain suspended in a cloudy liquid. For twenty minutes I paced the room, searching for some hidden purpose or meaning. But the brains were as silent as their thoughts.

Se Coucher was the most lavish theater of the bunch, yet one with the simplest offer imaginable—a restful nap. The portal brought me to the head of a grand hallway that ran for miles upon miles in a single direction. Doors on both sides opened to grand bedrooms that shimmered in the gaudy gilded style of the French First Empire. Each golden room contained an exquisite imperial-sized bed with billowing canopies, elaborate sculptures and engravings, and luxurious sheets and pillowcases weaved entirely of silk. Priceless comfort was this theater's singular promise. Slip naked under the smooth covers and stay as long as you like. Pleasant respite for weary Citizens who had no urgent need to leave the confines of surrogate reality.

I entered a random room and closed the door behind me. The burnished rosewood floor glowed with a sienna gleam in the light of six candles hanging from a center sconce. Thick, heaving curtains hung over night-blackened windows. A grand canopied bed sat at the back with a diaphanous lace veil hanging from its support frame. The lace fluttered at my approach.

I pulled it back. Before me stretched a silken duvet that glinted like a still pool of Mediterranean aquamarine. I took out my passport and removed my jacket and folded the one into the other and set them at the foot of the bed with my hat on top. Then I peeled back the cover and slipped beneath. The silk was cool and slick at first touch, like the surface of a refrigerator. I pulled the sheets to my nose and lay still.

I don't remember falling asleep, nor the attempt. The soft trill of a wind chime woke me, chasing away inscrutable dreams. I sat up and looked around. The chime sounded again, obscuring a muted buzz coming from my folded jacket. I crawled over a mountain of fabric and pulled out my passport. There was a message for me.

New Theaters Acquired.

I tapped through to the opening menu. The *Favorites* option had a small star beside it. I tapped it. A long list of theaters cascaded down the screen. I scrolled slowly.

The Shallow Sea

The Sunk-Cost Patriarchy

Pain Possession

Placebo Palace

The Death of Desire

The Relativity of Everyday Things

The Bystander Effect Revisited

War & Peace

Survivor Bias Island

Mind's I & Mind's U

Past Privilege

Your Double

Floodgate Effectiveness

Born Again and Again and Again

Symposium

The Cornerstone Principle

My heart sank scanning the list. This Little World wasn't among them. If only it had been so simple. I scrolled to the top and counted down. Sixteen theaters of the first sixty still in operation. A reasonable number. Something I could tackle in a few days if I was diligent. Sooner, if I was lucky.

I tapped through each theater, getting a sense of their purpose and—more importantly—checking the names of the designers, in search of Walsh, Francisco, MG, Saint, or Lopez. Any one of these would do.

It didn't take long to find a promising match: Francisco Lopez, Engineer.

. . . With our deadline days away, an acute anxiety about the purpose and effectiveness of This Little World began to fester. I worried that I was perfecting another social opiate, not a challenging work of personal psychology. I'd hoped to build a theater that exposed peoples' secrets to themselves, offering a chance for worthy introspection. But nobody reacted this way when confronted with their unbound Id. There were no epiphanies, no revelations. People wallowed happily in their own neuroses and begged for more. I asked Locksley for time to reconsider some of This Little World's core features, but he convinced me to keep it running as-is.

The success of the Forum depends on work like yours, he told me. This Little World will turn heads and get people talking. It's our flagship offer. So let's make some noise first, then figure out where to go from there.

A million pounds of pressure. I didn't love the idea that my theater should be the star of the Forum's launch, but I didn't hate the idea enough to say no.

Mikkonen tried spinning my success as only he could.

The technology that underpins This Little World is quite an achievement, he said. You have many reasons to be proud. And so few reasons to regret anything.

I feel like a hack, I said. An entertainer in a lab coat.

I feel quite the opposite, he said. You have made significant technological breakthroughs in the past few months.

Maybe, I said. But I'd rather not commit Henry Ford levels of damage while nurturing the mistaken belief that I am Marie Curie.

By that you mean . . .

There are bad ways to attempt good things.

I see, he said. Yes, that is certainly true . . .

11

I HOPPED THROUGH THE NEAREST PORTAL into *The Death Of Desire*, designed by Francisco Lopez, one of Delia's drinking buddies and fellow Engineers. I was finally chasing a lead that felt solid, like there was a big fish waiting for me at the end of a short line.

The Death of Desire had been one of the Forum's original theaters nearly four years ago, and its function—according to the description in my passport—was appropriately ambitious. Conceived as a means to alleviate the firm grip of addiction in all its cruel forms, it was a place where an alcoholic might come to wean himself off drink, or someone with a crippling sex addiction could break free of their carnal shackles. Advertised as a place of healing, it gave me a good first impression of Mr. Lopez. I imagined a selfless artist with great empathy and understanding, exactly the sort of company Delia Walsh would call a friend. But my first steps through *The Death of Desire* put immense strain on this early impression.

I emerged in what appeared to be a hospital waiting room. It was a broad rectangular space with low-tiled ceilings and lit by a lurid fluorescence. Rows of black vinyl chairs lined the room. Filthy floor to ceiling windows made up one of the four walls. Outside, a leaden sun threw shade over a bombed-out city, its tepid light straddling the line between day and night. Between the husks of crumbling skyscrapers, a constant wind spun cyclones of ash and filth.

I studied the dim room. There was a reception desk on its far side. A ruddy forehead topped by a nest of wild hair poked above the counter. Elsewhere I counted three others, all of them asleep in their seats in various parts of the room.

I walked to the counter, my shoes clacking like hammers on the scuffed quartz floor. The receptionist looked up with total disinterest. It was a woman with a mottled face and brown threads of wispy hair, wearing dark-rimmed glasses. She made no expression at seeing me approach.

"Hello," she said flatly. "Can I help you?"

"I don't know. What is it you do?"

"I check people in."

"For what purpose?"

"If you don't know, why are you here?"

I pulled out my passport and flicked if vertically. When the badge appeared, the woman blinked rapidly, but seemed otherwise unmoved.

"You know what this is?" I said.

"Yes."

"I don't mean to be rude," I said, putting the passport away. "I'm just looking around."

"Okay."

"So what do you do here?"

"I check people in."

"As you said. So what's the purpose of this place?"

"We offer severing services of all kinds," she droned. "We have a list of available options if you'd like to see it."

"Severing services?"

"Yes."

I waited for more detail, but none came. "All right, I'll see the list," I said.

She pulled up a laminated sheet of A4 paper and laid it on the counter.

> *Welcome to* The Death of Desire! *Severing Services Currently Available:*
> CORE EGO: *Shame. Love. Sadness. Empathy. "Self." Others by request.*
> PHYSICAL: *Pain, Five Senses (Tactile, Smell, Sight, Taste, Hearing), Hunger; Others by request.*
> *Note: Addiction treatments are still available. Please consult with one of our technicians.*

I stood back. The receptionist pulled her menu off the counter and stowed it.

"The mandate of this theater seems to have expanded," I said.

"What does that mean?"

"Would it be possible to speak with the designer?"

"Who?"

"Francisco Lopez. He designed this theater."

"I don't know anyone by that name."

"Someone else then?"

"There is no one else," she said, leaning to one side to check on the bodies cluttering her waiting room. "Except those hobos. But they don't work here."

"That list mentioned technicians."

She nodded. "Yeah. That's me."

"You're the technician?"

"Yes," she nodded. "It's not that hard. People tell me what they want, and they walk through that door. I push a button. Done."

She pointed to a nondescript swinging door to the left of her desk. A placard at its middle said *No Admittance Without Authorization*. I sighed and backed off, looking past the woman into the bowels of the office behind her. There was no life or movement back there, nor anywhere else in the space. Just the technician and her three hobos.

"Thanks for your time," I said.

I crossed the room, heading for the portal, my gut sinking into my shoes. My lead had evaporated as fast as it had found me.

Three steps from the door, I heard a wheezing voice.

"I know him," it whispered. "I know Lopez."

One of the sleeping men had awakened and was now reaching his bony arm out from under a tattered trench coat. Hair the color and shape of a cotton ball puffed out from beneath a newsboy hat fitted tightly over his head. As I approached he lifted his chin. It was a young face aged by accident and lack of care, pocked with sores and layered with yellowing flakes of skin.

I bent forward to hear him better.

"You know Francisco Lopez?" I said.

The man nodded painfully. "Since the early days," he said. "A fucking saint that man. Helped me kick opioids."

"Do you know where he is now?"

The man rotated his head slowly, as if to prevent it from tumbling to the floor. "I wish I did. I know he's working on new things. But we never stayed in touch."

"He doesn't visit his own theater?"

"Hasn't for a long time. Didn't like what this place had become."

"What was that?"

The man smiled a toothless grin and laughed, the laugh erupting into a wet cough that shook him. Gasping, he found some air. When he was breathing evenly again, he beckoned me closer.

"I was here from the start," he croaked. "The very beginning. Francisco had a dream. He wanted to help people, folks with addictions of all kinds. His mother was an alcoholic. Lost her when she was forty-seven. He was thirteen. So he built this place to free people of the impulses they couldn't control. The grip of addiction. Drink. Drugs. Sex. Anyone suffering could find solace here. Hope. And it worked that way for a while. It was a fucking miracle. I kicked heroin coming here. And little by little that loss of desire for the needle carried over to the outside. Lost all hunger for it in the real world too. Took a while. But it worked. It was incredible."

"Why are you still here?" I cut in.

He chuckled. "I'm getting to that. Something happened, see? Somehow, someone had the idea to selectively lobotomize themselves in ways never intended. A new breed of Citizen started showing up, looking to amplify thrills, not dampen them."

The man turned aside to cough, a ragged gurgling eruption that left him breathless. He panted for a moment, then continued.

"About six months in, there was a Citizen who wanted to eradicate his sense of shame. He was single, he liked solitude, he hated the idea of collective responsibility. And he was about to run for a prominent public office. Francisco obliged. I don't think he knew what kind of chaos he was unleashing when he did. He just wanted to see if it worked. The detached curiosity of a scientist. So the guy got his wish. He left here with an empathy-shaped hole in his head."

"It wasn't permanent, was it?"

"Not at first. But he kept coming back. Getting used to the feeling of not giving a fuck. Like my own rehabilitation, a little practice goes a long way."

"Where is he now?"

"He won that election, that's all I know."

"Is that what the lady meant by *severing services*?"

He nodded. "One of many. Once word got around that you could be freed of your shame, men from all over started making requests to remove whatever facets of themselves they found inconvenient.

Love, Humility, Fear, Lust. It was a new form of cosmetic therapy. Then came the fetish set, looking to target specific desires for sadomasochistic ends. Basic survival mechanisms, on the chopping block. Thresholds for pain, gone. Impulse control, eliminated. Adrenaline drained. Humans entered this theater and robots walked out. Didn't take long for Francisco to regret what he'd done. Called it *sociopathic medicine*. But it was too late. So, two years after he'd opened this theater, he handed the keys to someone else and walked away."

"You think he's still around?" I said.

The man shrugged. "I know he had other ideas. But who's to say? This whole experience might have soured him on the whole—"

Another violent fit of coughing cut him short. When he stilled himself, I extended my hand.

"I don't know what you've been through or why you're still here," I said. "But I can show you the way out if you want me to."

The man's vacant eyes quivered and he gave me another gummy grin. "No, no; I'll be fine," he said. "I'm something of a daredevil in here. Just had my immune system neutralized. Wanted to see what would happen."

"How's that going?"

"I feel like shit."

I stood back. "Yeah, you look it too."

He pumped a triumphant fist. "It's amazing what they can do nowadays."

"Take care," I said.

Coughing again, he gave me a wave and sank back into his seat and closed his eyes. I left as quickly as I could.

BACK IN THE ATRIUM, I collected my thoughts and checked my expectations. The reality of this place was slowly setting in. Finding Delia or anyone else here was not going to be as simple as striking up a few casual conversations. For one, the sheer scope of the Forum was daunting. In spite of the few crowds I had seen, I had to accept that the population here was quite vast. I'd have better luck asking people on the streets of Seattle if they knew my local bartender. Still, I had no other options just yet. It was time to put in some legwork.

Of the fifteen remaining theaters, *Pain Possession* seemed a logical next step. Designed by someone named Michael Grange, I had hopes this would lead me to the mysterious MG from the unpaid bar tab at Antony's. The theater itself promised a fascinating experiment in which countless imaginable pains were physicalized as objects that could be worn and removed and traded around like accessories to an outfit, perhaps as a way of experiencing in safety the vast catalog of human suffering. It, too, fit the mold of a radical early experiment gone awry. Now it was the site of the pain equivalent of a pepper eating contest, where Citizens gathered to challenge one another to endure the greatest possible pains for the longest amount of time. I asked around if anyone had talked to or seen Michael Grange. Not a single Citizen knew him.

With a sinking heart I continued down the list, entering theaters and asking after their designers. *Placebo Palace* was simply a giant stadium filled with chocolate candies. *Mind's I & Mind's U* was an experimental theater where people took turns transplanting their brains into the bodies of animals. *War & Peace* was just a comprehensive immersive adaptation of the Tolstoy novel—well-made but currently unattended. The host told me I was the first visitor in almost two years.

Exploring *Symposium*, I found a physical reproduction of ancient Athens, circa 400 BC. But the city was entirely empty. It took almost thirty minutes to locate the one grubby Citizen hiding within, living inside an oversized pithos in the middle of an abandoned market, a man who claimed apprenticeship to the preeminent cynic, Diogenes. Once a hedge fund manager from Venice Beach, this half-naked apostle now spent his days eating, shitting, and masturbating to his heart's content in a Hellenic ghost town.

He claimed he was happy, but spoke wistfully of the earliest, busiest days of the theater, when he and hundreds of aficionados spent their time living out the maxims of the pre-Socratics. Heraclitus, Anaximander, and Pythagoras were frequent favorites. Their program was simple—to live as they lived, think as they thought, and—as he put it—find some purity, away from the trash heap of modern life. Now that he was alone in a theater built for thousands, he felt honor bound to push himself to his mental and physical limits. Or at the very least, until his Forum membership was revoked for lack of payment. A cynic to the bitter end.

In theater after theater, the content I encountered was vastly different than the experiment's original stated purpose by a considerable margin. Most had mutated from reasonable attempts to prove a hypothesis into inscrutable distractions. But my wanderings were not without minor discoveries. I noted early on that the Forum's population was primarily made up of men, and that a majority of these men seemed embarrassed about the amount of time they spent here. It was always for good reason, they'd assure me. They had come to make something of themselves or to improve their lives. If only they could find the right theater they could attain an almost superhuman enlightenment. This is what kept people engaged, searching, yearning for change.

Late in the afternoon, I visited *Your Double*, designed by someone named Jude Synge. It billed itself as a psychological playground where Citizens acquired perfect doppelgängers of themselves to escort around a sunny reproduction of the greater Los Angeles area. These copies mirrored the original Citizen in every possible way, save for the knowledge that they were copies. In effect, all who entered *Your Double*, were twined in body and mind. Best friends with themselves.

According to the theater's summary, the intended effect was therapeutic: *Would you be friends with you? Are you as charming as you have always suspected? Are you empathetic to the degree you have always wished? Are you as effortlessly sexy as you believe? Are you interesting and funny, or just a dreary bore?* Your Double *will let you know. Experience the radical objectivity that comes with observing yourself from without. You'll never look at yourself the same way again. Come visit us today, and prepare yourself for total psychological rejuvenation.*

When I entered *Your Double*, it was dusk, and the sky was a battered crimson and the syrupy scent of night blooming jasmine floated heavy on the air. I was poolside at the Roosevelt Hotel on Hollywood Boulevard, a place I had been twice before in my younger days when this sort of pilgrimage made sense. The pool glowed a window cleaner blue, and with nobody swimming and no wind blowing, it was as smooth as a slab of dried epoxy. All around the pool were flat square sofas laid out in a grid with parasols plugged into their centers. Almost every seat was already occupied, and always by a pair.

The distant jangle of ice on glass caught my ear and my mouth went as dry as Death Valley topsoil. I walked out from under the eaves that surrounded the patio into rosy light and tiki flame. There was a covered bar at the far end the pool. My tongue craved the taste of a cold beer, virtual or not.

I weaved through the lounge chair archipelago, minding everybody's business as I passed. As advertised, the place was crowded with twins. Every man had his double. It was like wandering over the deck of a twisted version of Noah's ark, where God had provided everyone present with a backup version of himself. But these were not congenial pairs, and there was nothing therapeutic about the behavior I witnessed.

I saw one man reposing in swim trunks, a pair of shades shielding his eyes, as his double stood by feeding him hors d'oeuvre from a bountiful platter. Not a word passed between them. A second man was sitting on the chest of his perfect likeness, his hands wrapped around the poor double's throat. Every few seconds the man on top would release his hands so the double could gobble up some air before the original tightened his grip again. A third man was dragging his twin by a leash clipped to a dog collar fixed around the double's neck. A fourth was reading a book while sitting on his double as if it were a park bench. And on and on, one diorama of abuse after another, and not a single conversation worth eavesdropping on.

When I reached the bar, I fell against it and yawned.

"Hello, sir," someone said. "Would you like me to call up your double?"

I twisted toward the voice. A bartender had appeared from some invisible character spawner to wait on me. He was a handsome chap in his thirties with a shiny smile, smooth dark hair and clear brown skin. He had perfect posture but no clue what to do with his arms. They just hung at his sides like two towels on a rack.

"Not just yet," I said, leaning hard on the bar as I swept a look over the patio. "I'm just passing through. Getting a sense of the place."

I pulled out my passport and flashed the badge. The bartender registered it with the barest glimmer of a twitch, then smiled.

"Can I get you a drink?"

"*Cerveza, por favor*. Something cold and gold, your choice."

"*Si, muy bien*."

He backed away to rummage through the icebox. I continued to search the shadows and was not disappointed. A carnival of sadism and curious apathy writhed out there in the half-light like a demonic landscape painted by Bosch.

"Here you are, sir."

I reached for my wallet. The bartender raised a flat hand.

"No charge, sir."

I nodded and grabbed the beer and swigged, looking him over. There was a hollowness to this man, a plastic action-figure feel.

"Are you real?" I said. "Human?"

"No, sir."

"You're part of the theater?

"Yes, sir. I am an artificial host. My function is to sell drinks."

"You see a lot of action in this theater?"

"What do you mean by action?"

"Excitement. Energy."

"I have witnessed quite a few fights."

"What kind of fights?"

"Wrestling mostly. Hand-to-hand violence."

"Anyone ever die?"

"Yes, sir."

"By accident or deliberately?"

"Deliberately."

"Tell me about it."

"Which one?"

"The most recent."

"The most recent murder happened two days ago," he said flatly. "An inebriated gentleman was arguing with his double when a fight broke out. The inebriated gentleman smashed a glass tumbler over his double's head. He then dragged him to the pool by his hair and pushed its head into the water. The double drowned in four minutes and thirty-six seconds."

"You were counting?"

"I have direct access to the data."

There was a sudden movement to my right, a frenzied shuffle that compelled me to step back. It was a young man with spiked dirty blond hair, wearing green speedos and a Hawaiian shirt with a pink and yellow palm fronds pattern that hung open, revealing a body tight enough to break rocks against. He was bobbing and weaving like a windsock.

"Another triple Long Island, *amigo*," he said, spreading the whole sentence like a paste.

"You a regular?" I said.

The young man turned and overturned, looking around. It took a few seconds for him to locate me.

"What's that?" he slurred.

"Are you a regular here?"

"Oh yeah, every fucking week man," he said, raising his hand into devil's horns. "Best place to blow off steam."

"A few drinks, a dip in the pool," I said. "A nice heart-to-heart with yourself?"

He blew a strange laugh and his lips vibrated and he almost fell over. When he righted himself he laid two elbows on the bar and smiled.

"Heart-to-heart. Yeah, right." He lifted a finger and jabbed it at the sky. "There's no better feeling than looking yourself right in the face and just fucking punching it."

A tall sweating cocktail appeared in front of him. He reeled back, catching the edge of the bar before falling on his ass. When he stood up, he gave a sloppy salute and swept up his drink and piloted the straw to his mouth. He took a long slurping sip and winked at the bartender.

"Thanks, bro," he gurgled. "Put it on my tab."

"Of course," said the bartender.

The drunk turned to me and reached out. I think he meant to pat my shoulder, but he was short about three feet. His arm sailed through the air and scooped back to his side. He tottered, then stood upright.

"Live a little, bro," he mumbled, the straw back in his mouth. "Kick yourself in the balls."

He wobbled off, bouncing through the grid of sofas like a pinball hitting bumpers. I looked back at the bartender. He was standing stiff again, his eyes fixed on something interior and not of this world. The humming code of his being, maybe.

"Is that how it is most days?" I said.

"Yes, sir."

I finished my drink with three more flicks of the wrist and set the bottle aside. I tickled the air to bring the bartender closer. He drew his hands behind his back and leaned forward.

"What can you tell me about the Engineer who designed this place?"

"Jude Synge? He's a skinny man. Quiet. Some pent-up anger. Very intelligent."

"Have you seen him recently?"

"The last time I saw Mr. Synge was two years, five months, and seven days ago."

"Two years and five months is a long time."

"And seven days. Yes."

"Seems like a lot of Engineers abandon their theaters. Why is that?"

The bartender shrugged mechanically. "Engineers are like artists. They like to develop new ideas. Jude was no different."

"You ever meet his friends? Other Engineers?"

"Yes. Quite a few helped him test this theater."

"Delia Walsh? Or Francisco Lopez?"

He nodded. "I don't know Mr. Lopez. But I did meet Delia Walsh. She helped Jude improve the code for this theater."

"When was the last time you saw her?"

The bartender looked to the horizon, calculating. "Two years, nine months, two days."

"What was she doing that day?"

"Arguing with Jude."

"Any idea where she is now?"

"No."

"What about Jude?"

"Nine months ago he began work on a new theater called Saint's Country. That appears to be his most recent project."

My heart leapt at hearing the word *Saint*. One of the four names on Delia's postcard bar tab. I flushed with a newfound energy.

"Why's it called Saint's Country?" I said.

The bartender shrugged. "Jude's friends called him Saint. Saint Jude. I don't know why. I assume he named the theater after himself."

"Saint Jude."

The bartender nodded vaguely. "The patron saint of hopeless causes and impossible tasks."

When one door closes, another opens. I hit the bar top with a vigorous slap. "Thanks, buddy," I said. "I wish I could slip you a fifty, but I'm outta cash."

"Money has no value here. And I would have no use for it."

"All the same, thanks a million."

I gave him a wave and set off for the portal, keeping my head down as I searched my passport for Saint's Country and queued it up. Before stepping out, the sharp crack and shatter of breaking glass rang out through the darkness. Someone screamed, another shouted.

"C'mere you piece of shit! Wipe that fucking smile off your face!"

The voice was familiar.

. . . I finished porting This Little World into the Forum at three-thirteen in the morning, fewer than six hours before its grand opening.

No, not finished. No work of art is ever finished, only abandoned. One of Valery's perfect sayings. I find it applies to almost everything—art, relationships, arguments, life in general.

I abandoned This Little World at three-thirteen in the morning. I simply stopped working. I'd reached a point where I knew enough was enough. There was no reason to polish something beyond its capacity to shine. I'd never felt that way about any of my work. There was always some kernel of curiosity that kept me coming back. This was a remarkable milestone. To be so devoted and obsessive about an idea one minute, and utterly devoid of feeling for it the next—very strange. A sudden lack of interest, drained of all enthusiasm for a project I had been working on for most of my real career. I simply froze in that moment, swept away by wayward thoughts. I want a beer, I told myself. I miss Seattle. I haven't been laid in ten months. I should probably get a haircut. Etcetera. When I realized I wasn't thinking about the work anymore, I just knew I was done.

On my way out, I ran the full boot sequence one last time. This Little World fired up smoothly, ready for action. Everything looked good. Then I walked out.

It was the last time I ever set foot in that theater. In fewer than six hours, it would host a wave of its first proper guests. Not testers this time. A real audience. People primed for wonder by Locksley's sales pitch.

But I wouldn't be with them. I was already searching and yearning for something new. I just didn't know what . . .

12

DAYLIGHT DIMMED OVER LOW FURRED HILLS, fading the piney greens into dusky black. A dropping sun filtered its last bloody light through dishwater clouds. I sat high astride a horse, a brown chestnut beast with a wild mane and a slow gait. I had never ridden a horse before today, neither outside nor inside a surreal, yet by some generous algorithm I had been gifted enough instinct to carry on without fear. With each step the mare's shoulders dropped one way, and I shifted the other, wobbling only slightly in my saddle like a man drunk within his limit.

I was exploring Saint's Country, an accelerated simulation of the western expansion of the United States. My path had led me to Oregon country, where cowboys were in abundance, smoldering campsites were common, and gunfire was general all through the countryside. The simulated year was 1852. Next week another year would pass.

I'd been riding for an hour over rocky hills and through chittering forests in pursuit of Saint Jude Synge, the theater's primary Engineer and Delia Walsh's colleague. And for the first time in my investigation, my diligence had paid off. While watering on the Snake River I spoke with a pair of zinc prospectors who let slip that someone going by the moniker Saint had just passed through Fort Hall the day before. They hadn't seen the man with their own eyes, but word of his whereabouts was limping down the trail. They gave me a secondhand description of a cloaked rider heading west through the valley wearing a flat-topped hat pulled over a mess of light brown hair and a dark blue bandanna.

For many miles my horse and I followed a trail that offered no alternative but forward and behind. It led us down a rough hill and beside a shimmering river and up again to a high embankment half shorn away and lined with felled trees, like the monstrous antlers of some primordial wendigo. The sounds of unincorporated Oregon fussed in the arid air—a whitewashed wind blew through high lonesome trees, the melodies of meadowlarks bounced off shorn cliffs, the clip of iron horseshoes clicked a stone flecked trail, a wolf howled at the rim of a distant hill.

After following a crumbling ridgeline, we dropped again to the river's edge where the water ran fast and loud. We then rounded a tumult of stone protruding from the hills. The air in this shallow vale took on a gauzy tinge and it was there that I smelled the woodsmoke. My horse snuffled and shook her head. I reared back and whispered calm into her twitching ears.

Finding her some peace, I dismounted and led the mare off the trail to the river's edge. I tied her to a fallen log within reach of the water. She began to drink. Alone I hiked along the bank. A hundred yards farther on I saw the campfire, a twinkling star in the ripe black of night with a lone figure in a wide flat cap sitting astride a hacked stump, his back to me. I could hear the snuffling and cropping of another horse tethered somewhere outside the rimmed halo that made up this man's luminous domain.

I approached, closing the distance carefully, the rush of water obscuring my steps. At twenty yards I stopped. He seemed not to notice me. I waited to be sure. Presently I heard singing.

"*Cass, I long to see your face. Soft and mild, your dimpled grace.*"

It was a woman's voice. She crooned on.

"*I long to hear your siren's call. Sing to me, come bring me home.*"

I cleared my throat and called out. "Beg your pardon?"

The singing cut short, and the hat pivoted. A smooth slender profile cut against the flickering firelight. A feminine silhouette with a dark bandanna knotted around the neck.

"Who's there?" she said.

I raised a hand that only a hunting bat could see. "Name's John Pike," I said. "Just out of Fort Hall this morning. I smelled your fire, and it stirred a need for company."

"I see."

"You don't mind?"

The woman turned back to the fire. All I could see now was the shadow of her hat, propped like a devilish nimbus.

"I got beans here," she called out. "And beer."

"Thanks kindly."

I pushed forward, taking big steps to make a racket by which she could track my movements. Her eyes found me as I reached the edge of the firelight and didn't let go. They were sleepy eyes that glinted silver in the orange light. She offered me a seat on a large stone just across the fire. I sat and thanked her as I marked her scarf—a navy-blue twist of fabric. She held a slender stick stripped of bark and with it stirred the contents of a tin of beans wedged in the center of the campfire, its label blistered and blackened. She pulled the stick from the tin and jabbed at the fire. It sparked like a hammer to an anvil.

"It's a long way to Fort Hall," she said casually. "You've done some riding."

"Just a bit."

Her face was friendly and dirty, with rounded angles that could have gone either way, or some new way unfathomed. Her hair was wheaten and pulled back in a loose ponytail. She plunged the stick into the tin and drew it back and sucked the tip. The taste gave her pause. At last she looked at me.

"Hungry?"

"Thirsty more like."

"Beer's okay?"

"Definitely."

She laid her stir stick on the ashen stones at the fire's edge and rose and walked to the bank of the creek. She bent herself to the water where the necks of six bottles broke the rippling surface and she pulled up two and carried them clinking back to the fire. Cracking the cap from one she offered me the other. The dark bottle was scratched and chipped. I pried it open and took a drink. The beer was cold and hoppy.

The woman returned to her tipped log and took up the stick and went back to stirring, sipping from her own bottle every now and then. After a long silence she sniffed and looked at me over the flames with some baleful satisfaction. I took a small drink, then set the bottle by my foot and took out my passport. I held it up. The woman looked and smiled slightly at the auditor's badge that appeared.

"Just passing by," she said. "Right."

I tucked the passport away and took up my bottle. "I don't mean to break the spell of this place," I said. "But I was wondering if you could answer a few questions about your work here?"

She thrice tapped the rim of the tin of beans as if it were a bell.

"If I can."

"You're the one they call Saint Jude?"

She ducked her head and grinned and raised it up again. "That's right. Just Saint is fine."

"Patron of . . . what was it?"

"Hopeless causes."

"You were one of the Forum's first Engineers, is that right?"

"The sixth employee if I remember right."

"How many of you were there in the beginning?"

"There's just one of me and that's plenty," she winked, then sat up straight. "Almost one hundred of us. Most working on their own theaters. A few pairs too."

"But only sixty theaters on launch day?"

"Fifty-eight. Quite a few didn't make the cut."

"What were the criteria?"

"Some secret sauce known only to our director."

"Pritchard Locksley?"

"That's right."

"You designed *Your Double*. Was it your first theater?"

"In here it was."

"Are you still involved with its operation?"

"I am not."

"What happened?"

Jude sighed and batted at the waves of heat rising from the flames. "What always happens," she said. "The hooligans showed up and disproved my hypothesis."

"Which was?"

"I thought I could design a theater worth more than just escapist entertainment. A theater that balanced the head with the heart. *Your Double* was meant to be a place where people could face themselves with truth and honesty. And for a while it worked out. I thought there would be something liberating about facing yourself and talking to yourself like an old friend. Over time, the audience grew. And pretty soon they turned my little project into an amusement park for sadists. Once that happened, I wanted out."

"You couldn't fix it?"

"I tried. My hopeless cause. See, the average man will punch a bleeding hole right through your assumptions about the inherent kindness of human beings. But I don't blame them. They didn't break any rules in my theater. They just pushed it to its limit, carving big troughs through a garden I didn't cultivate with enough care."

I nodded. "So you abandoned *Your Double* and built this place instead?"

Saint smiled sadly and looked skyward at the pinholed heavens.

"I worked on something else first. Didn't work out. This is my third theater to date," she said. "I pitched it as a serious investigation of colonialism, but in truth, I think I just wanted a place to be myself."

"There's already a lot of mainstream cowboy fantasies on the market."

"Sure. But they always have a plot. Ain't none that let you just live as you please."

She raised up and drew her shoulders back to stretch. Then she leaned back upon her log and kicked a leg out and crossed her arms in front of her.

"It used to be that people had more agency in commercial digital playgrounds. For a time there were hidden rooms, shadowed haunts, forgotten corners where you could hang out and be yourself, or some other self, in a special place built by a dozen just like you. Maybe fewer—just one or two weirdos. Or maybe you were the only freak of your phylum on Earth. It didn't matter. There was always a place for you somewhere, in one of these alter worlds. A place that felt like it was made just for you. And that was a comfort beyond all measure."

She paused and looked about the bubble of firelight that pushed against the tarred black of night.

"Most of that's gone now. The old days are dead, bought and bulldozed by the corporations—Hypo, Kosmos, Inverse. They run the show out there. They dictate what experiences are possible, and the purpose of them. They run every surreal on earth except this Forum. But those of us who remember the early days, we yearn for that old feeling. So we make spaces we can lean into, if only for a time, and live the errant truths of our being."

"That makes sense."

"I'm glad. Anything else?"

I straightened up, ready to peel back another layer as slowly as possible.

"Is there a theater in the Forum called This Little World?"

Saint ignored the question and poked again at her bubbling beans. Tasting from the stick, she chucked it into the woods. Then she scooped up two larger branches and used them as pincers to lift the tin from the fire. Setting the beans aside, she threw the branches on the fire. They crackled in dry agony. The woman watched the steaming can for a time but made no move for it.

"That one shut down a while ago," she said.

"Do you know why?"

Saint looked up, her eyes narrowing. She watched me for a long time. Then her eyes flicked sideways and fixed on something behind me, just over my shoulder. A sharp crack from the brush turned me around, but I couldn't see a thing in the dark. My vision flared and throbbed with the campfire's blazing green afterimage. As the haze faded, liquid shadows cast by the sputtering fire danced amid the trees.

"Why don't you jump to your final question, Mr. Pike?" Saint said firmly. "And work backward from there. It'll save us time."

I turned back, thinking long and hard about how much truth I was willing to tell. When I looked at Saint, her eyes were fixed on me like two screws in sheet metal.

"You still frequent Antony's in Burlington?" I said.

Saint's brow lifted into a suspicious arch. "No, I don't."

"Well, I got bad news for you," I said. "You've got an unpaid bar tab."

Saint blinked a few times before bellowing a laugh that shook the trees. "You are not fucking serious."

"I am," I said. "But that's not why I'm here. Your name is on that tab with a few others. People I'd love to speak with."

"What names?"

"You, Delia Walsh. Francisco Lopez. Someone called MG."

"Okay . . . ?"

"I just want to ask them the same questions I'm asking you. About your work. The Forum's early days. How it all played out. And where it's going next."

"Interesting line of questioning for an auditor."

"I think so too," I said. "Who's MG?"

Saint bent to the tin of beans and pinched the rim a few times to test the heat. It pinched back. She blew on her fingers and shook them against the night. "If you don't have a name I'm not giving you one."

"Francisco Lopez, what about him?"

"Have you checked *The Death of Desire*?"

"First place I looked."

"And?"

"It's a lobotomy clinic."

Saint nodded her head solemnly. "Yeah. He was salty about that," she said. "We don't talk much but I know he's working on a handful of new things. He might stop by Antony's from time to time. But I wouldn't know."

"What about Delia Walsh?"

"What about her?"

"What was she working on when you last saw her?"

"Something ambitious. Something she said would piss off a lot of people. Her father included."

"Any idea what that could mean?"

Saint flared her nostrils and stared at me through the rising curtains of heat. "She was something of an anarchist. Devoted to the idea that the Forum and its technology should be free to all. An open-source public utility. But that's not how you make money, it's how you lose it. And the Forum is run and regulated by guys who really like money . . ."

Saint paused and her face flattened into a frown as she threw a second glance over my shoulder. I didn't move.

"You afraid of something, Saint?"

She looked back at me and her face softened. "Not in here," she said. "Not in my own theater. But out there, I don't trust anyone. Delia didn't either."

"Did something happen to her?"

"I'm sure it did. The question is what."

"What do you think?"

Saint took her time answering. "I think she's hiding in a Green Room. Waiting for something that may never come. Some sense of safety."

"Green Room?"

Saint's eyes narrowed to slivers. "They don't teach auditors about classified theaters anymore?"

"Not this auditor," I said. "Why would Delia be hiding in a classified theater?"

Saint took a deep breath and clasped her hands between her knees, keeping her eyes locked on the fire. "Delia saw the fatal flaw in this place long before anyone else. She saw it before we went live. But nobody cared. We were all having too much goddamn fun pushing the Forum to its limits."

"What fatal flaw?"

"What she called the desire line of technological progress. The idea that a new technology will always regress over time to some lowest common denominator usage. Something far more vulgar that its creators intended."

"Meaning what?"

"Meaning the purpose for which it was built will not be how it is used in the long term."

"Is that what happened to her theater?"

"That's what she thought. She said it was inevitable."

"What do you think?"

"I think she was right. The irony is, she never took her own advice. In spite of all that, she still thought she could change the world with her work. And that pissed off a lot of people. Important people."

"I'd like to talk to her if I can."

"Is that so," she hummed, "Well, good luck."

We sat amid the gentle crackle of burning wood, watching one another, guessing at what sort of creature the other was. I didn't want to go, but I had no further questions and I could feel that the end of our conversation had arrived, like the end of a long, rough rope slipping from my hands. I took a final pull off my beer and set the bottle at my feet and stood, moving sluggishly to avoid any misunderstanding.

"Thank you for your time, Saint," I said. "Best of luck on your travels."

"I have already arrived," she said.

I pushed into the reddened shadows of the woods. Saint watched me go, elbows on her knees, hands together.

I gave a last wave. "And thanks for the drink," I said.

She shook her head. "It was nothing."

I believe she meant it literally.

. . . I missed the Forum's grand opening. Not by choice exactly. I'd been napping after that last day of work, and woke midway through the afternoon. Later I found my phone tucked away in my refrigerator, its alarm ringing dutifully. I was always a heavy sleepwalker.

I puttered around my apartment for the rest of the afternoon, absent of feeling. Just decompressing. I thought I might catch hell from Locksley for not showing my face, but he never called. Around dinner I pulled a random book from my shelf and started reading. Moby-Dick. *No obvious connection to the noises crowding my mind. No connection to the vague ideas I'd been stewing. Maybe that was the point. To take to the sea and get as far away as possible from the damp, drizzly November in my soul.*

Around nine that night, after Ishmael had signed his papers for the Pequod, *I set the book aside and dragged myself down to Antony's. Most of the crew was there, raving and chattering about what they'd seen at the opening. I slipped onto a bar stool to listen.*

Did you meet the Danes? Francisco said. Paulsen and Sierke?

I did, MG said. The Black Hole *theater.*

Fuck me, Francisco said. That was wild. A joint effort with UWs theoretical physics department. Told me they had a pretty rough time getting up and running. They're happy with the result, but they hit a conceptual roadblock. The closer they got to a full resolution simulation, the more unwieldy everything became. And once they made it past a certain fidelity to reality, they couldn't harvest reliable data from inside the black hole.

That makes sense, Synge said. If you attempt a perfect replica of the fundamental laws of the universe, you have to abide by those laws. Information is destroyed when it enters a real black hole, so it stands to reason that you'd see the same result in a perfect simulation.

Couldn't you add some sort of extra output? MG said. To see what's really happening in there?

You could, Synge said. But that would be an intrusive violation of the laws of physics. An unnatural exception. Wouldn't be an accurate simulation, so what would be the point?

You might still learn something from that intrusion, I said, butting in.

Well look who finally showed her famous face, Synge said. Where were you?

I fell asleep, I said.

Did you visit InVisage? MG said, heading off an argument. The one where you explore the interior of a human body at any scale, up to the size of a protozoa. I spent half the morning inside, cruising the lungs and the lymphatic system.

Whose lungs? I said.

They ignored me.

What about the evolution of language theater? Francisco said. Can't remember the name, but the basic idea was genius. Pick two languages, set some cultural and social conditions, and punch in a general time frame. It simulates the outcome of these two languages commingling. Vowel shifts, borrowed vocabulary, the whole deal.

That's fucking wild, said MG.

Even crazier, Francisco said, Once the new language is rendered, the theater gives you temporary fluency. Just like that. I combined Cantonese and Irish Gaelic and set the simulation to simmer for four hundred years. Ten minutes later, I was speaking god knows what kind of sentences.

Holy shit, I said.

He tapped his temple with a frown. It's all gone now, he said. My fluency evaporated the second I left the theater. A weird feeling.

Synge sat tall and tapped a fork against the side of his bottle. The glassy ping shut us up. Let us not forget the main event, he said. This Little World.

He eyed me with a lurid smile, halfway between unfriendly and hungry. If he was angry about something, he didn't say so. I took the bait anyway, just to see where it would lead.

Why the main event? I said.

Synge rolled his eyes and shook his head.

Because Locksley closed the show with a guided tour of your theater, he said. Said something about it being the future of the Forum.

Synge crossed his arms and sat back, watching me. Everybody was watching me, waiting for my reaction. I nodded softly, and took a drink.

I should ask him for a raise, I said.

Everybody laughed. Everybody but Synge . . .

13

I EXITED THE FORUM as the clock struck seven. Slow, tired steps carried me up the long staircase back to the surface. It was nearly dark when I reached it. The trees and mountains that caged me in were asphalt black silhouettes against a night blue gradient. Across the open driveway, a black sedan idled, its cabin light aglow. I moved through an orchestra of crickets and owls, shoes crunching over dry stones, and peered in the car.

The driver was a bony man in a fitted black suit with an equine face and a shark fin where a nose should be. He had jet black hair shaved down to a fuzzy centimeter, a cut that looked more like a medieval coif cap than a proper haircut. He was reading a dog-eared paperback propped against the steering wheel. When I rapped on the passenger window, he marked his place with a slip of paper and stowed it, then unlocked the doors and waved me in. I slid into the passenger seat.

"Do you mind me up front?" I said. "I hate looking ungrateful."

"Not at all," he replied, his accent unmistakably English.

I shut the door, and he killed the dome light. Firing up the car, he turned it around and rolled us across the bridge onto the shadowed highway heading west.

For the first few miles I stared ahead in silence, fixated on the road that flowed beneath us like a swift river, ashen in the bright headlights. It writhed and twisted, the center line alternating between dashes and parallel stripes with a speed that suggested a secret message scratched out by some eldritch communicant hiding in the heart of the mountains. My driver maintained a pleasant aloofness during these spinning thoughts. If I showed some outward signs of worry, he said nothing. He just drove on, hands at a perfect ten and two, his chin raised, his relaxed face ready to smile at a moment's notice. When I sighed suddenly from lack of sleep, he tapped the dashboard to call attention to his onboard air purifier.

"A bit of fresh oxygen?" he said.

I waved my hand.

"I'm fine," I said. "The air up here is nice."

He smiled and nodded. "I often find that. Just let me know."

"Do you work for the Forum?"

"Not directly, sir. I run a private car service. Shuttles and sedans."

"Based where?

"Everett."

"Are you aware that I'm a federal auditor?"

"I am, sir."

"Have you signed any NDAs barring you from talking to me?"

"No, sir."

"Would you answer a few questions if I asked?"

"Within limits, I suppose I would."

"What sort of people make up most of your passengers?

"How do you mean?"

"Men or women? Younger, older? Retired?"

"Men mostly. Usually white. The age varies. But it's always people with money and time to burn."

"No working stiffs?"

"Rarely."

"Ever meet anyone, how should I say . . . famous?"

"Yes sir."

"Politicians? Celebrities?"

"Both."

"And their families?"

"Sometimes."

"Did you ever drive a senator named Walsh, or any of his family?"

"I'm not at liberty to say, sir."

"Did I just hit your limit?"

"Yes, sir."

"I respect that."

"Thank you, sir."

We carried on in silence.

WE REACHED THE CASCADIA just past eight in the evening. I thanked the driver and clawed my way out of the car, exhausted and worn out. The driver pulled away as soon as I was on my feet. I waited until he was out of sight before heading to my room.

Pushing the door open, I reached for the light switch. A breathy voice fluttered through the dark, stopping me.

"Welcome home, Mr. Stark."

I froze and peered in. A jaundiced light from the A&W directly behind me cut across the carpet, searing a path to the foot of the bed. A pair of glossy pumps bobbed in the shaft, fitted to a silky pair of crossed legs—gams so long and smooth you could have skied down them. A bluish cloud of smoke tumbled through the shaft, thickening as it came. A toasted sweetness hit my nose. The image of a woman slowly took shape in the shadows. She was tall and lithe, lounging on the bed in a black skirt and suit jacket, propped back on one arm with a billowing cigarette stem in her free hand.

I stepped through and shut the door and flipped on the light. The woman blinked and grinned as she raised up like a feline shaking off sleep. She took a short sip off her cigarette and blew it sideways.

"Fun day at the office?"

I pulled off my hat and waved it through the air. "Hello, Auntie."

On the desk beside the television was a bottle of Paddy's whiskey, two clean tumblers, and a bucket of ice. Auntie already knew my vices and I was past the point of being careful. I crossed to the desk and poured two drinks, dropping a single cube in mine. Auntie held up two fingers. I stirred the tongs through the ice, searching for two beautiful rocks.

"You went out of your way for the ice," I said.

She rolled her eyes. "A broken ice machine should be a felony."

"You come here often?"

"My clients do."

"They deserve better."

"They appreciate the anonymity. Fewer prying eyes."

I handed her a full glass. The ice chimed nicely. Auntie took it and stirred it through the air with a few flicks of her wrist and took a minute sip. I downed mine in one go and set it aside.

"You mind if I freshen up?" I said.

"I'd be thrilled."

"No rush?"

"None at all."

I slipped off to the bathroom to splash my face and loosen my tie. When I came back Auntie hadn't moved, but her drink was gone, and her cigarette was longer and the haze in the room was thicker. I peeled off my jacket and tossed it over the back of a chair and poured myself another whiskey. Auntie pivoted to watch me, drawing her legs up to one side, like a duchess riding sidesaddle. I showed her the bottle. She held up her empty glass and I filled it. Ice cubes danced where the whiskey landed.

I put the bottle down and leaned against the desk. My silence aroused something in her because she laughed suddenly.

"I heard they gave you a new name," she said.

I nodded once. "John Pike."

She grimaced. "A big ugly fish," she said. "Nothing like you at all."

I shrugged. "Feels like a character. Something to work with."

"You have quite an imagination."

"My best asset."

"So I've discovered," she said. "An imagination so rich it has you dreaming of living on Mars . . ."

"Toots told you?"

"He didn't just tell me. He asked me to set it up."

"I appreciate that."

Auntie raised the drink to her lips and sipped, watching me from across the rim. Then she licked her lips and cradled the glass, staring down at the melting ice.

"I haven't done it yet," she said. She looked up. "I'm not certain I should."

"You think I'm joking?"

"I'm on the fence."

I finished my drink and set it on the table and crossed my arms. "Six years go," I said, "This planet burned past a three-degree global temperature rise a few decades ahead of schedule. Twenty-nine countries now have nuclear warheads. Clean water costs more per ounce than corn. Surrogate reality addiction rates are doubling every eighteen months. And just last week I read a recipe for pancakes that called for cricket flour. In my humble opinion, Earth is in a free fall, and I want off of this rock before it hits bottom. Getting my ass to Mars is the only thing that feels like progress, like something worthwhile. So if there's an empty seat on the next settler ship, sign me the hell up."

Auntie clasped her hands and tapped her thumbs together. "I guess you are serious."

"I guess so."

"And what about Delia?"

"I'll find her. Just give me a few days."

Auntie bit her lip and shook her head. "That's not what I mean," she said. "Don't you relish the idea of seeing her again?"

"Does she want to see me again?"

"You'll have to ask her."

I cleared my throat. "As much as I would love to rewind the years, I know the danger of nostalgia. I'm not fooling myself a second time."

"Is that what happened?"

I scooped up the bottle and poured myself another whiskey and brought the tumbler to my nose. God what a scent. Maybe only thing on Earth I'd truly miss.

"I asked her if I would see her again," I said. "I wanted to. She said no. As far as I'm concerned, that's a closed door."

Auntie pursed her lips. She reached for her clutch and popped it open and pulled out a miniature pen.

"Toss me the paper there," she said, nodding past me.

On the desk propping me up was a pad of monogrammed paper. I flung it with a tight flick, and it spun to one corner of the bed. Auntie picked it up and uncapped the pen and scribbled something and tore the sheet free. Then she capped the pen and held up the paper.

"Imagine Red has a theater inside the Forum called Life on Mars. It's invite only, but I can get you inside. Visit tomorrow and talk to Xavier Sterne, one of Red's system designers. He has sway with the expedition selection committee. Make your case, and ask him to call me."

"Invite only?" I said. "Is it a Green Room?"

Auntie's mouth opened and her tongue did a little dance behind her teeth. Then she folded the paper in half and closed a fist around it. "What do you know about Green Rooms?" she said.

"I don't rat on my sources."

"Green Rooms are classified theaters, usually affiliated with something federal. No entry without authorized credentials."

"Who runs them?"

"Any number of organizations. The military, the CIA, DHS, private contractors with loads of cash." She paused for a moment, studying me. "Why do you ask?"

I shrugged. "Things might be getting a little weird."

Her eyes flared. "You think she's hiding in a Green Room?"

"I don't think anything. I'm just following the leads I uncover. What do you think?"

"It would be . . . surprising."

"Has Delia never surprised you before?"

Auntie's jaw pulsed and rocked back and forth. She stood. "All too often," she said. "But you need hardware to access a Green Room. What they call a Green Card."

"Green Card, Green Room. Lots of mixed metaphors here. So how do I get one?"

"They're not easy to come by but . . ." she said, her face turning to a scowl. "Shit."

"Voice that thought."

She opened her purse and stowed the pen, then pulled out a compact mobile phone. "Someone with a father on the Senate's Security Technology and Innovation subcommittee might have a shot at snagging one." She held her phone up like she was choking a small rodent, her thumb moving furiously.

"Are you asking Daddy Walsh if anything's gone missing?"

She shook her head, still typing. "Senator Walsh doesn't need to hear about any of this until you know more."

"I'd need a Green Card of my own. You think he's up for it?"

Auntie scoffed and continued typing in silence. A pert beep sounded. She stowed the phone back in her purse and wedged the purse under her arm.

"Not a chance," she said. "If word got out that his daughter stole a Green Card, he'd lose his spot on the subcommittee. Probably worse."

"Could I borrow one? You must know someone."

"It doesn't work that way. Green Cards are like keys. Coded to work with a single theater. If you don't have the right card, or you don't know the name of the theater, you're fucked."

"That ups the ante."

Auntie laughed lightly. "Was that a pun on my behalf?"

"Ante? Christ, no," I said. "I'm just feeling my odds get longer and longer."

She floated across the room and stood twelve humid inches from my face. With a cool palm she patted my cheek. "Don't fret, Stark. You'll manage or you won't."

She pulled open the lapel of my jacket and slipped the folded paper into the inside pocket and stepped back.

"For my favorite Martian," she said.

"Thanks."

She nodded once and crossed to the door and opened it a crack and slipped like a ghost into the cooling night. A moist wind blew into the room. The door closed and clicked shut and the room went quiet. I poured myself another drink and held it, watching the door, waiting for another surprise. Maybe hoping for one. But the door stayed shut.

I set my drink down, reached into my jacket pocket, pulled out the paper and unfolded it. Auntie's handwriting was tiny and tight and easy to read:

Life on Mars. Xavier Sterne.

I pocketed the paper and carried my drink to the bed and sat on the corner. I was starting to feel greasy, like I'd spent the day hiding in a dirty wool sock. After I finished the whiskey, I disrobed and hopped in the shower. It took a while to feel clean under its piddling stream, using soap that smelled like laundry detergent. After toweling off I threw on a white T-shirt and a new pair of slacks.

Back in the main room, I turned on the television and set the volume at something just loud enough to be ignored. Then I kicked off my shoes and stacked two pillows the size of dictionaries against the headboard and laid back. I flipped to the evening news and let the drone of disinterested anchors wash over me as I lay motionless and unfeeling on the bed. After an update on local affairs and a quick cutaway to the local weather, the lead anchor broke a special report.

"*In just a few days, Imagine Red's seventh colony ship will touch down on the surface of Mars, bringing with it a host of technological improvements and a renewed optimism for the future. Join us for a live chat with the crew of Cupid 7 as they approach their final destination.*"

I sat up and slid to the bed's edge. The news team cut to an interior shot of Imagine Red's mission control. As the narrator described the high stakes of their seven-month voyage, the camera swept slowly over the assembled team. They looked like shabby students who cared nothing for their physical well-being, but their eyes had the glint of perfectionists who obsessed over details invisible to the average man. I admired that kind of tireless devotion to work that took so much and gave so little. These men and women were artists of a kind, and the toll their work took on them was the price of greatness. I hoped one day to share in that greatness, in whatever way I could.

The Mars segment ended and went to commercials. I fell back and laid a pillow across my face, projecting myself into those images, dreaming of long days on the rough rusty sands, the soaring rocky hills, the pale orange skies. A new world, a new home. Freedom of a kind unknown since the age of exploration. I wanted that life more than anything I had ever wanted down here.

Well, almost anything.

. . . Two weeks after the Forum's opening, Locksley showed up at my door with a dozen white roses and a bottle of champagne. As he had predicted half a year earlier, This Little World was a massive hit. The most visited theater in the Forum by a substantial margin. He was right all along. I asked him why he'd been so confident.

We're living in an age of narcissists, he said. The average man is his own favorite subject. He finds himself endlessly fascinating and believes others do too. And now we have a tool that lets him explore his own sordid subconscious. What more could he ask for?

Health care and good schools, I said.

Locksley laughed but I knew he could sense my frustration. Perhaps he even wanted to say something to comfort me. But a man motivated by the acquisition of power and wealth will never understand the view of one motivated by empathy. So when he opened his mouth, the last thing I wanted to hear came tumbling out.

People want to meet you, Delia, he said. They want to know how that marvelous brain of yours works.

Dear God, no.

Some days later I told Mikkonen: This Little World was a mistake.

We were strolling the beachfront of a theater he had designed himself and recently debuted, taking in the simulated sun, breathing the simulated air, huffing the simulated sea salt.

I am curious why you feel that way, he said mildly.

Because it's premised on a massive fucking miscalculation, I said. I thought if I designed a theater that pulled conscious and subconscious thought streams from a user's mind, that I could kick-start some sort of introspective revolution. Like a digital ayahuasca trip. But it hasn't worked out that way. People are starting to get the hang of the rendering engine. They've learned how to control the output, like lucid dreaming. All it takes is a half dozen sessions and they're experts. Instead of making something that can help people, I've made something that can bring all their prurient fantasies to life.

Interesting, Mikkonen said.

I'm not opposed to prurience, I said. But not on this scale. Not so free form and unbounded. It's not what I want to contribute to the world.

Can you fix it? he said.

I'd like to, I said. But I'm not optimistic. Might be a cursed problem, a proposition with no viable expression.

Mikkonen nodded silently, processing what I'd said like someone who'd just been told the moon was made of cheese—the possibilities were endless, but the practicalities were rough. After a few moments of silence, his eyes brightened.

I share your concerns, he said. But Locksley believes This Little World is the most important theater in the Forum right now.

I shook my head.

I don't understand why, I said. It's generating buzz, not results. It's not fulfilling the Forum's mandate. It's a high-tech distraction.

Would you like me to tell you why? Mikkonen said.

I stared at him in disbelief. Mikkonen waited for my answer with a mute sort of obedience. Laughing, I stopped walking and sat down in the warm sand and crossed my legs. I gestured for him to do the same.

All right, I said. Tell me everything you know . . .

14

THE NEXT MORNING a brisk wind pushed me from the motel to the shuttle stop. I reached it in record time and waited in the tunnel to stay warm. The benches in the waiting area were empty and by the time I saw the shuttle puttering up the road no one had joined me.

Aboard the shuttle was a different story. All but a handful of seats were taken, and the air was clogged with noisy yammering. I took an aisle seat in the first row with a good view of the driver. It was a woman this time, about fifty with a glossy head of bobbed brown hair, and large everywhere except for her nose, which was as small as a cuff button. Feeling less social than yesterday, I sank into an open seat and folded my hands across my chest and crossed my legs and closed my eyes.

When we reached the Forum, I was the first to debark. On my way out the driver asked me what time I would like my car to arrive. I set a 9:00 p.m. departure to give me more time. She thanked me as a mass of hurrying men surged down the shuttle's stairs. Each jostled impatiently for the lead as they scurried up the Forum's outer steps. I fell in behind. At the top of the steps we passed between the columns.

Shadows gathered like a cold blanket. As we approached the door to the staircase, the crowd slowed and coagulated, feeding the narrow passage like a stony throat devouring us whole. Down we went.

The men ahead of me disappeared into the glowing portal. I took out my passport and navigated to the search bar. I typed out *Saint's Country*, hoping to speak with Saint again about Green Rooms. Before I could hit *Search*, the passport vibrated and rang with a sparkling chime. A message window popped up.

Meeting Request

Pritchard Locksley, CEO

Press Go to Accept

A cold call from the man in charge. Interesting and unexpected. It didn't seem out of character for the Forum's steward to want to speak with a Federal Auditor, but something about the timing and abruptness of the request felt defensive. I tried to remember if Toots had warned me to expect such a meeting—even if he didn't, it somehow felt inevitable.

Deeply curious, I pressed *Go*. A new message appeared.

Please proceed to the nearest portal.

I looked up. Locksley's name had appeared on the portal's lintel with his title just below. I pocketed my passport and adjusted my hat and tightened my tie. Then I pushed through.

LOCKSLEY'S OFFICE MADE A STUNNING FIRST IMPRESSION. I stepped from the glowing frame onto a transparent glass disc, twelve feet in diameter, held aloft by a steel pillar above a pool of burbling water at the center of a great circular room. There were no walls, only curved windows running around the circumference that looked out across three hundred and sixty degrees of blue sky and serrated, snow frosted mountains. Two dozen feet above me was a domed ceiling decorated with painted rural scenes of the Pacific Northwest—Mount Rainier on a foggy day, a spawning salmon leaping from a roaring river at the end of a fly hook, a distant sparkling view of the Puget Sound with an orca breaching beneath a cloudy sky.

A set of burnished steel steps led down from the platform, spanning the pool and coming to rest on a field of oat white shag carpeting. Further on was a thick glass desk with nothing but a portable computer tablet laid upon it. A taut figure with ropey muscles and skin the color of milky tea sat behind it, his legs propped over one corner. He wore bamboo sandals, linen clamdiggers, and a fluttering Hawaiian shirt. Looping curls of thick silver covered his head like a Christmas present topper. This was Pritchard Locksley.

Locksley raised an arm when he saw me and beckoned. I took one step forward and looked down. I was wearing slippers, not my own shoes. When I looked back at Locksley, he was on his feet and circling the desk, still on his phone.

"That's good news," he nodded. "We like good news."

He pulled the phone away and mouthed an apology. I gave him a wave and continued down the stairs.

"Look, I really need to go," he continued. "We'll circle back on this tonight. Cheers."

He tapped his phone and laid it face down on the desk just as I reached him. He cocked his head and greeted me with a crooked smile.

"Mr. John Pike," he said. "Wonderful of you to come."

He scooped up my hand before I could respond and shook with vigor.

"I'm Pritchard Locksley," he said. "Thank you for your time."

His voice rose and fell with aristocratic pomp, exactly as a man named Pritchard would sound. He pulled me forward as he continued to hold my hand, as if to grant me a privileged whiff of his excellent cologne.

Still gripping me tightly, he took a step backward. "I apologize for the ambush. I generally wait until the conclusion of an audit to meet face-to-face, but your request intrigued me . . ."

"The list of theaters?"

"That's right. It's an odd request from your agency. Very specific."

I pulled my hand from his. "It doesn't come from the agency per se," I said. "It's my own interpretation of their current interest."

"That being?"

I smiled and walked to the nearest window, faking an interest in the view. "They want to know if the Forum is fulfilling its original mandate."

Locksley joined me at the window. "I can assure you with great confidence it is. Exceeding it, in most cases."

"From what I've seen so far, I have little reason to doubt."

"Excellent."

Together we watched a current of cumulus clouds tumble through the sky and tear itself to shreds over the jagged peaks.

"Let me stress," Locksley said after a pause, "How grateful I am for our continued partnership. Without public funding, we'd be just another cynical surreal peddler."

He turned from the view and cast his steely eyes on me.

"I am proud to say we are something far greater now. I hope you and your department agree."

I faced him and raised my chin. "You run a vital enterprise," I said. "We know that."

"Vital. That's true."

"Are you proud of what you've built?"

His lip curled into an uneasy smile. "Another interesting inquiry," he said. "I am proud of the opportunities the Forum has afforded to so many, Engineeers and Citizens alike."

"*Opportunities* is a curious choice of words. Opportunities are not results."

Locksley puckered and touched a curled finger to his mouth. "The way I see it, there is potential energy and there is kinetic energy. The Forum is pure potential, and that's where my interest lies. What people do with the tools I provide is their business. They are the kinetic forces."

As he spoke, something on the window behind me caught his eye—a speck of hardened matter. He frowned and reached out with a wormy finger to scrape it from the glass. He examined his finger with confusion and flicked it away. His face brightened again.

"What have you seen so far?" he said.

"Quite a lot. Two dozen theaters or so."

"My Sysop mentioned the Narrated Life."

"Yes, my first theater."

"An impressive demonstration of our technology, don't you think?"

"I've never experienced something quite so bewildering."

"Yes, good."

Turning suddenly, Locksley strode back to his desk and bent forward. He pressed a finger to the computer's screen. A soft beep sounded.

"Jodie, please hold all messages and calls until I return."

A clear and calm voice answered. "Yes, Mr. Locksley."

Locksley straightened up and clasped his hands.

"Mr. Pike, I'd like to impress you further, and show you the full scope of what is possible here."

"I am at your disposal."

"Wonderful," he said, lifting an illuminated passport. "Ready to receive?"

—

LOCKSLEY DESCRIBED OUR FIRST STOP as the Forum's original blockbuster. Exodus, a theater visited over one million times since its premier three years earlier. It had spawned numerous sequels, all of which were still active and among the Forum's hundred most frequented theaters.

The premise of Exodus was a basic endurance test intended to challenge the physical limits of its participants, grafted to a light narrative drawn from biblical themes, but with all references to specific ethnic and religious groups removed. The story was simple and straightforward, meant to inspire and encourage participation. In the parlance of Forum developers, it was a *voyage theater*, a now popular subcategory built around the idea of long travels over punishing terrain and deadly obstacles. This first iteration challenged Citizens to cross an arid desert with only a single skin of water, a straightforward experiment in human survival.

"The data we gleaned from Exodus in its first few months was invaluable," Locksley said with pride. "And is now in the possession of the US military. It has been of enormous use to their understanding of desert survival."

The unexpected popularity of Exodus led quickly to a sequel. Exodus 2 was a repeat of the first's basic premise with an exotic change of setting—the ice-swept tundras and snowy mountains of Antarctica. Exodus 3—set in the Congo Free State—arrived a mere six months later. Exodus Fallout was set in a fictional postapocalyptic wasteland, while Exodus Resurrection took place in the Holy Land.

Taken as a whole, the Exodus series was impressive from both a technical and execution standpoint. But after an hour spent exploring various permutations of its core theme, I detected in its sequels a significant and persistent decline in quality, with subsequent entries prioritizing spectacle over substance.

"The scientific merit of this one seems somewhat negligible," I noted as we moved toward the exit of Exodus Stormchaser.

"It varies," Locksley admitted. "A few have slipped into the realm of escapist entertainment. But the sheer variety of these experiences has been a boon. We must cater to all kinds if we hope to keep the lights on."

It was a balanced answer—guileless and rational. But my question had rubbed him the wrong way. This was made obvious by his subsequent choice of theaters. They were serious, with outwardly scientific titles and themes—*Number Numbness*, *Eclipse Studies*, *Market Socialism in Theory & Practice*, *Wolves & Rivers*, *Studies in Fusion*. In these obscure laboratories, I met dozens of science-minded seekers conducting research they hoped would lead to new breakthroughs. They were men and women utterly devoted to their work, and perhaps somewhat addicted to their own experiments. Stays of upward of a month or more were fairly common.

Following lunch—a salmon barbecue hosted beneath a glass dome at the nadir of the Marianas Trench, lit by starry swarms of bioluminescent sea life—we visited *Creative Visions (Moderated)*, a theater dear to Pritchard Locksley's heart.

"This," he said with arms outstretched, "is the beating heart of the Forum. A playground with no established purpose or goal, except to entice your imagination and sate your curiosity. It is a studio of sorts. A place that offers unlimited creative freedom to any and all who seek it. You need not be an artist or engineer to make things here. You simply need a will to create."

We had entered what appeared to be an immense Florentine piazza, paved with white marble flagstones that stretched thousands of yards in all directions. What I saw on its horizons stunned me. Hundreds of magnificent, eclectic structures in all directions that rivaled the wonders of the ancient and modern worlds: A colorful two-hundred-story skyscraper made of whorled glass that looked like something plucked from the Great Barrier Reef; a Pokémon called Jigglypuff the size of the great Giza pyramid made of colored toothpicks; a tin robot more than a mile high with a head like a silver lion, two steel snakes for arms, and a mechanized horse for the body and legs.

For the next hour Locksley showed me around and introduced me to many of the theater's most active artists. During these brief encounters he always referred to me as his colleague, never as an auditor. I spoke to one man who was building a scale model of the Eiffel Tower, down to every last bolt and rivet, entirely out of recycled trash. Another was re-creating New York City using marshmallows of various sizes. A third was building an imaginative reconstruction of the labyrinth from ancient Crete, complete with a lurking Minotaur.

Locksley's enthusiasm for this theater and its ardent creators was genuine, but my patience was running thin. Standing midship on the quarterdeck of a working model of the pirate Blackbeard's famous galley, the Queen Anne's Revenge, and gazing into the horizon at a five-hundred-foot-tall singing automaton fashioned in the image of Leonard Cohen, I reasserted my role as auditor.

"I'd like to ask you about those original theaters," I said.

Locksley nodded and turned and hoisted himself on the gunwale, sitting with his knees hitched up, like a child on a swing. "Of course," he said.

"From my research I noted about sixty theaters in the beginning. The list I received yesterday had only sixteen. It's quite a gap."

"That's right," he nodded. "It's nothing unusual. The first theaters we built were demonstrations of the Forum's power. They taught us things; they led to new discoveries. But they didn't always achieve what their designers had hoped."

"I visited quite a few of these theaters yesterday. Almost all of them were a pale shade of their initial promise. Quite a few were hostile, in fact. Is that the fate of most theaters?"

Locksley slipped from the gunwale and clasped his hands behind him. He began pacing the deck. "An excellent question," he said with a sigh. "It touches on what I like to call the desire line of technological evolution—"

I flinched slightly. Just a quick torque of the neck.

"Desire line of what?" I said.

"Technological evolution."

Saint had mentioned this and said it was Delia's idea. Someone was lying.

"Sorry," I said. "Carry on . . . "

"It's a simple description of the progress of technology. Someone conceives of a revolutionary new product—Henry Ford and his automobile, for example. They imagine a perfect little niche for this new object—always benign, always intended to make some menial chore just a little more bearable. Henry Ford's faster horse, for example. Then they reveal the new product. An unwitting public laps it up and puts it to use. If successful, more and more people attach to it. They incorporate it into their lives until, without knowing how or why, they have made it a necessary part of their existence. It is no longer a solution to a problem that bothered them, but a shortcut around the problem itself. They soon find ways to use it for purposes never intended, a solution in search of yet more problems. The absence of a rule is still a rule, as I like to say. Now they cannot do without it. In Ford's case, we built cities and suburbs not for people, but for cars. Entire industries sprang up, devoted to the propagation and upkeep of cars. We created sports built around expert knowledge of cars. And we now accept a world organized at distances reachable only by cars. Henry Ford offered an invention to save us time, but it robbed us of so much more. Yet how could he have known . . ."

"And this is your idea?"

"That's right."

"You fear that's happening here, in the Forum?"

"It's inevitable," he said. "I suspect in fifty or one hundred years, on its current trajectory, this technology will serve purposes we cannot yet fathom from our present naïveté." He lowered his voice. "But not before the porn industry gets ahold of it. They're always at the vanguard."

"Quite a legacy."

Locksley threw up his hands and backed away, shaking his head. "You're right. I should be mortified. I had such high hopes for this place. But it's a free country. And when men have money, they spend it freely. Not on what makes them happy, but on whatever makes them feel powerful."

"Some people have ideals," I said. "Some even stick to them."

Locksley grimaced and shook his head. "There is nothing in this place that was not brought from the outside. The odd genius will flourish in here; the rest of these idiots will simply have fun."

"Nothing wrong with a little fun."

"No indeed," he smiled. "Is there anything else I can help you with?"

"As a matter of fact, there is," I said, queuing up a request I wasn't sure he'd like. "Would it be possible to get a list of your original Engineers and their current projects?"

Locksley froze, a pause so complete I wondered if the simulation had hitched or broken. He broke his silence with a twitch of his eyes.

"Any one in particular you'd like to speak with?"

"No, sir. I'd just like to speak with anyone who's been here since day one. Your best and brightest."

He drew a long hissing breath through his nose and exhaled as he nodded.

"My best and brightest," he repeated. "Quite a few have moved on to greener pastures, of course, but I will see what I can do."

"There's no rush. I have plenty of work to keep me occupied."

"Whatever you need."

He turned from me and stared out across the sterile gray geography of the theater, doing his best to hide his face as it trembled between irritation and calm. In the distance, a castle built of twentieth-century handguns glinted in the artificial sunlight. Breaking his meditative silence, he spun around with a burst of new energy and snapped his fingers.

"Would you allow me a small indulgence, Mr. Pike?"

"If you think it's worth my while."

With a wild grin he fished out his passport and began typing something. "I fear I have undersold the artistic potential of the Forum, and I regret that. You are not the usual sort of auditor, the kind that responds to simple metrics and promises of revenue."

Finding what he wanted, he invited me to tap.

"Give me one last chance to impress you," he said, his eyes glinting, almost pleading.

. . . Mikkonen spilled the big secret. Locksley wanted to make This Little World's codebase standard in all future theaters. That was his hidden agenda. He didn't care about This Little World itself. What intrigued him was a program that could scrape data from human minds and use it to render novel content in real time. He wanted the engine, not the finished vehicle so to speak.

I confronted him. I wasn't angry exactly, but I felt I had been considerably misled.

It's a milestone, Locksley told me later. The most groundbreaking piece of software I have seen in my career. I hope you're proud. I hope you understand how much further you have pushed surreal technology.

You might have told me what you wanted, I said. Before I slaved six months on a dud. Day after day I thought about pulling the plug and starting over.

It's not a dud, Locksley said. It's a brilliant proof of concept. The people who tripped in your theater won't soon forget it. They want to build off it. The offers I'm getting, the calls I'm taking, are off the charts. Scholars with proposals for experiments that would be untenable—unethical even—in the real world, are now possible with your work.

Okay.

And we'll go further, he said, his face flushing. Your codebase won't be confined to theaters. We can make tools. Available to every engineer, artist, scholar, and designer who sets foot in the Forum. People with imagination and passion can dream up new theaters with almost no technical knowledge. Your work will democratize the very process of creation itself. The age of experts will end. The age of artists is upon us.

Locksley, I said. You used to be immune to this kind of bullshit utopian prognostication.

I want to call it Cagliostro, he said, arcing his arm through the air. How does that sound?

Call what Cagliostro?

Our new theater tool, he said. Based on your code.

I didn't answer. His spiel sounded revolutionary in a way that implied an apocalypse was near at hand. The best I could manage was a sigh and a head shake. I was exhausted. I wanted to curl up somewhere and disappear into the wet earth.

You can sleep on it, Locksley said. But the wheels are already in motion. And I promise I will make you proud . . .

15

I FOLLOWED LOCKSLEY INTO AN INKY BLACK THEATER with no walls or ceiling, just a hardwood floor lit by a disc of light that vanished into a blinding darkness in all directions. A slow swaying waltz played from a source high above, a jazzy number from the previous century, drenched in reverberation and coated in dust. A disco ball hung from an invisible ceiling high above, spinning slowly and throwing off brilliant shards of light that rippled through shades of purple and blue and red.

Standing shoulder to shoulder, Locksley leaned in to whisper. “One of my protégées built this theater,” he said. “It’s a simple premise, but it will take some time to get the algorithm just right. Go on ahead, into the light.”

With a gentle nod he urged me forward. When I reached the halo’s fuzzy outer edge, a man’s voice called out across the darkness, sultry and calming.

“Welcome to *the Last Dance*,” said the voice. “Prepare yourself for an emotional experience unlike any other.”

The central spotlight brightened as a vaguely human figure began to materialize from a viscous cloud of swirling smoke.

"Call to mind someone you have lost," the voice continued. "The one that got away. An old flame consigned to a foggy memory. A loved one long absent. Imagine their face, their voice. Remember what they meant to you. Concentrate."

A memory of Delia sprang to mind, an image from our one day together—her sitting beside me in the car on my way home, a consoling hand on my knee, her face stolid and beautiful. The smokey shape at the center of the room began to ripple and coalesce into something more solid. It didn't take a genius to understand what was happening. This theater was summoning a replica of Delia Walsh in response to my thoughts. And if that happened, my cover was blown.

Locksley called out behind me. "You're a natural, Mr. Pike," he said. "Just let it happen."

I shut my eyes and forced my thoughts in a lateral direction, trawling my memory for alternate distractions. Another fixation, an alternate yearning, something simple and close to the surface. I found her easily, stalking the archives of my adolescence. I fixated, drawing the image closer until she was as clear as my memories of yesterday.

I opened my eyes. The formless smoke shuddered and pulled together, taking on color and shape. A tall woman with a curled bouffant of platinum blond hair appeared. She wore a black silk bustier dress that hugged every curve like a speeding Ferrari.

Locksley erupted with laughter.

"You are full of surprises, Mr. Pike," he said. "She looks familiar."

"Rita Hayworth," I said.

It was indeed Rita, pulled straight from the poster for *the Lady from Shanghai*. With a hand on her hip and a snarl on her lips, she waited with catlike patience for me to advance.

"Now begins the Last Dance," the voice intoned. "Embrace! For tonight is the night to make amends, right old wrongs, and tell the ultimate truth. Tonight is your last dance."

Rita sighed and raised her arm like the neck of a great swan. "Will you hold me," she whispered into my ear. "What are you waiting for?"

Approaching, I stopped short to search her face through the cool light and soft shadow. Rita stepped forward and grazed my cheek with a hooked finger.

"Come," she breathed. "Dance with me."

I opened my arms, and she pushed her body into mine, wrapping her hands around my waist and laying her head against my chest. She sighed. Her hair was luminous and smelled of lavender and honey. Her body felt wonderful and warm against mine. I closed my eyes and held her tight.

"I miss you," she whispered. "Do you miss me?"

"I suppose so," I said, my breath on her neck. "I miss watching your films with my father. Yours and Bogie's. Lauren. Mitchum. Those were good times. I guess they planted a seed somewhere . . ."

"Oh," she moaned. "That makes me so happy."

We swayed and the music swelled, and the dance lights throbbed like a pair of hearts beating as one. Rita's warmth flowed through me like volcanic lava running through my limbs. It was wonderful. A perfect, and perfectly ridiculous, feeling. And a waste of my time.

I pulled away. Rita took no offense. She sighed and swayed on, dancing alone to the sourceless music. As she spun across the halo of light, her body began to smoke and dissipate. In seconds she was gone, but the saccharine ambience remained.

A heavy hand clapped my shoulder and Locksley appeared with a schoolboy's smirk of prurient glee.

"You have a refined taste in women, Mr. Pike . . ."

"Pining for an imagined past isn't refined," I said. "It's just another kind of sadness."

Locksley tutted and threw his arms behind him. "Most men I bring here conjure the girl that got away their final year of high school. Men in their twenties, men in their sixties, damn near every one of them dreams of a young girl that never gave them the time of day."

I turned away, searching for the portal to leave this place. "Like I said, another kind of sadness."

Locksley nodded and pulled up his passport. "Maybe it's time to wind this tour down."

"Sure."

He looked down, smiling at his portable screen. "But first," he said. "How's your golf swing?"

WE STEPPED INTO A THEATER hosting a trio of eighteen-hole low-gravity golf courses on the surface of the Moon called Lunar Links. The portal spit us out on a long terrace overlooking a broad gray basin with rounded gray hills wrinkling the horizon. Broad glinting fairways with minute patches of drab green here and there and the occasional yellow sand trap. A handful of Citizens, casually dressed in slacks and polos hopped up and down the fairway, no bigger than fleas at this distance.

Locksley and I walked to the railing and looked out over the courses.

"The back nine in the sea of tranquility is superb," he said.

"Why aren't we wearing suits?"

He laughed. "It's a golf course, not a science experiment."

Smiling, he pushed back from the railing and walked to a small kiosk made of moon rock and ceramic tiles. Within was a rack of clubs and multiple buckets filled with pearly white balls. Locksley selected a driver and gave it a gentle practice swing. Satisfied, he looked back at me and offered it. I shook my head.

"I'm supposed to be working," I said.

"Me too." He smiled.

He hoisted a bucket of balls and carried them to a driving station nearby. I followed. When he reached the plot, he set the bucket aside and pulled out a single ball and teed up.

"There's nothing like a firm strike in one-sixth the earth's gravity," he said brightly.

He swung and connected. Good form, a solid crack. The ball sailed up the slope of the hill and vanished amid the sparkling lunar soil. He teed up another ball.

"What's your ultimate hope for this place?" I said. "When you've taken it as far as you can."

He stopped and stood upright, leaning on his club like a cane and cocking his head. "In what sense?"

"What do you want it to become? A better version of SR? Or something new?"

He took the question honestly, nodding as he considered his answer.

"God's honest truth," he said. "I would like nothing more than to open everything in here to everyone. The world deserves to see what we have built. The world deserves a tool like this. It would do more good than harm if it were an open-source playground."

"What's the worst you can imagine?"

He drew his head back in a sinister laugh. "No comment. Perversion is inevitable, but I believe we can do a lot of good as well. It's a shame how secretive we have to be."

"I imagine you could make a lot of money if the public had access to this place."

"I do like money," he shrugged. "But that doesn't change my belief in the rights of the average person to have access to something this useful."

"What about the—what did you call it—the desire line of technological development? Isn't some kind of abuse inevitable?"

"There will always be those who misuse the best of what we have to offer. But a small percentage of our users will continue to make works of wonder and magnificence. I believe it's a risk worth accepting."

"So what's keeping you from opening the doors?"

"Your employer, of course," he said.

Locksley struck and watched the ball sail. It disappeared over a distant hill.

"As part of the government's investiture in the Forum," he went on, "They have a clear interest in keeping it circumscribed, out of the hands of ordinary bumpkins. Top secret shit. Not suitable for public consumption."

"Do they decide who comes and goes?"

"Not exactly. But they do make access difficult. Lots of red tape. Thankfully, I have a few on my side who are working to, let's say, expedite our freedom."

"And who would that be?"

"Friends."

"Senators?"

Locksley paused then slowly straightened up. He hoisted his club onto his shoulder and gripped the handle with two hands, like a baseball player at the plate, waiting for the next pitch.

"That's a rather pointed question," he said.

"And a logical one."

"Or did I mean accusation?"

"You tell me."

Locksley shook his head. "Like you said, Mr. Pike—you have work to do." He walked his driver back to the racks. "Will you be all right on your own?"

"I should be."

"Good. Have a pleasant week. You may contact me through your passport should you need anything."

Leaving his gear behind, he marched back to the gleaming portal, typing something into his passport as he went. When he reached the frame, he threw me a perfunctory wave, then plunged through. Eddies of lunar dust swirled in his wake.

I turned for a last lingering view of the moon's landscape—the gleaming gray hills, the black shadows, the voided sky and its million spattered stars. Then I pulled out my passport and tapped it on. I paused, torn between resuming my search for Francisco Lopez, or tracking down Saint for more detail on Green Rooms and Green Cards. Neither lead felt particularly strong.

A flat chorus of laughter fluttered in from somewhere far away. I leaned over the railing to look down. On the links far below two golfers dressed like they had flown in from Mardi Gras bounded down the fairway to the next green, clearing fifteen feet with each leap. They were swinging their clubs with menace, like training wushu warriors in a science-fiction future, shouting and laughing and having the time of their lives. Suddenly I had a change of plans.

I tapped through to the search engine and typed in *Life on Mars*.

. . . Cagliostro—the Forum's new creation tool—came online quickly with Mikkonen's help. I pitched in from time to time, but it was largely an effort spearheaded by Locksley himself. In spite of that, he made sure I got full credit. Called it Delia's tool or Delia's code. Generous, but unnecessary.

I was more interested in content, not tools. A hammer is only as interesting as the house it builds. A little naive probably, but that's how I saw things then. I suppose I was holding on to any excuse possible to stay angry with Locksley. It didn't take much.

Unfortunately, because of this credit, Forum developers constantly swamped me with requests for help. Engineers and designers who wanted a quick tutorial came to me in droves. Maybe that was Locksley's plan all along. He didn't want people bothering him.

Even Jude Synge, my sometime rival, hit me up for advice. At university he had majored in computer science with a focus on bioinformatics. His interest in surreals was largely accidental and often reluctant, but the more we talked the more we found common ground. He told me surreals interested him only as a means to become more human, not less. I liked that approach.

His launch theater, Your Double, *was what he called a therapeutic theater. It was a novel space where users—or Citizens as we now called them—could interact with perfect replicas of themselves. The theater was up and running, but it was a far cry from what he'd originally envisioned.*

I had hoped, he said, that the experience of interacting with a double of oneself could provide an eye-opening, transformative experience, leading to the development of greater empathy, kindness, and generosity.

I'm right there with you.

I'm having trouble perfecting the cloning process, unfortunately. The doubles produced are about as smart as your average golden retriever. Hardly compelling as a twin.

But affectionate I imagine.

Sometimes, he smiled. But for the double concept to work as intended, I need a near-perfect facsimile of the target Citizen. My current theater manages the physical replication well, but there's something about the neurological data that gets messed up in the duplication process.

Of course, I said. Consciousness is the space between neurons, so to speak. The Forum's default renderer doesn't handle that sort of replication very well.

Can Cagliostro help?

Cagli—Jesus I can't even say the name.

Jude laughed. Not yours?

Locksley's.

Of course.

Anyway, I sighed. It should. This Little World captures the mental output of our users at 99.7 percent fidelity. Then it uses a hefty algorithm to generate or correct the missing .3 percent. It works well. Nothing uncanny or upsetting.

That's crazy, he said. The doubles I'm generating might as well be zombies.

We can fix that, I said. But don't mention zombies to Locksley. It'll give him terrible ideas.

Noted, Jude said. But I may save it for the sequel.

We both laughed. And just like that, we were colleagues . . .

16

I OPENED MY EYES TO A DUSTY OCHRE SKY seen through the spectral glass of an oxygen helmet. Jagged orange hills dotted with scraggly brown stones serrated the horizon. With effort and concentration, I took a few tentative steps. My formfitting environmental suit frustrated all grace, and to look sideways required the effort of my entire body. But the view was well worth the inconvenience. Far ahead was the broad, endless rise of Olympus Mons—largest volcano in our solar system. I was standing on the surface of Mars, as if it were the most natural thing imaginable.

Opposite the volcano's slope was a wide smooth plain with a white lattice tower marking the center of a prototype Martian colony. At the tower's base were half a dozen habitations, each the size of a garbage truck and shaped like bulbous white gel caps with round porthole windows and the Imagine Red logo stenciled on their sides. They sat just off the ground on short stilts planted in the regolith like a herd of overfed pigs asleep on their feet. Steadying myself, I threw a leg forward and made the tricky descent toward the colony, smiling all the way.

Up close, I saw that each habitation had a single entrance situated at one end of the tubular structure—sturdy air locks with hefty crank handles. I wandered, hopping from one habitation to the next, scanning for signs of the man I had come to see—Dr. Sterne. On the fourth or fifth habitation, I found an obvious tell—a sign above one air lock read: *Welcome all visitors! The Doctor is in!* A bright red arrow pointed at an illuminated red button. I climbed a short stepladder and slapped the button and leapt back. Thirty seconds passed. The button flashed once and turned green. I climbed the ladder again and twisted the crank. The door swung open, and I pulled myself in.

A serpentine hiss announced the beginning of the depressurization process. When it was safe to remove my helmet, I did so with some trepidation. The sensation of this theater was so visceral that its simulated nature was impossible to accept. My body rejected what my mind understood.

I was removing the rest of my suit when a voice crackled over an intercom.

"Mr. Pike. You made it!"

I looked around for a camera or a speaker, something to address directly. "Were you expecting me?"

"I was told you might stop by. Step on through."

I finished disrobing and passed through the back of the air lock into a tight hallway. The design of the space was no different than the cramped layouts of what I remembered of various International Space Stations over the past decades—narrow but efficient spaces designed for serious scientific inquiry. I moved down the hallway, getting accustomed to the lack of a suit in low gravity. Every step felt like an aborted leap. Doors to the right and left opened to two tight bedrooms. Further on the corridor opened to a slightly larger space.

I found the doctor in this final room, a fit man in his late fifties in a tank top and athletic shorts, caged in what looked like a robotic exoskeleton. His lank arms and bony legs pumped at a rapid pace—a form of resistance training to guard against the atrophy his muscles would suffer in low gravity. When I moved into his field of view he smiled at seeing me but didn't slow down.

"Welcome aboard," he said between labored breaths. "I'm Xavier Sterne. And I guess you're this year's auditor?"

"That's right."

He laughed. "You're my fourth, and you won't be my last."

I gestured at the exoskeleton. "That's for keeping your bones dense, I take it?"

"Exactly right," he said. "The most mind-numbing exercise yet conceived. And yet it may be the crucial factor between living or dying on this rusty red ball."

He pressed a hidden button and the exoskeleton let out a long deflating whine, then shut off. The metal frame relaxed with a shrug and the doctor extricated himself like a butterfly leaving its chrysalis. Once free, he reached for a small white towel hanging from the wall by a Velcro catch and ripped it free.

"How is it out there?" he said, patting down his face.

"Outside the Forum?"

"Inside, outside. Anywhere. I haven't left this place in quite a while."

"Don't you visit other theaters?"

"Not a one," he said proudly. "That would contaminate the data. But I hear it's quite something."

"That's dedication."

"That's science."

I looked around and ran a hand down the smooth curved wall of the habitation. "I love the simplicity of these things," I said. "How many have made it to the real Mars?"

"Enough to house one hundred and eighty colonists. Quite a way to go before they're all occupied."

"They're bigger than I imagined."

Sterne nodded and crossed the room. "Cozy too." He grabbed a mug from a nearby shelf and filled it with slow-falling water from a wall-mounted spigot. "I don't mean to give the impression that it's been easy for the folks up there. But we're on the right track. A single death after six sorties, soon to be seven. That's impressive."

"And aggressive."

Sterne downed his water and returned the cup to its perch. "We have to be. This planet is falling apart. And the people on it would rather digitize themselves than leave."

"It's easier to pacify fears than face them. Cheaper, too."

"Okay, but you can't save a species by escapism."

I nodded. "I'm arguing for the sake of it. I tend to agree."

"I know you do," he smiled. "You wouldn't be asking for a seat on the next shuttle if you did."

I nodded. "I think Earth's fucked."

"I think so too," he frowned. "But it's a long slow fuck. And that's part of the problem. People respond better to instant tragedies. If water leaks through the roof of your house, you fix it. If you break a bone, you bind it. But we're proverbial frogs in the water . . . as bullshit as that story is. We're dying slowly with idiot grins on our faces."

He laughed suddenly and I laughed with him, without knowing why.

"It's a nice irony here," I said, "You working in a simulation."

"How often have I thought that myself," he smiled. "But this is vital work, nonetheless. In real life, I am not fit enough to embark upon the great Martian exodus myself. But within this simulation, I can gather useful data for those who follow."

"Can't begrudge you for that."

"It's not so bad. We test new ideas here. Ideas they can replicate up there."

"A worthwhile use of this technology," I nodded. "Maybe the first I've seen."

"Kind of you to say so." He slapped his towel against the Velcro strip and cast a longing gaze through a nearby window at the rusted vista beyond. "I'm gonna ride this one out as far as I can."

His smile trembled as he contemplated that future. Was he wondering at the lonely years ahead? Or the years lost behind? Perhaps both. Years, months, days, minutes, seconds. Time was his life's currency, but the denominations hardly mattered. All were equally worthless in the end.

"What I wouldn't give to head up there myself," he said wistfully. "But that's for your generation, Mr. Pike. And those to come."

"There's nothing I'd like more."

"I'll pass it along."

"I may go by another name soon. Auntie can fill you in."

"I'll make sure to mention it," he nodded. "By the way, if you stick around, you can watch the Martian lander touch down. Just out there, on the landing pad." He scanned the sky through the small porthole. "It's a little marketing stunt the people at IR cooked up. Once a day, the lander comes down and out come AI replicas of the astronauts, currently en route to Mars."

"Some kind of meet and greet?"

"To pose for pictures mostly. It's a little gauche, but people seem to like it."

I opened my mouth to inquire further but a tinny alarm sounded suddenly from one of the bedrooms I'd passed. Dr. Sterne's eyes lit up like two miniature suns.

"I'm sorry," he said. "Don't mean to run you off, but that's the warning bell. My missus'll be on her way."

"You're married?"

"Thirty-eight years this December," he nodded. "She visits twice a week. Has done since I began nearly four years ago."

"Lucky man."

"I am," he said. "If you can find a partner half as patient, you've got all you need."

"I'll start looking."

He patted my shoulder and bounded back through the narrow corridor.

"Good luck, Mr. Pike," he said, departing. "We're an ornery bunch in here, but we mean well. I hope your final report will say the same."

He gave me a pumping thumbs up and turned into one of the bedrooms and shut the rounded door. I returned to the air lock with a smile, soaking in the ambient rumble of its generators and the hiss of the life support systems. It took me fifteen minutes to suit up and step outside. Once I was back on Martian soil, I took out my passport and cleared the search field and tapped exit.

Proceed to the nearest portal.

I hadn't taken more than ten steps when a shadow crossed swiftly before me, heading toward Olympus Mons. I squinted against the rosy sky in time to see a triangular gray shape drift down and away between two habitations to my right. I followed as quickly as my legs would move.

I stopped at the far edge of the Martian village. Here the ground sloped away at a gentle angle until it reached a flat tarmac disc with painted markings about one hundred yards away. A triangular craft hovered above the tarmac. I knew it by sight. This was Cupid 7, a perfect replica of the real Martian lander currently on the last leg of its trip to the real planet Mars. The lander descended like a downy feather to the landing pad. As it neared landfall, dust billowed, and rockets roared. When the rusty clouds of regolith had settled, the lander was on the ground. I jogged down the slope to get a closer look.

As I drew near, the lander's door cracked open like the single petal of a large flower. A stepladder telescoped to the ground and a figure wearing a cherry red astronaut's suit emerged, followed by a second and a third. These were the colonists now embarked on *Imagine Red*'s current voyage—or more accurately, digital facsimiles of them—ready to shake my hand and answer my questions about their mission in-progress.

My gut twisted. As much as I admired the project, I had no interest in meeting or interacting with these promotional ciphers. I could feel the artifice of the whole situation, the crude marketing angle. I understood its purpose—to drum up public support for an expensive and dubious interstellar colonization project—but I was already a true believer. I didn't need the T-shirt or the lunch box. I wanted a seat on the next rocket.

As the astronauts set foot on the landing pad to greet their audience of one, I backed off and turned to go, quickening my step as they hailed me. I ran as fast as I could, up the soft slope toward the habitation. Then I stopped.

A solitary figure stood at the crest of the hill, clad in the same bulky suit as me, a tinted visor obscuring the face beneath. I waved. The figure waved back. If this was Dr. Sterne he showed none of his earlier courtesy. I waited. The figure beckoned me closer. I trudged up the hill. When I'd made it halfway up the slope, the figure halted me with an open hand and laid its second hand on its chest. A crackling radio feed filled my head.

"Got word you were looking for me," he said. The voice was pitchy and distorted, but obviously masculine. "How 'bout a drink?"

He lowered both arms and waited. I didn't know how to respond. Sensing my confusion, he pointed to a red button on his chest the size of a half dollar. I pressed a hand to my own chest, imitating the gesture. The channel opened with a pop.

"Inside the Forum or out?" I said.

"Outside," he said. "You mind if I bring Antony?"

"I like Antony. What time?"

"Ten p.m."

The figure dropped his hand and the channel closed. He turned and strode off, disappearing beyond the basin's rim. I sprinted up the slope with great effort and passed between a pair of habitations, returning to what passed for this colony's town square. The man was gone.

. . . Months after the Forum's opening, I was still avoiding the place as much as I could. I didn't want to go back without a concrete idea for a new project. I wasn't one to sketch and prototype. I needed a strong motivator to get me started. Something I could throw myself into with confidence.

At first, I started thinking about memories. About retrieving them. Storing them. Playing them back. I knew it was possible with the right architecture. But the more I inquired into the nature of memory, the more I learned how malleable and incomplete it could be, the more I realized this idea's potential for abuse.

An example. My mother died when I was six. Old enough to feel the ravages of her loss, but too young to remember much that was concrete and unshakable. Until recently I would sometimes sit quietly in a dark room and scrape the barrel of my mind for stray memories of her. I even tried meditation, hoping that might unearth missing fragments. But that never happened.

When the Forum came online, I started to wonder if I could use this technology to see my mother again. I realized almost immediately how this was misleading. I would not see her as she was, but only as I remembered her now. A mythology of my mother, told through memories that had been rewritten with each retelling. Such a theater would only reinforce the narcissism already inherent in the natural act of remembering. The mother I remember today is not who I remembered five years ago, nor ten. She is the revised and incomplete version of the original input.

Since these early thoughts, dozens upon dozens of theaters have harnessed memories exactly as I had hoped to. All of them have succumbed to the same basic pathologies: fantasy, projection, wish fulfillment.

From memories my interest drifted to identity. Synge's theater Your Double *fascinated me for a while. The idea of facing down a perfect replica of myself was compelling as a marketing pitch. But I had my suspicions it wouldn't pan out the way Synge intended. There's too much novelty inherent in the idea, and no incentive to be honest or kind or generous. I didn't have any firm predictions about how his theater would evolve, but I had a gut feeling it would backfire. I think time has proven that true.*

But there was something to the identity angle that compelled me. It was nascent in This Little World. How to force people to face themselves, or evaluate themselves in a way that felt natural? In a manner that encouraged curiosity? Could I design something that pulled the user apart like a jigsaw puzzle and forced a reconstruction, piece by piece? Would that be worthwhile?

I struggled for months on this single problem. All the while, the Forum grew bigger and bolder, bolstered by my code and Locksley's flair for salesmanship. And with its success came big changes . . .

17

BACK IN BURLINGTON, I returned to the motel and tried to sneak in a quick nap before my date with the mysterious Martian. Failing that, I watched more television. Just before 10:00 p.m., I dragged myself from the bed and pulled on a clean button-up shirt and jacket and slapped on my hat and ducked out. I hopped in the Boson and rode it to Antony's.

When I arrived, Iris was behind the bar pulling pints from a steaming washer and wiping them down with a gray rag. The ornery veteran named Randy was asleep on his stool, head against the counter, his bony fingers wrapped around a pint glass with little more than a splash of golden backwash inside. The TV above the bar was tuned to a cop show set in a snowy northern town where the good guys wore parkas and beanies and the baddies committed crimes in wool sweaters with shotgun recoil pads sewn into the shoulders.

I took a stool at the end of the bar and gave Iris a wave when she turned to see who had come in. Sweeping wet hands down her apron, she threw a glance at Randy and raised a finger to her lips. I nodded and she tossed me a fresh coaster and piled on a Kokanee all in one motion.

"Welcome back," she said quietly. "John, was it?"

"That's right."

"You find Delia?"

I shook my head. "Not yet. We'll see what happens."

She crossed her fingers and returned to her work. I nursed my beer and watched the TV in silence. When she was done stacking pints, Iris swabbed the same dishrag over the bar. When she got to me, she stopped wiping and slapped her hand on a laminated menu and slid it across the counter, giving it half a turn.

"Hungry?" she said.

I shook my head, but looked anyway. Giant pizza pies, calzones, tomato pastas, cheese breads, the usual fare. Nothing changed my mind. Iris pushed the menu aside and crossed her arms, pushing a hip against the bar. She smiled lightly, her large eyes glowing like cool white moons in a sunny face. I felt better just looking at her.

"You look tired," she said.

"Do I?"

"What's keeping you up?"

"Nothing I can talk about."

"Top secret?"

I leaned forward. "A matter of national security."

"You're funny."

I sat up and shook my head. "Honestly, I'm not doing much of anything."

Iris opened her mouth to speak but the front door chime cut her short. She looked past me and her face brightened at what she saw.

"Hey, 'Cisco," she said. "Take a seat."

I turned. A polished gentleman in his thirties approached the bar. He had gelled wavy hair and sun browned skin. He wore a svelte, steel gray, Italian-cut suit and his eyes lurked unseen behind a pair of mirrored wraparounds. His nose was thick and bulbous like a root of fresh ginger, and his mouth was thin, a mere crack in a misshapen boulder. He exuded the energy of a man about to bet an enormous amount of money in a game of blackjack. When he reached the bar, he peeled off his glasses.

"How you doin', Iris?"

"I'm all right. What are you drinking?"

"Double bourbon," he said, brown eyes beaming. "Top shelf."

Iris nodded and rummaged around for her best bottle. The man took a seat at the bar's empty end and laid his glasses aside. Iris turned back, holding a bottle of Maker's Mark. The look on her face was an apology, but the man didn't mind. He tossed a billfold as thick as a book on the bar top. Iris set a tumbler down and started pouring.

"Doing good?" she said.

"Better than ever, darling," he said, watching the bourbon rise.

Iris shook her head as she grinned. She poured until the whiskey gripped the rim. The man took it carefully and sipped.

"Francisco," Iris said. "This is John, a friend of Delia's."

Francisco glanced at me, the tumbler at his lips. I nodded.

"John Pike," I said. "An acquaintance at best."

Francisco drank down half the glass and set it aside carefully and reached for the bottle to read the label.

"How much for the bottle?" he said.

Iris squinted and rubbed her neck. "Good question," she said, calculating. "I get about twenty-five pours from one of those. Three-fifty?"

Francisco peeled a five hundred from the billfold and held it between his fingers like a captured butterfly.

"Keep the change," he said. He looked sidelong at me and Randy, then tapped the counter with his free hand. "And bring two more glasses."

Iris grabbed two more tumblers and set them down. Francisco poured a splash in each and pushed them my way. I pulled mine aside and slid the other down the bar where Randy could find it later. I lifted my glass. Francisco did the same.

"Thanks for this," I said.

"Cheers."

He drained his glass and looked at Iris with weary eyes. "Iris my dear," he said, jerking his head toward the front of the restaurant. "You mind if we take this to a table? Is that all right?"

"Fine by me."

"Thank you, hon."

Francisco stood, carrying his tumbler and the bottle. I followed with my own drink. He guided us to a table at the front of the room, not far from the row of arcade cabinets where the squelch and squeal of looping electronic noises would mask our conversation. Francisco pulled out a chair and sat with his back to the bar. I took the far seat. He topped up my drink and pushed the bottle to one side.

"Francisco Lopez?" I said.

"That's right. You've been looking for me?"

"I've been looking for a few people."

"You don't want me to feel special?"

"I don't want you to feel spied on."

"Thank you," he smiled. "I hear you're this year's auditor?"

"That's right."

"But you're looking for people?"

"Engineers and designers. Some folks in D.C. felt previous audits suffered a few blind spots. We wanted to take a different approach this year."

"Okay. Approach me."

"*The Death of Desire*. That was your first theater?"

He nodded. "Years ago."

"What happened?"

Francisco anchored his elbows on the table and cupped one hand over the other, making a stand for his weary head. He hummed ponderously.

"It broke," he said finally. "I didn't test it enough."

"What if you had?"

"I might have weeded out the exploits and glitches. I might have restricted its systems. I might have done a lot of things."

"You still could. Why haven't you?"

He thought about that for a long time, as if the answer would define his entire personality. Then he just shrugged.

"I lost interest," he said. "Too many ideas, not enough years. So I walked away."

"What are you working on now?"

His face widened, revealing a rampart of perfect pearly teeth. He straightened up and pulled out his passport. After a few strokes he held it forward.

"Go on," he said.

I took out my passport and tapped. *Ping*. Another theater acquired.

"That's an invite to Anything Once," he said. "My new baby."

"What's the concept?"

"You know the old cliché, *I'll try anything once*?"

"I've used it myself."

"Of course you have," he said, leaning forward. "But did you mean it?"

"Not really."

He nodded and eased back. "And why is that?"

"Some things you can't come back from."

Francisco snapped his fingers. "That's the beauty of *Anything Once*, John Pike," he said, his voice low and feral. "In my theater you can try everything you ever dreamed—skydiving, opiates, orgies, ortolan, waterboarding, leukemia—and no harm will come to you."

"No risk?"

"None at all."

"Can you die?"

"Sure. Sometimes dying's the ultimate thrill. Drowning, burning, falling from a great height, taking a bullet to the head—point-blank, just to feel yourself shutting down. But it's temporary, like I said. You're always back in a few moments. Respawned."

"What about real death?" I said. "What happens if a person's body just gives out while they're inside? What then?"

Francisco wrapped two hands around his tumbler and rolled it between his palms. The liquor inside sloshed to and fro.

"Why do you ask?" he said.

"Maybe I'm worried," I said. "About our mutual friend."

"I see." He nodded and took another drink and stared into the rippling whisky that remained. "As far as I know, if your body gives out inside the Forum, you're a goner. In spite of the simulation, you're still tethered to your brain." He tapped his right temple with two stiff fingers. "Gonna be a while before someone figures out how to get around having one of these organic CPUs."

He laughed at his own joke and downed his drink. Then he picked up the bottle but stopped short of pouring.

"'Of course, if you could die in there," he continued, "And carry on living as a digital entity, I doubt you'd feel much different than one of those Amnesiacs."

"Amnesiacs?"

Francisco sat up and took a long breath that spoke his irritation. "Citizens who pay a premium to forget they're inside the Forum. Total immersion." He leaned forward. "Rich idiots running from trouble in the real world, mostly."

"It's a wild country in there."

Francisco slid down his chair a couple inches, relaxing a bit. "You think something like that happened to Delia?"

"It's a possibility," I said. "She hasn't been seen or heard from in a few months. People are getting worried."

"You saying this as an auditor or as a friend?"

"Both."

Francisco sat back and crossed his arms. He looked down at the table and back at me. "I know she was working on a new theater. I never learned the name."

"I heard that too. Something big. Disruptive."

Francisco's eyes narrowed. "Who said that?"

"Who do you think?"

"It's sounds like something Locksley would say," he scoffed.

"How so?"

"He flattered Delia every chance he got."

"You don't think she deserved it?"

"I'm not saying that. She's one smart fucking cookie. But for Locksley there's no line between the professional and the personal. And that can get ugly."

"Or violent?"

"Sure."

"You think he did something to her?"

Francisco wrapped two worried hands round his empty glass and squeezed. "Nah," he said, finally. "As much as I hate him, I can't see that." He drank until the tumbler was dry. "What about Mikko, you talk to him?"

"Mikko?"

"Mikkonen. Delia's partner."

"First time I've heard that name."

"A strange guy. Brilliant. I've never seen him on the outside, but inside he holds court in a theater called *Another Man's Shoes*. He designed it himself, a few years back."

"Good to know."

"He and Dee were thick as thieves. He had to be the last one to see her."

"*Another Man's Shoes*."

"I still go a couple days a month. Just to let off—"

He cut himself short and his eyes flared, fixed on something behind me. I turned. There was a man standing at the front door, a stout bruiser in a gray trench coat, looking rain soaked and grim. He had a single bristling eyebrow that ran from temple to temple and his five o'clock shadow looked like someone had sandblasted his face with coffee grounds.

"Evening," Iris called out. "You here for food or drink?"

"You got schnapps?" he growled.

Iris clowned a look of surprise and turned to the wall of bottles. "Pretty sure we don't . . ."

The bruiser grumbled and scraped the room with a scowl, fixing on me and Lopez at our little table.

"Where the hell do I get a schnapps?" he grumbled.

I shrugged and looked at Lopez. He was hunched over with his nose in his glass. I looked back at the bruiser.

"I'd try a hotel. Plenty in Bellingham."

"Fuck that."

The man turned and barreled back through the front door. The instant it swung shut, Francisco shot to his feet and hurried to the bar.

"Is there a back door I can use?" he whispered hoarsely.

"Through the kitchen," Iris said. "Is something wrong?"

Lopez turned and raised his hand. "It was nice to meet you, John," he called out.

"Hold on," I said. "Are you in trouble?"

Francisco pulled a weak smile, and glanced at the front door again. It stayed shut. Moving toward the kitchen, he shook his head rapidly. "I wish you great success," he shouted.

"Likewise," I said, watching him go.

Francisco broke into a run. He slammed through the double-action door like a linebacker and the door swung closed, knocking back and forth a few times before shuddering to a stop. I walked my drink and the nearly full bottle of bourbon to the bar and sat down. Iris wrinkled her nose.

"Odd guy," she said.

"What just happened?"

Iris shrugged. "'He's always been a bit twitchy," she said. "He probably shouldn't carry so much loose cash." She looked down and tapped the neck of the whiskey bottle. "You good with this?"

I pulled it close. "I am great with this."

She smiled and buttressed an arm against the bar and gave me a squint. "Are you one of those virtual fetish guys too?"

"Virtual fetish guys?"

She clicked her tongue. "Come on. You know. Like 'Cisco."

I shook my head. "Tell me."

"There's some private club up in the mountains," she said. "I know he's part of it. Delia was too actually."

"Sounds great."

She rolled her eyes and flopped the rag over her shoulder and laid a forearm across the bar. "I don't judge, John. Shit, I used to be a dancer. Men have dopey fantasies, and they'll pay anything to make them come true."

I nodded and ran my thumb in circles around the mouth of my beer. I felt childish keeping up my John Pike facade for someone unrelated to the case. But discretion was more important than honesty at this point.

"Where are you from, Iris?"

She shook her head and took a limp swipe at me. "Changing the subject means I'm right. Am I right?"

"I'll tell you later."

She licked her lips, waiting for more. I said nothing. She sighed and shifted. "Issaquah," she said. "Moved to Seattle after high school. Well, Georgetown. It's basically Seattle."

"You danced in Seattle?"

She nodded. "Downtown. A place called Deja Vu."

"Most of the girls there have stage names. What was yours?"

Iris grinned and pulled her phone from a back pocket. She tapped the screen to brighten it and held it up to show me the image of a radiant purple flower with a tiny starburst of yellow at its center.

"That's a violet," she said. "Get it?"

"Your stage name was Violet?"

She looked at the phone smiling, then clicked it off and set it aside. "I thought it sounded nice."

"Iris was Violet," I said dreamily. "A good title for your memoir."

She laughed and her eyes softened and got sad. She looked up at the TV and I did too. It was a cop show now. A guy in a suit was interrogating a weeping drunk in a dark room. Police in the next room over were watching through a one-way mirror, shaking their heads and lighting new cigarettes off the burning embers of the old. On instinct, I patted my chest. My own cigarettes were back where they belonged. I pulled out the pack and withdrew a single smoke.

Suddenly, Randy shot upright with a wheezing gasp, like he'd just been rescued from the bottom of Lake Washington. He looked around blinking, smacking his wet lips and rolling his sticky tongue.

"Where's my boys at?" he gasped.

Iris crossed to the fridge and pulled out a Budweiser. It was in Randy's hand before he could remember who and where he was. He drained half the beer before coming up for air.

Iris patted him on the wrist. "The war's over Randy. You're safe here."

Randy kept blinking and looking around. When he spotted the tumbler of whiskey by his elbow, he stared at it like he was contemplating a robbery. Eventually he looked at me. I nodded. He scooped up the glass and downed it like apple juice. Then he cleared his throat.

"You hear gunfire?" he said.

"You were dreaming, buddy," Iris said.

Randy pounded the counter with a curled hand. "The fuck I was," he growled. "I heard shooting."

"No," Iris countered. "You didn't."

I sat in silence, trying to tune out their inane back and forth. My thoughts drifted back to what Francisco had told me. Mikkonen. Delia's colleague. *Another Man's Shoes*. Suddenly all I wanted to do was get back to work.

I stood and slapped on my hat and took my wallet out.

"What do I owe ya?" I said.

"Leaving already?" Iris said.

I threw a twenty on the bar and folded my wallet away. "Been a rough day," I said.

"There's always tomorrow."

"In theory," I said, heading for the door.

She laughed. I did too. But I wasn't joking.

. . . Locksley wanted to congratulate me. But I was hard to get ahold of, and I hadn't been inside the Forum in months. Was I well? he wondered. Was there anything he could do to help? I told him I was struggling to maintain an interest in This Little World. I told him the success of that theater wasn't the kind of success that motivated me. I couldn't find a way forward. Maybe I was losing interest in the whole SR scene.

Locksley swooped in with his usual platitudes. Told me This Little World was drawing astounding numbers. That I should be proud of what I had done. I told him I was proud at one time, but that had passed. I told him the only thing that kept me going was the work itself. So long as I was solving problems I was fine. My best work was whatever I'd do tomorrow. The problem was I didn't know what I was going to do tomorrow. I felt empty.

Throughout my rant Locksley just listened. He offered no solutions. That was unlike him. For the first time in a while, he just let me talk. When I was done, he changed the subject.

I want to throw a party for you guys, he said.

Who, I said. The designers?

Yeah, he said. Something small. Just to let everyone know how much I appreciate the work you've done. The work you're doing.

I'm sure that'd be nice.

He gave me a time and date. A week later I showed up for the party at his Madison Park office with a bottle of wine. He met me in the lobby wearing a silk shirt, cologne, and contact lenses. He took the bottle and scanned the label.

We'll start with this, he said, waving me in.

Something felt off but I followed anyway. He led me to a fifth-floor terrace overlooking Lake Washington. He'd cleared the whole floor and prepped it for a candle-lit dinner—a tiny circular table with two chairs in the middle of a four-thousand-square-foot space. Crisp white tablecloth, crystal glasses, silverware, modal jazz piping in from hidden speakers. A personal waiter on standby.

This wasn't a party, it was a fucking date.

Locksley asked me if I wanted a drink.

I said yeah, to throw in your face.

He got defensive.

Come on Dee, this is a celebration, he told me. My way of cheering you up. Thanking you for a job well done.

I told him I was there to celebrate with my colleagues, exactly as he had promised. His dumb grin fluttered but held fast.

We can call them over, he said, No problem. I just wanted some face time with you first. My star pupil.

Pupil? I said. Fuck you.

I stormed out . . .

18

ANOTHER MAN'S SHOES, the brainchild of an Engineer named Mikkonen, advertised itself as an immersive empathy emporium. On paper the concept was simple—enter the theater and describe the sort of person or cultural group for whom you would like to gain a better understanding. After a few seconds and some rigorous calculations, you would become that person in every outward aspect, adopting the appearance and cultural currency of your chosen avatar in a setting built specifically for your enlightenment.

It was a theater originally conceived for rehabilitation purposes. An unrepentant racist convicted of a crime motivated by his bigotry could be sentenced to six months of immersive therapy here, taking on the guise of the very people he despised. A politician convicted of fraud might spend a mandatory three months in the shoes of the constituents he had cheated. A man found guilty of domestic battery would find his life inverted as a woman trapped in the same terrestrial hell he had inflicted on his partner.

It was no surprise to discover that this theater bore little resemblance to its original intended function. Beyond the gate of light, I stepped into sun and fresh air, onto a snaking boardwalk with a turquoise ocean view where waves roiled and surged against a glowing white sand beach. There were beautiful women and beautiful men everywhere, some strolling the path, others stretched out upon the sand or idling barefoot in the surf's breathing shimmer. Hedonistic vagabonds out for a hungry stroll. The weather and temperature were perfect for any kind of aimless action—walking or jogging, swimming or sunbathing. Even the tickling wind seemed to warm me as it kissed my face.

Farther inland, along a beachfront avenue, was an endless row of quaint tropical cabanas, each with a long terrace facing the ocean and teeming with sun-sweetened revelers who drank and swooned and danced to throbbing pulses of music that thickened the air. There were masquerade balls and chill-out spaces, nudist gatherings and open orgies, social mixers, concerts, art openings. Something for every taste within a five-minute walk.

I ambled down this street on a parallel boardwalk, at a loss for direction. I hadn't gone far when I passed a fit young man the spitting image of Marlon Brando in his 1950s prime wearing a pair of tight black square-cut shorts and a silken vest. As he passed me our eyes met. He winked and pulled a bright lopsided smile, further solidifying the resemblance. He didn't just look like Marlon Brando; he was Marlon Brando.

I turned to question him, but the words died on my tongue. Passing in the opposite direction was a crowd of stars from the turn of the century—three Brad Pitts, four Angelina Jolies, one Jennifer Aniston, and two Matt LeBlancs. For all their energy and verve they might have been on their way to a photo shoot. I stepped off the boardwalk to let them pass.

Now my attention was piqued. And to my dawning surprise I recognized almost everyone around me. Celebrities seethed from every corner and cabana, in all directions. Over the course of one minute I spotted three more Brads, two more Angelinas, three Selena Gomezes, two Halle Berrys, three Harry Styles, one Denzel Washington, two Zendayas, one Kendrick Lamar, two Charlie Chaplins, one Debbie Harry, one Maggie Cheung, two Princess Dianas, one Andre 3000, one Billie Eilish, one Nina Hagen, and a Tom Holland. Many other faces I knew by sight, but could not recall their names. I had stumbled into some eternal Hollywood soiree on the ever gold coast of Southern California.

My curiosity magnifying, I scooted across the boardwalk to a flagstone path that led up to the nearest cabana, a two-story adobe cubical with a party of about three dozen crowding its terrace. Here, too, the faces were as familiar as my own, yet from an era even further in the past, Hollywood's noir years—two Humphrey Bogarts, one Lauren Bacall, three Marlena Dietrichs, two Natalie Woods, four James Deans, five Elizabeth Taylors, and one Frances Farmer.

I turned to face the pedestrian traffic. A young man with a fountain of tawny hair passed by. He carried a skateboard fresh from its packaging under one arm. I waved him down.

"Excuse me . . ."

He stopped, hair bouncing like a show horse's tail. He had an angular, feminine face with eyes that hid a gigolo's spirit. He was barefoot and his collarless white shirt hung open to the sun, fluttering around a pair of short shorts of robin's-egg blue.

"River Phoenix?"

He smirked and ducked his head to one side and raked his fingers through his thick hairline like a fork through custard.

"Yeah man," he said, looking pleased. "Glad you noticed."

"I saw *Mystic Pizza* a long time back."

"*Mister Pizza*?"

"*Mystic*."

River sniffed and scratched the back of his neck. "Don't know it."

"One of his best."

River smiled stupidly. "Thanks."

"You know someone named Mikkonen in here?"

"Sure," he nodded with a sideways wobble. "Everyone knows Mikkonen. He's the boss man."

"How would I find him?"

River flipped his hair from one shoulder to the other to cast his gaze on a new vector. "Hangs out at one of the greasy spoons on Avenue F," he said. "Sometimes all day. Just reading."

"Avenue F?"

River pointed inland, tracing a path through the row of bungalows. "This road here is Avenue A. All other avenues run parallel. So one row back, that's Avenue B, the nightclubs. C is the hotels. D is the . . . " He trailed off, biting his thumb and mumbling to himself. "Shit, what is D?"

"I get it," I said. "Avenue F is restaurants."

"Restaurants are Avenue E. F is Diners."

"Just diners?"

"Yeah. The Hot Cup, that's Mikkonen's hang. Serves breakfast twenty-four seven. Has good coffee and a full bar."

I stepped back and searched for the nearest road leading inland. It wasn't far, just a few houses behind me at the junction of Avenue A and East 34th Street. Beneath the sign that marked the junction, a blond woman in sequined capris and a ripped black tee was lighting a cigarette. She looked up. Madonna, circa 1989.

"It's just a big grid," River said. "But it has everything you need to feel alive."

"How far does it go back?"

"Farthest I've been is Avenue Double-M," he said, pointing uselessly. "That's castles and palaces. Took a cab out there to an industry party."

"What industry?"

"Everyone here pretends they're in the middle of shooting a film. So we throw a lot of industry parties to blow off steam."

I nodded as if this were the most normal thing I had ever heard. "The Hot Cup, Avenue F." I said. "Is it left or right?"

He looked around and shrugged. "From here, shit. I have no idea. I've been wandering all day, not a clue where I've been or where I'm going."

"No plans?"

"Hope to get laid."

"Is that a typical day?"

"That's every day."

"Thanks for your time, River."

He flicked a salute and tossed his skateboard to the pavement. He mounted it with a swoop, but his foot clipped the edge, and he wobbled a few feet before tripping off. His feet slapped the street, and he skittered to a halt. I turned and headed for the inland avenues.

The layout of this theater was just as River had described—an orderly sediment of amenities that felt more like an amusement park than a city. This made perfect sense. Everything here was artificial, custom built for the fulfillment of collective fantasies. There were no economic principles at work in this fantasy land, no forces competing for money and attention, nothing to govern the ebb and flow of ideas and capital and real estate. It was a simulation in which desire was the only fungible resource.

When I reached Avenue F I saw diners for miles in both directions, each one a unique specimen, each with a colorful sign that soared against the sky like an avant-garde lollipop. They blazed with perky names like Charlie's Hovel, the Two-Bit Cafe, the Double Z, Ralph & Betty's, the Char Shack, Fries & Pies, and the Soft Spot. As I soaked in the warm light of these beacons, the sudden thought of an omelet and hash browns rumbled my stomach. I pressed my hand against my belly and walked on. A few minutes in, a taxi passed and pulled to a stop a few dozen feet ahead. A couple stepped out, a man and woman robed in finery that suggested early twenty-first-century royalty. The man let the woman pass and she pranced to the entrance of the Golden Rod. He looked up at my approach and I fell into the easy smile of John Legend. I pointed at the cab.

"You mind?" I said.

"All yours."

The woman called to him from the café.

"They've got our booth!" she shouted.

It was Beyoncé, holding the door open. John waved and tugged at his tie and trotted up the path. I opened the cab's rear door and swung inside. The cabbie watched me through the rearview mirror. He waited until I had settled.

"Good morning, sir," he said.

"You know the Hot Cup?"

"Of course."

"Let's go."

A STRING OF BELLS TINGLED as I entered the Hot Cup, a typical American greasy spoon—plaster stucco ceiling, unpainted wood wainscoting, booths upholstered with fading red vinyl. It looked like any old roadside diner between the two Portlands and nothing more. No panache or flair. Just a place to eat eggs and browns and toast, safe from the rain and the wind.

The place was active but not busy. I crossed to the counter and set my hat down. A tower of waxy pies rotated in a scratched glass case. A hairy, balding cook with a caterpillar mustache stepped from the kitchen, wiping his hands on a stained white apron.

"Sit anywhere. Plenty of space."

"I'm here for Mikkonen," I said with a cool, offhand shrug.

The cook's head rotated to the right, but he stopped himself and looked back at me.

"Don't know him," he said.

It was a nice try, but he'd already tipped his hand. I looked where he had. At the back of the diner was a circular booth tucked in the corner. There was a man sitting there alone, face half hidden behind a full color broadsheet newspaper. A cup of black coffee steamed in front of him, beside a face down mobile phone.

"Hey," the cook said. "Buy something or get out."

I gestured to the man in the back booth "I'll be quick," I said. "I owe him a hundred bucks."

He slammed his hand down on the counter. "Order something or get out."

"One black coffee."

The cook mumbled some blue curses and stormed into the kitchen. I crossed to the booth. As I drew near, my shadow fell across the man's raised newspaper. The newspaper lowered an inch, revealing a thin face and a pinched pair of wire-rimmed reading glasses.

"Mikkonen?"

"Yes?"

I lowered myself into the opposite seat and laid my hat on the table. Mikkonen folded the paper and laid it by and removed his glasses, holding them in his fist. I held up my auditor's badge.

"A minute of your time?"

He stared at my passport for an odd length of time. Then he sighed and laid his glasses on the table.

"A minute is fine," he said.

I unbuttoned my jacket and sat back. Mikkonen watched me with a curiously blank look. He was as skinny as a scarecrow with sandy greased hair that ran down the back of his neck and gathered into wet strings at its nape. He had a friendly but tired face with drooping puppy eyes and a prickly mustache that poked out from his face like a stiff hairbrush. He wore a casual dress shirt unbuttoned to the sternum that lay like a jacket on his bony shoulders. Around his neck was a loosely wound yellow scarf. He had a gentle charisma, but I didn't recognize him as anyone famous. In a theater where A-list celebrities outnumbered the roaches, this novel face was a pleasant surprise.

"I'm not here to cause trouble," I said. "I'm just looking for someone. Someone close to you."

He nodded knowingly, as if I were rehearsing a script he had already read. "Okay."

"I just want to know that she's safe."

"That is kind of you."

"You know who I'm talking about?"

"I do."

"I was sent here to bring her home. But I've seen enough in the last few days to know how difficult that would be. Just knowing she's alive and well would be enough."

"I see."

"Can you help me?"

"In what way?"

The diner's doorbell string chimed like a glass full of ice. A trio of Willie Nelsons entered and shuffled around the foyer, searching the walls for a free booth. I crossed my hands and leaned in.

"People tell me she was working on a new theater."

"What people?"

"Old friends. Colleagues."

"Ah."

"Can you get me in?"

Mikkonen cocked his head. His nose twitched. "No."

"No, you can't, or no, you won't?"

"No is no. Why bother qualifying it?"

I fell back, drumming my fingers on the table. "The truth is," I said, "Her father wants her back in the real world. But I'm not so adamant. I just want to talk to her. If I can tell the senator that much, I think he'll be satisfied."

Mikkonen chuckled softly. "A satisfied politician. Does such a creature exist?"

A porcelain roar filled the room. At the front counter a dozen coffee mugs had tumbled to the floor and shattered. The hairy cook was already on his knees scrabbling through the shards.

"Jesus, I'm so sorry," he moaned.

A tall blond woman stood over him, staring down at the mess. Her back was to me, but I could see from her black silk skirt, her flowing white blouse, and the ermine scarf that she had class. She held out a twenty-dollar bill, waiting with saintly patience for someone to pluck it away. As broken mug fragments fell clacking into a bucket, she let out a long chilly sigh and glanced about the room. Her face gave me chills. It was Rita Hayworth, straight off the set of *the Lady from Shanghai*. If this had been any other theater, I'd be certain she followed me here from Locksley's theater, *the Last Dance*. And even then, I couldn't rule it out.

"My fault," she announced to the room. "I spooked him."

The cook scrambled to clear the mess, his ass in the air and his pants nearly slipping off. Rita bent forward like a blade of grass in the wind and stuffed the twenty in his sweaty crack.

"Keep the change, sweetie."

The cook flinched and looked up. He laughed nervously. "Thank you, Ms. Hayworth," he said, looking skyward like a fretful puppy. "Thank you."

Rita spun around, almost writhing, and floated out the front door with a sassing of bells. Mikkonen cleared his throat. He took a quiet sip of his coffee and set it down gently.

"Quite a spectacle," he said.

"It must drive you mad."

He cocked his head. "Mad?"

"You designed this theater. You can't be happy with what it's become."

Mikkonen pressed his hands together in prayer and kissed his fingertips. Then he shrugged.

"Market forces, nothing more."

"That's your excuse?"

Mikkonen turned up his hands as if surrendering. "That was an explanation, not an excuse."

"You think there's a difference?"

"I do," he said. "The fault lies in my shortsightedness. I assumed the best in people. But most have no interest in fixing what is wrong with them. They only want a break from themselves from time to time."

"Is that what Delia's doing? Taking a break?"

"It could be."

"You don't know, or you're not saying?"

Mikkonen yawned and looked at the cook, who had just finished cleaning up and was hauling the bucket of shards to the kitchen. Then he opened his spectacles and put them on. He grabbed the broadsheet and snapped it open.

"Delia is exactly where she wants to be," he said. "And if it's Daddy Walsh you need to pacify, tell him she's doing fine."

"That's not gonna fly. Not without proof."

"Proof of what?" someone said.

A hard hand like an oversized talon clamped my shoulder and held me down. I looked up to see Pritchard Locksley's leathery face swing into view.

"Hey pal," he smiled. "Funny finding you here."

"Is it?" I said.

Locksley turned to Mikkonen. "You behaving yourself?" he said. "This guy works for Uncle Sam."

"Hello, Mr. Locksley," Mikkonen said from behind the opened paper. "Welcome back."

Locksley jabbed a finger at Mikkonen and flicked it a few times between us. "I didn't know you two knew each other," he said. "That's wonderful."

"We don't," Mikkonen said, still reading.

I slid from the booth, grabbed my hat, and stood. "And we have a lot less in common than I'd hoped."

Locksley took a step in my direction. "Stay for coffee, pal," he said. "You might hear some war stories."

"You don't want me hearing war stories, Mr. Locksley," I said, turning to go. "I can't keep a secret."

Halfway to the door I passed the cook ferrying a steaming cup of coffee to the table. When he saw me leaving his face dawned with rage. I shrugged.

"Give it to the old guy," I said and walked out.

2

. . . In that first year, the Forum grew like kudzu in a Georgia summer. Hundreds of new Citizens joined every week. I don't know where Locksley was getting these people, but they weren't pulled from the street. Most were dudes with tech industry ties. A handful were scholars. Very few were artists. Not my scene.

As the Forum's population grew, so did its theaters. A hefty percentage of new Citizens started building their own and sharing them around. The tool Locksley had commissioned from my code was just that good. And as much as I hated the results, it was fascinating to see so much creative energy unleashed. And so quickly. Someone with a clear idea on Monday could be up and running by Friday. Of course, the majority of these new theaters were fetish dungeons, adolescent novelties, and stoner daydreams. But there were quite a few goofy distractions that made an amusing first impression.

What if you had eyes on your knees?

What if what you saw as the color blue was what I saw as red?

What if you were invisible?

I stayed far away from these gimmicks and steered myself toward the few remaining theaters that grappled with difficult questions. The ones that challenged me. The ones that tossed me into the depths of a fascinating problem and forced me to swim.

Hitch a ride on a single photon and cruise the universe.

Evolve a new species of mammal in one afternoon.

Learn a new language via total immersion.

Like a teenager browsing random playlists of unfamiliar music, I was hungry for new ideas. Something to inspire me or jolt me from my boredom. My own imagination had dried up. I was suffering an intellectual drought I had never experienced before. I did keep busy—working as a consultant, helping new Citizens navigate the Forum's robust systems. That brought some satisfaction. But it wasn't enough.

The following summer, after a year of vacant idleness, I found myself reminiscing about the past, about my earliest versions of This Little World. The janky beta build, a pre-Forum surreal. I began to wonder if I still had the archival feeds for those original sessions. With old-school SR tech, I could watch the feeds directly using a standard surreal deck. I could relive what the volunteers had experienced, like looking at someone's old journal in four dimensions.

Something drew me back to this idea. A desperate search for inspiration, I guess. Or the sickness of nostalgia for my better days. I didn't care. I just wanted to spend time in that space. To go back and get a taste of my beginnings.

On a slow weekend I drove back to Seattle and tracked down my old servers, in search of the hard drives that still had session feeds from my early tests. When I found them, I pulled up footage from the Starbucks Beta and started browsing. There was a ton of content to sift. Thousands of hours of surreal feeds. Hundreds of sessions, hundreds of people, mostly volunteers in those days. Hundreds of names I didn't know, a few I did. But one name was conspicuously absent. Pritchard Locksley.

That couldn't be right. I knew for a fact that he'd sat for me three times during our Beta sessions. But all his feeds were gone. On closer inspection, I found gaps in the session timelines. Places where a session should have been running, now mysteriously void.

I double-checked the session logs to be sure. To my surprise, I discovered that Locksley had taken twenty-four separate trips in my Beta Build. Twenty-one more than I was aware off. Twenty-one without my knowledge.

My first impulse was to call Locksley and ask him directly. Why are your logs missing? What the fuck were you doing? But I knew I wouldn't get a straight answer, not from him.

I drove back to Burlington that night. I drove straight to the Forum.

I knew what to do . . .

19

I LEFT THE HOT CUP to glower beneath a salmon and tanzanite sky. The sun was gone and the streetlamps had popped on and the foot traffic was heavier than when I'd gone inside, fifteen minutes earlier. Imposter celebrities shuffled between their last distraction and the next in a world where everything was always available and nobody knew what day it was.

I crossed the street, dodging Matthew McConaughey on a mint green Vespa and passed all four members of the currently hip girl group Gem Fatale in close conversation with the Jackson Five. When I reached the opposite side, I hopped up a set of short steps into a diner called Syrup Central. Through the door, a pasty Timothée Chalamet in a wallet cap greeted me and suggested an empty booth at the back. I pointed to the long counter by the window overlooking the street.

"I prefer a view," I said.

"Awesome, sure."

I made my way to the front and took a stool. Timothée scuttled in beside me and slipped a menu under my nose, a vivid catalog of the dishes they offered. None of the hundred supersaturated photos looked appetizing. I pushed the menu away.

"Just a coffee. With a splash of cream."

"Sugar?"

"I would have said sugar."

Timothée wilted like I had just licked his nose. "Sorry. Coming right up," he said, pressing the menu to his chest and scurrying away.

I laid my hat aside and crossed my arms over the counter and fixed my gaze on the Hot Cup. With the sun going down, I could see through its glowing windows. Mikkonen was still at his table, listening impassively to his new companion. Every now and then Locksley's arm would swing into view, animated like a monkey flinging shit. If he was yelling, nothing on Mikkonen's face confirmed it. Their conversation went on like this for quite a while: Locksley swinging, Mikkonen staring.

About the time I realized my coffee was taking an eternity to reach me, the bewitching scent of a flowery perfume clouded my nose. Before I could turn, a soft finger grazed the back of my neck and slid along my shoulder and down my arm.

"He's not worth the attention, sugar."

A breathy mid-Atlantic lilt. I looked down at the hand. Five long fingers, slender and pale with strawberry tips.

"Who are we talking about?" I said.

Hard heels clicked behind me as the roving finger reached my hand and jumped away. It was Rita Hayworth, as lovely and aloof as ever. Rose red lips pulsing like a beating heart, flowing platinum dunes of pinned up hair, skin as creamy as milk in a farmer's pail. A breathing statue carved from living marble. I was staring at her, but she wasn't looking at me. She was watching Mikkonen and Locksley.

"Mikkonen's a crafty man," she said. "Be careful what you tell him."

I slid back to get a better view of my new friend. "He acted tough," I said. "Usually a sign of weakness."

"Not always?"

"Sometimes it just means they're tough."

Rita flashed a spicy smile, looking me over like I was something she wanted to chew on. "I'm not bothering you, am I?"

"Bothering can mean a few things."

She patted my wrist. "You're cute."

I nodded, throwing a quick glance across the street. Nothing stirred in the Hot Cup.

"Forget about Mikkonen," Rita said. "He won't help you. He can't."

"What about Locksley?"

Rita's face sunk into something halfway between a pout and a scowl. "Most definitely not."

"Why's that?"

"He's never helped anyone that wasn't of some use to him."

"I can think of a lot of ways a Federal Auditor could be useful to him," I said. "And still I get attitude."

"It doesn't matter anyway," Rita said, slapping the air in front of her. "Neither of them knows where Delia is."

"Who's Delia?"

Rita opened her mouth and tongued the corner of her lips. "Just another girl," she said. "I can get you close if you're still looking for her."

I grunted. "What does 'close' mean in a place like this? Everything here is just one door away, but everyone seems lost."

Rita looked down at an empty stool tucked under the counter. "You haven't invited me to join you."

"Be my guest."

She smiled daintily and removed her pelt scarf and folded it twice to lay it on the counter. Then she pulled out the stool and smoothed her hands down her skirt and backed onto it like a reversing truck, giving me a long full look at her bumpers. Crossing her legs like a pair of giant scissors, she spun to the side and looked me over, a gentle smile that grew over time.

"Thank you," she said.

"I saw you at the Hot Cup," I said. "I guess you saw me."

"Heard you too. Your voice carries."

"Was I that obvious?"

"I'll put it this way," she said. "Everyone but the dishwasher knows you're looking for Delia Walsh."

"All part of the plan," I said. "So how do you know her?"

"From the diner mostly," she said, nodding out the window. "The Hot Cup's been her hideaway in the Forum for a while. Hers, Mikkonen's, a few others. They were a pretty tight group for a while. Talented dreamers."

"For a hideaway, this theater seems a little crowded."

Rita shrugged and leaned forward to look at the translucent image of herself in the window. She scraped the corner of her mouth with a pinky nail.

"When you don't look like yourself," she said, "You can hide anywhere."

"And who are you?"

"I'm Rita Hayworth."

"Why is that?

She laughed and struck a subtle pose against the dimming daylight. "Why the hell not?" she moaned. "Just look at her."

"I'm looking."

"Yes, you are."

"You chose a good era," I said, staring at her hair.

"I think so, too," she said. "Her platinum years were much more interesting. Red hair never translated in black and white."

"Is there a young Orson Welles wandering around somewhere?"

"A few svelte Charles Foster Kanes, I think. By *Shanghai*, Orson was already a bit puffy."

"They were married around then."

She laughed and wagged her chin. "I'm not a strict role-player."

"And who are you without this mask?"

She pursed her lips, searching my face for a motive. "A concerned friend," she said. "Don't let it bother you."

Spunky Timothée Chalamet interrupted with a bright "Hello!" He slid a mug of steaming khaki coffee under my nose and pressed the tips of his fingers together.

"Here we are," he said. "A cup of joe with a splash of cream." He stepped back and gestured at Rita. "Something for the lady?"

"Nothing for me."

"A glass of water maybe?"

"What did I just say, champ?"

Poor Master Chalamet ducked and bobbed away. Rita fixed her eyes on me and studied, her eyelids raising and lowering like a butterfly sunning its wings. I hooked a finger through the mug's ring and pulled it close. Before I could drink, Rita leaned forward and puckered her lips and blew a gentle breath over the surface. The coffee shivered. I took a sip. The perfect temperature.

"Tell me about her," I said. "About Delia."

Rita took a long replenishing breath and laid her arms across her lap.

"She was a friend. A brilliant friend. Bold and beautiful. With big ideas and the talent to make them happen."

"Was?"

Rita touched her mouth with two fingers. "Sorry. That sounds sinister. I haven't seen her in months. I don't think anyone has."

"Months is a long time in here. Long enough for every trace of someone to vanish, I imagine."

"Yes and no. All traces in here are just digital noise. They can vanish in a second, but were they significant of anything to begin with?"

"So, how can you help me?"

"I can tell you where she spent almost all her time in the last year. The name of the theater."

I took out my passport and laid it screen up on the counter. "Perfect. Tap me in."

"That's not possible."

"Why? Because you're making this up as you go along?"

Rita pulled a sour look. "Shame on you. I'm trying to help."

"Sorry, Rita. I've got trust issues."

Rita smirked. "Because Delia has a Green Card and her new theater is off limits."

"How'd she manage that?"

"Her father, I assume."

"Stolen?"

"Almost certainly."

"All right, so what's the move?"

"You'll need a blank Green Card. Once you do, I can fix it with the right credentials."

I flattened my face at the suggestion. "I'm not exactly at the top of the ladder when it comes to security clearance."

"It's the only way to reach her."

"Fine. Assume I can swing one. Then what?"

"The *Mind's I*," Rita said carefully. "That's where she's been working for the last year. On some radical new idea."

"The *Mind's I*?" I tapped on my passport and hit the search bar.

Rita laid a soft paw on my wrist. "It won't show until a Green Card is active."

"If I can find one."

"That's right."

With a slight kick of her heels, Rita slid off the stool like a pancake from a skillet and rose to her full height. She grabbed her clutch purse and pulled it to her breast.

"Convinced?" she said, batting her eyes.

I wasn't, but I didn't feel like derailing this train just yet. I had a hunch that playing along would get me further than shutting her down. Drawing out the silence, I looked back across the street. Locksley was on his feet now, standing beside Mikkonen's table. He was still swinging his arms, but not with violence. Mikkonen was half listening, eyes fixed on his cup of coffee.

"What's in it for you?" I said.

"Only the assurance that Delia is alive and well."

"That's kind of you."

"How long will you need?"

"Twenty-four hours," I said. "Just to know if it's possible."

"Good. We'll meet again, right here."

I pushed back and stood and held out my hand. "Thanks for the lead, Ms. Hayworth."

"Goodbye, Mr. Pike," she said with a sugary grin. "Until next time."

My nerves crackled at the sound of the name Pike. I hadn't introduced myself to her or anyone in this theater. I'd been cautious not to.

"I'll be in touch," I said.

She leaned forward and dusted my cheek with a kiss. Her swirling flowery perfume filled my nose and fogged my memory. I closed my eyes to drown in the scent. Spectral visions of blue jays and bunny rabbits crowded the stage of my mind. When I opened my eyes, Rita Hayworth was gone.

I waited at Syrup Central for another twenty minutes, just enough time to finish my coffee. Then I slapped my hat on and hurried out the door. The sky was a chalky black and the streets glowed a lamplit yellow. A troubling doubt gnawed my insides, a wary intuition that told me Mikkonen was still the man to follow. Rita's appearance had the stink of a setup. Maybe someone with access to *the Last Dance* had watched my feed and decided to fuck with me. The obvious culprit was Locksley, but he'd been with Mikkonen the whole time. If it was in fact Locksley at all—hard to be sure in a place like this. It was time to proceed with greater caution than usual.

I crossed the street and skipped up the Hot Cup's front steps and peeked through the glass door. The booth Mikkonen had occupied was empty. Only his paper remained, folded neatly on the seat.

I returned to the street and hailed a cab, asking the driver to take me back to the beachfront, as close to the portal as he could. He dropped me off where I had met River Phoenix and zipped off without asking for money. Strolling the boardwalk, I took out my passport and ran a search for the *Mind's I*. As expected, nothing came up. I stashed it and moved on.

The night was alive and humming with crowds swarming the streets and packing the beach as thick as they had ever been. Up and down Avenue A, cabanas twinkled like holiday dioramas. The party was eternal in this wonderland, and the beauty was free.

I walked quickly toward the theater's exit, looking out across the moonlit beach and the heaving mercury tinted waters beyond where the surf crashed with a beautiful rustling. Human cries that could have been screams of terror or squeals of surprise echoed through the grayed out night. It wasn't worth it to find out which.

. . . I was shaking when I entered the Hot Cup. Mikkonen saw me, looked up from his newspaper. I stomped over to his table.

I have a favor to ask, I said.

He folded the paper and set it aside and laced his hands.

All right, he said.

I slid into his booth. He watched me with his typical disinterest.

I don't think you'll agree to what I want, I said. But I need you to know why I'm asking before you say no.

That is very considerate, he said.

Answer this question, I said. If you can. How often does Locksley visit This Little World in the Forum?

Mikkonen gave me an empty stare.

I'm not allowed to share personal information, he said. That would violate the privacy protocols we have in place.

Give me a range, I said. Is it more than ten?

Mikkonen said nothing.

More than fifty?

He said nothing.

Over one hundred?

Mikkonen's lips pressed together, and his eyes fluttered with the wild action of a moth trying kill itself against a halogen lamp.

He is rather fond of your theater, he said finally.

Jesus Christ, I said. I need to know what he's doing in there.

Could you be more specific?

It's a hunch, I said. Based on experience. Based on what I know about him. Two years ago he covered his tracks but not very well. Deleted old beta feeds, manipulated data. The recordings are gone. And for some reason here in the Forum we don't have feeds at all. No records at all. No transcripts for research purposes. Nothing.

Mikkonen nodded gently. It's no conspiracy, Delia, he said. Recording data feeds in here would be unmanageable. The resolution and fidelity of the Forum would generate over three terabytes of information every second.

I nodded, grinding my teeth. I knew he'd say that because I knew the difficulty involved. I just wanted him to get a sense of how angry I was. And how desperate for answers.

What if I watched a live feed instead? I said.

He raised an eyebrow.

A live feed of . . . ?

What if we duped This Little World and slaved the copy to the original. When Locksley enters This Little World, I enter the duplicate. Now I'm seeing what he sees, without his knowledge. It's taking a joyride on his id, like a furious little homunculus in his forebrain.

You're right, Mikkonen said. I don't like this idea. So why ask me?

I didn't say I wanted your help, Mikko. I said I wanted a favor.

That being?

You know everything that goes on in here. You know the name of every theater and who designed it. When someone shuts down a theater, you know. When a new theater goes online, you see it. Right?

Yes.

So I'm asking you to keep quiet.

I see.

Pretend you didn't see anything. If I'm wrong, I'll fuck right off. But if I'm right . . . well, I hope I'm not right.

Mikkonen said nothing. His eyes roamed my face in search of some ulterior motives. But I was as serious then as I had ever been.

Well? I said.

I am calculating the risks, he said. Please be patient . . .

20

IT WAS LATER THAN I EXPECTED when I exited the Forum—just after nine-thirty—but my ride was still waiting for me. The driver with the English accent stood propped against the door of his sedan, reading from his phone, its ghostly light conjuring the illusion of a bodiless head levitating in midair.

I took a seat on the Forum's perimeter steps, fished out my smokes and lit up. After a few calming drags, I took out my phone and switched it on. A window popped up to tell me I had a new voicemail from Billy Brighton's wife. I stared at the name for a moment, aching with a tiny regret. More likely than not, Billy was still logged in, cosplaying as a cop in his neo-noir fantasy. And his wife Melina was probably waiting by the phone, counting on me to drag him out. There was no explanation for what I was doing now that would satisfy her. But I had a good feeling her husband would hold on for another few weeks at least.

I tapped past her message and brought up my recent calls and scrolled through to the number that rang me the morning after my first meeting with Auntie. I called in.

A warm, woozy voice answered. A voice I recognized, and one who recognized me.

"Mr. Pike," Toots said. "How's the audit going?"

Rainfall and traffic churned in the background, laying a bed for the rhythmic clock of clogs on a sidewalk.

"Hiya, Toots," I said. "It's going well. And today I learned a few things that were left out of my tutorial."

"Such as?"

"Green Rooms."

"Right," he said, taking a long time to collect his thoughts. "What do you need to know exactly?"

"How to find one. How to get inside."

"You think that's necessary?"

I took another drag and blew it over the receiver. "Starting to," I said. "Is there any way you can hit me up with a blank Green Card? Something I can use when the time is right?"

Toots laughed. "Blank? Are you fucking nuts?" he said. "That'd be a security nightmare."

"What if I got you the name of a specific Green Room? Could you get me access?"

"Auditors don't usually get security clearance of that caliber," he said, "And I'm not in a position to change the rules."

"Don't usually or don't ever?"

"I've not seen it happen."

"Shucks."

"Let me read the tea leaves here. Would you say getting ahold of a Green Card is paramount to concluding your work as an auditor?"

"That's some potent tea you're drinking."

"Jesus," he muttered. A gurgling motorcycle passed him by, eating up the next few sentences of an earnest string of excuses. When I could hear him again, he concluded with ". . . see what I can do. But no fucking promises."

"Thanks, buddy. I'll wait for your call."

"Might take a while," he grumbled. "Keep busy."

"Roger that."

I hung up and closed the phone and checked again to make sure it was dead. Then I finished my cigarette and flicked the butt to the gravelly ground and stood. I crossed to my driver's car. Hearing me approach, he stowed his phone and stood to attention.

"Nice night," I said.

"Good evening, Mr. Pike."

He opened the front passenger door and stepped to one side.

"Thanks for waiting," I said.

"And where are we going tonight?"

"Back to the motel. I got a long night of waiting ahead of me."

"Very good, sir."

He smiled and bowed his head, still holding the door. I ducked to enter. That's when I felt a hard chill sting the nape of my neck. I stopped. Something clicked. I closed my eyes, waiting for the boom and the blankness. The driver's breathy voice tickled my ear.

"You've got a rendezvous, John Pike," he said. "Back inside."

"They allow guns in there?"

"They make exceptions. Move."

I obeyed. He pushed me through the gate and goaded me down the long stairway. As we approached the portal, he pulled up my jacket and took a firm hold of my belt.

"Take out your passport and hold it over your shoulder," he said. "Nice and slow where I can see it."

I did. The screen lit up. The driver tapped his passport against mine. A chime sounded. I glanced at the screen. *La Casa Roja*.

The barrel dug into my neck like a bovine stun-bolt. A swift, icy pain trilled down my spine and across my skull. I stumbled but a hand caught me by the arm. The pressure reappeared between my shoulder blades. I straightened up, arms raised.

"Face forward," he yelled. "Now walk."

LA CASA ROJA WAS A NIGHTCLUB THEATER—a murky cave with reflected red light drafting down like a bloody mist from hidden high-set sconces. The walls were tiled with fractured facets of mirror and obsidian that gave the illusion of a building suspended in the act of shattering. Two levels of terraces with low tables and cushy chairs encircled the entire room.

The driver and I had appeared at the topmost terrace. A long flight of stairs fanned down before us to an empty dance floor, like a slow flow of molten lava. Above the dance floor hung a pair of coral-like chandeliers in a messy fractal effulgence. A long ebony bar lay like a wriggling eel at the back of the lower floor. On the left and right walls were deep booths, as black as wells of ink that resisted illumination. A languid pulse of music thumped against the floor and up the walls, more felt than heard.

The driver prodded me again.

"Arms out."

I T-posed, looking every bit our savior on the cross. The driver's hands slipped under my jacket. He ran his palm along my lower back, then slipped his fingers under my belt and swiped left to right. Finding nothing he stepped back and tapped my shoulder with the gun's hilt.

"Now turn around."

I did so, coming face-to-face with my driver again. He was handsomer inside the Forum than out—a stronger chin, darker whiskers, a thicker brow, and taller too. He pressed the gun to my forehead.

"No sudden moves," he said.

"Did I forget to tip last time?"

He flashed a toothy smile that looked more expensive than his car and reached into my jacket and ran his cold fingers up and down the inside of my thighs, fluttering them a little to see if I'd flinch. Finding nothing there either, he ran his palms down the sides of my pants. When he finished he took a step backward and lowered the gun to a lazy height. At the ready but less aggrieved.

"You think those gun exceptions apply to me?" I said.

"Can't be too careful with Uncle Sam," he said, flicking the barrel at the stairs. "Go on down. They're waiting."

"Who?"

"They."

He shooed me again. I stepped to the edge of the stairs and looked out across the club. It was dark and humid, but I could just make out the patrons, people huddled in intimate groups and tucked away in veiled corners and crouched into high-backed booths. I was still scanning when someone whistled far below. A high-pitched note that swooped through the room and landed in my ear. I searched for its source and spotted a skinny arm waving from a distant booth under a warm halo of light.

I descended, strutting down the steps like I was born to this scene. The driver followed. When I hit the bottom, my shoes squeaked over the dark hardwood. We crossed the dance floor and navigated a garden of tiny circular tables and miniature stools to a row of booths along the club's right wall. The seat backs rose over five feet and looked like the plush interiors of escape pods jettisoned from some imperial starship. I walked to the far corner, guided by a treacly amber light spilling from the final booth. As I stepped into view of my hosts, I saw a pair of hulking goons the size of refrigerators seated in the booth. One had the face of Robert Mitchum, the other was the spitting image of Lenny Montana, exemplar for mafioso muscle on the silver screen. Seated between this duo was a string-haired beanpole with a push-broom mustache staring me down with a tired look that bordered on annoyed.

"Mikkonen," I said. "Did you change your mind?"

Mikkonen gestured to an empty spot in the booth. "Shut up and take a seat."

I took a step back and pocketed my hands. Robert Mitchum scowled.

"He told you to sit," he barked.

"I heard him."

The refrigerator Montana grimaced and stabbed at the table with a meaty finger.

"Do it or we break you!"

Mikkonen laid a gentle hand on his shoulder. "I can handle this," he said.

The goon fell back.

"I don't need handling," I said. "Just say what you need to say."

Mikkonen made a tutting sound and reached for a pack of cigarettes lying on the table. He lit one and blew a thin rail of smoke across the booth that beckoned as it slowed and curled in the air. He offered me one. I waved it away.

"I've got my own," I said.

I patted my jacket, but the pack wasn't there.

"Do you?" Mikkonen said.

"Why can you smoke, but I can't?"

"Administrator's privilege."

I gestured at the driver standing at my shoulder. "And the hand cannon? Is he an admin too?"

Mikkonen tutted and looked past me. "Did he say anything?"

The driver stepped forward and shrugged. "Wanted me to drive him to his motel. Made a phone call before that. Asked someone about a Green Card."

Mikkonen's eyes widened slightly.

"A Green Card, that's curious," he said. "Quite unusual for an auditor."

"I'm a new kind," I said. "Nosey and annoying."

"And obsessed with Delia Walsh," he said coolly. "That's hardly new."

"Who?"

Mikkonen wrinkled his nose. "You seem to enjoy this arch personality you have cultivated." he sighed. "A pulp anti-hero, total and complete. No surrogate reality required."

I shrugged. "Personality is just a shaggy dog story we tell ourselves. Why not have a little fun with it?"

"You see? Cynical and trite." He paused for another drag. "I saw you talking to Rita Hayworth earlier. A funny coincidence after the scene she made at my diner."

"It wasn't a coincidence. She was looking for me."

Mikkonen ashed his cigarette into Montana's drink. "What did she tell you?"

"I'd rather not say."

"What did she tell you?"

"You'll hate yourself for asking."

"An acceptable risk."

I pulled off my hat and ran my fingers through my hair and slapped it back on. "Well," I said. "She told me your mustache looked like a dead ferret."

Montana shot to his feet and pounded the table. "Don't nobody talk to Mikko like that," he growled, nostrils flaring. "You hear me? Don't nobody—"

With feline speed, Mikkonen snatched up his greyhound and launched the drink at Montana's face. The goon gasped and clapped a hand over his eyes, too late to stop the sting.

"Take a walk," Mikkonen growled, pointing at the stairs.

"Aw, Mikko . . . "

"And don't come back without your manners."

Glistening with a hangdog frown, Montana edged out of the booth and stood tall. At nearly seven feet he was a boulder with legs. He plowed his shoulder into my temple as he passed, knocking me sideways. When he reached the foot of the stairs he took them slow and lumbering. I looked back at Mikkonen. He frowned and lifted his cigarette, hooking his free arm into the crook of the other.

"Here is what happens next, Pike," he said. "My man will take you back to your motel. Then you drive to Antony's. When you get there, I want you to pay off your bar tab."

"My bar tab?"

"That's right."

For the first time in a long while I was speechless. Such a random request, I couldn't parse it. I hadn't even mentioned Antony's. I scanned Mikkonen's gentle face—his sad eyes, his mop of stringy hair, his thick wet underlip, his drooping mustache. It was a face that lacked all guile and meanness, in spite of our sinister surroundings. He was a man who seemed perfectly serious and quietly desperate.

"Is that a code for something more sinister?" I said.

"No," he said, shaking his head slowly. "It means pay off your tab."

"What happens if I don't?"

He sniffed and shrugged. "You are welcome to find out."

"Quid pro quo," I said. "You answer my question and maybe I play your little scavenger hunt."

He crushed his cigarette into the table. "Negotiations have ended, Mr. Pike," he said, raising his chin and glancing past me.

Too late I realized what was happening. That's when the bottle exploded against my temple. In a split-second shock of lightning, I reeled, a hot throb swelling my head as a curtain of darkness fell, heavy and cold. I fell with it.

. . . I got the duplicate theater up and running in a matter of days. Then I waited. About a week later, Locksley entered This Little World. He strolled in like a man going to the gym. A man on a routine.

I entered the duplicate. Following him in, so to speak.

That evening I called Locksley in a rage. As soon as he answered, I unloaded. I gave that motherfucker both barrels. Barely let him get a word in.

You fucking dirtbag, I screamed. If there was a law that covered this kind of violation I would write the statute on a rope and wrap it around your neck and squeeze until your brains shot out your ears. You're a liar, you're a lecher, you're a narcissist, and you strung me along like a battered kite. So now I have the double indignity of feeling stupid and violated all because the only thing about me that matters to you isn't inside my head. It's considerably lower.

Hold on, Dee. What are you—

You want to play dumb? You want me to believe you're confused about something? Fine. Let me be perfectly fucking clear: I know your habits in This Little World. I know because I just watched a perverted tryst with a woman who looked suspiciously familiar. She was about my age, my height, and she had my face. Fucking sick, you fucking coward. A craven misogynist whose dreams of reinventing the wheel for the betterment of mankind ended when he stuck his greased dick through the axle hole and proclaimed his mission accomplished. Well congratulations. Now I have definitive proof that This Little World is exactly the abject failure I feared it was. You rode it like a fucking riverboat through the swamp of your psyche, and made a fool out of both of us in the process. So here's the deal—This Little World goes offline, effective today. That's my prerogative, right there in my contract. I work independently, at my leisure, under my rules. And if you refuse, or try to take punitive action, just remember who pays your bills. I have the receipts, and I will show them to anyone I please. A notable US senator first and foremost.

Delia, I—

Fuck you. Leave me alone. And if you see me anywhere, turn and run . . .

21

AN AMORPHOUS WEIGHT held me down as I woke, as if I lay trapped beneath the stones and ironworks of a collapsed cathedral. My head was throbbing, and my mouth had an acidic flavor—the taste of pain. I focused on my breathing and opened my eyes to a smeared sunlight with no apparent source. A minute passed before I understood that a white cotton sheet lay over my face. I dragged this aside and the sunlight burned brighter. I closed my eyes and waited, breathing slowly, searching for a better feeling. Gradually the weight lifted.

When I had the strength, I sat up. I was back in my room at the Cascadia Inn. The curtains were drawn back and a gorgeous golden light poured into the room. Someone had disrobed me down to my boxers and undershirt, and the light felt warm and liquid on my bare skin. My suit lay in a crumpled heap on the chair beside the writing desk. Rubbing my eyes, I yawned so wide my jaw hurt. I threw my legs to the floor and stretched. My joints clicked and popped.

I closed my eyes and rubbed my temple. Mikkonen's final instructions reverberated in my head. *Go to Antony's. Pay your bar tab.* An absurd request, but so specific I couldn't resist. I rose and moved to the window to look out.

It was a gorgeous day, late afternoon and more lovely than autumn had a right to be. The air was heavy and sun-soaked with scintillating shades of gold light. A formation of Canadian geese cut across the clear sky. My borrowed Boson was parked just outside, but now it had friends parked in adjacent spaces—a Volvo station wagon, a Maserati, a Ford truck.

I dragged the drapes shut and picked through strewn clothing and dressed myself in my crumpled threads—a faded forest green button-up under a gray herringbone suit. I couldn't find my hat. Instinct told me it wasn't worth the effort to look. Before heading out, I checked myself in the mirror. I looked about as fresh as a man who'd spent a winter's night in a lion's cage. Good enough. I smoothed my hair down and walked out the door.

HAZY DAYLIGHT WARMED the pizzeria's tinted windows. In the half glow, every scrap of furniture and every shard of carpet glowed with a surprising newness—smooth crimson upholstery on the seat cushions, newly laid wood grain veneer on the tabletops, a freshly laid carpet. The telltale odor of stale beer and baking dough was gone, replaced by the pungent off-gas of newly installed carpet and a tang of fresh paint. Antony's had suffered a hideous makeover in my absence.

I crossed to the back of the parlor and stepped up to the bar. There was no one around, not even Randy asleep at his post. The television was off. The clock above the liquor rack read 6:43 p.m. I took a seat and waited. When nobody showed I got up and crossed to the kitchen door and pushed my head through. The kitchen was empty. I called to the back.

"Iris?"

Getting no answer, I stepped through. The kitchen wasn't just empty; it was shut down. I peered down a short hallway that led to a stock room at the rear. Employee lockers stood snug against the back wall, all of them closed. I walked down the row, opening any that didn't have a padlock. They were empty.

When I returned to the dining room, Iris was standing behind the bar in front of a running sink, scrubbing down a dozen pint glasses as if she had been there all along. I approached the bar and crawled onto my usual stool.

"Iris," I said with a bored drawl.

She glanced over her shoulder and smiled. She slapped the faucet off and dragged her hands down her apron and turned to the bar.

"Hey, John. What can I get you?"

"Do I have a tab that needs paying?"

"Not sure, I could check."

She backpedaled to the register and punched it open and peeked inside. Shaking her head she shut it again.

"I don't see anything," she said. "But that doesn't mean you don't."

"What's it mean?"

"It means I don't see anything," she said, fluttering her lids. "Can I get you a drink?"

"Sure," I said. "The usual."

She answered with a happy snort and hunched down to open the refrigerator. Her hand froze on the handle, and she laughed and dropped her head before looking back up.

"Sorry," she said. "Remind me?"

I waited a second to see if she'd remember but she didn't. I waved my hand. "You know what, forget it," I said. "I'm drinking too much anyway."

"You sure?"

"I'm sure."

She stood and leaned forward on her folded arms. "Takes a brave man to admit that."

"I wouldn't call myself brave."

She crossed her arms and pushed her hip into the bar. "You doing okay?" she said.

"Well enough," I said. "You have your phone on you?"

"Why?

"I think I know where she is."

"Who? Delia?"

I nodded and held out my hand. "Come on, I'll show you."

Iris hesitated, then walked to the cash register. She took up her phone and unlocked it before handing it over.

"No funny business," she said. "I'm low on data."

"Of course not."

As soon as the phone was in my hand, I turned it off and switched it back on to see the lock screen. A saturated landscape image of Mount Rainier at sunset, so lovely and generic it was probably a standard stock photo that came with the device.

"That's new," I said.

She cocked her head. "What is?"

I showed her the screen. "You had a picture of a pink rose here yesterday. What happened?"

Her face contorted for a second before settling back into a smile. "I changed it. Last night."

I snapped my fingers. "What am I saying," I said. "Not a pink rose. A purple violet."

"Right," she mumbled. "Like I said, I changed it."

I laid the phone down. "Makes sense," I said.

She eyed me strangely. "Do you need my phone or not?"

I sat up and pressed my hand to my breast to feel through the jacket. Still no cigarettes. I spun around on my stool and scanned the restaurant. I could see it so clearly now, what I had already felt. The falseness of this place. No ancient tobacco tints, no patina of human breath, no moldy corners, no grease stains or wear and tear on the fresh carpet. This wasn't Antony's, it was an ideal replica. I turned back to the bar and looked at my host. It wasn't Iris standing there, but some fidgeting facsimile who was now searching my face for the extent of my waking suspicion.

"I'm still inside the Forum, aren't I?" I said.

Iris drew her head back. Her chin bunched in folds. "The what?"

I slapped my palms against the bar and pushed off the stool. I looked around the restaurant, checking the details. It all seemed so obvious now, the artifice was undeniable.

"Still in the goddamned Forum."

Iris crossed her arms. "You sure you don't need a drink?"

"Who are you really?" I said. "Auntie? Locksley? Mikkonen?"

Iris did her best to look surprised, but the act was canned. "You're nuts," she laughed. "You know that?"

I laid both palms against the bar to feel the wood. It was too smooth, too perfect. I took a deep breath and let it out and gave the thing talking to me a hot look. "The real Iris knows my usual is a Kokanee," I said. "And she has a picture of a purple violet on her phone."

This Iris—whoever she was—opened her mouth but no words came. She just stood there, jaw hanging loose, tongue running over her bottom teeth. Then she shook her head and crossed her arms leaned back against the steel sink.

"Well, shit," she said. "We underestimated you."

"I'm not that smart. You're just sloppy."

Not-Iris held out an arm for self-examination. She raised her fingers and wiggled them. Then she crossed her arms again and shrugged

"You didn't give us much time."

"Is that my problem?"

"It will be."

"Is she safe?"

"Who?

"The real Iris. Tell me you didn't hurt her."

"Fuck off," she scowled. "Who do you think I am?"

"I used my three guesses. Do I get a fourth?"

"Take as many as you like."

I shook my head and slid off the stool. "I'm not in the mood, actually. I have places to be."

Walking to the door, I reached into my pocked. My passport wasn't there. My heart skipped. I pressed my hand to my chest then searched my other pockets.

"Shit."

I turned around. Not-Iris laughed. She reached beneath the bar and pulled up exactly what I was looking for. My passport flashed between her dirty fingers.

"I guess you want this?" she said.

"It would help."

Not-Iris dragged her chin back and forth. "You're not going anywhere 'til you give me exactly what I want."

"Delia."

"Delia what?"

"That's my fourth guess."

"Wrong again," Not-Iris growled. "Now hand over your Green Card."

I relaxed suddenly and started laughing. This clown was playing chess five moves ahead on someone else's game.

"You find this funny?" she sneered.

"I don't have a Green Card," I said. "I never did."

Not-Iris's face flushed and the veins in her neck bulged. She was getting tired of me. "So why the fuck did Mikkonen send you here, Stark."

The room froze over with an icy silence. Not-Iris knew my real name. That narrowed things down considerably.

"Why do *you* think I'm here?" I said.

"I know this is where Delia came with her colleagues. Scheming and planning for years and years. So how the hell do you fit in?"

"I wish I knew."

"You do know. Spill it."

Not-Iris's face bunched up like a ball of rubber bands and she bent sideways to reach under the bar. I stepped back, ready to run, but Not-Iris was faster. She had a gun, and it was loaded—a hefty hand cannon built for punching holes in the sides of buildings. I raised my hands just a little below my shoulder line, a noncommittal surrender.

Not-Iris sneered. "You talked to Mikkonen earlier, a real heart to heart. Then the first thing you did was come here. If you don't want to tell me why, it don't bother me none. But we'll find out why sooner or later."

My gut flipped at the idea of people turning Antony's upside down, innocents in a war they didn't sign up for.

"You're sniffing around the wrong hydrant, doggie," I said. "Antony's is just a nice place to have a strong drink."

"We'll see about that."

I was about to snark again, when someone interrupted.

"Don't bother with this one, Pike."

Not-Iris and I turned in unison. Standing at the kitchen door was a familiar beanpole with a fuzzy mustache and sleek long hair. It was Mikkonen, wearing a polyester disco shirt with a soaring lapel and pattern of yellow and green paisley swarms. He strode across the dining room, his bold blue eyes fixed on the woman. Not-Iris's eyes narrowed but the gun didn't stray from its bead on me.

"That's far enough, Mikko," she said. "Or this asshole gets it between the eyes."

Mikkonen stopped and fell into a wide stance like a gunfighter, his passport held like a surrogate pistol.

"You made a mistake, Citizen," he said calmly. "That disguise of yours is running on my code."

A twist of worry contorted Not-Iris's face. Mikkonen took another step. The gun swung from me to him.

"I guess you want the first taste of this," Not-Iris said.

"My code," he said. "Stolen from my theater. Line for line."

Mikkonen cocked his head to one side and lifted his passport. He retracted his thumb like a miniature cobra looming over the screen.

"I can shut you down, any time I like."

Not-Iris's eyes bulged in their sockets. "You son of a—"

Too late. Mikkonen tapped. Not-Iris shuddered, let out a throttled cry that jumped three octaves, and broke apart in a digital storm. Her body flattened and pixelated, as if she'd been absorbed by a television. A flickering series of longitudinal scan lines ran from head to toe. A second later she blinked out of existence, leaving a black void the exact shape of her body hanging in the air. A second later the void expanded, filling out the shape of a much larger person. Colors reappeared and soon there was a new image standing where Not-Iris had been. The image of a man—a man with a face I knew well. Muscle in a suit with sawdust for brains. It was Toots's stocky partner, Agent Wallace of the FBI.

Wallace flickered, then popped into three dimensions like a balloon inflating instantly. He had attained his true form, but the transition hitched, and his body seemed to reject the pose he had spawned with. His head jerked back, and his knees buckled, and his arms flung skyward like some celestial puppeteer bidding him dance. The gun he'd been pointing at Mikkonen spun from his hand and arced backward, smashing the neck of a top-shelf tequila before hitting the counter. It discharged on impact, a sound like a sledgehammer on an oil drum. I ducked, but the bullet had already passed me by. Wallace swayed woozily on his feet and shook his head, a fat pointer finger digging for the pain in his ear.

This was my window to move, a split-second safety valve. I clambered onto the footrest of the nearest stool and used it as leverage to launch myself over the bar top. Wallace turned, still confused. I rolled over the counter and fell behind the bar, sticking a sloppy three-point landing on the perforated floor mat.

Wallace perked up and searched the bar for something to hit me with. I scrambled to my feet to find the gun. The discharge had sent it spinning back to the cash register where it was hanging perilously off the counter's edge. I lunged and fell short, hitting the floor. My hands broke my fall just as something exploded above me against the side of a cupboard. Shards of glass showered my head like a jagged hail. Raising an arm to shield myself, I looked up. The stray gun was peeking over the counter. I reached again, pushing myself up.

"Son of a bitch!" Wallace roared.

I hooked the barrel between my index and middle finger and fell back down. The gun fell with me. Tucking my shoulder in, I landed hard on my side and somehow the gun settled in my hands. Pulling it close, I rolled onto my back. Wallace was at the other end of the bar, reaching for another pint grenade. Before he could wind up another pitch, the grip was in my hand. My finger hooked the trigger. Wallace cocked his arm. I had no choice.

The gun bucked and roared, punching a hole in the ceiling just above the big man. Wallace flinched and the pint dropped from his hand and shattered behind him. I dragged myself to my feet, holding the gun steady.

"Hands up," I said hoarsely. "And back off."

Wallace dragged his arms skyward and sneered. He was pissed off, but he wasn't desperate. He took a few giant steps backward and gave the bottles in the rack a sidelong glance. I raised the gun higher and tugged the hammer with my thumb, but it slipped off. It caught the second time and clicked.

"One wrong move," I said, "And you get a new skylight."

Wallace gurgled with a hateful laugh. "First time you ever held a gun, Stark?"

"Shut up and walk."

When we were free of the bar, I flicked a look at Mikkonen. He was on the ground, bunched against the frame of the kitchen door. He had a sour look and one hand clapped over his left shoulder. A racing stripe of blood ran down the arm and dripped to the floor. Hit by the first discharge. I looked back at Wallace. He had backed into the corner of the room and was crossing his arms and grinning stupidly, the look of a man who'd just eaten a baby and liked it.

"Wasn't me," he grunted.

"Mikkonen," I said, watching Wallace. "How is it?"

"Hurts like hell," he gasped. "This might be a permadeath theater."

I stepped sideways to close the distance between us.

"Permadeath?" I said.

"In most theaters, taking a fatal bullet would kick you back to the Atrium. In a permadeath theater, it's brain death."

"Why the fuck is that an option?" I said.

Mikkonen winced and rolled his injured shoulder. "Some experiments demand the possibility of actual death to be effective."

"Fucking science," I said.

Eyeing Wallace, I hooked my free hand under Mikkonen's good shoulder and hoisted him to his feet. He rose with a gasp and steadied himself. Wallace stewed in the corner, watching us with a laconic leer.

"Is this one of your theaters, Wallace?" I said. "A place to get rid of people you find inconvenient?"

"You're not my lawyer," he scowled. "I ain't saying shit."

He was playing tough, but his eyes never left the gun in my hand. And he wasn't running.

"You're scared of this," I said, holding up the gun. "Tell me you're not."

"I'm not scared of nothing."

"If you weren't, you'd rush me. Maybe I'd shoot you. No worries. You'd just reappear somewhere else. But you're not doing that. You're frozen solid, thinking about how much a gun like this could hurt in a place like this."

Wallace tried to hold his grin, but there were little devils on his shoulder pulling his cheeks to the floor. I took a step and leveled the barrel at his face.

"I'd like my passport back," I said.

"Fuck you."

I fired. A close shot that kissed his aura. Wallace flailed, his arms curling over his head, and he collapsed in a heap. I waited. Still on the floor, his elbows parted, and he peeked through. The barrel stared back.

"The passport," I said. "Or the next one rents that tiny room in your head."

Wallace shuddered with adrenaline-soaked anger. He clambered to his feet and reached into his pocket and pulled up my passport. It gleamed cleanly. He flicked it like a playing card across the room, and it sailed past me, clattering beneath some chairs.

"Aw," he said flatly. "Not again."

"Mikkonen," I said over my shoulder. "Where's the portal?"

"Do you know where the Burlington shuttle would be?"

"Just down the street."

"It's there."

"Good. Open the front door. This guy is going for a walk."

Mikkonen heard the order, but hesitated. He looked worried. "Are you letting him go?"

"Not a chance."

Mikkonen nodded and peeked under the hand clapped to his shoulder. Then he shuffled to the front of the restaurant. I took a few steps back and waved Wallace ahead.

"After you."

Wallace looked around for a different option. There wasn't one. He fell into an unhappy cant, like a hobbled horse. His head tracked me as he passed.

"You're too late," he growled. "You gave it away."

"We'll see about that."

He scowled and moved past. When he was well ahead, I swung wide and snapped up my passport from the floor and followed. Mikkonen had already stepped outside and was holding the door open. Early evening light poured in like melting sorbet. Wallace shambled through, stepping into the bright. His arm jumped to shield his eyes, and he looked around. I could see his gears turning. Before he could split, I stuffed the gun between his shoulder blades.

"See that Boson," I said. "That's you."

I pointed. Wallace looked and took an angry breath and walked on. When I reached the car, I veered to one side and spoke some magic words.

"Trunk open."

The Boson's rear hatch lifted with a sarcastic hiss. Wallace looked gravely at the vacant trunk, then turned his furious eyes on me.

"You're not fucking serious," he said.

"I am fucking serious."

"I won't fit."

"You will," I said, prodding him with the gun. "One way or another."

He bared his browning teeth and grumbled and raised a leg just high enough to drag it over the lip of the trunk. Then he tipped forward and poured himself inside. I pressed the barrel of the gun against his second loafer and pushed. Wallace balled his fists and pulled them to his chest. He looked like a baby stuffed into a suitcase. When I reached for the hatch to close it, he snarled.

"You think you can get away with this?" he screamed. "I'm FBI. You're a video game cop."

"I'll take that risk."

I slammed the hatch. He roared a litany of attenuated obscenities that somehow sounded nice behind so much steel.

"Will you leave him there?" said Mikkonen.

I circled to the driver's side and opened the door. I set the heavy handgun on the seat, hoping it was enough weight to trick the sensor, and leaned in.

"Engine start."

The car lit up quietly, ready to roll.

"Drive to Seattle, FBI headquarters, no stops."

The dash screen illuminated with a map, course plotted. I slammed the door shut. The car pulled out of the space and rolled through the lot to the street where it waited for an opportunity to merge like a well-trained dog. Then it was off, down the street and gone.

Mikkonen looked confused.

"FBI. Was he serious?"

"He was."

"And he knew your real name."

"Sounds like you might too."

"Yes," he said. "For a long time now."

"How long?"

"We should rest for a moment."

I took a deep breath and sat down on the curb, palming my knees. Mikkonen sat beside me. We exchanged a mutual look of silent relief. His expression was empty but relieved, and there was something about his slight frame and innocent face and funny mustache that made me confident that the danger had passed.

"Is Delia okay?" I said finally.

"What do you mean by okay?"

"Christ. If I have to explain, the answer must be no."

"She is where she wishes to be." Mikkonen said, lifting his head and staring blankly at the horizon. "And if she wants to be found, she will allow it."

"I just want to know that she's safe."

"Is that true? That is all you wish to know?"

He didn't look at me, but the intensity of the question bore down on me like a dark pair of eyes. I said nothing and stood, and Mikkonen did too. We crossed the parking lot and hit the sidewalk and ambled north in the fading daylight. It was already darker than when we had stepped outside. We stopped at an intersection, waiting for the light to change in our favor. I looked around at the oversaturated unreality of this place—at the rows of tidy houses behind chain link fences, the canopy of trees rusting orange and red, the range of blue mountains beyond. And high above, a sky of waterlogged blue—a more-perfect-than-perfect replica of mundane reality.

By the time we reached the shuttle stop, the sun had slipped away, and the stars were floating overhead like sleepy fireflies. We marched up the stairs to the cube and down its central tunnel to the benches on the far side. The portal was right there, where the shuttle bus would have stopped in the real world. I offered Mikkonen the right of way, but he didn't move. He waited in silence, watching the horizon's final colors fade and cool.

A soft breeze brushed my face and fluttered my jacket. I closed my eyes to enjoy it. They got the wind right, I thought. Simulated or not, it felt good. Or was I just settling for second best? After so much time in the Forum, maybe I had grown to accept these artificial foundations and facades as real enough. Maybe I was a creature of the Forum at last, a shade in a world where *good enough* was good enough. The high fidelity of reality was no longer my high-water mark. Perfect had been our enemy all along.

Mikkonen took a deep breath, and through a long exhale, straightened up like a sunflower drinking in the light. He looked stronger now, and satisfied, though his eyes remained shadowed with fatigue. He prodded the browning wound at his shoulder.

"You all right?"

"A simulated injury," he said. "How strange."

"You won't take it with you I suppose." I nodded at the portal.

He flapped his arm and then seemed to forget about the wound entirely. "Certainly not," he said.

I crossed to one of the benches and sat and threw my arms back to buttress my wobbly frame. "So," I said. "What was that about paying a bar tab?"

He blinked a few times, then took a seat beside me. "I suspected someone was following you," he said. "Watching you move through the Forum. I needed a way to lure them out. It turns out I was correct."

"Why a bar tab?"

"Because you do need to pay off your tab."

I sat up and folded my hands in my lap. "I don't get it."

"You have a debt to pay at Antony's Pizzeria," he said drolly. "If you want to find Delia, I suggest you settle it."

I knuckled my closed eyes and shook my head to scare off a growing fatigue. "I'm not sure I understand, Mikko."

"I am not sure I do either."

"I don't have a tab at Antony's. I've been there twice in my life."

"I believe you. Nevertheless, this is what I have been asked to tell you."

"By who?"

A silence stretched between us. Mikkonen said nothing, keeping as still and silent as a Greek statue stripped of its paint. A milky, mute glossiness hovered behind his fixed eyes.

"All right," I said. "I'll see what I can do."

Mikkonen rose and gave a curt nod, then crossed to the portal. He stopped a foot before it and made a half turn. "If you manage it, I will meet you in the Atrium," he said. "Tomorrow, at any time."

"All right."

"I hope that is not too much to ask, considering all you've been through."

"Well," I shrugged. "We got the bad guy, didn't we?"

"Not all of them," he said. "But they never mattered anyway."

He gave a slight bow and then exited the theater, making no sound nor casting any shadows as he passed through the wall of light.

I counted to five and followed.

. . . An old writing chestnut argues that the climax of any good story should be surprising but inevitable. Locksley using This Little World as a fantasy bordello does not qualify as a good story—not surprising, certainly avoidable.

But his abuse of my work did prove a valuable lesson. It was a point Locksley and I had often discussed—new technology, given enough time, always strays from its originally intended function. Large-scale contact with reality will mutate its purpose into something both stranger and simpler. A lowest common denominator effect. I remember my father told me that when he was in college the internet was touted as the great information equalizer. Unfettered knowledge and wisdom for all the world. Now it's a morass of commercial activity and artificially generated lies. Bottom of the barrel shit. So it went with my poor theater. It began as a tool for confronting personal fears. It ended as an amplifier of prurient dreams.

But there was one tidy irony buried in this tragedy. In my quest to unmask Locksley, I finally hit on a new idea for a theater. The concept came fully formed, clearer than anything I had dreamed up before. When I told Mikkonen, he agreed to help. We got to work.

As the new theater came together, my urge to reconnect with old colleagues amplified. A psychic need for a dose of kinship. Something I hadn't felt in a while. So I started going to Antony's again, two or three nights a week.

Everyone in that little gang was still riding high on the Forum's success. In the years since its opening, they'd gone on to design countless new theaters, many of which were doing better than their originals. It was encouraging to see. Like witnessing the start of a new movement to which I was only peripheral. Their own Nouvelle Vogue.

But that didn't stop them from endlessly needling me for stories about my mystery project. Synge—now going by Saint—was always the most insistent.

Mikko says you're deep into something new, he said.

I am, I said.

Give us a pitch, he said.

Well, I said, swinging my empty bottle like a dinner bell. I have reduced my newfound dislike for surreals to a single word.

Beautiful, he said. Let's hear it.

Agency, I said.

Saint snorted. Only the essential quality of our medium, he said.

MG butted in. You want to make a theater that removes agency from the user? he said. Entirely?

I'm this close, I said, pinching a centimeter of empty air. When you give a user agency to act inside a theater, you are also giving them permission to act badly, or not at all. They can abuse the rules just for the fun of it. The absence of a rule is a rule. No human activity is immune to this behavior. Politics, games, cultural norms, automobile traffic, languages—it doesn't matter. In every case, rules are simply advisory. There is no moral obligation.

I get that, MG said. I had to shut down Horrorcore for exactly that reason.

That was yours? Francisco said, unnaturally surprised.

Over time, I continued, the novelty of any brilliant idea eventually wears off. People get bored. They push boundaries. They test theories. They break things just to prove they can. It's happening already. Everywhere in every theater. And that's a problem. If we're artists, anyway. Because an artist's job is to extrovert some aspect of their personality into the world. To show the world what it means to be them, one more unique human being among billions. One kind among many. That's the hardest, most honest job of all.

Right, Saint said. So what are you planning next?

I think I just told you, I said . . .

22

IT WAS MID-AFTERNOON when I stumbled into the natural sunlight of the real world, a light altogether too hard and yellow to pass for anything but a cheap downgrade of the Forum's syrupy vibrance. I was alone outside the gate, and it was too early to count on a shuttle being anywhere close by. I jogged over the tarmac lot and crossed the wooden bridge that spanned the river and stepped out onto the two-lane highway that led to Burlington and beyond. It was vacant in both directions with the same dead look as a dried lava flow. A ragged wind riffled the pine-furred mountains and filled the valley with a low groan, a sound close enough to the rumble of a running engine to give me pause.

I didn't have time to wait around. Someone was on their way to Antony's, and I was about seventy miles behind. I turned west and started walking, my hitching thumb cocked and ready to raise at the first westbound car.

Two hours later, my ride dropped me off outside Antony's. I pulled a twenty from my wallet and told the kid to spend it on weed. He thought that was funny and sped off laughing.

There were three cars parked out front of the restaurant—a beat-up blue coupe, a dusty black flatbed truck, and a spit-shined Ferrari Testarossa from the late twentieth century, vanilla white and gleaming like melted ice cream in the sun. If this car didn't belong to Wallace's accomplice, I'd eat it, tires and all.

I marched up to the front door, wound up with enough energy to kick it off its hinges. Out of courtesy, I opened it.

If someone had erected a gleaming lighthouse at the center of the restaurant with a million-candlepower halogen lantern blazing at its precipice, it would not have attracted more attention than the tonsured, tinsel curls and ruby red Hawaiian print shirt currently sitting at the bar making small talk. It was Pritchard Locksley, in town on a rare sabbatical from his virtual kingdom. He and Iris were deep in a conversation that was making her smile. She didn't even notice me until I was right behind him.

"Hey John," she said brightly. "We were just talking about you."

"He's a name dropper," I said, stepping in behind.

Locksley's shoulders stiffened and his head rose.

"Is that you, John Pike?"

I pushed into the bar and leaned forward with the sunniest smile this side of Mercury and turned toward the man. I barely recognized him in his real-world incarnation, a testament to the beautifying filters he was running inside the Forum. Outside he was ruddy and pockmarked with port-wine blemishes and flaking skin. Yellowed fingers thrummed against a bottle of Kokanee like two spiders racing up a wall. Two throbbing red lines ran across his cheekbones toward his ears, impressions made by the glossy oxymask hanging from his neck. An accessory that probably cost more than a year of my rent, it was the same milky color as the Ferrari outside. Probably the same brand too.

Sitting up straight, Locksley gave me a tired side-eye and took a dainty sip and wiped his lips with the thumb of a trembling hand.

"Heya, Pritch," I said. "Drinking local?"

He lifted the bottle and looked at it like it had just appeared in his hand. Then he gestured at Iris.

"The lady recommended it," he said.

Iris beamed. "I said it was your usual," she said.

I pulled a stool out and sat.

"How long you been here?" I said.

Locksley sighed and his head dropped. He began to laugh. "Not long enough."

Iris smiled and bounced a look between the two of us. "How do you two know each other?"

"Well, let's see," I hummed, looking Locksley over. "We work for the same boss, we both like low gravity entertainment, and we have a mutual fondness for Orson Welles's films. Especially the noir stuff. *The Stranger*, *Touch of Evil*, and that other one with the blond redhead."

I tapped my fingers on the bar. Locksley played dumb.

"What's the name?" I said.

"You got me."

"With Rita Hayworth, you don't know that one?"

Pritchard glared at me, and we locked eyes for a long time and to his credit the man did not break. But this charade was boring me. I faced forward and slapped the bar.

"How about a Scotch." I said. "Something fancy."

Iris nodded and turned, sifting through the bottles.

"Something fancy," she mumbled.

"Wallace is a good brand," I said. "Strong and simple." I looked back at Locksley. "You want a glass of Wallace, Pritch? It goes down easy."

Locksley's face drained and he bared his teeth. "Shit."

He stood, kicking his stool back, and scooped his coat off the stool beside him. Iris was still fiddling with the well. She held up a bottle with a peach label.

"Nothing called Wallace," she said. "But Maker's is popular."

"That'll do," I said, still watching Locksley.

Iris brought the bottle to the bar. When she saw Locksley putting on his coat she slapped on a frown. "Finished already?"

"He is," I said. "But he may not realize it."

Locksley ignored us and yanked the zipper to the middle. He pulled out his wallet and threw a hundred-dollar bill on the bar.

"This should cover it," he said.

Iris nodded. "More than enough."

She plucked it up and moved to the register and made it ring. Locksley started walking, steam shooting from his ears.

Iris looked back, hand over the till. "Your change?"

"Don't bother."

Iris looked at me. I put a finger to my lips. When Locksley was almost at the door, I gave him a parting gift.

"He's FBI," I shouted. "Did you know that?"

Locksley froze, his hand reaching for the door. I stepped away from the bar and walked to the front of the restaurant. "Was he Rita too?" I said ponderously. "Or was that some other lackey on your payroll? Doing her damnedest to squeeze a Green Card from me?"

Locksley grimaced and turned away, lurching like a car with the clutch locked. I was two steps away now, staring at the bush of his glinting gray curls. He shifted on his feet and tensed up. Maybe he thought I was going to hit him. I wanted to.

"The funny thing is," I continued, "I don't have a Green Card. In fact, I was hoping you might be able to swing me one."

He shrugged with some annoyance. "Whatever strange fantasy you're acting out," he said, "It's got nothing to do with me."

I stepped closer and he reared back. "Here's my real question," I whispered. "Are you working for Wallace? Or is he working for you?"

"I don't know anyone by that—"

"I'm patient, not stupid. Which is it, Pritch?"

"No comment."

"Fair enough," I said brightly. "Just stay out of my way and steer clear of the Forum for a few days. If I don't see you, I'll tell my friends in DC that you're running a tight ship. Updated with facts friendly to you."

"Facts," he said flatly.

I looked him over then took a generous step backward so he could feel some measure of freedom from my goading. It seemed to help. He took a long breath that rattled on the way out. His shoulders drooped as he blew, tension sliding off his back like a satin robe. When he turned around he looked almost friendly.

"You want to know the facts?" he said.

"If you know any."

He looked back at Iris behind the bar. "Not here," he said before turning and pushing through the door.

I looked at Iris and held up two fingers. "Two minutes," I mouthed. She nodded and I went out.

Locksley stood in front of the vanilla Testarossa, gazing across its roof at a cluttered horizon of telephone poles and power lines and rooftop air-conditioning units. I looked down at our smeared silhouettes reflected in the waxy hood. He was fidgeting in a way he couldn't control.

"Yes," he mumbled. "I've been looking for Delia Walsh. I'm worried about her."

"You know what? I believe you."

"It's true."

"I know you know her pretty well," I said. "You worked with her for years. My read is that something happened between you. Something ugly. And now you feel bad."

Locksley's chin hardened like a walnut, and his nether lip began to tremble. He slammed his hands into his pockets to steady them.

"I have nothing but the highest respect for Delia Walsh."

"High enough to prevent her father from finding her?"

"I didn't say that."

"Wallace would have told you why I was here."

"Yes."

"But you had to find her yourself."

He took a long time to answer. "Yes."

"Knowing her father might never know where she was."

"I would have told him."

"You say that now . . . "

Locksley's face twisted with rage. "Because it's fucking true," he said. "Senator Walsh and I are close friends. I would never hold back from him."

"Okay," I nodded. "But as far as I can tell, Delia doesn't want to be found. I wonder why that is?"

Locksley worked hard to maintain a statuesque defiance, but within seconds he shrank and shook his head. He was searching for a way out of his own past, but for that he'd need a time machine.

"Yes, I crossed a line," he said. "It didn't feel like it at first. But when she found out, she made it abundantly clear that I'd fucked up. That's when she pulled the plug. Sabotaged everything she'd accomplished."

"This Little World?"

Locksley nodded. "She struck gold. She made it possible to push the Forum to places we'd never dreamed. The whole damn thing runs on her code now. But she didn't see that as a victory. Maybe she was right."

"Right about what?"

Locksley chewed on his lower lip for a moment, working through a layman's answer for me. "She saw the fatal flaw, right from the start. I should have too, but I couldn't help myself."

"The flaw in what?"

"In us, our species." He paused and pressed his fist to his lips and swallowed air. Then he cleared his throat. "Delia warned me countless times. The reason you built this place, she told me, is not the reason it will endure. It will open a Pandora's box of idiocy, petty amusements, and perversions. Of lowest common denominator debauchery. It's a cycle as old as human history." He held up his hand and stared at his raised thumb. "Like sub-dermal implants, she told me. You know this story . . . ?"

I looked at my own thumb and the jagged white scar that hid nothing. "Tell me," I said.

"When subdermal implants were introduced a decade ago, peopled hailed them as a revolution in personal data security."

"I remember."

"Do you remember the violent amputations that followed? Men and women losing their thumbs to desperate thieves with bolt cutters? Criminals trading key rings of thumbs like USB sticks?"

"All too well."

"Subdermal implants were invented to free us of one burden. But their adoption created another. So it goes with all innovations. In technology, in politics, in life—a problem solved is another problem made. We live on a hamster wheel of brinksmanship that will not end until we innovate ourselves to death. Delia knew her first surreal would suffer the same fate, and she was right. About the Forum too . . ."

He looked at his thumb again and tucked it away under his fingers, an embarrassed little fist.

"How about I cut to the chase," I said. "If you had a Green Card could you find her right now?"

He shook his head. "She was working on something new, but she never told me what."

"If you're looking for a Green Card, you believe she's hidden away in a classified theater."

"I do," he nodded. "It's the only thing that makes sense."

I stepped off the curb and walked the length of the Testarossa, eating it up with a hungry look. "It must sting," I said. "Pritchard Locksley, the man who shepherded Delia's career, who gave her every opportunity, now a pariah without a clue where she is or what she's doing."

He pressed his palms to his eyes, as if massaging the memories of a time long gone. Then he lifted his chin in an attempt to regain some pride.

"It's true I supported her," he said. "I built her up. I saw genius at work. But she hated what I needed to do to keep the Forum running."

"Sell it out?"

His lip curled. "You sound like her."

"More than one person told me her ideas ran contrary to what you and her father were aiming for."

"That's not how I'd put it."

"How then?"

"The Forum is my life's work," he said, nostrils flaring. "My magnum opus. And it will only get bigger, day by day. That is my legacy. That is our legacy, mine and Delia's and everyone else who helped put this together. Nothing they have done or could ever do would change my mind about that."

"Of course."

"You don't believe me?"

"I do believe you. What I don't understand, is what her father would be so worried about."

"James Walsh is one of the few senators with a long-term vision. He knows how much the Forum will be worth when it weans itself off the public teat and goes private."

"Something Delia doesn't want?"

Locksley sighed and looked at me with a melting sadness.

"Delia is a contrarian. And she pushes things to their limits." He paused and shuddered, like a man who might regret what he's about to say. "Her father is worried that her more recent work might sour the public's perception of the Forum. That people might see it as a dangerous and unstable place. Something that might get you lobotomized or killed."

"Worried that his daughter might ruin a big investment?"

"Something like that."

"What about you?"

"I don't care what Delia does. There's room in there for everybody."

"The porno hustlers and the theoretical physicists and everybody in between."

Locksley nodded and stooped his shoulders. "Look, I'm tired," he said. "And I've said more than enough."

"You have," I said. "Thank you."

I straightened up and walked past him toward the restaurant.

"She's a willful woman," he shouted. "Always ten steps ahead."

"Maybe we should leave her there," I said. "In the lead."

"Maybe."

"As far as our other friend goes, I'd steer clear of Wallace for a while. He won't be happy the next time you see him."

"Where is he now?"

"Halfway between here and nowhere."

Locksley yawned. "Actually, I'd rather not know." He fished a fob from his pocket and clicked it. The Testarossa chirped. "Goodbye, Mr. Pike. Enjoy the rest of your stay."

He circled to the driver's side, pulling his oxymask over his head. He opened the door and tossed the mask inside and followed after. The door shut on its own. The car barked once and roared, growling like an amorous lion. It shot backward through a tight curve and rebounded, speeding through the lot. I watched until it leapt onto the road and blasted down the arterial. I went back inside.

A bourbon waited for me in a neat tumbler on a cocktail napkin with a glass of water and a second glass of ice nearby. Iris was washing dishes again. She pretended not to see me as I took a stool. Down the bar, old Randy lay like a lump of strewn laundry atop the counter, fast asleep. I set my hat on the counter and unbuttoned my jacket and lifted the glass. I sniffed and sipped and swished it around to coat my teeth. When I looked up Iris was staring at me. She gestured at the door with a soapy hand.

"That was weird," she said.

"It sure was."

"You gonna tell me why?"

"One of these days."

She wiped her hands on her apron then removed it entirely and hung it from a hook on the wall. "I doubt I'll care tomorrow," she said.

I took a sip and set the glass down and cleared my throat.

"Do I have a tab that needs paying?" I said.

Iris tilted her head. "I don't think so," she said. "You always pay cash."

I nodded. "That's what I thought."

Iris ran her wrist across her nose and grabbed a few drying pints and began stacking them. Watching her work, I knocked back half my bourbon. A sweet caramel burn ran down the length of my tongue, just the way I liked it. Cradling the glass, my thoughts drifted to Delia and the day we'd spent together. I wondered if there was something I'd missed from that day—a scrap of conversation or a key detail—but I couldn't think of anything. I hated this part of the job. When facts were scant and memory alone was the key to cracking a case. Four years of drinking and dwelling on the past had transformed my memory of our encounter into an ideal version of itself. For all I knew, Delia Walsh didn't even remember Kennedy Stark.

But if she did—

"What about Kennedy Stark," I said. "Does he have a tab?"

Iris froze for a second, her mouth agape and her eyes roaming over my face. Then she crossed to the register and punched it open. Pulling the tray from the drawer, she took out a small, white envelope folded over on itself. She brought it to the bar and unfolded it in front of me. Scrawled across the sealed flap someone had written *For Kennedy Stark* in a blocky font.

"Last time Delia was in, she asked me to hold this," Iris said. "Said I was to give it to the man who asked for it by name."

I took up the envelope and held it, reading and rereading my name in a hand that must have been Delia's. She hadn't forgotten. I stuffed my finger between the flap and the body and tore it open with an upward hook and blew inside. The envelope yawned open. Inside was something thin and stiff. I pulled it out, a smooth green shingle of plastic the same size as a Forum passport and just a few millimeters thick. No distinguishing marks. Affixed to the card was a yellow stickie with a message in the same handwriting as on the envelope.

I remembered. Did you forget?

"About what you expected?" Iris said.

I laughed loud and painfully, happy tears swelling behind the hurt. "I don't know what I expected."

Iris scooped up her dishrag. "Well, if you do see her, tell her we said hello."

"I will."

Iris moved to the end of the bar and started wiping it down. I turned the inscrutable card over and over in my hand. It bore no marks whatsoever, no indication of which theater it might activate. Maybe I'd understand more once I was back in the Forum. But I had to act fast. There was always a risk that Wallace would return, with or without Locksley's blessing.

I slid the card back in the envelope and tucked it away in my jacket and finished my drink in celebration. As the whiskey went down, a strobing light from the television caught my eye. Another ad for the imminent Mars landing. Touchdown was in two days, around 9:00 p.m.

Iris caught me watching with longing. She leaned on the bar with a locked arm, and tilted her head toward the TV.

"Living on Mars," she sighed. "It's never gonna last."

"You don't think?"

She yawned and shook her head. "I watched a documentary about it a couple weeks ago. Seven hundred years is too long to wait. We'll all be dead in, like, a hundred."

"What happens in seven hundred years?"

"They said that's how long it would take to . . . what's the word they used? To make it more like Earth."

"Terraform?"

She snapped her fingers. "Terraform, yeah. You're smart."

"They said it will take seven hundred years to terraform Mars?"

"Yeah, if they started, like, today. Because they have to melt all the ice, and then build some kind of giant space condom to block radiation from the sun. Because the sun's rays knock away the atmosphere. And then they have to turn the dirt from red to brown or whatever. It's a huge job."

I shrugged. "You have to start somewhere."

Iris laughed randomly and straightened up. "No you don't."

"What do you mean?"

"We could decide the Earth was worth saving. Use all that fancy technology and stay down here."

We both looked back at the TV. The Mars ad was long gone.

"I wish that were true," I said.

"Isn't it?"

"I don't have high hopes."

Her eyes narrowed. "Would you live on Mars if you could?"

"Definitely."

"Why?"

"A change of scenery. A change of purpose."

Iris nodded, fascinated at the creature sitting across from her. A snuffling grunt drew her attention away. It was Randy, face down, twitching and mumbling incoherent syllables.

Iris touched his shoulder. "Randy, you okay?"

Randy sat up with a snap. "VC in the bush," he barked. "Get the fuck down!"

Iris squealed. "Jesus, Randy. You're nuts."

"Hold on," I said firmly. "Did you just say VC?"

Iris raised a hand to her mouth. "He dreams a lot."

Randy shook the last of his sleep away and smacked his lips and swiped his cheek with a floppy hand. Iris set a beer in front of him and he snatched it up on instinct and drank. When he slammed the bottle back down he looked around. I snapped my fingers to get his attention. He looked at me, unable to focus.

"What did you just say?" I said. "VC?"

He blinked and squinted. "When?"

"You said VC. You yelled it. *VC in the bush.* You mean Viet Cong?"

His eyes narrowed as he reached for his beer. "That's classified," he said.

"Come on man, that's bullshit."

He took another sip. "It's not bullshit," he said. "I was deployed near Keh Sanh. Won't say where though. They could lock me up."

My stomach twisted and a dull pain shot from my belly to my head, kicking me off my stool.

"Jesus Christ, Randy," I said. "Are you telling me you fought in Vietnam?"

He sniffled and bent forward, his voice low and hoarse. "'Nam and Laos. But like I said," he winked, "That's classified."

I stepped forward and clapped a hand on the back of his neck and squeezed with a slight pressure. There they were. Lodged against his spine just below the skin. Two tiny capsules. SR contacts.

"Fucking unbelievable," I mumbled.

Randy flailed his arms, trying to shoo me off. "Hey!" he shouted. "Fuck you and get your fucking hands off me."

I stepped back. "You run military surreals, Randy? You got a fondness for the classics?"

Randy gurgled and stuffed the neck of the bottle into his mouth and mumbled something around it.

Iris frowned. "What's going on?"

"SR identity delusion," I said "He thinks he fought in Vietnam. Almost a century ago."

Iris looked back at Randy and wrinkled her nose. "Oh . . ."

I stood there just staring at Randy, seeing him now as the sort of guy I'd be paid to pull out of a surreal if anyone cared to pony up the fee. But even he didn't know what was wrong with himself. This was a whole new side to an industry that was already at ease with a small percentage of casualties paving its long road to success. Now more than ever I wanted out. Out of the industry and off the planet.

I pushed my drink aside unfinished. With a curt goodbye, I walked out.

. . . *Work on my new theater took longer than I expected. More than three years after the Forum's opening we were still working through some of the more difficult hurdles. But I was focused. Determined. And nobody was interfering. That was surprising.*

Locksley had all but vanished actually. I hadn't seen him for months, inside or outside. Lucky me. I heard rumors that he was spending more of his time outside the country, courting international investors and God knows what else. A petty part of me wanted to believe he was avoiding me, but what improvement would that fact make to my life? I was lucky to be free of him, one way or another.

That luck ran out eventually. Guys like Locksley can't tolerate defeat for too long. The next time I saw him, he had convinced himself that he was the aggrieved party. That he was the one who deserved an apology.

I'd parked my car a block from my apartment and was walking home when I heard a man shouting my name at some distance. A hoarse feral sound. When I reached my building I stopped short of the front stoop. Locksley was standing at the top, loose limbed and wavering, leaning forward against the windowed door. I could smell alcohol from a distance of maybe fifteen feet. As I watched he began pounding his forehead against the reinforced glass with a slow steady repetition. There were cracks in the glass already, a spidery radial pattern. After a dozen hits he shouted my name again and begged me to open the door. I backed off, putting a parked car between us for safety. Locksley beat the door with a meaty fist and screamed my name a third time. Then he reached for the door's handle and gave it a slap. It spun freely on its axis. Broken. At that point I walked away and circled the building to the rear. I snuck in through the back door and entered my first floor apartment without him catching sight of me. I moved to my bedroom and listened through the window. Over the next few minutes he screamed my name continuously. Eventually he left the stoop and wandered up and down the sidewalk, wobbling and pacing. I stayed still in the darkness of my room, obscured. He paced the sidewalk for a few minutes, then crossed the street. He picked up something from the opposite sidewalk and staggered back. It was a loose brick. I recognized it just in time to flee into the hallway.

The window broke with a terrible crash. That's when I called the police. Throughout my call, he screamed my name. I was lucky the window stood eight feet off the street. He had no way of entering. And he was lucky too. The broken glass would have torn his hands to shreds. He just stood outside, ranting and bawling until the police arrived. They scooped him up and hauled him away. I came out only after he was gone to answer questions.

Do you know this man? said the officer.

He's my boss.

Do you have any kind of relationship with him? he asked. Outside the office.

We don't, I said.

Would he say the same? the officer said.

I'm sure that man is capable of saying anything.

I'm not sure what that means, the officer said. Do you or don't you have a romantic relationship?

My jaw tightened so hard that my teeth hurt.

We most definitely do not . . .

23

I DROVE THE BOSON BACK to the Forum just after dark and parked out front. I had no time to lose and no interest in following their protocols. I hurried down the long staircase and pushed through the main portal. It was the latest I'd ever been inside. I thought maybe I'd walk into the middle of some after-hours audience. A coked-up, bleary-eyed coterie of nighthawks gathering for the commencement of an evening of sadomasochist activities, or a sect of digital pagans preparing for an evening seance. But as I prowled the Atrium in a simulated dusk light, the Forum appeared mostly as it always had. The same hush, the same sparse crowds halfway between one adventure and the next. Only the simulated sky had changed, tuned to a cooling navy night to match the state of the outside world. It was the first time I had noticed the influence of reality on the Forum's functioning. The central Atrium was as close as one could get to the outside without being there.

I found Mikkonen easily, stretched on his back on one of the perimeter benches, staring up at a simulated Milky Way as it sparkled in the darkening canopy. When he heard me coming he turned his head and raised his hand. I waved back. He looked skyward again and drew his hands up over his sternum. I took a seat by his bare feet.

"Waiting long?" I said.

"Not really."

"It took me a while to sort things out."

"I have not been in this Atrium for quite some time," he said. "Tonight, I watched the sun set from here. A simulated sun, but very well rendered in my opinion. I find it fascinating to let time slip past like this. A slow, relentless draining."

"When was the last time you were outside?"

He raised up on his elbows and looked at me down the length of his thin frame. "I have never been outside."

It took me a moment to understand what he was saying.

"You're an AI," I said.

He cocked his head. "I assumed you knew."

I shook my head. "People said you and Delia were close friends. It never crossed my mind."

Mikkonen absorbed the observation. He laid back down and shut his eyes. "We worked together for a long time. It was the closest I have come to feeling what you would call friendship."

"I suppose Delia felt the same about you."

"I hope so. She was not fond of many in here."

"She seems like the sort of woman that turns unhappy clowns into suicidal muses."

Mikkonen nodded. "Insecure men desperate to martyr themselves on the altar of her indifference."

"I was just talking to one, actually."

Mikkonen smirked like a dead man waiting to wake at his funeral. "Pritchard Locksley," he said.

"Easy guess."

"An unpleasant overlord."

"Pretty sure he and Wallace were working together," I said. "Hoping to squeeze a Green Card out of me."

Mikkonen ruminated for a moment, staring at his hands. Then he spun sideways and sat up, his eyes dark and intense. "Classified theaters are the one thing Locksley has no control over inside the Forum. But he is working very hard to overcome that limitation."

"What happened between him and Delia?"

"The details are not mine to share," he said. "I will say that Delia was smart enough to keep him at arm's length. But he made her and many others very uncomfortable."

"And then she disappeared," I said. "I don't like the timing."

"Only to work on her new theater," he reassured me.

"Is that where she is now?"

Mikkonen considered his answer carefully. "If she is anywhere, yes," he said.

Another evasive answer, the latest of many. But this one sounded sincere. I pulled out my Green Card and held it between us.

"Will this get me access?" I said.

Mikkonen's eyes brightened. He nodded. "Yes."

"How does it work?"

"It attaches to the back of your passport. A simple magnet."

"And how do I find the theater?"

"There's the rub. You'll have to discover that for yourself."

"You don't know it?"

He unhooked his hands and ran both palms over the top of his head like he was taking a warm shower. "I helped Delia build the framework for her theater. And I know its purpose, but she never told me the final name, nor its location."

I looked down at the Green Card. I turned it over in my hand. "Why wouldn't she tell you?"

"I think this little game she's been playing goes some way to answering that question."

"You consider all this a game?"

"It feels like one, no? The clues, the passwords, the intrigue. I believe Delia was well aware of what might happen following her disappearance." Mikkonen stretched and straightened up. His eyes narrowed and his lips pursed. "Even if I knew the name of her theater, even if I had a Green Card as you now do, I could not enter. There is a fundamental incompatibility between what I am and what Delia is."

"AI versus human?"

"Correct."

"Looks like I'm the man for the job then."

"It seems so."

I turned the card over and showed him the yellow stickie. "There's a note here . . ."

I remembered. Did you forget?

"Any idea what it means?"

Mikkonen smiled. "How obscure. Unfortunately, I do not. You might try our personal laboratory. For privacy, we did much of our research and testing in a theater called 4M. I have already given you the necessary permissions."

"A theater called Forum?"

"The number 4, the letter M. A pun."

"Forum. Right. And what is that exactly?"

"Just what it sounds like. A fully operational Forum within the Forum."

"You're kidding."

Mikkonen squeezed out a robotic, staccato laugh. "It always sounds supernatural to non-Engineers," he said. "But like all sufficiently powerful computational platforms, the Forum is Turing-complete. It can replicate a second version of itself within itself. With enough time, one could build a Forum within a Forum within a Forum, *ad infinitum*. Each generation suffers a slight loss of computing speed, but it is perfectly legitimate."

"Okay. So let's say I visit 4M. What am I looking for?"

"Enter 4M and navigate to a theater called *The Dungeon*. It was our workshop for many years, away from prying eyes. Where she tested her final build before migrating it to a classified location."

"You think the clue to her new theater is somewhere in your old workshop?"

He shrugged stiffly, as if it were an animation he chose to play at that specific moment, and not something he casually felt. "Delia told me the answer was close at hand. But I haven't looked, knowing that I could never visit for myself, knowing that this theater was not intended for me."

Knotted by excitement, my stomach rumbled.

"All right," I said. "Let's try this."

He rose and we walked in silence to the nearest portal a hop away. I pulled up my passport and tapped through to the search field. I typed 4M. It appeared alone in the search results. I pressed it and the lintel above the portal lit up.

"Okay," I said. "We're in business."

Mikkonen smiled a crooked smile and his mustache quivered. "*The Dungeon*. Remember."

I pocketed my passport and for some reason gave him a thumbs up. He returned the gesture without irony.

"Good luck," he said.

I ENTERED 4M, stepping from one Atrium to another. It felt like I had simply taken a giant step sideways in the same location. The Atrium of 4M was identical in all ways to the Forum's Atrium—its brusque Hellenic strokes, its airy expansiveness, its antiseptic calm—and yet something was markedly different. There was a low hum that suffused the place, hardly audible yet deeply felt. The whole place seemed to flicker with the same swirling warmth as a grainy strip of celluloid film. It was hard on the eyes, and my first steps made me nauseated. I stopped to reorient myself. Massaging my temples, I looked for something in the distance to fix on. I settled on a pair of Citizens about fifty yards away, standing just outside one of the countless preview portals with the familiar large screens suspended above them. They were talking and gesticulating with spastic gestures and jerky movements, as if trapped in the nitrate of an early-twentieth-century silent film. A mesmerizing but uncanny look.

It took a moment to sync my brain with the frame rate of this Forum-within-a-Forum. When I moved forward, the sensation was akin to marching along the bottom of a swimming pool. My motions were recognizable, but wholly alien to experience.

I pulled up my passport again. It looked somewhat blockier in my hand, rendered at a slightly lower resolution than my original. I pulled up the search engine and typed in *The Dungeon*. It popped up in a list that included *Sex Dungeon*, *Dungeons and Devils*, *The Dungeon Masters*. I cued up and locked it in. The lintel above the portal didn't illuminate right away, a symptom of the truncated speed of 4M. But when it did, I was ready.

CONTRARY TO THE NAME, *The Dungeon* was a cozy and eclectic space. A room about the size of four train cars stacked side by side with a ceiling around twelve feet high, it looked like a carpenter's workshop from a steam-powered century. The walls and floors, beams and pilings, were all made of a smooth and smoky oak, held in place by iron nails and finely cut mortises. A central, square pillar about five feet wide on each side had built-in shelves from floor to ceiling, every one stacked with books and boxes and spiral-bound notebooks.

This rustic underlying framework was offset a few centuries by a collection of state-of-the-art computer equipment scattered around the room. One side was entirely obscured by a wall of LED monitors arranged in a gentle concave like the inside of an insect's compound eye. There were swooping strands of fiber-optic cables strung like cybernetic cobwebs from one end of the room to the other. Tucked away under rough-hewn tables and benches were sleek black computers with blinking lights and humming fans.

I walked slowly through the space, floorboards creaking. Flowering plants and shrubs in small pots added another vector of beauty, alongside the heads of stuffed animals. Amid moist orchids and arching ferns and rustling ficus plants, more than two dozen taxidermy trophies populated the space. Many were affixed to the high beams that crossed the high ceiling, others stood on sturdy pedestals in unobtrusive nooks—an American black bear, an inquisitive beaver, a shy fox, an impossibly large moose, a stoic wolf, a wary snake. A strong smell hung in the gelatinous air, a swirling bouquet that fused the acrid tang of overheating computers with the dusty musk of animal fur.

I turned to the wall of monitors. There was a desk off to one side, cluttered with books without dust covers, dog-eared journals, pens, notebooks, loose sheets of paper, stained coffee mugs and a few empty bottles of beer. The papers were marked up with hastily scribbled notes and figures and equations, a frenetic variation of the handwriting on the envelope addressed to me. I read what I could, but there was nothing personal here—just the inscrutable symbols of a coder at work. Nothing I could follow. After a few minutes of pawing at the mess, I succeeded only in tidying it up. A neat little stack of papers and books to mark the progress of my investigation.

Stepping sideways, a reflection of light from the darkest corner of the desk grabbed my attention. I stared at the space, but the shadows there were impenetrable. I stepped closer, squinted, and reached for something squarish. My fingers tapped a smooth glassy surface, and the object fell back with a clatter. I clawed around until it was in my hand and pulled it into the light.

It was a framed text, half a dozen lines of verse printed on a thick paper with an elegant serif font. I tilted it to find a better light.

My brain I'll prove the female to my soul,
My soul the father; and these two beget
A generation of still-breeding thoughts,
And these same thoughts people this little world,
In humours like the people of this world,
For no thought is contented.

WM. SHAKESPEARE, RICHARD II,
ACT 5, SCENE 5, LINES 6–11

The sense of Shakespeare's poetry had always eluded me, and it was no different here. But the source of Delia's early inspiration was plain as day—This Little World, taken from this soliloquy. I read and reread the lines with the hope of dislodging some secret meaning, but I couldn't make heads or tails of them. For all I knew, this was simply a keepsake, a memento from Delia's past, not a hint at the future. I set the frame down gently, exactly where I'd found it and continued my search.

Opposite the bulwark of monitors was a wall entirely obscured by a heavy curtain. A long narrow table with two chairs was arranged before the curtain in such a way as to give a perfect view of whatever lay beyond. I glanced at the wings and looked for the drawstring, but saw nothing. On the long table were two keyboard and mouse pairs, both plugged into computer workstations nearby. Between them was a large gray box with five mushroom-style push buttons built in, each one a different color—Yellow, Green, Orange, Blue, and Red—and a black pointer knob with two settings labeled *Open* and *Close*. It was currently set to *Close*.

I switched the pointer knob to *Open*. The curtain jerked and split down the center and the two halves swayed as they shunted apart, opening to reveal an expansive two-tone landscape of featureless grays—a single dark plane that could only be called the ground, and a lighter gray plane that served as the sky. A faint grid of thin lines covered the floor in what looked to be one-meter increments. Apart from this, there was nothing out there. It was a bizarre space—empty and infinite, featureless and dull.

I returned to the console and flipped the pointer knob to *Close*. The curtains swung shut with a polite whir. The shivering light faded, and the room's shadows thickened. In the renewed dimness, I crossed back to the desk beneath the wall of monitors. If this was Delia's workspace, as it seemed to be, it was the only place I was likely to find anything useful. I opened drawers and sifted through uncountable sheets of paper and spent pens and stray paper clips. In a bottom drawer I found three pairs of eyeglasses. In another, a pair of 3-kilogram dumbbells and an elastic hair band.

Empty-handed, I shut the drawers and stepped back. The longer I stared at the piles of books, notebooks, and scratch paper on the desk, the larger my dread grew. This was a sifter, I feared—a job that would require time and patience and many hours of careful research, going over every line for clues about Delia's hidden theater. My heart sank at the prospect of returning here for weeks, perhaps months, on end, scrabbling through scraps for the tiniest of leads. It wasn't the sort of investigative work that excited me, not the kind of thing you read about in detective novels certainly. It was police work, desk jockey shit, something for the intern.

My frustration growing, I took the envelope from my jacket and poured out the Green Card. The yellow stickie was still firmly attached. I read it again, prying each word apart from its neighbor for some hidden meaning that had eluded me.

I remembered. Did you forget?

I remembered. That is to say, Delia remembered me. This was the meaning I took from her message, discovered inside an envelope addressed to Kennedy Stark. Was there another way to read it? And *Did you forget?* No, I never did. In four years, not a week had gone by where Delia didn't cross my mind. Should I have looked harder? How could I tell her I hadn't forgotten her? How could I prove I would never forget?

And then it dawned on me. She didn't mean, did you forget *me*. Three days earlier, I'd found a scrawled message in her car on a random receipt. A number I'd been instructed not to forget. I pulled it from my jacket, the receipt—a digital replica in fact—that I had taken from Delia's SUV.

Don't forget: 5.5.11.

I knew these numbers. They weren't a date after all. I crossed back to the cluttered desk and scooped up the framed Shakespeare quote. Act 5, scene 5, lines 6 through 11. By itself, line 11 read *For no thought is contented.*

I hurried from *The Dungeon* and returned to the Atrium of the original Forum. Taking out my passport, I pulled the Green Card from my pocket and searched both for the angle of interface, but it wasn't immediately obvious. On a whim, I held one against the other. The Green Card snapped into place. A few seconds later, the passport lit up. A message appeared. *Security badge detected.* I dismissed the message, and this brought up the search engine. There was a new icon at its head, a small green shield. I tapped the search field and typed *For No Thought Is Contented* and hit enter.

An icon appeared to indicate the passport was thinking. Then the name appeared. I looked up at the Atrium's portal. There it was, glowing in warm green letters.

No Thought Is Contented.

I burst into a shaky laugh. Hiding my passport, I lifted my hat and smoothed my hair and straightened my tie.

Delia Walsh, I whispered to myself. *It's been a while . . .*

No. No rehearsing. Honest conversation this time.

I drew a deep breath and took the plunge.

Just past the portal an electric
force hit me, followed
by a sudden
shock-
-ing
pain

. . . The moment had arrived. I was all but finished with my new theater. I needed only to switch it on. But doing so was a wild card. What I was attempting had never been done before, and there were potential dangers I couldn't completely eliminate through simulation.

Potential dangers to me, I mean. Not the user. I didn't know if I would survive the interface. I didn't know how long I could sustain myself as a simulation within a simulation. It was all theory at this point.

Assuming it did work, assuming my theater functioned exactly as designed, there was the next issue of how to reveal it to the world. I wanted my first visitor to be someone I could trust. And someone who trusted me. I wanted them to be open to a radical experience of empathy unlike anything they had ever experienced. I wanted to know that their feedback would be genuine. But I wanted the experience to be a complete surprise. Entering with an agenda might skew the effect.

That's when I remembered you, Kennedy.

Almost four years ago, you'd been hired to follow one of my old professors, Mr. Koontz. His wife told you she was worried he'd been unfaithful. That was part of an elaborate and kinky role-play they'd arranged to celebrate their 20th anniversary. I didn't understand then, I'm not sure I do now. But they were having fun. I don't begrudge them.

The point is, when Koontz came to pick up his badge for the Beta test for This Little World, he told me you were close behind. Said he'd been having weeks of fun trying to give you the slip. But you were good, he admitted. Couldn't shake you. Then he grabbed his badge and skittered out the fire escape.

That's when you came in. Interrupted my reading. Put on a little act. Fairly natural. It was fun to watch. I'd never interacted with a private detective before. You said your name was Sam. I knew it wasn't, but I played along. Gave you a badge and directions to the Beta test. You said you'd see me later.

To be honest, I didn't think you'd show. But you did. And you tripped in This Little World for over an hour. And to be honest, Kennedy, you were the ideal subject.

Yes, there were complications. You had a seizure. One of my assistants pulled you out. We called an ambulance. They took you to an ER downtown. You were in and out in twelve hours. I called to make sure.

A few days after your accident, I loaded up your session feed. I watched it.

Kennedy, I mean it when I say this: If I'd had more volunteers like you in those early days, I might not have given up hope on This Little World. Reviewing your feed, I saw a man cracking open at the seams. All your anxieties about the state of the world, all your worries, they manifested into a symbolic narrative. It was perfect. I'd never seen a feed so blatantly surreal yet so focused and with a finely crafted rising action. A tragedy nearly worthy of Aristotle.

Strangest of all, you dreamed of exiting the surreal, inventing a complete tête–à–tête with me, debriefing yourself in your own fantasy. We talked, you unburdened yourself, reflected on your fears, audited your sorrows. What was the phrase you heard me say . . . lonely but not alone? Your words in my mouth.

I'd thought to contact you at some point so you could walk me through your experience, just as you dreamed. But I worried about breaking the illusion you'd lived through. Would revealing the truth diminish the effect? I couldn't decide. A few weeks later I moved to Burlington to work here, putting my old life behind me.

So when the time came to decide who should be the first visitor in my new theater, your name was high on my list. The kind but wayward soul who would always do the right thing if given the chance. That was my read from watching your session. I hope I'm not wrong.

Once I'd chosen you, all that remained was how to get you inside without opening the door to Locksley or any other craven hacks. So I made a few phone calls, pulled a few strings. Mikko and I concocted this little game. I hope it's been worth it. I hope you can forgive these years of silence. Now that you can experience me as I am, I hope you understand how hard I have tried to always be the best version of myself. I think that's probably true for everyone, but I've never been anyone else.

Now that you're here, sharing this mind with me, maybe you have a clearer view . . .

24

WITHOUT UNDERSTANDING WHY OR HOW, I found myself standing in the Forum's Atrium again, disoriented and weakened by the draining sensation that I had just returned from a voyage of many years. Exhaustion weighed on me like a lead apron. I wanted to lie down where I stood and drift into unconsciousness. Yet somehow, in spite of myself, I made it to a bench and stretched out and closed my eyes, reflecting on the impossibility of what I had just been through.

I had found Delia Walsh by becoming her.

Or more precisely, I had just stepped into Delia's active mind, with my own taking a back seat to her consciousness like some passive parasite ruled by its host. The transformation from me into her was total, without a shred of myself present. My own—what to call it? . . . ego, personality, consciousness?—had been silent throughout the experience, leaving me without agency or input. I had been Delia Walsh, with Kennedy Stark on hold. Yet now that I had returned to myself, I could recall the experience with incredible clarity. I remembered Delia's musings and dreams, her ideas and anxieties, her joys and rages. From her earliest days to the moment she stepped into her new theater, I had access to all of it, in the same foggy way all memories are recalled. I knew what it was to be Delia Walsh, as if her life had once been my own.

I lay on my back with my eyes squeezed shut, inert and fatigued, trying to make sense of everything. A presence fluttered beside me. I opened my eyes. It was Mikkonen, sitting beside me like a man at prayer, his hands clasped and laid across his lap. He looked down with a canted head, his face puckered and questioning.

"Well?" he said.

I didn't know how to say what I wanted, so I stated the obvious.

"I found her," I said.

Mikkonen smiled at the shakiness of my voice. His hand levitated to his chest, and he held it there. "And?"

I shook my head. My thoughts were as slick and empty as a used oil drum. I sat up and smoothed my hair back and stared at my feet. Mikkonen edged away to give me room, waiting and listening.

I breathed in, then out. "I never really knew her, did I?" I said.

"In what sense?"

"Four years ago I had a seizure in This Little World. I thought Delia pulled me out and cheered me up. I thought we spent the day together, talking and reflecting on what I had been through. I felt so comfortable with her. She was everything I ever wanted in a friend, a woman . . ."

I shuddered through a sharp intake of breath. It was all so embarrassing—to admit that the foundational myth of my present was based on a surreal delusion. I beat my forehead with a pair of fists.

"But it was all a product of my own imagination," I said. "I spent the last four years hoping I would spend a second day with her. But there wasn't even a first."

Mikkonen's hand moved from his hand to my knee.

"How well do you know her now?" he said.

I blinked and looked back at the portal. *No Thought Is Contented* glowed green on the lintel. Mikkonen followed my gaze, but without a Green Card he wouldn't see what I could. I closed my eyes again and pressed my hands to my face, recalling and reviewing all that I had seen and felt.

"As well as someone knows themselves," I said. "I became her."

"Is that what it felt like?"

I dropped my hands and looked him square in the face. "I disappeared and Delia Walsh took over. But it wasn't like watching her from afar, because I didn't exist. It wasn't me *watching* her at all. There was *only* her. Nobody else."

Mikkonen's eyebrows lifted and his eyes brightened, and his face glowed with beatific joy.

"And somehow . . ." I said, forming this thought carefully. "Somehow she's still here. Still with me." I tapped my forehead. "I'll carry what she gave me to my grave. The gift of her."

Mikkonen smiled with satisfaction. "Wonderful."

"I remember everything about her life as if it had happened to me. Her aimless childhood. Her early interest in Surreals. Her wild dreams and big ideas. Her time in school. Meeting Locksley, meeting you. This Little World. And . . . everything else."

"She worked hard for what she wanted," Mikkonen said seriously. "In spite of the cost to herself."

"She wanted to share her story," I said. "In a way that couldn't be misinterpreted or abused. I think she succeeded." I paused for a moment, chasing an uneasy thought. "I can't imagine where this technology will take us next. What Locksley might do . . ."

Mikkonen's eyes narrowed, "Mm."

I didn't say anything else for a while. Mikkonen didn't either. He seemed to sense my need for silence. I wrung my hands together, still processing. A wave of uneasy energy radiated from my chest into my limbs. I rose to my feet suddenly and stared down the Atrium's infinite expanse. Mikkonen watched with a clinical detachment.

"Is everything all right?" he said.

"I'm not sure," I said. "I don't know what to tell her father. I mean, can she come back from this? Or is she . . . you know . . . is she gone?"

"What did she believe?"

I shut my eyes and fell into her memories, looking for the answer to my own question. It didn't take long to find it.

"She thought there might be a way out," I said. "But it didn't seem to bother her, one way or the other."

"That's what I gathered."

"I guess it's up to her now."

Mikkonen nodded. "As always."

I nodded recklessly, then pulled out my passport. I flipped it around and ran my finger over the attached Green Card.

"Will you now deliver that to Senator Walsh?" Mikkonen said.

I held it up. "The idea certainly amused her," I said. "I just might."

"I doubt he is prepared for what he will find. "

"Poor guy."

I checked the seam between the badges, then applied a light lateral pressure. The Green Card popped off easily, sliding across the passport like a playing card. I pocketed the passport and held up the card.

"I'd give it to you," I said, "But now I understand why you can't visit."

He turned up both hands. "Incompatible operating systems."

"She really likes you, Mikko," I said. "I could feel that."

His eyes flickered with a cool fire and his throat constricted, as if he were swallowing something large and angular. Then he stood and bowed his head ever so slightly.

"That is nice to hear," he said. "Thank you, Mr. Stark."

He paused for a moment, his lips parting ever so slightly. Then he smiled and turned and strode down the length of the Atrium as if he were touring the most beautiful garden in the world. I watched him go until he was just a speck against the stone pillars. Then I took out my passport and cleared its memory. The word *Exit* appeared on the lintel. Never had one tiny word sounded so beautiful.

THE NIGHT WAS HEAVY, and the air was brisk when I left the Forum for what I hoped would be the last time. The moon was high and full, and I navigated by its silvery ambience to where I had parked the Boson. I checked my phone for the time. One-twenty in the morning.

I fired up the car. The radio snapped on to a faraway station, filling the cabin with fuzzy bebop from a signal half swallowed by the mountains. I listened for a while to prancing trumpet lines and bouncing bass notes to let a better mood find me. Then I shifted into gear and set off.

When I pulled up to the Cascadia Inn, I found the door of my room hanging open a few inches. I put my ear to the split and listened before giving it a gentle toe tap. The door creaked inward. The lights were off inside but the glow from the A&W behind me was bright enough to see by.

My room had been turned upside down. Blankets and sheets on the floor, pillows pulled from their slips and tossed away, drawers hanging open, papers in disarray, and my clothes strewn like party confetti down the hall that led to the bathroom. I pushed inside and made my way to the writing desk and reached inside the wastebasket. I pulled out the empty bottle of bourbon by the neck, brandishing it like a club. Padding softly, I moved down the back hall, past closets emptied of all my things. When I reached the bathroom, I flipped on the light.

There was no one here. I set the bottle on the counter and looked around. Someone had dumped my bag of toiletries on the floor and made a general mess. On the mirror above the sink, the tacky residue of dried shaving cream spelled FUCK YOU in a fungal scrawl. Two of my disposable razors had been arranged on the counter with a tidy symmetry, their double razors clogged with curling fringes of pubic hair. Sleeping peacefully in the toilet bowl in a cloudy yellow brine was my toothbrush.

This invasion had all the hallmarks of an adolescent mind on a power trip. Wallace, no doubt. Just after he'd cornered me in the Forum. In spite of outsmarting him there, I didn't feel like sticking around to see if he'd come back for a second attempt.

I flipped off the light and went back to the main room and pulled off my stinking threads. I sifted through my strewn clothes and picked out a clean shirt with relatively few creases. Looking for my darkest suit, I found it under the bed. I slipped it on and jumped in front of the bathroom mirror, smoothing myself where I could. My gray fedora wasn't the best match, but it was all I had.

Freshly outfitted, I sat at the bed's edge and opened the nightstand. My credit cards were still there, sliding around loose in the drawer but the Bible was gone. An odd courtesy on Wallace's behalf. I tucked the cards in my wallet, then pulled out my phone and sat back against the headboard. I dialed Toots. He answered with a scratchy hello that broke open into a loud, gouging cough.

"Two in the fucking morning?" he croaked. "This better be good."

"I'm coming home," I said.

"No shit?

"No shit."

"Is Delia with you?

"Not exactly. But I did find her."

Toots coughed again. "Why does that sound so ominous?"

"It's complicated."

"Come on, Pike, where is she?"

"Call me Stark. My cover's blown."

"Goddammit."

"Don't worry about it. We'll talk tomorrow."

"Give me something better than this, brother. You woke me up."

"I don't believe that."

"It's the principle."

"Have you heard from your boy Wallace?"

Toots growled and shuffled something around. "That's an odd question."

"Yes or no?"

"That meathead won't answer his phone."

"He's working for Locksley on the side. Keep an eye on him."

"Jesus Christ, you are really winding me up."

"I'm headed home now," I said, sounding tired even to myself. "I'll call you tomorrow."

I hung up and started packing. I pulled my strewn clothes from the floor and took my empty toilet bag from the bathroom and crammed them into my valise like I was stuffing a holiday turkey. In five minutes, I was ready to jet. I pulled out my room key and pitched it onto the bed. Then I smacked the light and hoisted my bags and headed out.

HOMEWARD BOUND ON A MOONLIT DRIVE down a smooth freeway. Occasional cars crept past me like stalking nocturnal creatures, intruders in an otherwise hypnotic solitude. A slate gray sky glowed above, yellowed occasionally by the pulse of staggered streetlamps, their narrow penumbras driving back a liquid black otherwhere that churned at the road's shoulder. A fatal sadness chased me down this last road, the feeling that I was driving into some version of my past, to a time before halting, before surreals, before Delia Walsh. I stared up at the starry night, wondering which pinprick of light if any was Mars. Now more than ever, I was ready to leave this world behind.

I crossed into King County around 3:00 a.m. Ten minutes later I crested the long high hump of the ship canal bridge. The silicate towers of Seattle shimmered like starlight on the black horizon. I took the first exit and cut west through Amazonia to my neighborhood, where the streets were empty of everyone but a few shambling figures in musty overcoats and mossy beards, hauling duffel bags and pushing shopping carts with squirrelly front wheels. Revenants of the night who feared the day's coming as keenly as young men feared war and women's laughter.

I parked the Boson in a reserved space in front of my building, risking a ticket someone else would have to pay. I grabbed my bag from the trunk and went inside. Neither man nor mouse stirred in the halls. I padded down the worn carpets and up creaking stairs to my apartment. My keys jangled with a noise so clear I feared I would wake the whole floor. I opened the door quietly and stepped through.

The lamp in the main room was glowing. It was unlike me to leave it on. I set my bag down and leaned sideways to peer into the studio. Beyond the bed, a familiar leg with a stiletto heel bounced off a sturdy thigh. I cleared my throat and entered.

Auntie looked up from her whiskey and smiled. She was sitting comfortably in my easy chair in a billowing yellow blouse and tight black trousers. Her dark hair was pinned up in a frayed bun that looked like a young palm tree. The open bottle on the table was one from my reserve—a thirty-year bourbon I'd been saving for a special occasion. I guess this was it. Beside the bottle was a second empty glass and a sequined clutch purse.

Auntie took a pert little sip from her drink and gasped like a cracking soda can. "You have good taste," she said.

"As do you."

She pinched the neck of the bottle and turned the label toward her, looking down with a nostalgic smile. "My third husband always had a bottle of this on hand. He never touched the stuff, but he knew I was much nicer with it nearby."

"How long before that stopped working?"

Auntie pushed the bottle away. “He’s not worth another word.”

“Who are we talking about?”

She nodded with approval. I chucked my hat and coat to the bed and crossed to the table and poured myself a glass. Auntie watched me in silence, like I was some endangered species of monkey. In a way I guess I was. Drink in hand, I stepped back to remove myself from striking distance. Auntie took another sip and looked around the room.

“A modest hovel,” she said. “Lots of books and magazines. If I didn’t know any better, Kennedy, I’d say you were ferociously last century.”

“If that’s an insult, I’ll take it.”

“Not at all,” she said, uncrossing and recrossing her legs. “Men like you are so rare. So committed to stability. Suspicious of the ephemeral. A disciple of slow learning.”

“Bland, you mean.”

“Don’t be hard on yourself.”

“I’m just tired.”

“Of what?”

“Looking for love, I guess.”

“Aw, fear not,” she tutted. “There must be someone out there who suits you. If you’re willing to wait for her.”

“Is that your best *Hang in there, kid*?”

“I suppose it was,” she said, her eyes darkening. “Now . . . where is Delia Walsh?”

I shook my head. “Not yet,” I said. “Not before you tell me how much you know about Agent Wallace of the FBI.”

Auntie’s eyes narrowed and the four corners of her face pinched together. “Toots’s partner?”

I nodded. “Face like a leather tote bag, yeah.”

Auntie set her drink on the table and nestled both hands in her lap. “Go on.”

"He ran some interference in the Forum," I said. "Tried to stop me from finding Delia. Nearly killed me in the process. He's a dangerous man and he's still out there."

Auntie looked around the room, biting her lower lip and thinking curses that could be read on her face.

"I'll look into it."

"That's it?"

"It's all I can do right now," she shrugged. "Now, back to the matter at hand. Did you find her?"

She stared me down. I waited to see if her face would break. It didn't, not a wrinkle. I downed my whiskey in a breath and walked the glass to the table. This made Auntie visibly impatient. I reached for her whiskey and drained it too. She didn't flinch. I set the tumbler down hard and looked her in the eye.

"Do you have a pen?" I said.

She laughed, eyes fluttering, and pulled her phone from her clutch and tapped it on. "Like I said, a man of the previous century. Tell me."

"*No Thought Is Contented.*"

She reared back without typing. "What's that?"

"The name of a theater."

"Is she inside?"

"So to speak."

Auntie lifted an eyebrow. "No riddles please."

I ignored her and crossed to my bed and reached into my jacket for the Green Card. I held it up.

Her mouth opened with a delighted little gasp. "Ah-ha."

"You were right," I said. "Give this one to Daddy Walsh, and let him know that if he goes inside, he'll find his daughter."

I tossed the card and Auntie caught it, snapping it out of the air. She looked it over with awe and care.

"A word of warning," I said. "Daddy is not going to like what he finds."

"No?"

"It might sour a lot of people on the long-term prospects of the Forum as a vehicle for entertainment."

"Maybe the senator should decide what's best for him."

"Sure," I shrugged. "Just a warning."

Auntie raised her phone and tapped the screen and put it to her ear. She played with the bottle of whiskey as it rang. I heard someone answer.

"It's me," she said. "Stark says he found her."

A thin voice on the other end replied. Auntie pulled the phone from her ear. She eyed the screen and read off the theater's name, then put the phone back to her ear.

"Classified, as we suspected."

The voice on the line raged momentarily, then quieted. Auntie eyed me and her lips broke into a thin leer.

"Yes," she said. "I trust him."

The thin voice answered quietly.

"Perfect," she said.

Auntie hung up, looked down at her phone and started typing again. I tossed my tie on a heap of dirty clothes in the corner of the room and snapped open my collar and crossed to my bed. I fell sideways onto the mattress, fatigue following me like a dragging chain. I stretched out and crossed my hands behind my head and watched her. Auntie slipped the phone into her clutch and stood, holding the Green Card at arm's length.

"I will verify this and get back to you," she said, smoothing her skirt. She strode across the room. "Until then, Mr. Stark."

"What about Mars?" I said.

She stopped. "You spoke with Dr. Sterne in the Forum?"

"I did. He seemed amenable."

"Good. I suppose someone at Imagine Red will contact you," she said, adding, "If it all works out."

I sat up on my elbows. "That's all the assurance I get?"

"I'm afraid so."

She made for the door. I watched her go until she reached for the knob.

"Wait," I said.

She stopped again without turning. "Something else?"

"Why did you hire me?" I said. "Of all the halters in Washington, in North America, why me? Do you know why?"

Auntie turned, a quivering smirk dancing above her chin. "Delia had your business card, remember? Her father found it. He suspected you might know something."

I shook my head with a condescending smile. "It was Delia. She hired me."

Auntie stiffened and crossed her arms. "No, Mr. Stark; I did."

"Only because Delia orchestrated it. She wanted me to find her, nobody else. So she made me the most likely candidate. She had a friend get one of my cards. She sent a few emails, mentioning me and my importance to her work, knowing how easy they'd be to scrape from her server. She even sent a letter through the post, five days before disappearing, that she fixed to bounce back for lack of proper stamps. In it she mentions a future meeting with me. That was a lie, but it sounded damn convincing. Maybe you opened that letter yourself. Maybe the senator did. Doesn't really matter, it did the job. You came to me, just like she wanted. Any of this sound familiar?"

Auntie's jaw worked back and forth. She opened her mouth, closed it again, then cleared her throat. "How do you know all this? Did she tell you herself?"

"She shared it with me, so to speak."

"I see." Her cheeks tensed. "You should have brought her directly to us."

"I did the best I could."

"Good night, Mr. Stark."

With that, she opened the front door and shot through. The door shut and her footsteps receded fast. Pretty soon the only sound I could hear was my heart beating in my ears.

. . . The evening before I switched on my new theater, I stopped by Antony's to see the gang and have a drink.

Might be my last, I remember thinking. All my creative energy focused on morbid thoughts. Always so catastrophic.

I said nothing to anyone when I arrived. Just rolled in as usual, reticent and tired and thirsty. The gang greeted me with waves without breaking the flow of their conversation. I climbed onto my stool. Realized only then that it was always free when I came in. Did they keep it for me? Or just an unconscious habit. Strange I had never noticed before. Pinched my heart a little. Did I really want to risk losing all this? Leave this behind? Yes. What else would I do? Nothing. I was built to walk this road, this and only this. Lonely, if not alone.

Some of us carry questions in our hearts that burn hotter than suns, questions for which no answer will ever suffice. Asking them is our respite, our substitute for prayer, and the answer unheard is the afterlife we can never achieve.

The usual? Iris said, swooping into view.

Sure, I said, managing a smile.

I looked down the bar. Saint, Francisco, MG. And two more faces I didn't know. New recruits. Another pang in my heart. Out with old. The next generation of Forum Engineers was already upon us. Sharp and savvy, probably attuned to Locksley's updated and expanded vision. Whatever that was.

Iris returned with a bottle of Kokanee. I pulled a folded envelope from my pocket and held it forth.

Iris, I said. Can you keep this for me? Somewhere close by?

She took it and read the front.

Kennedy Stark? she said.

If anyone by that name comes here to pay off a tab, I said, hand it over.

That's it?

That's it.

Do I tell him who it's from?

He'll know . . .

25

THE FOLLOWING DAY, a second summer kicked in. A warm late September with just a spritz of moisture and faded beams through shattered clouds. Even the gag tide had drawn back some ways, just a faint sour note on an otherwise fresh wind. Exactly the sort of fine weather that makes Seattleites quit browsing real estate in Southern California.

I left my apartment as early as possible, hoping to run a few errands before lunch. The Boson was still in front of my building in the no parking zone. No ticket had been issued. Leaving it there, I walked the few blocks to my own beater. When I reached my sedan, it was buried in fallen leaves, and a yellow tire clamp had been affixed to the front wheel. I brushed away the leaves. Four parking tickets stuffed under the wiper poked up like an oversized flower. I reread the street signs and came to the same conclusion I had when I first parked here. Some municipal voodoo was at work, magic I didn't have the energy to contest.

Errands could wait. It was too nice to be driving anyway. I left my car and walked south to Mercer and wandered into lower Queen

Anne's commercial sector. I downed a coffee and read the morning paper at my usual spot then hopped across the street to a local café where the breakfast herd was gathering. I poked my head in the door and snapped up a weekly broadsheet. On the cover was an anthropomorphic cartoon rendering of the planet Mars, its blushing face squinting in pain from a rocket lodged firmly in one eye, an image appropriated from an old silent film a century and a half old. A caption on the front read *We're Changing Mars. Will Mars Change Us?* I folded the paper and wedged it under my arm and walked out.

Backtracking half a block, I strode farther west down Mercer, passing a record shop and two more cafés and the Seattle Repertory Theater. I cut south into Seattle Center and wandered beneath the rust-colored boughs of overhanging trees and across gray macadam and yellowing lawns. I stopped at the edge of a man-made crater at the center of the park, two stories deep, at the bottom of which was an old fountain that hadn't worked in almost a decade. I took a seat at the top edge of the crater and set my coffee beside me and snapped open the paper.

The featured article was a think piece devoted entirely to dismantling the received rationale for embarking on a mission to Mars by implying that humans who moved to the red planet would quickly evolve in a direction that separated them from their earthbound cousins. Interstellar speciation as a scare tactic, an odd angle of attack. The timing of the article was no accident, of course—Imagine Red's seventh landing was tonight. Out of respect for the astronauts and my adoration of the project I was predisposed to hate the piece, but the article itself gave me a whiff of an entirely new stink of cynicism. It concluded by arguing, quite gleefully, that human society as we knew it was already beyond saving, in spite of our recent success in space. It pointed out that the resources we would need to successfully transport and establish a workable society, infrastructure, and economy to the red planet was financially and chronologically infeasible.

It would be better and far cheaper, the author claimed, to invest in a technology that would allow every man, woman, and child to transfer themselves—meat, mind, and all—into simulations of our own devising, so that we might navigate our futures with assured accuracy and maximum benefit.

It was a familiar argument. So familiar that I flipped back to the article's first page to find the author of this clandestine pro-Forum puffery. There in bold beneath the title was a name I had missed the first time around—P. C. Locksley. My stomach churned and my chest tightened at seeing the name, a visceral reaction triggered by the immediate overlap of Delia's experience with Locksley, and my own. I closed the broadsheet and folded it up and walked back to my building, tossing the paper into the first recycling bin I passed.

Standing on my front steps I checked the time. It wasn't even eleven. The Mars landing was scheduled for 9:00 p.m., give or take a quarter of an hour. Plenty of time to get in a few hours of work, if I could stomach it.

I jumped into the Boson and hit the ignition. That's when I noticed a parking ticket tucked under the wiper. Punching the gas I drove off, working the wiper and the washer fluid to give the ticket a good drenching. By the time I reached Ballard, it was a sodden pulpy strip.

I parked in front of my building and hopped out and looked up at my office. Dark windows in the daylight. I walked to the front door, jostling the keys in my pocket. The same ruddy itinerant was asleep in the vestibule again, a reflective space blanket thrown over him like a piece of crumpled foil. His head lay on a plastic bread bag filled with dirty clothes. I opened my wallet and pulled out a short stack of twenties and tucked it in the crook of his elbow.

Circling the building I entered through the back and climbed the stairs and trudged down the hall. Old hardwood floors welcomed me back with pained creaks. I unlocked my office and slipped inside.

Rounding the L-bend to my desk I flipped on the lamp. The answering machine was flashing, seven blinks in a series. I sat and hit play. The machine spooled and squeaked, and the speaker crackled. The first message was from a sergeant I knew down at the Seattle Police Department.

Stark, you fucking bum. I know you're there, pick up. Where else would you be? Not on a case for Chrissake. Come on! Stark?

There was a brief pause.

All right you piece of shit. Hide under your desk if you have to. I want you down at the station immediately after you crawl out of your own ass. We got some questions for you.

The second and third messages were ghosts—hang-ups with just a fraction of dead air between the beep and the click. The fourth message was the sergeant again.

Stark, Jesus! Where the fuck are you? I'm driving to the Cavern, and if you're not there I'm buying the room a round and charging it to your tab.

The fifth message started with a hissing silence that ran for about ten seconds. Then a doddering old voice I didn't recognize broke through.

Mr. Beadle? Hello? Are you playing games with me, Mr. Beadle? Are you? Hello? By God I won't stand to be mocked, if that's what this is. Is that what this is? You're mocking me? Maybe you're recording this, thinking to embarrass me on the internet. Is that what you're thinking? Oh by God, I'll sue you for libel if that's what you're gonna do. By God all good and holy, I will sue. I will. Just you . . . just you wait.

A wrong number.

The sixth message was the first legitimate inquiry of the bunch. A woman from Lake Forest Park suspected her husband was carrying on an affair with some surreal version of Queen Victoria. The very idea made me smile. This spurned wife wanted pictures and recordings to serve as exhibits A through Z in the divorce proceedings that would inevitably follow. I wrote her number down as she said it, and waited as she recited it four more times for my benefit, as if this wasn't a recording but a live broadcast.

The seventh message was the bartender from the Headlamp Tavern, Andy. Bless him.

Hey, buddy. Haven't seen you around for a second. There was a cop in here earlier, asking about you. Got me a little worried. I'm keeping a shot of Jameson warm for you in a little baggie under my armpit. Love you, pal. Let us know you're okay . . .

His timbre was so gentle that I could feel myself blush. Good old Andy, it was nice to know he was back where he belonged. His message finished with a *toodle-oo* and the message beeped.

I wiped the machine's memory and swiveled 180 in my seat and kicked back, planting my feet on the back wall. I ruminated on the sudden strangeness of my life and the improbable augmentation I now carried with me—the memories and life of a woman I once believed I knew, but never knew at all. I had forged a simple fiction of her to suit my fantasies and ease my anxieties, a fiction that only flattered and fed my worst impulses. Now that I knew the real Delia, so to speak, all those easy fictions had fallen away, replaced by the sweet bitterness of a complicated reality.

I glanced up at the Imagine Red poster gleaming like a dimmed sun above me. *Imagine Life. Imagine Home. Imagine Red.* Speaking of comforting fantasies, I thought, smiling. Still, thanks to Delia, I now had a chance, however small, however insane . . .

Just then the floorboards outside my office groaned. I spun around and sat up. The door squealed. I reached for a drawer and opened it quietly and pawed through the junk inside, searching for anything hard and heavy. Creaking footsteps approached. My fingers grazed the hilt of a small folding knife. I pulled it out and pried it open.

A faint shadow slid across the floor and up the far wall to the windows overlooking the street. A protuberant stomach in a crinkled suit appeared, followed by the brim of a bent fedora. Wallace rounded the corner, bringing his meaty hands and sweaty mug. He carried a Smith and Wesson Governor—a snub-nosed beast carried legally by no FBI agent on Earth. Wallace leered when he saw me and looked down at the blade in my hand. He laughed from somewhere deep inside his liver.

"You gonna butter me, Stark?"

I twisted the knife in the air like I was digging through a wall of cork. The blade glittered in the afternoon light.

"I'll try . . ."

He stepped closer. "That was a mean trick you pulled."

"I did my best."

"Not good enough."

"Guess not."

He took another step and raised the gun. "Goodbye, asshole."

"You want a Green Card?" I said quickly. "I found one."

Wallace squinted and ground his teeth like he was chewing tinfoil. "Bullshit."

"If you really think so, pull the trigger."

He hesitated and looked down at his gun.

"How much did Locksley offer you?" I said.

"Plenty. What's it to you?"

"I know where the card is. Why don't we squeeze him for a little more?"

Wallace pinched his face so hard he looked like a deflated basketball. "Why don't you shut the fuck up?" he snarled.

He raised his arm and locked his elbow and took a bead. I sat back and closed my eyes. The sound of creaking wood opened them again. Wallace heard it too. He blinked and looked back at the front door. From my angle, I couldn't see what he was seeing, but I could tell it made him uneasy.

His face brightened suddenly, and he lowered the gun. "Hey, pal," he said with a laugh. "Just following up—"

The crack of a pistol cut him short. Wallace's hat did a backflip as a thin flap of forehead peeled back and fluttered like a soggy toupee. His fingers straightened and his body stiffened, and his gun tumbled to the floor with a thud. He stood frozen for a moment, swaying like a scarecrow in a steady wind. Then he lifted his foot to take a step. A second shot cut him down. Toppling backward, the base of his skull cracked against the windowsill. Blood spattered as he hit the floor. He lay flat with his arms flung out and his head pressed hard against the baseboard in a way that made him look like he was trying to kiss his own shoulder. A nimbus of red blossomed beneath him.

Silence overtook all. At last I heard footsteps, softer this time, more cautious. I peered over my desk and looked down at the gun lying at Wallace's feet, a million miles away. My hand tightened against the knife's hilt, and I inched sideways to the windows, hoping a missed shot might break the glass and draw some attention my way.

Another gun rounded the corner. A Glock this time. FBI standard issue. Toots came with it. Our eyes locked.

"You alone?" he said.

"I was," I said. "Now it's a crowd."

His lip curled like he'd find that funny tomorrow. He flicked his gaze this way and that, searching the corners of the room. Finding nobody, he holstered his weapon and bent down to pick up Wallace's gun. A pair of leather gloves covered his hands. My first thought: no fingerprints.

"That real leather?" I said.

Toots nodded and lifted the gun. He stood back and took aim, but not at me. He lifted his chin as he stared down the sights.

"You like that poster?" he said.

He meant the stylized picture of Mars hanging behind my desk. *Imagine Life. Imagine Home. Imagine Red.* I glanced at it and shrugged. Toots fired.

Glass shattered, erupting in a radial spray. The frame hopped once but managed to hold and came to rest at a slight angle. Now there was a new dark hole with frayed edges a few centimeters west of Olympus Mons. Toots laid Wallace's gun down exactly where he'd found it, tweaking the position a few times. When it was just right, he stepped back and looked up at the damage he'd done. It was good. He circled to the far side of Wallace's body and ducked slightly to get down to a pistol's point of view. He nodded again, satisfied.

"Looks about right," he said. Then he rose up and pointed to the door. "Wallace came in posing as a client," he said. "You let him get as far as right here. He pulled the gun and fired."

Toot's pointed on a vector that flew from an imaginary gun across the desk and through my head, into the wall.

"Praise Jesus, you ducked just in time," he said.

"I knew what was coming."

Toots wagged a finger. "No. He caught you by surprise. You were lucky."

"Inches from death."

Toots looked down at the body, sucking air through his teeth. "This little shit," he grimaced. "I should have known."

"I tried to tell you . . ."

I shrugged in place of finishing. Toots sniffed. Pulling off his gloves, he circled the body and crossed to my desk.

"We'll squeeze out of this one," he said. "Wallace wasn't well liked." Toots reached a hand into his vest. "I stopped by your place a few hours ago to deliver this," he said, holding it up. "When I couldn't find you, I came here. That's when I noticed Wallace casing the place from his car a few doors down. I decided to hang back. When you showed up and Wallace got out, I followed."

"Jesus."

"Just Toots, thanks," he smiled. "Here."

He held out the envelope. My eyes narrowed.

"What's this?"

"Your rent for the next ten years." Toots slapped the envelope against the corner of my desk.

"I told you I didn't want money," I said.

Toots glanced over my shoulder at the damaged poster. "Yeah I know," he said, "I'm just being generous."

"And Senator Walsh, has he seen her?"

"He's on his way to the Forum as we speak."

I grimaced. "He's not going to like what he finds."

"That's not my concern, nor yours." Toots shook the envelope. "Just take it, pal. Before someone changes his mind."

I took the envelope gently, like it was something made of tissue. When I peeked inside, a stack of bills as thick as two thumbs peeked back.

"Thanks," I said. "This helps."

Toots nodded absently. He was staring at the damaged poster of Mars again. The new bullet hole already looked at home, like a fresh crater from an impacting meteor. Cocking his head once, Toots gestured.

"You are on the list," he said. "As promised."

My gut fluttered. "Seriously?"

Toots blocked a sudden yawn with his fist. "Don't get your hopes up," he said. "There're five thousand applicants in that pool. And I doubt you'd pass the physical. Not without some effort."

"I'll take up jogging, swear off smokes," I said. "Whatever it takes."

He stared me down, eventually shaking his head. I swallowed and threw my hands to my head and started laughing. A hard, painful laugh, coming from the aching core of me. Toots was glad to see it.

"The Boson outside," he said. "That the one we gave you?"

I nodded.

"Bring it back on Monday," he said.

He turned away and his arms jumped akimbo as he looked down at his dead partner, just a rind of a man now, freshly squeezed on the floor of my office.

"All right," he sighed. "Time to call this in."

. . . Why switch on now? Mikkonen said. Why not wait for him to arrive?

It was a good question. It might take weeks or months for my plan to unfold. For you to enter the Forum. And if not you, someone. One of these days. I didn't have faith in my father to sniff out the clues I'd left behind. But someone would eventually. Maybe his fixer. Or his goons on the SPD. Or the vamp who vets his underlings.

In any case, I didn't have to activate my new theater when I did. I just wanted to. I wanted to be alone for a while. Alive with my thoughts and nothing else. Free of physical want. If all went according to plan, I could leave at any time, this prison where I live. But maybe, I thought . . . maybe I wouldn't want to.

To get used to it, I told Mikkonen. To acclimate to life in the dark.

Can you move around normally? Visit other theaters?

I don't know, I said. But it's not something I want to try. Too many unknowns.

I'm not sure I understand, he said, his face twisting. If he will be you, then where will you be?

I smiled.

These are the questions worth asking, I said. Have patience.

Can you come back from this?

In theory, yes, I said. I'll let you know if I do.

Mikkonen stared at me for a time, mouth parted slightly. It was the closest he had ever come to speechless.

Perfect empathy, he said at last. That's what you call this?

That's right, I said.

Why does that interest you? he said.

Because I am tired of explaining myself to other people, I said. And I am tired of other people explaining themselves to me. I want to know if there is a path around all the confusion people have about each other.

Maybe I can erase all the fictions and fantasies about who I am and show them a mind unmediated. My whole self, extroverted in four dimensions.

A process, Mikkonen said, that necessarily requires liberating people from themselves.

That's right, I said. What better way to empathize with someone than to become that person, wholly and completely. Temporary unmediated self-annihilation. One soul overtaking another. Become someone other, fully and completely. No vicarious thrills. No voyeurism. The Other becomes the Self. Subject from Object. And the result is pure empathy. I hope so anyway. Wouldn't that be something worth exploring on a larger scale, with more and more people? My gift to a world in pain. What is it like to be a bat? asked Nagel. Why leap to that question? What is it like to be anyone but yourself? What is it like to be Delia Walsh? Would it improve a person? Expand their understanding of what it means to be human? I like to think so. I have to imagine it could. The dream of the arts made real through science. Wouldn't that be something?

It is certainly something, Mikkonen said. But I'm the wrong entity to ask . . .

26

THE COPS SWARMED MY OFFICE LIKE LOCUSTS ON MAIZE, but Toots handled them beautifully. He flashed his federal cred and dazzled them with a play-by-play that had just enough action and just enough foggy detail to sound real and inevitable. The capper of the tale had him revealing that Wallace was already under investigation for trafficking drugs through tunnels dug beneath the Canadian border. That sealed his reputation.

The cop's captain showed up fifteen minutes after the first batch and took aim at me straight away. After all, it was my place, and there was a dead Fed on the floorboards. I played dumb and morose, giving one syllable answers and no lip, with Toots running wingman, filling in whatever details I could not. That approach disarmed the captain faster than I expected. Pretty soon he'd forgotten I was in the room, preferring the taste of what Toots was serving up. As it turned out, the captain had already had a few run-ins with Wallace over jurisdiction clashes around the city. He liked the guy about as much as lemon juice on a canker sore. Luck was on my side.

I stuck around until 6:00 p.m., answering whatever questions I could. Eventually some guys from Toots's bureau showed up to sweep away the local boys and there was a bit of a back and forth about who was in charge. For the first time in a long while I saw law enforcement actively fighting to take a case, and not batting it around like a radioactive bomb. A slow month maybe. Or maybe there was something about a dead Fed that attracted more local interest.

Eventually I was given leave to go. I thanked Toots with a handshake and a nod and made my way out. Turning at the door, I caught the police sergeant giving the dead man a contemptuous little kick in the ribs, a half-smile breaking over his pudgy face.

Pulling my hat down, I turned around and went out.

ANDY WAS TENDING BAR AT THE HEADLAMP when I got there, propped forward on his elbows talking to the nose of a young Asian man with a kind face, a faux hawk, and arms contoured like fire hydrants. The guy was wearing a T-shirt that was either too small or vacuum sealed. I crept to my usual stool and waited for Andy to notice. It took a few minutes. When he finally looked my way, it was only because he seemed to sense something amiss at the wide edge of his perfect view.

"Kennedy," he crowed. "Holy shit, babe. It's been ages."

He touched his friend's wrist to excuse himself and slid down the bar.

"Got your message," I said. "Thanks for checking up on me."

"I tried, my God," he said frowning. "I even stopped by your office."

"Just to look for me?"

Andy flicked his eyes at his friend and flashed a smirk. "Well, Danny lives in Ballard. But I would have anyway."

"I believe you."

He dropped to one elbow. "Are you good?" he said.

I nodded. "I'm fine. I was working up north." I pulled out the thick envelope Toots had served me and laid it flat on the bar top. I tapped it with a single finger. "A paying gig I couldn't refuse."

Andy leaned forward on bare forearms and pushed his nose down toward the envelope, snuffling around.

"Is that a million dollars I smell?"

"Might be," I said, scooping up my drink. "Somewhere between Rockefeller and Gates I think."

"Super. You want a round for the room?"

I looked around the empty bar. "It's just me and your friend?"

Andy nodded, "I'm drinking too."

I shrugged. "Why not?"

Andy pirouetted away and started picking through the bottles in the well like they were bowling pins, looking for the cream of the crop. He returned with a double bourbon crackling with a few rocks of ice. Then he looked down the bar. His friend Danny smiled and waved. Andy waved back.

"Get you something else, babe?" he said.

"I'm good with this," Danny said.

Andy winked and poked my forearm. "Danny works at an ER downtown," he said. "Has the wildest stories."

"One's about me I'll bet," I said, taking a sip.

"Shit, what happened?"

"It was years ago," I said. "What are you guys up to?"

Andy twisted and looked back at a clock hanging behind the bar. "I'm working 'til close," he said. "But we'll probably watch the landing on my phone tonight."

I nodded. "That's my night."

Andy stood and stretched. "Crazy to think there's a city on Mars right now."

"More like a village."

"Still. It's cool."

I bobbed my head and poked a finger in my drink and slurped it dry. "It is," I said, "But a lot of shit has to go right for it to work."

"Didn't peg you for a pessimist."

"I wasn't yesterday."

Cradling my drink, I peered into the roiling whiskey. The round glass and the rippling amber liquid gave off a planetary glow. It looked like Venus, but I thought of Mars. I thought of the lander, the astronauts about to touch down, the colonists already hard at work like busy interplanetary ants. How lucky they were to be on the cusp of an adventure so tenuous. How fierce and courageous. Like Delia, in a way. With the breadth of her memories now resident in my head, I understood better what it was to be fearless and ambitious, led by a compulsion to create and push boundaries, no matter the cost. I was ready for my chance on the red planet. With her courage and her convictions and her drive paving the way, I was more ready than ever in spite of the danger.

Andy nudged my arm. "What's got you smiling so big?"

I bit my lip and wagged my head. "Just thinking about the future," I said. "Where I am now, and where I'd like to be."

"Hopefully doing what you do best."

"What's that?"

"Being kind."

I sighed. "Well," I said, raising my glass. "Amen to kind."

"Amen," Andy said.

WHEN I GOT BACK TO MY APARTMENT, I tossed the envelope on my bed and didn't look at it again until I had showered and shaved and emerged from my chrysalis. After drying off, I pulled on a comfy pair of blue jeans, a black T-shirt, and a pair of brown loafers. Then I took the envelope and dropped into my recliner and pulled out the dough. I counted the amount twice, then shoved the money back and set it aside. It was enough cash to pay for a long hiatus and come back to work feeling energized.

Around eight-thirty I turned on the television to see how far the lander was from touchdown. I was fortunate to have checked early. The landing was predicted to occur in eighteen minutes, about fifteen before the advertised spectacle. The precision of orbital mechanics and rocket equations were reliable to be sure, but they couldn't be expected to adhere to the needs of prime-time television.

As the landing module Cupid 7 made its final orbit, I threw a frozen pizza in the oven, popped open a bottle of red wine, and poured myself a heavy glass. Fifteen minutes passed quickly in this fraught process of preparation, and by the time I was sitting in my lounge chair with a slice in hand, the count to touchdown had commenced.

As the Cupid drifted down through the hazy atmosphere, the network shifted among three camera angles: one fixed on the landing crew, of whom three of the seven were in view; another at an angle level to the Martian horizon; and a last pointed straight down at the planet's surface. I wasn't interested in seeing the astronauts strapped into their seats as the majesty of the Martian landscape slipped past with its blazing palette of reds and oranges and sunny golds. There was no action in the cabin, no drama on the faces of the men and women about to make history, no movement. Just calm looks and slow hands. If any of them were worried, none showed it, exactly the kind of thing that makes terrible television.

The people in charge of the broadcast must have realized this too because the final three minutes were a mesmerizing spectacle of wonder and beauty, pulled from cameras embedded in the lander and on the surface: long quiet shots of Mars's virgin horizon, rusted peaks upon which water had not flowed for millennia, and vast plains of soft untrammeled regolith. The only sound audible was the steady flow of transmission from the Cupid to Earth. It was not a two-way signal, we had been told, because it took upward of five minutes for a signal on

Mars to reach the Earth and vice versa. This meant a ten-minute gap between any question and answer, far too long for mission control to comfortably guide their astronauts to a safe touchdown. The men and women of Cupid were landing this on their own.

For these final minutes and seconds, I listened intently to the radio chatter. I could hardly breathe:

That's good spot. (Garbled) Yes. (Pause) 700 at 25 is good.

Cupid's looking good. Hope you're enjoying this Control.

Not too many rocks. All clear.

600 feet, down at 19.

We're going manual.

These voices captivated me for their lack of opacity. Just jargon and numbers that sounded like a coded sacred language spoken by otherworldly gods.

540 feet, down at . . . angle is 30. Down at 15.

Nice. Nice, 400 feet, down at 9 (feet per second). 58 (feet per second) forward.

No problem.

350 feet, down at 8.

Okay, you're pegged on horizontal V.

Come on now. Need to slow it up.

All right. One and a half down. Ease her down. 270.

Singh, how's the fuel?

Thirteen percent.

Looks like a good area here.

I see a couple deep shadows. Try to get ahead.

230 feet, down at two.

Slow it up. Slow it up.

17 forward. Coming down a little fast.

Gonna be right on the lip of that crater.

200 feet, 9 1/2 down.

I don't like that speed. Ease it up some.

Roger.

120 feet.

Ease up. Ease up.

I see a good spot. Take it there.

100 feet, 14 down, 11 forward. Eight percent fuel.

No dammit. Ease up!

Thirty seconds.

What did you—

Fifteen seconds.

No, no, no.

Hold on. Hold on.

Pull out! What are you doing?

The signal died suddenly, like oxygen rushing from an airlock. Silence. There had been a real terror in that final question. A woman's voice, stern but shaky. Her final words hung in the empty air. I held my breath. My heart was hammering.

Seconds later a clear voice broke through, someone from mission control.

We . . . ah . . . we seem to have lost contact with Cupid.

My heart lurched. One by one concerned voices floated over the airwaves. A panel of experts convened to assess the situation.

We're not sure what's happening now. It could be a simple transmission malfunction. Certainly our hopes and prayers go out to the crew. We're going to stay on this as long as we can . . .

They stayed; I could not. The suspense was unbearable. I grabbed the remote and silenced the television. My head hurt and my breathing was erratic. I sank into my chair and looked out the window and stared out at the apartments across the courtyard. A few lights were on, but nobody stirred. I waited. Desperate for something to happen, for someone outside to scream, giving voice to my shock and sadness. Or to enter my apartment with a bouquet of flowers and admit that the botched landing was an elaborate joke, executed for my amusement.

But nothing happened. Nothing but the silence. I withstood it as best I could, my mind afire with thoughts of doom, reeling at the loss of yet another comforting fantasy. How many could I endure in one week?

I sulked in a daze for God knows how long. The rattle of my phone against the table knocked me free. I rose up wearily and crossed the room. When I looked at the screen, a feeling of dread ran me through like a hot lance. A text message from Billy Brighton's wife. I opened it.

Mr. Stark, please. Please tell me you've found my Billy. Please tell me he's coming home. You're the only one who can help him.

As I read these words, an image loaded in—a photo of two identical, adorable toddlers seated at a small dinner table, both holding spoons dripping with gobs of ivory white ice cream or yogurt, their beaming faces slathered in the same. Another message followed.

If you could show him this, maybe it would help. He loves his kids, I know he does. Tell him they ask about him every day. Tell him they want him home. I want him home . . .

I scrolled back to the image. The kids looked ridiculously happy and unreasonably calm, their fresh youth inoculating them against the travesty of their father's absence. My throat tightened. I inhaled and shuddered.

You're the only one who can help him, her text said.

No. That wasn't true the first time I lost him. It wasn't true now. I was sloppy and he'd given me the slip. Hard truths. I was just a two-bit halter who fell into the job out of boredom. A man with limited talents and an inflated sense of purpose. I was a dead end. Billy's wife could do better. She might as well hire another . . .

A sudden idea seized me. A train of thoughts I'd never had. A depth of intuition that seemed to spring from nowhere. A holistic understanding of surreals and the code that ran them. Another gift from my time with Delia. Her memories, her knowledge. There was an answer in there, somewhere . . .

I shot to my feet and grabbed the Boson's fob and left my apartment in a flash.

Ten minutes later I was back in my office. I snapped on a desk lamp for minimal light. Then I booted up my Hypo SR console and loaded a new session of the Five Borough Blues.

Before entering the surreal, I fired up a VPN and logged into a private server Delia had set up years before using an ID and password only she knew. Now I did too. I searched this server until I found a sniffer program that she'd written to pull personal data from commercial surreals—a quasi-legal tool she'd used for mischief as a teenager, and later for research, during the development of This Little World, now perfectly suited to the task before me. How I knew all this—where to find it and how to use it—surprised me. But it came second nature, these impulses, these ideas, like the muscle memory of a classical pianist.

I loaded the program in parallel with Hypo and synced them. Everything was ready. I hooked up, laid back, and dove in . . .

BACK IN THE *FIVE BOROUGHS BLUES*, I found myself standing outside room 601 once again, waiting for the sound of gunfire to invite me in. The hotel's exchange vents still rattled, and the reek of summer trash hung thick in the air. But the gun never popped. I put my ear to the door. A man was gibbering on the other side, unfurling an annoyed string of curses and muted exhortations. I reached for the knob and turned it.

I entered room 601 for the second time this week. Whitewashed walls and warm lights welcomed me back. Billy Brighton was here, slouched forward in his favorite recliner, head in hands. The gun was a merciful distance away, laid on the table beside him.

"Fuck this fucking case," he mumbled into his palms. "Fucking sick of this shit."

Beside the gun was an unfolded piece of paper with the number 109 scribbled across the middle, or 601 if you held it upside down. Poor kid. Still tripped up on the most basic details.

I stepped forward and raised both hands. "Billy . . ." I said gently.

He lifted his head. His eyes were raw and gleaming wet. "You again . . ." He gestured vaguely at the corner of the room. "I didn't kill him this time," he said. "Just a hard knock on the head."

Beyond the foot of the bed a set of legs in pinstripe trousers, capped by a pair of leather shoes, lay face down on the carpet. Billy laughed once and fell back in his chair.

"Gonna wait for him to wake up," he said, "Finish this shit once and for all."

I closed and locked the door, then walked around the bed. The man in the fancy suit and shiny shoes looked better this time. Only a small streak of blood colored his silver hair. I watched him closely. His fitted suit gently rose and fell, sliding over shoulder blades that drew apart, then back together in a slow, steady rhythm.

I stepped around the napping man and walked to the open window. Its curtains bucked in a warm wind. I pulled the window closed and secured the latch and walked back to Billy. He had sunk down deeper into the chair and his eyes were closed. With his finger to his temple he tapped out a simple rhythm while humming a tuneless melody. I stood over him.

"Billy," I said again.

His eyes opened with the speed of a garage door. "Hm?"

"I'm taking you home."

He puckered and shook his head. "I gotta get this right."

"No. You don't."

"Thirty-three fucking tries. I can't just walk away."

I dropped to one knee and held his gaze. "Sunk cost fallacy, my friend. The truth is you can. You can stand up and walk out that door at any time. Don't waste the days you have left. Return to what's real."

Billy laid both arms down on the armrests and held them loosely like a drowsy king. "This is real. It's real experience, like anything else."

"Don't kid yourself," I said. "You're in here because you're running from a reality that doesn't stack up to your dreams. You want a life that's less real, not more."

Billy sneered. "What do you know about me?"

I reached for his hand and took a firm hold. The room flickered on contact. A split-second loss of power, then back again. Billy didn't seem to notice, but in that instant my mind lit up with an ocean of data, pulled from the sniffer running in the background.

"I know where you are right now," I said calmly. "You're in a motel in Issaquah, the Evergreen Model. Room 203. Logged in through a Hypo Pro console, firmware 3.2.7. You've been there five weeks and three days . . ."

Billy yanked his hand back like he'd just been stung. "What the fuck?"

"You're paying your Hypo fees through a Bank of America account in your name alone, probably something you're hiding from your wife. Weekly withdrawals of one hundred and twenty dollars. At that rate you'll be broke in seven weeks. But that doesn't account for motel fees and food expenses, assuming you want to stay alive."

"How the fuck did you do that?"

"Do you want to stay alive, Billy? Or are you walking a slow road to the end?"

"I don't want to die. I just . . ."

"You want things to be easier. Less complicated."

"I don't know. I guess."

"You want to feel like you're moving forward, into a future that makes sense."

"Yeah."

"I know you're hurting. I know you want this to be the cure. This place, this fiction. But the truth is, this is where dreams die. This is someone else's story, and you're in it because it's easier than telling your own."

Billy shuddered and made a low honking noise, choking on the tears he fought to hold back. "What's my story?" he said.

"You're Billy Brighton. The only one in the world. A crack real estate agent with a talent for making friends. Married to a woman who loves you like crazy. With two kids that love their father more than anything in the world, except maybe a bowl of vanilla ice cream."

Billy's sob broke through. He wept, gulping thick lungfuls of air. I lay my hand on his knee.

"You've still got time," I said. "So much time to make your own story. So much time and so much life. To go where you've never been, to see what you've never seen. I can show you how. I can get you started. But I need you to leave this place. Meet me in person."

He wiped the wet from his cheeks. "Am . . . am I in trouble?"

"Not a bit, kid. Log out now and I'll come find you. With a large pizza and a six pack of your favorite beer. We'll just talk. Then I'll take you home."

He nodded without saying anything for a long time. Then he said, "Okay."

I patted his knee. "You'll wait for me?"

He sobbed, wide eyes welling. "Yeah. I'll wait."

"I'll be there, pal. You'll see."

I stood and held out my hand. He took it and I pulled him to his feet, a dead weight gaining strength. He sniffled and coughed as I led him to the door. On our way out, he glanced back at the unconscious cipher on the floor.

"Will he be okay?" he said.

"He's ones and zeros. He'll be fine."

I guided Billy down the hall to the elevator, and we rode it to the lobby and walked out into a humid New York night. Together we found an exit on the corner of 6th and 23rd, and he logged out without a moment's hesitation. A good sign. In a blink Billy was gone, waking to the real world.

Before following, I took a last look around, absorbing in the sights and sounds and smells of a simulated New York City. It was pleasant, but it didn't fool or fascinate me anymore, not the way surreals used to. A few days in the Forum had cured me of all cheaper illusions. I could sense the artifice of these commercial surreals in every detail. I could see the edges of the simulation, its boundaries and limitations.

Satisfied with another case completed, I stepped back and glanced up at the lovely unreal night. False gray clouds slid across the silver disc of a painted-on moon. I scanned a scatter of blinking stars that weren't real, searching for a tiny red planet that wasn't real, with tired eyes that weren't real either, yet filled with a newfound hope that was.

EPILOGUE

LOW ABOVE THE RUSTY MARTIAN PLAINS and ancient jagged boulders hangs a gritty ochre sky. Powdery regolith stirs in a thin wind, blurring further the already hazy heavens. At a great distance lurks the gently sloping cinder cone of Olympus Mons, vague in its looming outline.

Where the wide plain rises to a low knoll sits a tight colony of capsule-shaped habitations on sturdy stilts, eight in total, arranged in a circle. A white steel tower rises from the center of this false courtyard, its peak alight with flashing lights that beckon to exhausted travelers. The doors of these habitation pods hang open, as do the hatches of their interior airlocks. The quiet storms of Mars have coated their insides with a fine film of orange dust. Otherwise the pods are empty. Those who once lived and worked there, who held so much hope in their promise, are gone.

As the winds pick up, a low rumble agitates the air. A compact shadow sweeps across the ground and crosses the abandoned colony—a lander performing its programmed descent.

Beyond the deserted colony the lander slows and eases down. Rockets bloom with iridescent flames to slow the craft, fires that surge and flutter. Billows of oxidized dust churn in its wash like a burning fog. At last the lander touches down, dead center on the platform. The rockets go dark, and the noise subsides.

Mute moments pass with none to absorb the uncertainty of the moment. Then a hiss cracks the silence. Pressures equalize. The lander's hatch swings open, and a stepladder unfolds to the ground. Three astronauts emerge, decked in slender polished suits of gleaming cherry red. Hands aloft, they wave and turn, turn and wave, as if the object of a thousand cheering spectators.

But there are no crowds to greet them in this simulated world, nor colleagues to welcome them home. Yet still they wave and smile and scan the crowds that could have been, their surely beaming faces hidden behind golden domes of glass, celebrating what some say is the greatest purpose of humankind. Artificial ambassadors of an evaporating future, they wave and turn and wave some more. To celebrate, to bask, in spite of truth, to dream.

ACKNOWLEDGMENTS

First and foremost, my deepest gratitude to my wife, Kloé, for her patience and constant encouragement, and for gifting me the Olivetti typewriter that set this story in motion.

Hugs and kisses to my kids, Calvin and Elsa, for endless joy and inspiration.

Blessings to my mother and father for always encouraging my extracurricular diversions, and to my brother, Brendan, for never distracting me from them.

Gratitude to my tenacious agent, Charlie Serabian, for taking a chance on me, and to Liseanne Miller for running a tight ship at Global Lion.

A special thanks to Diversion Books, and to my editor Toni Kirkpatrick, for giving this book one last gentle nudge across the finish line.

Finally, thank you to my earliest readers for their generosity and wisdom—to Marc-Olivier Bouchard for his advice on world-building and tone, to Tyson Theroux for his comments on structure and character, to Bryant Moore for positive vibes, and to Jordan Lees for his encouragement from afar.